FANCY FARM

BY

NEIL MUNRO

AUTHOR OF
'JOHN SPLENDID,' 'THE DAFT DAYS,' ETC.

POPULAR EDITION

WILLIAM BLACKWOOD & SONS LTD.
EDINBURGH AND LONDON

FANCY FARM.

CHAPTER I.

THIS was our notion of a man, in Schawfield—that he should look like Captain Cutlass. This was our standard of gentility—a race as old and rare as Captain Cutlass's, a voice like his to kindle and command, and yet so kind for natural incapacity; an eye so brotherly for honest rags, a heart without guile, a hand to scatter, and a passion for home. When we were boys, and reading worldly books on Sabbath, hidden in stable-lofts or crouching in the heather, all the gallant men-at-arms were Captain Cutlasses—the knights, the scourgers of buccaneers, the great old sea commanders. When we grew older, and a hat or necktie was to buy, we took our cue from the wear of Captain Cutlass. As lovers with the village girls in evening woods, owl-haunted, rich in secret moonlit groves, we kept us decorous by some influence that came from meetings with the Captain; as men of the world (in our rural way) our mouths were wondrous clean, and often we drank but little, for that, we were told, was the way of Captain Cutlass.

No saint, remember; saints are, for the most part, women, invalids, and elders—the virtues that come to some of us late in life being naught to brag of, only a moral rheumatism; Captain Cutlass knew himself so well, and the hazards of his place, that all his life he feared the devil and fled temptation. 'Faith! 'tis the only way for some of us; come, good fellows, let us drink one toast to Captain Cutlass,—*Non inferiora secutus*—following no inferior things—as his motto went on the white stone over the ashlar pediment of Schawfield House.

It was only behind his back we called him Captain Cutlass—a nickname he had heired at second-hand, like Schawfield itself, from a grandfather who used the weapon woundily in some old sea-fight, when British sea-fights were in fashion. Here, nicknames run in a family like corner-cupboards and curling-stones, and the Schaws of Schawfield are like to be Cutlasses for generations to come, even if they never breed a sailor. His name and dignity were, properly, Sir Andrew Schaw, and to hear of his oddities and exploits made stupid people call him a little daft. I wish his kind of madness was more common.

Yet what was the world to make of such a baronet, who was on terms of gaiety with any random creature he should meet upon the road, played pranks so droll, indulged so queer a fancy, laughed so heartily at the solemn rituals of society, had the heart of a boy when his hair was grey; never kept a carriage, or went to London; married——

Ah! the cat was nearly out of the bag there—just a little prematurely; but, after all, this is not to be the story of that escapade; what I contemplate is the diverting history of his great experiment in training the Ideal Wife.

"He's so easy-osy a man in other things you would think he would take his chance like other men and grab the bonniest," said the wives of Schawfield village, which presented some deplorable results of a fashion of wooing so primitive.

"Mind the man's motto, though, 'Nothing but the best!'" said Mrs Nish of the Schawfield Arms, who bought her napery on that principle, and had a passion for necklets and brooches made of the same material as her parlour mantel-shelves and timepieces, so that she sometimes clattered in her movements like a quarry. "It's not every day a laird's in the marriage market, and Sir Andrew's braw enough, and young enough, to pick his lady at his leisure the way I pick my hens. Besides, he's had his lesson, honest man!" and she would sigh profoundly, dewlaps quivering, buttons straining like to burst across her bounteous chest.

There it was,—the origin of Sir Andrew's great experiment; he had had his lesson, honest man! and Schawfield village knew it, as I sometimes think it knew the utmost penny Schawfield paid in interest on his mortgages. There are no secrets of the country mansion hid from the neighbouring village anywhere so long as there are gallant lads and laundrymaids for them to make love to. The odd thing is that my lords and gentlemen should go on believing that high walls and acres of surrounding policy can foil the wings of gossip,—a free wild bird that flies farthest over parks and desert places. I have seen it nest in a charter-chest behind an iron door.

For two years he had borne the burden of his error, carrying it gaily like a man, and lost it with a pang. She died, did Lady Jean, without a single look or word or act from him to show he had grieved for anything in their brief time together, except the prospect of her absence. A poor little wisp of a thing, to be petted and borne with; she put the lap-dog off her bed or a moment on the day she died, and drew her husband's head beside her on the pillow.

"Andy! Andy!" she said waefully, "I've known about you and Lucy all along, and you've been—you've been the very prince of husbands."

"What!" said he abashed. "Who told you?"

"It was Aunt Amelia," said she, "but she meant no harm."

"She never does," said the baronet, "but I wish she could have spared you. As God's in heaven, Jean, I have been happy!"

"Oh, Andy!" she exclaimed—a feckless body—"I must look a fright with my hair cut, but I would die with joy if I could think you really loved me."

"Love you, Jean!" he said, with his arms about her; "I have seen you sleeping and have heard you breathe in dreams, and for all those days and nights we have been companions: it would be a bonny-like thing if I did not love you."

She sighed and toyed with a lock of his dark hair, and mournfully looked in his eyes. "Ah!" she whispered, "it was not that way I was thinking of. You are a man who loves all things living, and would die to save a dog from hurt, but—but I'm so selfish I would like to think I had not much misled you, and that you prized me a little more than all the rest, and never rued you married me."

"I never rued aught in my life, but my sins," said the gallant Captain Cutlass, "and that I was not a better husband."

"I could not have had better," she protested. "Tell me you were happy."

"As the day was long!" said my brave Sir Andrew, and he lay beside her till the hour of the turn of the tide, when she hung for a moment breathless on the

verge of things, and then released herself of life and
care in one contented sigh.

Some hours he spent wandering about the farm like
a man demented, pained as if he had lost a limb, feeling
soiled as though the slough of despond were veritable
mire; then up and saddled the mare, and rode like
a fury for the old home. It is ever in the body or
the mind to some old home we go with all our triumphs,
failures, pains, as the red hind in her travail makes
for the hills where she was calved. He swept through
the fallen leaves of the winter-time, trampled dock and
bracken, tore along the canters through the woods,
sought fervently the upper valleys where the winds
blew free. It was the spring: the larch was hung
with tassels; all the woods were sweet with the tang
of pine, the chuckling thrush, and the flurry of honey-
moon wings. There had been rain in the early morning;
no speck of dust was on the world, as clean as if it
had been new created, and the burns ran merrily,
merrily, twitching in fun at the lower flounces of the
lady ferns that bent adoring over them. Each mossy
cliff dropped gems, and every dyke was burning with
the pale flame of primroses that surely grow in Schawfield as they grow no otherwhere,—so soon, so long,
so unmolested, as if a primrose crop were the single
aim of nature. Along the hunting roads where the
hoofs of the horse sank soundless in the turf, the coney
scuttled and the foumart flashed. A ruddy patch of
hide was stirring in the thicket; he saw the dappled
fallow nibble leaves in the enchanted clearings; wood-
doves murmured; willow-wrens laced the bushes with
a filigree of song so fine it would have missed the ear
of a traveller less observant. Life! Life!—Lord, how
he felt the sting and splendour of it in his every sense!
So had he ridden in the old bold days, capless and

young, and this a sample of the glorious world; so had he felt himself a part of the horse between his knees, a part of the turf on which they thudded, a part of the windy pine, of bird and beast, of scent and song, omnipresent and eternal, like the living air!

And then——and then he felt ashamed of his health and his forgetfulness, even for a moment, in that magic air, of her he had left behind in Fancy Farm, remembering she had never shared his sense of wellbeing, and could not realise the wonder and glory of life for soever little a space in the bewildering desert of time. It was not the spoiled and feckless wife he saw, the aimless languid Lady Schaw, but the girl she was once, pretty as a flower, Jeanie Jardyne, who had been one time happy with her young companions. Of her slim, sweet, girlish form he thought, and the winds of the Indian sea blowing her flowing garments; a way she had of clinging on his arm as if they strayed alone in a world inimical; evenings with her in the woods while still she had her bridal mystery; peaceful nights when she was lying by his side.

Nobody met him that day in his woods and avenues, for the folk of Schawfield ever evade an eye bereaved, knowing when company is an infliction and condolence a wound; and he had seen no face of man when, climbing the brae at Whitfarland, he emerged from a bank of whin upon the prospect of the sea.

For a moment he checked the mare, took off his wide grey hat, and, breathing deep of the landward breeze, stared at the archipelago. Silver and green, with the pillars of birches and their tender plumage, the lesser isles were lying like fairy gardens in the Sound, and far away—far, far away,—sailing among the sunset's gold, were the great isles of the Hebrides. He looked upon them like their first discoverer—a lean man, a

clean man, smirched by no town reek nor sallowed by
greasy foods, late hours, and the breathed atmosphere
of herded populations; tan and ruddy, satin-skinned,
brown-haired; an eye that quested like an eagle's, and
swooped on distant things as does the seaman's eye
or the old hunter's. No flesh-pads spoiled the structure
of his shaven countenance; his teeth were drift-white,
his ears close on his head and pointed a little like
a faun's; his nose looked like one on which a sculptor
had spent great care and a memory of antique marbles;
his hand in repose was like a woman's, but tightened
on the reins raised up cords of steel. The cut of his
grey clothes and the fashion of his scarf gave a hint
of the dandy.

Below him the sea surged noisily, the leafy banners
of the little isles streamed multitudinous; a gannet
poised, and tern sloped piping shrilly down the wind.
He glanced behind him at the mansion woodily recessed
—his ancient proper home,—got off the horse, inhaled
the salty perfume of the tide on the wrack-strewn
beaches, then passed through the sea-pinks to the shore,
where he stripped a sunburnt body behind the shelter
of a rock, and walked to the edge of the bay, and stood
a moment with his arms held high, his eyes ecstatic
on the far horizon.

A moment later he was breasting the waves, swimming with mighty strokes, the sea-weeds trailing across
his lips, the salt spray in his nostrils.

CHAPTER II.

In Schawfield village one funeral pall of thick black velvet, heavily fringed, did duty at our funerals for two hundred years, so that velvet, like the lilies of Lent which, till later years, we saw in kirkyards only, is ever associated in our minds with mortuary sentiments. The books of the kirk-session still bear record how Quinten Hogg, a vintner and an elder, going on a jaunt to Edinburgh, was commissioned there to buy "twenty ells, with fringe and tassels conform, for the common town's use, inasmuch as the old mort-cloth is sore moth-eaten and abused." But, twenty years ago, in revolt against the charges of the session for a pall that had long since earned its cost, some thrifty folk in Schawfield started a Mort-cloth Fund, and bought a rival pall, which lowered so much the cost of obsequies that death, in the words of pawky Cooper Leckie, was almost popular.

"And quite right, too; we must be movin' wi' the times," said Mrs Nish of the Schawfield Arms, till the craze for economy in the shows of grief began to threaten her monopoly of the hearse, and then she was all the antiquary—for old times, old manners, and the mort-cloth in which the lairds and all the ancient people of blood had been happed at last without regard for a half-guinea more or less.

Her hearse in its day had been the glory of the parish. Golden angels romping among golden clouds

played cheerful-looking post-horns upon every panel;
great ostrich plumes cocked and nodded upon the top
of it, like Highland soldiers' bonnets; and texts like
"So passeth away all earthly glory" were in the Latin
tongue on scrolls upon its gables. It was the only
funeral waggon (except the poor man's cart) for more
than thirty miles, and its engagement called for a certain
ritual of bargaining, since the cost of its hire depended
upon things that might seem irrelevant—as the season,
or the price of wool or oats, the social plane of the
departed, or the money he had left—the latter only
open to conjecture.

A man with a melancholy eye, and his natural voice
restrained to a pious whisper, would come into the inn
at gloaming, lean over the zinc of the tiny bar, and
mournfully ask for a glass of spirits.

The landlady would sigh her sympathy as she turned
the faucet over the half-gill stoup, and poutering her
bosom like a dove, till the stone-work of her necklet
went like a mason's yard, would indicate that all was
known to her,—the peaceful ending and the very hour
of it, the last words, and the doctor's diagnosis.

Then the bereaved, with short despondent sips at the
glass, as one for ever henceforth indifferent to earthly
appetites,—"Ay, Mrs Nish, he was a game ane, but he's
gane, and that's the lang and the short o't. Slipped
awa' at an awkward time for us, wi' the hay no' cut and
the weather broken. Forbye, we lost a calf in the dam
last week,—a maist unlucky summer! Poor John!"

"Here we have no abidin' city,"—and the dewlaps
would be wagging like a barn-fowl's wattles. "Your
uncle was an honest man, and it's aye a consolation that
he died respected. I wouldna wonder but ye'll want
the hearse?"

"I wouldna say but we might; the guidwife kind o'

mentioned it.   I think it's pomp and vanity mysel', and
Uncle John was a man o' nae pretences : the cart would
suit him fine.   There's nae great grandeur called for wi'
a man's remains."

"Deed no !   At the best we're a wheen o' worms !"

"But the guidwife's aye for a bit o' style ; ye ken
yoursel' what wives are, Mrs Nish.   She bade me ask
what, aff and on, might be the hire o' the hearse for
Friday."

"Poor body !   She'll be the ane to miss him ; he was
so evendoon and regular————"

"As regular as the clock !   She used to say she could
boil the kettle on him.   And he was aye that fond o'
you !   His wife, ye mind, was your husband's second
cousin.   What did ye say about the hearse ?"

"It would be fifteen shillings ; is the mistress well ?"

The bereaved, with a dramatic start,—" My God !
mem, fifteen shillin's !   David Watson's widow last week
paid but ten, they're tellin' me."

"I'm no' denyin' 't, but ye see she was a widow,—
for widows it's always ten ; puir things ! it's their only
consolation."

After this fashion haggled the customers for Mrs
Nish's hearse : her long experience had given her the
skill to guess, in the first few sentences of such an interview, within a shilling or two of what was a proper fee
for the vehicle ; only once or twice had she given the
bereaved her lowest terms, to be shocked a little later at
the news of handsome legacies.

"Folks 'll get an awfu' surprise when I die," said
Makum Ross, the merchant, to her slyly, once ; he was
a miser whose aim in life was to die worth fifteen
hundred, which, for his sins (that, like all the worst of
sins, had cost him nothing) he meant to bequeath to the
Free Church.

"You'll maybe get an awfu' surprise yoursel', Makum," said Mrs Nish, with sinister meaning.

"Dod! she's sharp in the tongue, but I'll hae repartee for her yet," he had remarked, chagrined, as he left her presence, attended by the wild guffaws of farmers in for a wool market, and he had the laugh against her at the end, if a sense of humour goes with middling honest Scottish merchants to the shades. When he died his sister came to the inn.

"Makum and you were aye good frien's; he thought the world o' ye," she said to Mrs Nish, who hated to do business with her sex.

"A worthy gentleman!" said the landlady, "ye'll miss him sore, but ye have aye the consolation that he died respected. Ye'll be ettlin' on the hearse; I'm glad it's just been newly painted. I never saw it look so braw,—five books o' genuine gold Willie Crombie took to the cherubim and seraphim, and ye never saw such trumpets!"

"It wasna the hire o' the hearse I ca'd about," said Makum's sister, with a bitter woman's satisfaction, "it's an awfu' pity about his will,—every penny to the kirk, but a hundred pounds for a parish hearse to be kept for the use o' a' and sundry by the Mort-cloth Fund!"

So passed away the glory of Mrs Nish's hearse: its rival cut her prices down to the cost of plain post-hiring, and would have driven the seraphim and the cherubim completely from the field if it had not been a hearse of startling new design, with no black plumes, and sides of glass, which made a burial "far mair melancholious than there was ony need to be," as some of the natives said, who were used to obsequies where the leading *rôle* was not so ostentatious. "It's makin' a parade o' the departed! And there was something nice and cheery in the look o' the golden angels wi' their trumps," said they.

Fat days then for the Mort-cloth Fund! Its revenues accumulated till they became a kind of incubus, which was finally made less on one occasion by a Mort-cloth Ball. Behold the folk of Schawfield jigging, then, in Mrs Nish's hostelry. Watty Fraser with his fiddle, perched high in the nook of the big bow-window, shut his eyes, and pumped with ecstasy from the unseen source of the music that bubbles and gleams eternally about the world: 'twas as if he tickled the young girl Joy, and made her laugh. The floor rocked under the mighty tread of the country dance and the beat of the strathspey. A velvet pall should have been hung for banner under the chandelier,—*memento mori*,—the innocent cause of all this gaiety, but Schawfield had its sense of the proprieties; it called the dance the Jubilee Celebration, and the pall was absent, in the darkness of its kist within the vestry of the silent kirk, under the mourning unforgetting trees. Play up then, Watty! another dance; give us "The Miller o' Dron" or "The Wind that shakes the Barley"; landlady, make the old mell gurgle, and send in another bowl; are we not young? and it is long till morning.

In a little room behind the bar, to which the scuffle of the dance and the stampede of the young men charging across the floor for partners came like gusty rumours of the sea each time the door was opened to let in another loaded tray, four or five worthies sat, too fat, old, or sedate for dancing, doing their best to lower the credit side of the Mort-cloth treasurer's intromissions.

"That's right, Johnny! be always comin' in with it in quantities; it'll no' go wrong," said Fleming of Clashgour, the farmer, whose bosom ever swelled, and whose interest in another world than that of nowt and sheep invariably awoke at the sound of jingling glasses.

"Man! there's one thing vexes me," said Jamie

Birrell, the Writer, plowtering with his toddy-ladle, and his rosy face all glistening. "It's that the Captain's such a recent widower; he would have fair delighted in the evening's entertainment."

"I havena seen him dance since he was married," said the banker. "The last time we saw him shake a jovial leg was at his home-comin', when he led the Grand March and Triumph wi' his cook. 'I never saw her equal at an *entrée*,' said he, with another fling—though it's known very well he could live on brose himsel' if his frien's were well set up in dainties; and he waited on her at the supper like a titled lady."

"Makin' her mighty blate and ashamed o' hersel'," added the lawyer. "That's the worst o' Sir Andrew's democratic cantrips; they're well meant, but cursedly embarrassing to the folk he plays them on. The cook would have been better pleased wi' a touslin' frae the gardener. But what can ye make o' the selfsame gentleman? He's droll, and that's the lang and the short o't" ("droll," in Schawfield, signifying something approaching amiable lunacy). "If he wasn't droll there wouldn't be all this surplush in the Mort-cloth Fund, and we wouldn't be having our ordinar' Friday night sederunt spoiled by idiots posturin' to Watty Fraser's old birch fiddle."

It was the year—it was indeed the very week—on which the new schoolmaster came to Schawfield,—a poor east countryman with no head for a dram, as it turned out later; but as yet this fatal disability was undiscerned, and he sat with the other worthies in the parlour, looking desperately jovial, but sinfully, slyly pouring most of the mercies down the table-legs.

"I don't understand," he exclaimed in his high-piped voice. "It's not the laird who's giving the party, is it?" And Clashgour, with a "Ha! ha! that's a good one!"

rumbled into convulsive laughter at the notion of the laird signalising his release from the wrong wife by a ball.

"Not exactly, Mr Divvert, not exactly," said the lawyer drily. "The circumstances would scarcely warrant that with strict propriety. To let you know, his wife —peace with her!—died some months ago, and, as baronets most properly pay more for their burials than common folk, there was a sudden augmentation of the Mort-cloth Fund that only such an occasion as this could restore to its old sufficient and safe balance in the Union Bank. Do you take me, Mr Divvert—do you take me?"

"Good Lord!" cried the dominie, "I was not aware of the circumstances. Might it not seem a bit incongruous to Sir Andrew if he learned that his hearse and mort-cloth fees paid for—paid for our conviviality?"

"That shows ye don't ken Captain Cut—Sir Andrew, nor his story," said the lawyer, "and that ye don't ken Schawfield very well either, or ye would know that there's little chance of any rumour reaching Sir Andrew that would vex him. By the blessing of God, it's the semi-jubilee year of the Mort-cloth Fund, and ye're expected to assume that it's that we're celebrating. Not that the Captain's feelings need on this occasion be very scrupulously considered, for the death of his poor departed in the spring was of the nature of release for both of them—at least, it might be so considered by any other husband than Sir Andrew. How he would look on anything, I would not take it on me to jalouse; and he may be breaking his heart for her for all I know to the contrary."

Still the dominie looked bewildered and the company mysterious, nodding their heads like mandarins.

"A delicate woman,—the wrang ane a'thegither!" hinted the banker with a wink.

"A' a mistake! Maist deplorable!" conveyed Clashgour in a husky whisper. "But he was game, man, game, and stuck to it like a man!"

"I have never heard a word of it," said the schoolmaster.

"Of course not," agreed the lawyer. "It's quite between ourselves in Schawfield,—a kind of family affair, —and I trust it will go no further."

"I'm nothing if not discreet," the dominie assured him, so eager for the story that he choked on the first honest gulp he had made at his toddy-glass.

"There was a time, two or three years ago, yonder," said the lawyer, settling back in his chair, "when two sisters, daughters of an Indian officer, came for a month to a lodge that's over the way by Whitfarland, with their father. Jardynes they were called——Lucy and Jean Davinia. I'm no great judge of the sex myself, but here's our friend Clashgour, he's made them a kind o' a speciality. What do ye say, Clashgour?"

The farmer raised his hands in the gesture of a man whose admiration almost stifled words. "A clipper!" he exclaimed with fervour. "Such a carriage! and such style!"

"Just that!" Mr Birrell broke in impatiently. "If ye get off on that key there's no stopping ye. Premise, Mr Divvert, that one was a most extraordinar' fine young lass, the other in mind and body no way to compare wi' her. In the ordinar' course the laird should have called on the Jardynes, but the customary bee was in his lordship's bonnet about the folly of social calls and suchlike ceremony,—and he left the duty to his aunt Amelia. She came back loudly singing the praise of the bonny sister. As her swans are apt to be geese in the long-run, Sir Andrew was no way impressed by her account of what he missed by refusing to go to Whitfar-

land, and was only to be set right on that point the very
day before the Jardynes left for India. It was the Sabbath: he had been to the kirk, in one of his droll re-
lapses into an interest in the faith of his fathers, and he
saw the lassie worshipping. . . . I think mysel'," said the
lawyer in a pawkier key, stroking his rosy face, " that a
woman never looks better than under these particular
circumstances, if one is young enough to have an interest
of the kind and it's not too devout an hour for the observer. What do you think, Clashgour? Ha! ha! You're
winkin', eh? At any rate, the lady took the Captain's
eye, and I daresay he was not the only one that day for
whom she spoiled Dr Cleghorn's sermon. The Captain
dragged his aunt forward for an introduction when the
kirk had skailed, and—well, that's the reason why we're
here at the Mort-cloth Ball."

Jamie Birrell was, in his way, an artist; he liked in
debate, or speech, or story to keep his hearers balanced
for a little on the brink of climax, and the eager interest
of the dominie's eye was ample ministry to his vanity.

" Awfu' unfortunate! Might hae happened to ony
man!" said Clashgour, spilling the surplus snuff from a
tiny ivory spoon on the terraced front of his waistcoat
as he fed a capacious nose, and, lest the narrative should
be spoiled by clumsy interpolation, the lawyer hurried
to its close.

" Sir Andrew walked and talked for five-and-twenty
minutes with the sisters; found the one a tonic to his
wit and a joy to his carnal eye, and the other but her
feeble echo. He went home, I'll warrant, with his head
bizzing, and it looked like the end of it, for the Jardynes
sailed in the morn's morning. But the ship they sailed
in met with stormy weather, was wrecked near Madras
under circumstances that filled the newspapers, and Col-
onel Jardyne was drowned. Full of compassion for the

orphan girls—particularly the tall one—Sir Andrew sent Miss Jardyne the condolence of his Aunt Amelia and himself, and it was the start of a correspondence."

"I understand! I see! I see!" cried the schoolmaster, and the company watched his face with zest, and still nid-nodded like mandarins.

"Miss Jean Davinia Jardyne could be a most clever hand at a letter, it would seem; it was not many months till Sir Andrew and she were plying an ardent correspondence wherein every thought she revealed was born companion to his own convictions. He proposed, ram-stam, by telegraph; was accepted, and the lady came home in the care of a relative that he might marry her. If it was not at the kirk door he met her first, it was gey near it, and he saw his Aunt Amelia's blunder — *he had brought home the wrong lass !*"

"Bless my soul, you don't tell me he married her!" cried the dominie, and the company nodded on like mandarins.

"In faith he did! You would not doubt it for a minute if you knew him. You see the fault had not been hers, save in the one dubious particular that she had got the inspiration for her letters to the Captain from her younger sister, who, in correspondence with another lover, and one she was to marry some months later, had put a vast amount of genuine feeling into her sister's pen. The Captain, always kind, said never a word of his disappointment, but put a plausible face on his reception of his unexpected bride, and married her there and then without letting her know he had so cruelly been deceived."

"It beats all! What a quixotic creature!" cried the excited schoolmaster, taking another sip of toddy, —with a properer enthusiasm for the manifold and fantastic quirks of human nature he might, as we sometimes thought in Schawfield, have been as good as his neighbours at the bottle, and lived as long as they did. "And yet, do you know, there's a likeable side to a folly of that kind. I could not do it myself, but I admire the man who's fit for it. It shows, do you know, a noble abnegation." He aired the sentiment—guileless Mr Divvert!—as if it were a new philosophic truth now for the first time discovered, and the mandarins looked each other in the eye, uneasy to find the Forfar body was so shallow, shallow!

"That is an idea that whiles occurred to ourselves," remarked James Birrell slyly. "You'll find few in Schawfield, Mr Divvert, who would call Sir Andrew anything but the perfect gentleman."

"See him on a horse!" suggested Peter Wyse.

"Or sailin' a boat, or swimmin'," said the banker in tones even more admiring.

"Hear him laugh!" said Clashgour, "it's smittal—his laugh; and he can get on better terms wi' a stranger in ten minutes than maist o' us could get in a fortnight, even across a bottle."

"And you're only on his surface even then," remarked the lawyer, shutting a mouth like a letter-box. "The rarest qualities of the laird are only gotten at on close acquaintance; he has a thousand hare-brained notions I daren't air myself, or my business would go to stramash, but sometimes—only sometimes, mind ye!—they find a curious pleasant agreement in my mind, and look like convictions a body would die for, if one was young enough, and living wasn't so much more comfortable, being a thing one's used to."

Watty Fraser's fiddle jinked drowsily over the measures of "The Haymakers," slurring whole bars, content to give only the accent to the dancers. "It's near the end, I can hear," said Clashgour regretfully, thinking of six miles on horseback that must be covered before he got home to bed.

"He's young,—he'll likely marry again," remarked the schoolmaster, already affected by the Schawfield interest in Sir Andrew's future. An hour ago he had been itching to be home; now he would bide till broad daylight if he could gossip about the baronet.

"I wouldn't wonder," said the lawyer, yawning. "Wha's for hame? . . . If I was him, and o' the marryin' kind, I would tak' Norah!"

The company, all but the Forfar alien, looked at him with some surprise; he seemed to realise, himself, in a second, he had been too free, and shut the letter-box mouth with a snap of some ferocity.

They all streamed out into the lobby among the retiring dancers, and out into the street.

Clashgour scrugged down his cap upon his fore-head, threw a reluctant leg across the saddle, audibly commended himself to God, and, glucking horribly with ale as he posted to an easy trot, disappeared up the lamp-lit lane that led to the dark surround-ing country full of brooks, declivities, and other hazards. "There gangs a d—n good horse!" said the banker, buttoning his topcoat, listening to the clatter of the hoofs on the broken causeway. "It'll take him hame some day deid; Clashgour should be tee-total." And himself meandered home with a sappy sense of wellbeing, apparently possessor of himself, as he could not wholly be in other hours, having for the nonce a poet's exaltation, thinking the world magnificent! magnificent! Young folk, wrapped against the morning chill, walked off from the door of the inn with the rhythm of the fiddler still in their feet; their chatter and laughter sounded down the street, and sank to whispers in the closes. Watty Fraser, with his violin wrapped in baize, an Orpheus half-asleep, and a portion of art's reward—a knuckle of ham in his coat-tail pocket,—sought his attic. The solemn little town took on for a space a revel spirit, as the woods wake up and twitter sometimes just before the dawn. Quick, one by one, the windows darkened in the inn, as Mrs Nish, the canny woman, hurried about the house like a virgin anxious of her oil; and the last of the merry-makers, having drawn a final glass before the bar, were left outside a banging door. High on the steeple clanged the hour of five, and echoed among the hills, and Divvert, counting the strokes incredulously, realised that every peal smote him inside the skull with a pang of headache.

"Dash it!" he said to the Writer, "I'm little used to hours like these, nor to all this toddy. I was wiser sleeping among my books," and Mr Birrell chuckled. He listened to the dying rumour of revelry down the street, and looked at the sky, where an old moon sliced her way through a welter of night and cloud. "Books!" said he. "With less devotion to the books, Mr Divvert, you would have had a better head for toddy. This is Life—Life! the thing that all you sober cloistered gentlemen most deplorably miss the fun and splendour o'. On such a night stood Dido—stood Dido—how is it, now, the Captain puts it? . . . Never mind: the main thing is, we're livin', and there's mony a body deid, puir souls, includin' the Captain's lady."

"This Norah!" said the schoolmaster, pressing his brow. "Who might Norah be?"

"Norah," repeated the lawyer, cocking his head to the side with a forensic glitter in his eyes. "Did I, by any chance, make reference to a Norah?"

"In the room, you know. You said if you were him you would marry her."

"Did I, faith!" said the Writer, "I trust I put it more grammatically, not to say more respectfully; and, whether or not, it was an unpardonable liberty. Mr Divvert,"—he patted the teacher with a fat impressive finger on the chest,—"the lady's Norah only to her admiring friends, and among the most reverent o' them's one—James Birrell, M.A., Edinburgh. To all else she is Miss Grant, Sir Andrew's ward and second cousin, and to be named with due discretion."

"Man! you might be in love wi' her yoursel', you're so particular," said Divvert, turning up his collar, and the Writer looked at him sternly in the rays from the fanlight over the door of the Schawfield Arms.

"Mr Divvert," said he portentously, "you have something yet to learn of delicacy and the general situation. Understand!—the general situation. I have at my age nothing at all to do with love, nor love with me. I am Sir Andrew's man o' business, and you will kindly delete from your remembrance anything I may have said in there among my personal and discreet friends. The party I named is a lady,—so was the dear departed,— and we must consider feelings." He put his hand upon the teacher's shoulder, and, with his mouth close to his ear—"Let all I said in there be quite delete," he whispered with profound impressiveness. "You are not yet in the local atmosphere; you cannot understand the general situation. By-and-by, with the favour of God, you'll realise that here in Schawfield we are all one family, from the laird himself to Watty Fraser, and we must be loyal. Whatever we are, let us be Scottish gentlemen."

So saying, the little lawyer shook the teacher ceremoniously by the hand, and entered his house a few doors from the inn; and Mr Divvert, with a head confused by toddy and a diplomatic atmosphere he could not comprehend, went round the back of the church to his lodgings.

"They're very sly!" said he to himself as he went to bed. "What harm could it have done had Mr Birrell been a trifle more explicit? Oh mighty! but they're sly, sly!"

CHAPTER III.

THE Mort-cloth Ball was ancient history, as all hilarious joys appear when a season or two has gone, and the wedded life of Sir Andrew Schaw seemed infinitely more remote to the village folk, for whom the Lady Jean had always been an alien. Norah sat one day with her cousin by an open window that looked out from Fancy Farm upon a landscape she had learned to love in every changing aspect of it; she had been arguing with him, playfully, upon a topic almost stale between them, and at last, impatient of his perverse views, had stamped her foot and, quite forgetful of the dozen years of difference in their ages and the fact that a month ago she had been, in the eyes of the law, an infant in his care, had bluntly called him silly.

He watched her flounce across the room, with admiration. "You make me think, lass, of a cat," said he. "There is something feline in the way you put up your back and show your claws upon occasion."

"A cat!" she exclaimed.

"Tut! tut!" he said, "don't scratch; you know how fond I am of cats. A cat is the only creature that can enter a room with absolutely unconscious dignity, be fierce without awkwardness, and idle without becoming fat — not that there seems any danger of your becoming fat or idle either."

The lady smiled; the flash of temper that had

momentarily lit her eyes and flushed her brow died out, and she sank into a chair with a gracious easy irrestraint of every limb that really justified her cousin's hint at the feline.

"You're not so happy in your compliments as Mr Maurice," she exclaimed.

"Well, you know I have neither his privileges nor his practice," said Sir Andrew. "How, if I may ask, does the bard of passion and of mirth in his appreciative moments designate your charms?"

"Is it fair to tell?" she reflected audibly, looking out of deep green eyes that seemed sometimes black.

"I am persuaded that Dulcinea's eyes must be green emeralds," said Sir Andrew irrelevantly, quoting the Knight of the Rueful Countenance. "There is no harm, I am sure, in disseminating pure poetry, and in any case, as almost *in loco parentis* even yet, I have some little claim to know if the compliments that are proffered to my late ward and cousin are base metal or the true Parnassian gold.

"I am, it seems, in bearing, like a Virgilian goddess, a priestess carrying sacred vessels."

"Heavens! he could say the same of our milkmaid, Lizzie, carrying the cogues of pease-meal and milk to the calves. I prefer my own comparison—of the graceful and mysterious cat."

"And, sitting, I have—what does he call it?—the hieratic aspect of some old Madonna."

"Ah! the dear lad! what a sad evidence that poets and lovers should derive from life, and not from literature or art. You are too cold to Master Reginald, Norah; a swain so devoted and so fervent, though so confoundedly obvious in his compliments, does not deserve the snubbings that your playful and whimsical affection too often bestows on him. With a little more encouragement the lad could show you he has the stuff of a grand passion under the copy of Keats he always carries in his breast-pocket. I dragged him out on the yawl a week ago, and sailed him an hour or two along the coast with the sea coming over the coamings, and I liked the fellow's eye—there was no moment of quailing; but the idiot spouted Byron! Great Neptune!—Byron at such an hour—with the nor'-easter coming down in black squalls and a lost reef-pennant! I was ass enough to give him the tiller, while I went forward for a moment, and he let her gybe. . . . God nearly had us there!"

"Oh!" cried his hearer, "you horrify me! It is the first time I have heard of it; you must not—*must not* do such dreadful things."

He had risen, and was pacing the floor; the wind blew in from the open window, laden with summer scents, bearing the sounds of the valley—the reapers' hone, the plunge of the river on its weirs, and the scream of plovers. It blew through her beautiful and abundant hair, and seemed to pale the burnished olive of her pure and healthy cheek. Her eyes stared troublously; she had risen to her feet, and clasped her hands together, sucking her breath through sleet-white teeth, her lips apart and shuddering.

"Ah!" he said remorsefully, "I shouldn't have mentioned it; and I promise you I'll never give him a tiller again."

"You make—you make me furious!" she exclaimed, stamping her foot. "You should never have had him on board; you should never have let him take the tiller; you know very well he knows nothing about it. Had you—had you drowned Reginald!"

"What!" cried the Captain mockingly. "The author of 'Aphrodite!'"

> 'I spurn the sea-billow and mock at the gale,
> For thee, Aphrodite——'

The devil take it, Norah! why should a man throw off poetry of such a briny flavour if he doesn't know enough not to let a boat gybe in dirty weather? I like the lad that he seems not to have thought the incident worth mentioning to you. No doubt he's storing up all his emotion over the affair for a sonnet in the new book. How, by the way, goes the *opus?*"

She looked sideways at him distrustfully, still in a regal humour. "I don't know, and you are deliberately leading away from the subject we were engaged upon, which was certainly not Mr Maurice and his poetry."

"Deliberately,—now, Norah! you give me credit for a slyness I don't possess. Reggie's gybe came into my mind quite irresistibly with a twinge from a broken rib I got from a swinging boom in consequence of it."

"A broken rib!" she cried with knitted brows. "That accounts for your interviews with the doctor. You are the most secretive mortal surely ever breathed. Was it necessary to conceal such a thing from us?"

"No, not absolutely, but judicious. Discretion obviated explanation and alarm, and all the fuss Aunt Amelia would certainly have made about such a thing. A rib is neither here nor there; remember the indifference of Adam to one completely lost."

"Is it painful?"

"No more at present than Adam's was; if wives were always to be got so easily,"—he stammered as one confused, remembering; flushed, and sighed. "Norah," he went on in a new voice altogether, quietly, wistfully, "does the house not seem, even yet, a little lonely? Something chilly in the morning, eh? We are so quiet here. Silences, lapses, pauses,—I can't ride them down, —not if I rode the mare till she foundered. Would you imagine there would be so much difference? Oh! a man wants a wife! I'm possessed of devils,—the worst of devils,—old remembrance and remorse, and the days are full of ghosts."

"Go swimming, Andy," said the girl, suddenly all softened with a pity that welled up in her eyes, and made her bold lips tender and tremulous.

"Swimming!" he cried, flinging up his arms. "I've swam, and behold the sea hath lost its ancient efficacy! Once it could wash away all care, cool the fever of foolish nights, dispel the phantoms of the mind, cleanse, console, invigorate; now, by the Lord! it might be ditch-water! A man wants a wife, a little wife to look at, hear, be kind to. I came to-day on a silly novel, pushed at the back of the escritoire in her room, some day, perhaps, when she heard me coming, and was afraid——"

"No, not afraid, cousin; Jean was never afraid of you; she knew she had no reason; probably shame, poor dear, to be found disappointing you."

"That tawdry volume gave me as much emotion as if it had been part of herself. . . . Ghosts!" He ran his fingers through the thick hair over his temples. "Do you ever realise how bogey is the world?—so much is left behind of folk departed. Their breath is in the wind; their cast-off clothing keeps the shape it took from the pressure of their bodies; the sound of their voices and their footsteps goes for ever through this unchanging space. It isn't only that, but there are ghosts of touch, and hate, and appreciation; Jean's gone, but a wraith of her haunts Fancy Farm, where I hope she was not so unhappy, and whatever she cared for here has an air about it that belongs to her, and whatever she touched—even the stupid novel—is haunted by the spirit of her hands."

He turned his back upon the girl, and looked out at the piling clouds that billowed silvery in the west against a sky intensely blue. The house of Fancy Farm

—once a simple steading, but in recent years a little aggrandised with new wings pierced by low wide windows, gables corbel-stepped, and the deep verandah —stood upon a brae that gave the loveliest prospect of the valley. The brae sloped down in turfy waves that ended at the river, which went flowing over its granite weirs with a gushing sound that seemed to cool the day, and made its neighbourhood melodious; and over the river lay the tawny meadows, populous now with men and women and children making hay. Beyond, the old plantations, garrulous with rooks, and over them the steeple of the village.

"I'm afraid of getting tired of this place, Norah," he exclaimed, in an altered mood again. "Tired! tired! It was all very well when it was Jeanie's Fancy, but now I'd give ten years of my lease of life to be back in Schawfield, and in the sound of the sea. Yon's the place! I should never have leased it to our English friend,—a decent fellow, but"—he snapped his fingers and grotesquely puckered up his face—"Schawfield is thrown away on him."

"At two thousand pounds a-year," said Norah, twinkling.

"Yes! yes! that's the confounded thing!" cried her cousin impetuously; "the poor devil's not getting anything like the value for his money. He misses the romance of the place: he has only got the house and shootings, and the sunsets, and has not the key to its magic garden; he has not the faintest hint of its old associations. I'm defrauding Beswick; I've half a mind to return him fifty per cent of his rent."

"Yes, why don't you?" asked Norah, looking at him through drooping lashes, and her cousin laughed.

"You know very well!" said he. "It's simply be-cause I don't happen to have a thousand pounds at present at my disposal. What money is in my name is in the oddest corners of the world,—digging gold in West Australia, lumbering in Newfoundland, trapping and tracking furry things in Athabasca. It's feeding men and blazing trails out of the weary worn-out world into the regions of romance."

"And, incidentally, it's not getting much in the way of dividends," said Norah, laughing. "Andy, as a speculator, you're a perfect child!"

He actually flushed, quite pleased as at a compliment; shook with the soft chuckle that made Maurice always think of old Melampus in among the thickets, and stroked his chin. "Ha! So! Of course! of course! That's what I want,—the child's illusion, wholesomest and cheapest of all joys. ' Unless ye become as one of these——' But not so very childish, Norah; some day Athabascas will do well. We are growing the finest fruits at Fort Macfadyen, near the Arctic circle. What a world! What a world! Magnificent! Here am I, to the carnal eye, lounging about Fancy Farm, the prosiest of lives, but a wraith of me's paddling a canoe and singing chansons on the Mackenzie, or shooting moose and bear for supper. Great value! Great value for my money! And just yesterday I had a splendid adventure,—fifteen hundred pounds sterling of me struck a new reef on the Witwatersrand." He rubbed his hands ecstatically.

Norah sighed patiently. "What a guardian I've escaped from!" said she. "I'm glad the what-do-you-call-thems did not permit you to venture my money on such fairy enterprises. You go into the Stock Exchange as if it were a playhouse."

"So it is! So it is!" cried the baronet, quite delighted at the idea. "That's the way to look upon it,—like a play; or a poem! That's why I'm sorry for

poor old Beswick; he takes his Works in the deadliest
earnest, looks upon them as a kind of soulless congeries
of mechanism for grinding out,—not splendid things, not
steel for railways, ships, and bridges, but gold for his
daughter's Paris bonnets and his own wearisome luxuries,
including Schawfield,—but without the privilege of the
magic garden. By George! I'd let him have the house
and shootings for the rest of his lease for nothing if I
could have but the privilege of a hut on the place, and
a guarantee that he wouldn't talk Commerce when he
met me. I was foolish to let Schawfield, when I think
of it. I could have scraped along,—if it weren't that it
would involve shutting up the lodges, and paying off
a lot of men; I couldn't very well do that,—such decent
fellows; almost all of them have been with dad. But,
if it weren't for that, I could have rubbed along without
letting."

"You never required to let," said Norah, calmly
regarding him.

"Never required to let! Good heavens! what would
happen to Schawfield as a whole if I didn't? It takes
every penny of Beswick's rent to pay the interest on the
mortgages."

"You never required to let," repeated Norah firmly.

"Ah!" he exclaimed, "you're back at it again; you
mean, I could have taken some of your money?"

"Borrowed it, and paid me back when the dividends
come from the fairy and romantic speculations," said the
intensely practical and frank young person.

"There have been one or two rogues in the family,"
said Captain Cutlass, straightening himself, "but of late
we have run to common decency. I like the element
of imprudence in your proposal, but I thought we had
settled long ago it was not for a moment to be seriously
considered. My dear Norah, you have yourself to think

of,—and your future. You will marry, and the most
attractively poetical quality about Mr Reginald Maurice
to me is that he hasn't as yet made a farthing by the
Muse or anything else."

"Mr Maurice, so far, hasn't done me the honour of
asking me to marry him," said Norah, reddening, and
with flashing eyes the Captain failed to see.

"The blate wooer!" exclaimed Sir Andrew gaily.
"As I have said, you treat him rather cavalierly."

"Because I am indifferent."

"He's not."

"But I am; that is the main thing."

"But, my dear Norah, you confessed a decided passion
for the fellow to me, and——and Jean."

"Oh!" cried the girl, rising from her chair and
clenching her hands behind her back, "I should never
have said so to you; you do not understand."

"Upon my word!" said Sir Andrew. "I believe
I really did not understand my duty as your guardian,
or I should have brought Maurice to the scratch about
you when·I had the right."

She stared at him with her lips apart and breathing
deeply, her heavy chestnut eyebrows more than custom-
arily close together, her fingers playing the tattoo of the
devil on the table she had drawn her chair to, conscious
of a tremor of her legs that might betray her even while
she sat. It was a mercy that Sir Andrew Schaw, in
Norah's presence, ever was a man considerably abstracted
—rapt in inner visions; often it annoyed her, now she
saw it gratefully. With an effort she quelled the
coward flesh of her, and compelled in her voice an
ironic accent.

"You are, clearly, in a hurry to get rid of me," said
she.

He did not look; he did not contradict her.

"Norah," said he, "I want a wife," and she hurriedly
snatched a volume from a pile upon the table and began
to turn its pages noisily.

"You're more than usually irrelevant to-day," said
she. "I think we might dispose first of my pro-
position."

"That's disposed of finally," said he, in a tone that
left no room for argument; "Schawfield House is out of
the question, and I must make up my mind to be content in Fancy Farm. But the ghosts must be dispelled.
Can't you help me to a wife, Norah?" This time he
looked at her wistfully, and she found some passage in
her book extremely fascinating.

"I'd as soon recommend you neckties," she remarked,
with an attempt at playfulness.

"And I know exactly the sort of wife to suit me," he
proceeded.

"Listen a moment to this," she interrupted hurriedly,
with a laugh, and read a passage in the book. He
listened, laughed politely, though, indeed, the humour
of it was not great; plunged again into more important
things. "She must be good and wise and beautiful."

"Mormon! It is not one wife you want, but three,"
said Norah. "The age of paragons is ended. If I were
you I should confine my requirements to a single one,
which might console me for the absence of the others."

"As what?" he asked, and she looked embarrassed.

"What's wanted most in Schawfield—money," she
replied, with an effort at an air of badinage.

"I'd prefer that she had none; my ideal lady hasn't
a single penny. I go out, like Quixote, this very hour
to look for her," he said, rising to the door, and Norah,
looking after him, shrugged her shoulders.

CHAPTER IV.

IF Sir Andrew Schaw was "queer" to all his social compeers,—Scottish lairds with ancient Scottish names, who had English mothers, and had gone to English schools, and were Episcopalians, and, in character and accent, undistinguishable from the Englishmen they rode with half the year in Rotten Row,—it was not his fault, but due to his heredity. "The Siccar Schaws" was the bye-name of his folk from far-back years, and the steadfastness that name betokened was in no way else more manifest than in their nationality. They bided, most of them, at home, and married Scottish women; they bred true Scots, who might go round the world in English fighting-ships (with a piper in the poop at even-fall), but ever came back at last to Scotland, there to dwell content among the ancestral woods on the shores of the Scottish sea. The family's hereditary calling made the thing inevitable; no home had they away from Schawfield, save the narrow cabins of their sovereign's ships; no chance to let the glamour of the city sink within them; for years on the wastes of ocean, passing between their stations, or sweltering in clammy latitudes, the one spot of earth that rose to their inner eyes unutterably sweet because of its associations was the native parish where the lapwing whistled and the cool winds blew.

The first Captain Cutlass—he who won the appellation—kept a flat blue bonnet in his shore portmanteau, and put it on whenever he had crossed the Border on his way to the North from Plymouth. " Thank God ! " he would say with fervour.then; " nae mair, for a while, o' those damned mim-mouthed gentlemen ! " And his eye rejoiced, as the coach proceeded, at the sight of brick-built and flat-chested dwellings giving place to houses built of stone,—their grey tones blending with the landscape and the careening clouds. The second Captain Cutlass had been nurtured too in the Scottish sentiment; loved and rejoiced in his English seamen, but could not stand, as he professed, the English climate. " Sunshine and stour ! " he summed it up with an honesty that would have much astonished any Continental with a Continental standard of a climate. And Cutlass Tertius, my eccentric hero, absorbed the same sentiments almost as soon as he supped porridge. They sent him to the local grammar-school, and finished him in the College of St Andrews ; they drove him all the way from Schawfield to the Solent, and saw him on his ship, as if he were a convict banished, without allowing him a sight of the siren London. Such times as he returned from his naval duties, he flew North without a pause,—having seen the world widely, strange peoples, solemn temples, cities clamant, spacious harbours; and the first thing he would do when he got home, this sailor, was to mount a horse, dive into the sea at Whitfarland, or walk the roads with some ragged gangrel.

When his father died, Sir Andrew left the Navy. " Fifteen years of it, and never a shotted broadside ! I'd be better reading old Epictetus," said he, and settled down to working his estate. With falling rents for his farms, and a distaste for shooting-tenants, he found it a rather barren patrimony, but never once did you hear the man lamenting. He came home from the sea with that air of mystery and romance that landward people always look for in the mariner; stories were common of his carry-on in foreign ports,—all lies, as it happened, but for some the lies invested him with charm. At first his people, hearing of his quixotic follies, made some efforts to exploit him for their own advantage, and, faith! at times, he was a marvel of credulity; but it's ill to take the trousers off a Hielandman, and laird and tenants settled down at last to a pleasant understanding based on mutual affection.

A man he was who, in some cranny of his being, kept a wild-flower soul inviolate; nothing could harm him, ache nor care for long distress him: a man with a tutored mind, he thought, was master of his fate and of the world, and every catastrophe could be resolved to nothing in an honest sleep.

We saw him, as I said, in those days, like a creature of our books, so debonair! so frank! and so ubiquitous! At early morning, when the frost or dew was still upon the lawn, he could be seen among the sheep-folds of the upper glens, smoking his pipe with shepherds; at noon no glade of the forest could be so hidden and remote, but we, bird-nesting, gathering white hay, or seeking red-pine roots for firewood, were not liable to find him there before us, standing in the grass like a woodland deity in an old pair of sailor's leggings, and he knew us all by name. At evening sports on the village common Captain Cutlass had been more than once the champion; he was often the soul of farmers' parties.

At first they were abashed at this curious condescension in a gentleman, who spoke Scots like themselves, and vastly wondered that he was so careless of the company of his social equals in the shire, and then at last ascribed it all to his want of money. Money he had, 'tis true, but not enough for a country magnate;

and he never seemed so happy as when it took the form of scrip for some romantic enterprise that never brought a penny.

He leased the House of Schawfield, and retired to Fancy Farm, that had been for long a dower-house in the family; bred, not unprofitably, red Highland cattle with enormous horns. His aunt Amelia — a florid, bustling, sentimental body, who had never had an offer from a man, and long had ceased to hope for any—was his housekeeper. They were joined in Fancy Farm on the first year of his wedded life by Norah, in her teens, the orphan only child of a Highland cousin, with the true Schaw disregard for money, of which her father and mother had left her more than Captain Cutlass, as trustee and guardian, was inclined to look upon with patience.

Upon his easy-going and eccentric way of life his mistaken marriage had made hardly any difference. Lady Jean and Aunt Amelia between them, apostles of convention, tried to reconcile him with Society, but at their garden-parties it was ten to one he would be missing, or, if he did appear, it was to shock some sense of things "correct" or convenable, as when on one occasion he brought with him an Italian image-seller he had found in Schawfield village. The Italian had a tenor voice of the purest gold, and sang divinely, but his greasy rags estranged from Fancy Farm for ever after half the men and women Aunt Amelia and the wife had set their hearts on cultivating. And then they filled the house, at seasons, with the kind of folk they thought might be a compromise between the vagabonds he loved and the gentry they thought better company for him,— with an occasional poetic soul like Maurice, who had made a hash of life in a picturesque and cultivated manner, nourished himself on thoughts sublime and other people's viands; painter fellows, not particular about their clothes; actors even (Norah made some wonderful acquaintances): in short, they sought to cloy him with a rural rendering of the "Vie de Bohème," but he only laughed at them, and, when they were most wonderful, would quit them for the woods, an hour of conversation with the village smith, or a game with children.

Children!—ah! they were a passion with Captain Cutlass, and they always understood him. 'Tilda Birrell, the Writer's sister, understood him, too. "Fiddlesticks! what the man wants is a brisk young wife," said she, "and a wean or twa o' his ain to keep him in amusement. He's just a great big boy, and fine I mind o' him and his fancy rabbits!" Yes, he was aye the great big boy. I know, when we were bairns, and he came home from the sea with brass-bound jackets, there was no company he sooner sought than ours. For a moment or two we feared him,—so tall, so straight, so Englified and well-put-on, but he would stand upon his head, or crawl all-fours in a way to make himself ridiculous, and then we knew he was not grown-up inside, and was only a naval masquerader. We would speak to him at first in the English of the schoolroom,—all our vowels thinned, our "r's" with the dirl awanting, and our "ings" fastidious; he pretended he could not understand, and, himself relapsing to the Doric, led us back without our knowing it into the old vernacular, that came to us in moments unembarrassed.

Many a tale he told us, gathered about him on the grass at Cairnbaan; many a nest we found together; many a trout we guddled. Together we plundered his father's apples; he taught us all to swim, and a little of equestrian menage. To be unhealthy—even were it only with a headache—he esteemed a kind of crime;

'twas lucky we were wholesome creatures! A straight back, a high chin, a light foot, and a fearless utterance were, for him, the first of virtues. Books he would sometimes laughingly contemn, yet somehow, by his knowledge of them, made us prize, and well he knew it: it was but his cunning. If I have some acquaintance now with Shakespeare, it is since I sojourned once with Andrew Schaw in a Scottish Arden, heard the voices of "The Tempest" crying round his yawl, and laughed at his Scots perversion of the sinner Falstaff.

And a man so humble of his own capacities! "I'm a splairger!" he would say. I hope my readers know the meaning of the word. It stands for the dauber dilettante, and, in his case, did a manifest injustice to his power, which lay in the line of making life itself a picture. "I'm a splairger," he would say, as he watched some tradesman skilfully handle tools; "I've the splairger's dreams, man! and would be master of every art and craft and a don at all accomplishments, even if it was only playing draughts. But there's nae determined goal for the splairger, Alick; and you're the lucky man, content to mak' a perfect horse-shoe. The splairger's only master in his mind, and there I'm a perfect marvel! I've played at a score o' things, and tired o' them, and finished naething, the time that you were makin' the shoes for a thousand horses."

"Tuts, Sir Andrew, you that can dae onything!" said the smith to him on that occasion——the smith, who had had his visions too, though defective of a leg. "If I had a' my limbs aboot me, it's no' at this tinker o' an anvil I would be, but sclimbin' masts oot yonder round aboot the Horn, and you have seen it!"

"A great muckle jabble o' water!" said the Captain airily; "there's naething in it, and there's hardly a mast nowadays to sclim'; you see mair life here in your

smiddy. Try my tobacco, Alick. I once went round
the Horn on the *Bellerophon*. We lost a sailor over-
board in dirty weather, and I fell after him."

"Oh, I heard about that!" said the blacksmith sagely.
"Ye have the medal."

"Just that! but the point is, it's a curious thing
about the sea," said Captain Cutlass, "that in itsel'
it's a gentle creature, quiet as a bowl o' milk. Before
I dived, the weather roared about us, whoopin' in the
funnels, whistlin' round the yards—a noise that seemed
to dominate the world and deafened us so much we
had to bellow in each other's ears. But when I left
the ship and rose to the surface of the sea it might
have been Whitfarland Bay on an autumn Sunday—
a silence that, coming with such suddenness after the
turmoil of the deck, was like a swound. Man! I was
astonished; and then I saw that it a' fell in wi' my
philosophy—that everything is in oursel's, and naething
is outside oursel's, except appearances."

The smith hung on his bellows' handle and surveyed him, wondering. "Ye would be a gey wet
man that day, Sir Andrew!" was his comment; "but
a' the same I could be daein', if I had my leg, wi' a
little sailorising. I ken mysel' there's naething in it
but imagination, but that'll no' hinder the delight o'
dreamin' o't." And at that Captain Cutlass grasped
him by his calloused hand and shook it in a frenzy
of appreciation.

"Right, Alick!" he exclaimed delightedly, "that's
the way wi' me. I'm a' for the things untried. A
horse-shoe's fine, but once ye've made them perfectly,
there's mony another thing to ponder on. At least,
I think so," added the cautious Captain. "I can
only guess mysel', since I never brought onything to
perfection,—no, not even Schawfield!"

That, for long, had been his most abiding dream, his great ambition,—to have the estate of Schawfield in its way perfection. Coming home from the sea, where a ship was his little kingdom, and everything aboard of her was tidy, in its place, and order and economy of means to ends a law, ropes flemished down, and never an Irish pennant, he wanted to see the land he heired, and every farm and cot upon it, in the same trim order. For this, at first, he spent his money like water,—building, fencing, draining, repairing; but the money seemed to go through a sieve, and he found that an estate is not a ship, since it has no bulwarks. It was lucky his cash was almost done! Before he had wholly ruined himself, he saw that "ship-shape and Bristol fashion" could never be said of any Scottish property so extensive as his own. When he was tutoring his tenants at Braleckan in the matter of flower-gardens, his tenants six miles off were ruining the land by a neglect of the strict rotation of the crops, or letting their braes revert to whin and bracken. If he built them fences, they none the less light-heartedly helped themselves in winter to the healthiest, straightest firs in his young plantations. Cattanach, his factor, used to be distracted. "The laird's clean daft," said he; "I would squeeze the devils; that's the only way to get the best from them, and, if he did, they would think the more of him."

But there, of course, Cattanach was wrong — Sir Andrew Schaw was the idol of his tenantry, and, when he found that Schawfield could not be transformed into a battleship, he found a comfort in his own philosophy. "After all," he said, "I believe I would hate to see the place perfection after any human plan; arable land is admirable, but I like to see the brackens." It was in vain the factor pointed out that the tenants let their lands run wild from no such æsthetic principle, but only out of idleness; Sir Andrew had a kindly eye even for indolence, at which he professed himself (untruthfully) past-master.

Whatever happened, nothing marred the charm of Schawfield, nor for long dispelled the happiness its owner found in every acre of it. Save for the neighbouring hills that massed upon one side, it had a curious English aspect due to trees for which five generations of the family had had a passion. The western portion marched upon a bight of the Atlantic, which had made the Schaws all seamen; the seals played among the rocks below the mansion; night and day you heard—sonorous and majestic, like a murmuring of History—the voice of breakers upon distant beaches, and through the terraced gardens went continually the salt sea airs. Inland, the estate spread from the hill-slopes over an enormous plain that had harboured the earlier Unknown Race, whose standing-stones and cromlechs sanctified the fields. Cells of the Culdees, old Cistercian chapels, churches of the Living God, had flourished there since these lichened menhirs were uplifted in a faith whose meanings baffle us, but the menhirs still were standing, and the chapels were in dust. Those stones, so old, mysterious, and speechless, entered someway into what Sir Andrew, as a youth, had cherished as his faith. He wandered round them often when he should be in the kirk, and thinking many things, but mostly of the flight of time and man's futility. Oh! a daft young soul, I grant you! Likely you and I were wiser in our time.

Sea - shore and inland plain, hill and forest (for Schawfield from end to end was six or seven miles), hamlets and farms, a loch or two, the river and many burns;—you would, being a stranger, coming upon Captain Cutlass eating bread and cheese contentedly along with some road-mender, hardly credit him as laird of these.

CHAPTER V.

"I'M going to look for a wife," said Captain Cutlass, leaving Norah shrugging her shoulders; and, of all places to begin the quest of an ideal, he went first to his lawyer's office, carrying in his hand, with the true Cutlass nonchalance, which never boggled at doing tasks the world might think undignified, a salmon he had caught that afternoon.

"Here's my fee, forehanded, Mr Birrell," said he, throwing down the fish; "you never got prompter, cleaner pay for a consultation," and the Writer, knowing his man, was not a bit astonished. Lifting the salmon by the cord that bound it head and tail, bending it to a silver arc, "A bonny bit fish, Sir Andrew," he exclaimed; "you have been lucky on the river. I am much obliged to you indeed; it will delight Miss 'Tilda."

"I want to talk to you on an unusually delicate and important matter," said Sir Andrew, sitting down in the dingy little room that looked out upon a graceless prospect of blank old walls surrounding the small back-yard of Birrell's office. Pigeons and sea-gulls perched on the ridge of a neighbouring tenement which over-looked the walls, whereon the mother-of-thousands grew profusely, and gave the only evidence, except the sky, of a free, wild, joyous world beyond. The chamber, dark and dusty, lined with books and boxes, odorous with old crumbling wax and mildewed paper, would have been abhorrent to Sir Andrew if there had not been this vision of the birds, and the presence of the lawyer, in many respects unlike his trade—whimsical, humorous, only in the body prisoned there, in spirit as often as not in escapades.

"I'm always at your service, Sir Andrew," said the Writer, a very different man from the one we saw in a bacchanal hour in Mrs Nish's parlour.

"What's your views on matrimony?" abruptly asked the baronet, fiddling with the pens that lay before him on the table.

"A most reputable institution; there are those it well becomes, Sir Andrew," answered the lawyer. "I confess as much heartily, because, in my own position as a bachelor, I might naturally be thought to have a prejudice. But you might as well ask me what I thought of the landscape of Patagonia."

"Ay! you never married, yourself," said Sir Andrew. "I have sometimes wondered at you for that, since you are a sociable, sensible, healthy man, who must naturally have had the thing suggested sometimes to his mind."

The lawyer chuckled: the lips that could shut like a letter-box were capable of a puckered fun that, spreading upwards like a flowing tide, rippled in wrinkles round his twinkling eyes. "You're not the first that has wondered, Sir Andrew," said he. "Without much vanity I fancy I can swear my state has bothered more than one amiable dame in Schawfield. They have been quite vexed for me—some of them,—and have not hesitated to say so. My sister, herself, has for thirty years been preaching to me the duties of man and the bliss of conjugality, but that was Miss 'Tilda's strategy: she wrought on my contrairy nature, and knew herself so good and cheap a housekeeper that there was little chance of me, with my eyes open, putting a wife in her place."

"Oh! the housewife part of it! That's secondary," said Sir Andrew airily. "Marriage is only bliss when it's irrational, and not of the nature of a mercenary bargain—darned hose for a kiss."

"So it is—at five-and-twenty," admitted Mr Birrell; "but we cannot aye be five-and-twenty, and a scrupulous attention to the darning of hose and such-like is a wonderful compensation for the departure of the transient raptures which I'm told attend on the irrational unions you mention. But then," proceeded the lawyer hurriedly, realising he had touched a vein that had too personal an application to his client, "I'm no judge of darned hose or the raptures either, though I have safeguarded myself these many years by giving no contradiction to my sister's romantic story of a disappointment she ascribes to me in early manhood. Oh! a wonderful strategist, 'Tilda!'" And again Jamie Birrell chuckled. "You were not thinking of a wife for me, Sir Andrew? I can resist them single-handed, but if there's any with the backing of the laird——" and he looked at his client with his head to the side, and a droll expression of surrender and despair.

Sir Andrew, with a sudden movement, reached the window, which he opened. Out upon the sill stood one of the pigeons, which came, without timidity, upon his hand, as it had often done before. He stroked its feathers, put his lips upon the sleek, small head, and for a moment of abstraction searched into the mystery of its bead-like eyes for the soul of that other life which birds inhabit.

"Here's another client, Mr Birrell," said he.

"Wanting separation likely," said the lawyer. "A law-chamber's no place for pigeons of any kind; it might as well be the gled's nest." And he watched, with the sympathetic interest of one country-bred, the

Captain taking from his pocket a little of the seed he often kept there for his rambles, and putting it before the bird, which he placed again outside upon the sill.

"No," said Sir Andrew, "I had no design of marriage for my agent, but I'm at a stage where his counsel might be interesting. The Farm's a lonely place without a wife; all my old phantoms come about it, making night and morning unco glum. Doubtless you have thought of the possibility of my marrying again?"

"I'll not deny it has occurred to me, Sir Andrew," said the lawyer quietly. "You are a young man yet—exactly the age your father was when he married Lady Margaret, your mother. I mind it as it were but yesterday."

"You think it would be wise?" asked Sir Andrew, with that confiding innocence that made folk like him, since they knew instinctively it came from a humble heart, afraid sometimes of its own promptings.

"I would think it very wise, incumbent almost, in the interests of Schawfield," said the lawyer.

"I was very happy in my last marriage," said the baronet quite honestly, with a tender thought of Lady Jean, whose failings he had long since quite forgotten, and the lawyer nodded a pathetic acquiescence. "She taught me many things, and not the least that affection is the main thing—better, more enduring, than your raptures."

"Still-and-on," said pawky Jamie Birrell cheerily, "one may have a turn of the raptures too, falling back on the affections when they're done. Half the folk I see marrying in Schawfield burn themselves away in the rapture stage, and have not an ember on the fire all the rest of their lives."

"You don't know anything about it, Mr Cynic," said Sir Andrew, "for you stand outside."

"I daresay not," admitted Mr Birrell agreeably, "that's the way I mentioned Patagonia; but it seems I know enough to be considered worthy of your consultation," and he chuckled. "Do I know the lady, Sir Andrew?"

The baronet looked embarrassed. "That's the point," said he; "I do not know her myself. I am only at the preliminary stages of the adventure, and I have yet to find if there's any woman who will have me."

"Pooh! the country's full of them, Sir Andrew; any other person than yourself would have seen for the last twelvemonth that all the roads to Fancy Farm have been unusually gay with ladies."

"Calling on my aunt," the baronet amended, but with a note of fresh surmise.

"On Miss Amelia perhaps," agreed the lawyer, "but with an eye not altogether blin' on your estate, and, if I may say so, on Miss Amelia's nephew. The fact that I stand outside, as you say, Sir Andrew, makes me the more observant of such things, and I have been amused, in my bachelor way, at the assiduity with which the country swells—as we say— have paid their calls upon your aunt since you became a widower."

"It would be hard for me to think myself so desirable or the sex so designing," said Sir Andrew; and again Jamie Birrell chuckled, rubbing his chin.

"Desirable!" said he, with a sweeping glance at his client from head to foot. "Lord bless me! I'm here, a done old atomy, with no accomplishment except to draft a deed, and I havena been neglected in their kind attentions. An old and honourable name, a property the finest on this coast, a mansion — if you lived in it — fit for any princess, indeed, Sir Andrew!"

The laird laughed, and, breaking in upon his agent's inventory, reminded him that all those exceedingly desirable things might be thought too dear if burdened with a husband generally considered somewhat crazy. He had no illusions about the estimate in which his neighbours held him.

"And, as to the sex being designing," continued Mr Birrell, "what in the world else is it? 'Tis the women make the matches: I've seen it these five-and-thirty years, and I'm amused to watch lads going courting wi' a gallant air as if the adventure was all in their own hand, while all the time they are the bound unconscious choice of creatures who could wile the mavis off the tree; and what for no'? I am not blaming the ladies, Sir Andrew,—nothing else was meant by nature and the God who made them. They do not realise themselves their powers to cajole, though they see it in all other women, but it comes to them quite natural—like giggling. For that reason I call them designing, not in any spirit of complaint, since no pair ever came together yet without a plot, and it would be stupid to deny all overtures except on the part of the man."

Thus the garrulous James,—he was on to an old and favourite theory of his he had learned from his sister 'Tilda, who, to do her justice, never denied she had done her best herself to get a man, and still was ready to set out on the hunt again if she saw a likely quarry. The baronet for once in his life was listening with impatience.

"As there's no lady in the offing yet," said he, "there can be no cajolery in this case."

"I'm not so sure; I'm not so sure!" cried the lawyer sharply. "If I was in a jail and felt the slightest of the pangs of love come on me, I would have a keek at the keyhole to see what besom had her eye on me. Lord bless me, Sir Andrew! we're on a funny topic. It's the first time I am sure it was ever broached in this writing-chamber, and it was not opened yesterday."

His client now was striding up and down the room and addressing himself less to his agent than to some visionary corps of objectors. "No cajolery! no cajolery!" said he. "I'm so sure that affection's all, and the raptures a mistake, that I'm determined to seek a wife on strictly rational lines. I'm a little too old for the romantic." Mr Birrell put up a deprecating hand. "I'm too old for the romantic, and it is something else than the raptures I want."

"H'm!" coughed Mr Birrell, a little disappointed in this new phase of a gentleman whose every act was usually the expression of romantic impulse, and right well became him. "There are many considerations not improper to a judicious marriage,—especially where an old estate is involved. You are wise, no doubt, to keep them in your mind."

"What are they?" asked his client sharply, and Mr Birrell, with gravity, began to tally them off upon his fingers.

"First, there is social relevancy; second, some regard for the financial situation——"

Sir Andrew laughed. "My dear James Birrell," said he, "you're as bad as my cousin Norah: you lay stress upon the very things that least concern me. Did you think my consultation was preliminary to an affair of marriage settlements? By the Lord! I would marry a wench from a burgh tenement, with not a second sark to her back, if the fancy took me!" And the speaker, sitting on the corner of the lawyer's table, waved a restless leg.

The lips of Mr Birrell pursed, and he had difficulty in

refraining from a laugh. "Sir Andrew," said he, "you'll pardon me, but a step like that would scarcely be accounted so deliberate and rational as you profess to be in this matter. There's a certain inconsistency—a certain inconsistency. Dod! that would be sheer romantics!"

"It might be common-sense," protested the baronet. "I'm grown dubious of your thoroughbreds, and a strain of the peasant might not be a bad thing for the Schaws."

"A strain of good bawbees would suit a hanged sight better!" said the lawyer frankly, and, by a sudden impulse, he became more homely and outspoken with his client, as his age, experience, and relations with him in the past quite justified. "Man! I wonder to hear ye, Sir Andrew! I thought for a moment, there, ye were come at last to a sober understanding o' our situation. I tutored ye as a boy; I gaffed your first fish, and taught ye how to catch it; I was in the confidence of your father, and have watched ye like a son; and—I'll say it, Sir Andrew, though it may seem a liberty—there's whiles you have disappointed me by your throughither views."

"My dear old friend!" cried Sir Andrew Schaw impulsively.

"If you would but settle down!" said Jamie Birrell, stamping about the office. "Lord! if ye would gie over eccentricity and take up some genteel vices—even if it was avarice or the dram—that might mak' ye mair like other men in your ain situation, I would be thankful. But, these—these vagaries of yours—cutting all your social equals in the shire and lowerin' yoursel' to an equality with common tenantry and all that Radical nonsense,—it's fair ridiculous! Besides, it's costing money,—money we can ill afford in the present state of rents through all the country. We're sailing pretty close on the wind, Sir Andrew,"—James Birrell, in such moods, always made

himself a partner,—" we're sailin' devilish close on the
wind; these fancy speculations we have made of late
have no way bettered the situation. Our income, net,
now's hardly enough to keep us goin'."

" I haven't missed a meal, nor had an empty tobacco-
pouch," retorted the ridiculous baronet, " and you really
mustn't miscall my speculations. I assure you I find
them perfectly satisfactory."

" Not so sound as the investments of Clashgour. I
heard him say the other day that when he saved a
pound, he clapped it to another nine and bought another
coo!" And Jamie Birrell, with wondrous mimicry,
suggested the aspect and utterance of the cautious
farmer. " The welcomest news ye could bring to me,
Sir Andrew, would be that you had found a wife with a
pickle money; that's the truth for ye!"

" Beswick's daughter, perhaps?" said the baronet, with
a merry eye, and " Hoots, man! now you're haverin',"
said the lawyer. " I would not stipulate she must be
ugly, and Mr Beswick's daughter is as—— "

" Is as much entitled to our respectful allusion to
her as if she were a beauty," said Sir Andrew hastily.
" Handsome is as handsome does, James Birrell; and
I'm ashamed to have mentioned the lady's name in a
way to make you think for a moment I was disparaging."

" Oh! I'm no critic,—no critic," said Jamie Birrell,
" but she's no' our style; she hasna the advantage o'
bein' Scots to begin with, and that, in our family, has
always been considered an essential. There are plenty
more, wi' looks, and youth, and wit, and the bawbees
too, that would jump at us like a cock at a grosset.
The like o' us wouldna be fitly matched except wi' a
fine young beauty. I'm for the thoroughbreds, as ye
ca' them, and, *inter alia*, for the bawbees too; we
wouldna need to go far to look for the combination,"

and he shot, unobserved by his client, a sly little glance from the corners of his shrewd grey eyes.

"You harp too much on the money for my taste," said the baronet, and Mr Birrell spluttered, losing patience.

"Pshaw!" he exclaimed, "there ye go, Sir Andrew! clean against common-sense! Of course we could talk of such matters in circumlocutory terms even between ourselves, and never let on the filthy lucre was to be considered for a minute; it's the way that's always done in our position, I know, and I have done it wi' a straight face mysel' wi' other clients, but I'm no' going to risk it wi' you, who are aye apt to forget the money *is* the main thing. Ye needna deny it, Sir Andrew; for one in your position,—for an estate like ours,—we darena lose the chance o' a good connection. It's needed in the interest o' the land and o' our people mair than in our own; only a nabob could afford to deal wi' tenantry in the way we do, and I warrant we'll never be recouped by the dividends on Athabascas and the like. . . . Man! I ken the very wife for us!" he blurted out.

Sir Andrew lost his interest in the doves outside, and turned about with curiosity. "Indeed!" said he, "where is she?" and the lawyer regretted his precipitation. "I could tell you that," he said, "but I'll leave ye to your ain devices, and I'm certain sure if the lady wants us, by-and-by she'll have us; that, as I say, is the fate o' men. It was not for counsel from me you came to-day, Sir Andrew; I'm wondering why you did."

Sir Andrew laughed, as he rose to pursue his quest of the Ideal. "To tell the truth," said he, "I hardly know myself why I came to you, unless it was for the crack, and this adventure that I'm on is wholly out of your line. Put it that I came, as I sometimes do with my schemes, to put my poetical whims to the test against honest prose. I wondered how the world, which you represent so shrewdly, would regard a plan for training a wife before I married her."

"That's no' poetry," said **Mr Birrell** emphatically, "it's damn nonsense, by your leave. Ye might as weel talk o' trying to train that fish, before it was dead, to swim tail foremost!"

CHAPTER VI.

CAPTAIN CUTLASS had scarcely reached the head of the
street when the Writer was laying the tale before his
sister 'Tilda, who kept his house for him in the flat
above his office. He should have been more circumspect,
no doubt, but country lawyers sometimes are like that
—mum to the world about the secrets of their trade,
yet with a fireside confidante in petticoats, and Jamie
Birrell had the utmost faith in 'Tilda. His faith, in
general, was justified, but in any affair of love and
courtship women must be talking, and Miss 'Tilda, as
repository of the Captain's secret, was perhaps less
reticent than usual. Whether it came from her or not
—and, indeed, it may as readily have come from Fancy
Farm, where were other women,—the parish, two days
after he had been at Jamie Birrell's office, knew of the
Captain's latest whim.

The knowledge of it added to our admiration, and
gave his every movement greater interest. In his
common moods, when the silence of the forest or the
rumour of the sea sufficed him, his excursions took him
to the west, and we seldom saw him then in Schawfield
street. Now for a while he was attracted to the busier
country east of us, and every day we heard him " sound-
ing through the toun," as the old song says. Upon his
client's reference to a village wench the lawyer had
discreetly kept his thumb, even to his sister 'Tilda, and

the village had no cause for vain imaginings on that
score, yet never a girl came past the Captain on his
horse but she felt self-conscious. Lost to them all for
a time was the old, aloof, disinterested admiration; he
was now a hunter, and their faces flared. Not without
other reasons either, for his new deportment hinted at
his secret even if James Birrell had never blabbed to
'Tilda. His eyes, of old abstracted, or seeking far ahead,
more apt to fall with smiling recognition on a man or
child, now readily swooped in the wake of a fluttering
petticoat, or sought, with some unuttered question, every
bonny face. There were plenty of bonny faces in the
village : if he had a special interest in any one of them
he never showed a preference, but he seemed to find a
pleasure in them all. " Go out, my dear, and take a
walk to yourself," said mothers cunningly to their
prettiest girls, whose one reward, except the physical
good they got from the fresh air and the exercise, was
a sweep from the great grey hat and a pleasant word
from the cavalier. Never before had the dressmaker of
Schawfield had so poor a season ; gowns were no longer
fit to wear unless they came from town, and the church
on Sunday, when the doors were opened to let out the
congregation, and the sun shone in on the dim interior,
was revealed a gorgeous spectacle of artificial flowers
on women's bonnets. Good Dr Cleghorn, the minister,
was overjoyed at the increasing popularity of his morning service ; he was, perhaps, the only man in Schawfield who was unaware that not his sermons, but Sir
Andrew's pew, was the attraction.

For Sir Andrew pursued his quest—or he was sore
misjudged—even to the Tabernacle. With the sweetest
of eyes, demure, beside him—Norah's, he never seemed
to see them, and sent his own discreetly roving while
the congregation gathered, yet no one came who could

restore the thrill he had felt when Lucy Jardyne, with
the olive cheek of an Indian clime, had first disquietened
his bachelor worship.

Aunt Amelia, not yet in the secret, gladly saw his
new engagement with society, and with an unbreathed
blessing watched him sally forth on his horse each afternoon; but Norah said, "Saddle me an ass, so they saddled
him an ass and he rode thereon," as from her window
she watched her cousin pass on a quest from which, each
evening, he came back less satisfied than the prophet
of Bethel.

It was to her he came from his rovings, comically sad
at the poor results of his efforts to get in sympathetic
touch with that society of the shire on which he had
looked for years indifferently. At one place he had met
a charming creature—flushed with health and gaiety,
but a chatterer—a chatterer! "She could speak in five
languages, Norah, but she could not hold her tongue in
one. If women only knew! It is in silence they most
command us. By heavens! I would teach the power
of silence in every village school, and——"

"You need not shout," said Norah quietly over her
embroidery; her own long spells of silence now were
obvious even to Sir Andrew.

In another house he had met a lady who was quiet
to taciturnity, and shared his views on Music, Art,—
on everything.

"I know," said Norah, smiling; "Ma'mselle Echo;
in two hours of her company you would discover she
had no ideas of her own."

"I discovered it in twenty minutes," said the baronet.
"Her taciturnity was wise. A dear, good girl, but I
couldn't do without the spice of opposition."

There was the daughter of Mrs Ludovic Brooks, too;
for a day at least he had let his fancy play about her

splenuid golden hair, and a certain unplumbed depth of
sentiment, suggestion, pathos, and passion she could put
into her singing of some old Scotch songs; but her
speaking voice was shallow beyond description, and in
any case her countryside cognomen of The Nugget,
having reference to her prospects as the heiress of a
fabulously wealthy mother, was enough to cool his ardour. It was not so he put it, of course, to his cousin
Norah—all she got was a glimpse of the possibilities
if Mabel Brooks had been less auriferous and more
artless.

One thing only he gained from his revived association with his wealthy neighbours—confirmation of his
thought that he was by his very nature out of key with
the shire's gentility, and that if there was anywhere
in the land a wife for him, he must look for her somewhere else than up long avenues or gravelled carriage-
drives. It took months to convince him, though; the
autumn passed, weaning him a little from his purpose
by her beauty, making human love for the time ridiculous. Then Schawfield was sufficient—the days when
fleecy mists, half heat, half moisture, rose lazily from the
hills and the wide plain which they swathed for hours
after the dawn; and each day brought a richer colour
to the woods, the braes, the fields. There were noons of
trance when Fancy Farm seemed fairyland, its gardens
almost sick with the perfume of sap-glutted flowers
that could no longer hold upright their drunken heads;
when the dark hollows of the plantings seemed all caves,
and tenanted with elves; when a hush prevailed that
gave the world the spirit of eternal Sabbath. 'Twas
then the cromlechs and the Pictish mounds saw most
of Captain Cutlass, worshipper of nature, pagan dreamer,
poet inarticulate, and the lonely, solemn, scented pine-
woods shed upon him then some radiance of wisdom,

calmed him, rid him of the phantoms that arise in quiet and lonely hearts.

Norah sometimes spoiled those rapt emotions,—Norah provokingly coquettish, alive, and human, at a game of tennis in the court, or rambling between the shrubberies with her poet. Looking on them, he realised uneasily the mischievous, mad, actual world, wishing he were ten years younger—why, he could hardly say, unless that he might be another Maurice.

Winter came with plashing weather that appeared to soak to the very core of Scotland; he was out all day in oilskins: then came frost and moonlight nights, all glorious, that took him to the sea. The highway ran behind the house of Schawfield, which lay out upon a promontory, but a lesser private road went winding round the bay, and many a night his horse was there, and he enraptured with the sound of the surf upon the sands, its crepitation on the rocks, the glimmer of wan, vexed water under a reeling moon. The promontory and its great old trees lay westward like a giant cliff against the moonlit sea, and the lights of his boyhood's home were on the face of it; sometimes he heard Miss Beswick's harp. Leaving his horse, he would walk for hours through the deserted policies, revisiting each spot endeared by old experience; then, when the woods were sad with the cry of owls, would gallop home.

To be out at night, to seek communion with the rainy dark, or stand by lochans where the lone star steeped; to thunder down the avenues, or burst, a spirit of disorder, from behind the peaceful woods—these were the cantrips of Captain Cutlass.

Sometimes, in the middle mirk of night, as we lay asleep in Schawfield village, we would be roused to hear the clatter of his horse's hoofs. It seemed to half-awakened youth the very *avant-garde* of the Apoc-

alypse; but our elders, turning on their pillows, said,
" Hark! the Captain! Keep us! such a hurry! I
wonder if he has been luckier to-day." He, passing
through a street deserted, guessed at each dwelling's
secret, envied sleep so early and so sound.

It was the merriest winter ever was in Schawfield,
for the hunt was up by reason of the laird's example,
and the lasses who made no impression on the laird
consoled themselves in other quarters. Every other
week a bride's-cake in the baker's window, and Watty
Fraser rasped his way through fiddler's rosin at a rate
incredible. Never before was there such massacre of
hens, such scarcity of worn-out slippers, such a run
on white kid gloves. Wherever he went at dusk
between the hedges round the village, Captain Cutlass
came on lovers, and they kept, all winter in his forest,
something of the giddy rapture of the pairing spring.
Girls' voices on the hunting roads, heart-whole laughter
by the side of wells, the clang of the iron gates, which
had, all of them, kissing wickets,—the world seemed
wholly a world of wooers. Yet he was lamentably out
out of it. The age of desperate love is forty: at forty
women must have love or priests, say the philosophers;
at forty, men unmarried, feeling the last kick of the
tyrant who impels to sweet alliances, and knowing that
youth is gone, are more vehement than youngsters, and
the fever of activity that so often seizes on them then
and seems a greed of material possession is really due
to an illusion that success may be as good to kiss as any
woman. But Captain Cutlass knew a great deal better;
he had long ago decerned that success—as the world
esteems it—is the poorest consolation for the absence
of delights that are in the grasp of any lad and lass.

" The stupid fellow!" said Miss Birrell to herself, each
time she saw him passing, from her upper window that

gave her a command of all the doings of the world. She said it not unkindly—rather like a mother.

She was a little, russet, bird-like figure of a woman, with a bullfinch beak, eyes that nothing escaped, and her only saving grace as a gossip lay in the fact that scandal lost its acrimony in the emulsion of her great good-humour. "As sure as death! James Birrell," she would say, with an emphasis that seemed less vulgar to the ear than the slang of modern ladies, "if I had a shop I could make my fortune, for I understand human nature. Everybody likes a good listener, and I'm grand, James, at the listening, with such small conceit of myself that I can't afford to be the judge of other people."

Lacking a shop, Miss Birrell did very well at gossip in her parlour, and was soon to find that Norah Grant was now called in to help her cousin find a wife. "Fancy that!" she exclaimed. "Upon my word, the laird's gane gyte completely! I wish I had him by the ear! Oh, men! men! But this is such a place for clash; there may be nothing in the story."

"It's not a carried tale at all," said Mrs Semple, her informant; "it's only my observation, and putting two and two together. She was round this week with him at half a dozen places where Sir Andrew would never call alone, and she's keeping Fancy Farm so throng with lady visitors that I'm told it's like a Dorcas meeting."

"It's not every girl that would take the trouble," said Miss Birrell with an oddly innocent expression.

"H'm," said Mrs Semple, "I'm sorry for yon Mr Maurice. It's a pity he hadn't a better trade than poetry; he'll never be very fat off what he makes at that."

"I'm sure I have no idea what he makes at his poetry, but he would never be very fat on what I buy of it," said Miss Birrell. "But I'm no judge, and the laddie must have some good parts or he wouldn't be so great a favourite with Miss Grant."

"Are you sure he's so very great a favourite ?" said Mrs Semple dryly, and Miss Birrell saw that Mrs Semple was not Mrs Simple.

"I can only judge," said she, "by what I see; it must be plain to yourself he's hardly ever off her face, and she has him there in Fancy Farm a dozen times a-year. Poetry's not a very exacting profession, I would think, for it seems to leave a lot of time for gallivanting."

"I can't understand what she ever saw in the creature. She's a match for any man, and it would be far more like the thing if she married Sir Andrew.'

"Her cousin !" said Miss Birrell.

"Only second; neither of them could do any better. She's more the manager of his house than his aunt Amelia; he could not get a bonnier lass or a better if he searched broad Scotland, and she couldn't get a finer man. And then he's poor, and she's well provided for——"

"It's the one consideration that would keep Sir Andrew Schaw from thinking of her as his wife."

"Quite so, but that need not prevent her from thinking of Sir Andrew for a husband," said the banker's wife; and alarmed to find gossip already so close on what she thought a secret of her own, Miss Birrell produced a cup of tea and changed the subject.

At supper that night the lawyer had an intuition of some restlessness in 'Tilda's mind. "What's the very latest news ?" he asked, and she told him of Norah's new employment.

He heard of it with no great satisfaction. "But I suppose she'll find him somebody," said he. "If she played her proper cards she would not waste her time with Maurice."

"Pooh!" said Miss 'Tilda. "You men! You cannot
see the very nose in front of you; it takes the like of
me and Mrs Semple——"

But not another word on the subject could he get out
of her.

CHAPTER VII.

CURLING weather had come, and lasted long enough to make the unslacking outer world of Commerce wonder what was wrong with Scotland, whose business correspondence was gone all ajee, whose English cheques for days incredibly remained uncashed, whose industry seemed mysteriously suspended. "What's the matter? Is it drink?" impatient city houses asked by telegram, and got their first prompt answer at a cost of sixpence—"No, it's curling; nothing doing till a thaw."

A noble frost! The weather-cocks were faithful to the North for weeks; by night the dome was strewn with shimmering hosts of brittle stars that seemed to crackle in the cold; the sun went down each afternoon empurpled by the weather; the bone-dry countryside was hard as tempered metal; and the highways tinkled underfoot like glass. Poor sheep, trembling in the fanks! birds chittering on unsheltered boughs! But strong landward men were happy in that weather. Schawfield was become a place where work was only for women, and their husbands played as in the glorious ancient days of mastery. Only the village baker, hoary himself as if with frost, smashing the ice on his sponging-tubs, or cleaning his oven-sole with a frozen scuffle, was compelled to his daily tasks by the appetites of men, which ever grow more exigent in sport and cold. The blacksmith threw aside his leathern apron, damped his fire, put a rubber ferrule on his timber leg, and spent his days upon the ice. Heaven favoured Divvert with an epidemic of the mumps that closed his school. Merchant bodies balanced their books at night; farmers, with their cattle steaming snug in byres, gave no glance at their fields from that first morning they had hurried past them behind a cart of curling-stones. Even Dr Cleghorn, on a Friday, dragged himself back to the study from the Whiggate Loch with anguish.

Sir Andrew curled, as the blacksmith said, like a man who had done it for a living all his days, and the Hunt was off so long as the wind was North. Norah and Maurice skated on the long, wide river-pool below the bridge. Sometimes, coming home at night, with a weariness that was like a balm to every bone, the baronet would stop, unseen, upon the bank and hear their merry voices echoing under the limey arch. They seemed to occupy another world: he might have been a ghost, so distant did they seem from him, engrossed in young delights. The very night, o'erwhelming and contemplative, appeared to stand outside with him and murmur "Passing!—passing!—passing!" He would go into Fancy Farm to a Spartan meal and a remonstrant Aunt Amelia.

"Come back earlier to-night," she counselled him one morning; "Norah and I are expecting visitors." He was so keen upon his practice for a bonspiel that their interchange of comprehending glances quite escaped him, and it was like him that he should never ask who the visitors might be.

"Oh, I'll be home early," he assured her. "In any case you need not delay dinner."

"You can't stay curling after dark, at least," said Miss Amelia.

"Dear Aunt," said he, "there are such things as

candles, and the weather looks like changing. I'm
entirely in the hands of providence—and Paterson."

"Paterson?" she repeated on a note of question.

"The eminent poacher," said Sir Andrew, laughing,
as he donned his curler's bonnet; "he is skip of our
rink to-day."

He walked to the loch; the weather looked like
anything but change; John Frost had taken the universe in his hands and squeezed from it the final drop
of moisture. In a windless air the woods seemed
turned to phantom trees on which no green should ever
come again, but beautiful, most intricate! Old snow,
drifted in the ditches, showed the tracks of birds
and the devices of those eerie beasts that lope across
the fields at midnight; a fine wild Arctic sentiment,
a hint of chaos, and the chilled and puckered landscape of the moon was everywhere—in creases of the
plain, no longer flat, but showing dip and mound with
purple shadows, in frozen little waterfalls and icy
columns in below the banks. A scent, unnameable, of
earth congealed, and rotten leaves, corrupt no longer,
but all cleansed by the arresting and aseptic agent,
gave to the day a tonic quality that made him feel
omnipotent, and set him whistling like a boy.

The loch was in a fold of the foot-hills, hid behind
a wood of sombre pines. As he walked between
their naked columns with his footsteps deafened by
the fallen needles, and while yet a good way off, he
heard the booming of the ice, responsive to the
channel-stones; the tiny glen appeared to hum as if
its ribs were tightened cords plucked to some inner
resonance by the jocund gods. A moment came to
him there and then which seemed to concentrate the
gladness of a year—an ecstasy that was like an inward
ache, that rare and curious mood when we seem on

the verge of knowing immortality while yet in our fleshy cells.

He shouted at this wizard portal of the spirit, like a boy again, half fearful of its loneliness and mystery, and the echoes of his voice went clanging like to shaken brass against the precipices. A few steps more and he stood above the loch, and heard the players on its surface crying in the vigour of their game.

"Come awa', laird!" cried his poacher skip; "we're tired waiting on ye, and the factor's got your stanes!"

"They couldna be in better hands," replied Sir Andrew; "let him finish the end"——and he watched the majestic Cattanach, ponderous on earth, on ice mercurial, deliver a well-laid stone. "A little more elbow-in and he would hae been a better man!" he added hastily as he saw the stone go narrow.

"The same might be said at ony time o' friend Clashgour," said Cattanach, prone to Celtic jibings at the farmer who was never ashamed of his prowess with a bottle. "It would make a splendid motto for his heid-stane."

Sir Andrew took that place in the rink which his factor had kept open for him, and all forenoon 'twas he who kept the poacher's side on the road to victory; rapt in the game as if to curl were human destiny; caressing the Ailsa stones as if he loved them; sending them to their object with an impetus that seemed unfit to carry them half the way, yet had behind it the unseen propulsion of that iron wrist. Withal he played in silence——a thing unusual in the roaring game, and his stance upon the crampit had a curious kind of grace unlike the humped contortions of his comrades.

"Man! laird, ye play like a perfect lady!" cried the rapturous poacher; "ye put doon the stane and it goes to the mark itsel'. Soop up, Macrae! Soop up! I like ye weel, Sir Andra!... Tut! tut! ye idiot, ye've given him the shot! I beg your pardon."

Sir Andrew laughed: in the roaring game even a Scottish earl may be an idiot to a poacher who can play. James Birrell, defying rules, and trotting behind his stone with his head side-tilted and his legs in writhing sympathy with the inward curve of his Crawfordjohns, played wretchedly, but always claimed for his poorest shots that at least they lodged a caveat, making a "bonny guard." Clashgour used his broom with an intense ferocity, as if he were mucking byres, and would have sworn like a trooper if the minister and laird had not been there; the poacher skipped with a seaman's shouts that rang among the hills; Tam Dunn, the post-boy of the Schawfield Arms, drew to an inch, or clapped on guards with all the surety of some uncanny mechanism.

"Tam Dunn! Tam Dunn! ye're my very brother!" cried the ecstatic baronet on whose side he played. "Ye're a curler!"

"I might be waur, laird!" said the post-boy, grinning modestly.

Divvert, glad of a sport wherein, for once, he could be equal with the folk to whom as yet in other things he was an incomer from whom little was to be expected, was master of a twist that promised to establish his reputation; the minister with his black coat ludicrously walloping, and a cap with flaps tied over his ears that he might not hear, as he said, the objurgations of Clashgour, bent low upon his knees at each delivery as if he sent his stone upon its mission with a silent intercession; the blacksmith, skipping from end to end of the rink with his wooden leg more serviceable than an ordinary member, called it "Jessie" in a jovial spirit, half irony, half affection.

"Two up again, Jess! You and me for bonny curlers!" he would say, with a comical stamp of the rubber ferrule on the ice.

A meal had come to the loch at midday: hot scouse from the kitchen of Mrs Nish, still scalding, they had placed the pots below some coverings on the ice to await their appetites, which as yet were lagging behind the passion of the game. When they went at last for the pots they were invisible—the holes they had melted for themselves the only evidence of their fate! Ribaldry for the stupid man who had drowned a dinner; a hasty messenger to Mrs Nish again, and that marvellous lady rose to the situation! The men of the rinks stood on the banks devouring mightily; a world of drift and rime was round them; pinched black trees against the white expanse of brae and moor; a region tenantless, without a single smoking chimney, and, save for their gobbling and gabbling, silent as the very death. Sir Andrew, standing apart a moment smoking, put his hands upon his ears and looked upon the scene as he would on a picture by Wilkie, Van Ostade, or Teniers. He had again his old familiar illusion—of men, and hills, and weather, Time itself, at pause, eternally arrested, as it might be, in a gesture; he saw with clarity all life and the seeming habitable globe a bubble bearing on its iridescent upper sides brief images of things exterior. "I do not know—I cannot guess——" he told himself; "but here we are, knowing each other's voices, dare we be anything but loyal to each other?" A passion for his kind for the time possessed him, and he loved (as he told me later, I always give but his own daft fancies)— he loved the very crutch of Alick Brodie!

And now there came, with the resumption of the game, the first step of another cantrip of the Captain's (if follies have beginning in some special hour), an escapade on which depends this story. Had Tam Dunn played a poorer game that afternoon, or been a man with extravagant views of what was requisite in a post-boy's headgear; or had the teacher Divvert not unhappily (or happily, as the case may be) recalled a play of Shakespeare, Sir Andrew Schaw might never have found his ideal lady. 'Tis sure, at least, he had not found her under circumstances quite so ludicrous.

Destiny (always presuming some starting-point in that mesh wherein men struggle like the herring of the trawl-net, thinking they are free) decreed that after the meal upon the bank the afternoon should open with a change of rinks and players, and the baronet was skip against the skipping of the post-boy. They had chosen sides, and Sir Andrew pledged himself to pay for a hat for his opponent if he won the game.

"And what if I should lose?" asked the cautious post-boy.

Sir Andrew had for a moment the gentle thought to make the wager applicable either way, but he could not hide from himself the probability that the cost of a hat was like to make a serious hole in a post-boy's wages.

"In that case, we cry quits," said he. "The hat's a prize."

"Na, na," said Tam, "a wadger's aye a wadger, and I hae a hat already. I'm thinkin' I would be better aff, sir, if I had your heid instead o' your hat."

Sir Andrew smiled; he knew the compliment implied was one which in many quarters would be regarded as more polite than it was judicial. "You're better wi' the hat," said he; "it's likely to be more in fashion. Wi' my head ye wouldna have so good a reputation as a steady driver."

"Oh, I've seen ye drive, Sir Andra!" said Tam Dunn.

Clashgour, who, chosen in another rink, stood with his besom ready to join in, and bold with ale, ventured in bucolic humour his opinion that the prize would be more worth playing for if Schawfield House and property went with the hat; and Divvert, caught up in this intoxicating air of a democracy where all men spoke their minds and baronets were in the vein for banter, made allusion to the nightcap, which in "The Taming of the Shrew" was a symbol of the tinker's changed condition.

"*Paucas pallabris!* let the world slide, sessa!" cried Sir Andrew, slapping his leg; "I see a better wager; thank you, Mr Divvert! I'll not endow Tam Dunn with Schawfield—that would be a scurvy trick upon an honest curler; but the lord shall be Christopher Sly. I'll be the post-boy for the rest of the night if Dunn defeats me."

The joke, to all but Jamie Birrell, had no meaning, and it sent them laughing out upon the ice: the lawyer had an uneasy recollection that so many of Sir Andrew's follies started just as airily as this. Himself in Sir Andrew's rink, the thought of the possibilities made his playing worse than usual. Somehow he felt that he played for his client's dignity, and in his very carefulness he often failed to reach the hog.

"Play up, man!" cried his skip; "like Dr Cleghorn, ye're ower often out o' the parish. See, Mr Birrell, my besom's on the tee."

But Mr Birrell, with only a vague surmise at the story of Christopher Sly, and a knowledge that Sir Andrew never gave his word in vain, so ruminated on the outcome of the match that he played as if he were blindfolded. And the post-boy playing like a warlock!

"O Lord! Jessie," said the blacksmith to his wooden

leg, in a colloquy apart, "the law's very fine, but we were better wi' the poacher!"

And the hours went past, and the dusk ascended; wild geese withdrew across the pines; owls challenged from the woods. 'Twas not as if the Night came on, but rather as if Day withdrew and fled behind the hills; suddenly the players felt the dark.

One end more and the play was done: Tam Dunn came off the ice a victor. "Five up, Sir Andrew; no' bad curlin'," he remarked; "it took us a' oor time," and the lawyer in the dusk cocked a wondering eye at his client.

"That's a hat for ye, Tam," said the baronet.

"I have a quite guid hat already," answered the post-boy. "I got it a couple o' year ago, and a second would be rideeculous superfluity. It's no' that often there's a funeral."

Sir Andrew threw his stones upon the bank and then shook hands with the conqueror. "I congratulate you," said he; "the best side won, and the hat is yours. What hae ye got to do the night?"

"O Lord!" said Mr Birrell to himself with hands uplifted.

"I've to feed twa horse and tak' anither pair in a carriage to Duntryne to meet a lady comin' wi' the boat," replied the post-boy readily, well aware that Sir Andrew had an interest in everything.

"Phew!" the baronet whistled, "I hadna bargained on a hire, my Christopher; at the most I thought to be bedding horses. Still, there's the wager, so I'll trouble ye to let me hae your whip. If I'm to be at Duntryne to meet the boat it's nearly time that I was yokin'."

Cattanach, at that, retired behind the company and gave his views in Gaelic to the stars; James Birrell choked in a spasm of dumb vexation; the others stand-

ing by, incredulous that even Captain Cutlass would
play a prank so foolish, laughed at Tam Dunn, who
scratched his head and wondered that a gentleman so
temperate should have such droll ideas. "Dod! ye
werena in earnest, sir," said he; "I wouldna hae ta'en
ye on if I thocht ye were in earnest."

"I was never mair earnest in a' my life; didn't I
gie my word?" said Captain Cutlass, leading the way
through the planting.

Twenty minutes later, in the light of a tin lantern
spraying radiance from its pin-holes, he and Tam Dunn
between them yoked the horses in the stable behind the
Schawfield Arms; the baronet took the reins, and with
a flourish of his whip quitted the yard, dashed past the
inn, and down through the nigh deserted village street.
The lighted little windows of the open shops glowing
out upon the trodden snow did not betray him to the
passers-by, and his Kilmarnock bonnet was drawn down
upon his brow. Rumbling through the street he chuckled
to himself with real enjoyment, wondering what his aunt
would say if she could see him in his latest escapade.
But when the tenements were left behind, and he was
in the darkness of the open highway, with his lamps
revealing hurrying hedges that seemed made of coral,
he found the icy nature of the road demanded all his
skill in driving, and a kind of stubborn vanity kept his
mind engaged. Lord, but he loved a horse! No whip
for him! He thrust it in its socket, and with hands
that seemed to feel each slip of the hoof before the horse
itself was cognisant, he kept them up and going, talking
with them cheerily in the darkness.

And yet he was somewhat late of coming to Duntryne; the steamer was in and gone again on her other
calls along the coast, and the quay was quite deserted,

save for the muffled figure of a woman standing under its single lamp beside a little pile of baggage.

He saw her face as he descended, touching his cap as the man would have done for whom he was the deputy.

"Are you from Schawfield?" she asked him, a little sharply.

"Yes, madam," he answered meekly, still Tam Dunn. "I'm sorry if I have kept you waiting."

"I've been waiting here for nearly half an hour; you've made a pretty mess of it!" said the lady, throwing a rug into the carriage, whose door he had opened for her. The lamplight struck him full in the face as he lifted part of her baggage; something of race in the shaven countenance woke her interest, and she hastily took out her rug again. "I love the night," said she, breathing it with a gusto that he liked to see. "It's not so very cold, and I prefer to ride outside." Before he could say a word she was vaulting to the box.

This, indeed, was a little more than he had bargained for, but he thrust the baggage where he would have put the lady, climbed to the seat beside her, carefully wrapped the rug around her and drove on.

"To the devil with Mr Birrell as a curler!" to himself said Captain Cutlass.

CHAPTER VIII.

"I HOPE you're a safe driver!" said she, quite pertly, snuggling beside him in her furs.

"Middling, middling!" replied Sir Andrew, clicking to his horses. "But I'll be better able to say when the journey's ended." He expected some natural feminine apprehension at a speech so sinister, but his companion seemed in no way put about.

"You're not a very punctual one at any rate," she pointed out with a mischievous little laugh. "I was almost starving, waiting on that quay."

"I'm sorry," he said; "the road for part of the way's a sheet of ice, and it took me longer than I calculated. The horses have been out to-day already; Mrs Nish makes the most of them!"

"Mrs Nish?" said the lady, wondering.

"Of the inn, you know; they're hers. She's mistress," explained Sir Andrew.

"Oh!" said the lady, after a little pause. "Then— then you'll be Mr Nish?"

He laughed. "Not I!" he answered. "Husbands in these parts are not so ready to play second fiddle. Mr Nish, poor soul! has lost his interest in horses; he's dead those twenty years."

"Then you—then you——" she began and hesitated.

"I'm her post-boy; just Tam Dunn," replied Sir Andrew quickly, determined to play his part in the farce to the evening's end, and a movement of his companion's shoulder, which was close against his elbow, showed him she received the news with some surprise.

"Do you know?" she remarked with a ripple of amusement, "I—I took you, just for a little, for a gentleman."

"It's possible — in the dark!" he said. "There's often very little difference between a post-boy and a gentleman in the dark."

"I feel much safer with a post-boy—driving," said the lady, and sank deeper in her furs; and for a mile they drove through the night in silence. He wondered who she was and why she came to the Schawfield Arms —a stranger—in such weather. There was something pleasant he found in her propinquity, and he was glad she had not taken her place inside. Only an engaging touch of devilry he concluded would have sent her up beside him. Now and then as the carriage swept round a corner her shoulder came softly up against his side and rested there a moment. Her furs, her hair, or her clothes exhaled at times a faint, sweet, alien perfume, more like a memory of the East he had seen than an actual scent; he hated common perfumes! Against the radiance of the carriage-lamps he saw his breath and hers commingle in a vapour. Heavens! what a world of silly social barriers, that breathing the same air and alone in the vast night-vault they should comport themselves like poor dumb creatures apprehensive of each other. For himself, he could have chattered like a brook, but he realised that upon him depended a post-boy's reputation.

The rumour of the tide on the shores of the long sea-arm they had left behind had died away before she spoke again. "I'm thinking of Miss Skene," said she reflectively, "and if she isn't sorry now she made up her mind to stay on the steamer."

"I beg your pardon," said Sir Andrew, baffled by this irrelevance.

"Miss Skene; you know I was with her?" explained his companion. "I was going with her to Schawfield, but it is so dark a night, and she didn't know how the roads might be, and as there's no inn at Duntryne, she determined to remain upon the steamer and drive to Schawfield from the next pier in the morning."

"I'm sorry," began Sir Andrew, and his companion quietly laughed.

"Not I," she said. "She's perfectly comfortable; she'll see to that! If she'd been here I shouldn't have got to sit outside. And I love—I love—I love to be out in the night!" she exclaimed with a feeling of almost childish rapture.

Her mood infected him a little, though every nerve had to be at the service of his horses. He, too, loved the night, and no longer rued his bargain with Tam Dunn. Her frankness manifestly came from a wholesome simple heart, and for the first time he began to build up to his inner vision something of a portrait made of the hurried glimpse he had got of her at the quay. She was as tall as Norah, with an open and expectant countenance, which doubtless would be pretty in a friendlier air; quick, fearless, sparkling eyes, with a hint of banter in them; a definite chin; and a confident stretch of a yard from the ground to the nave of the wheel by which she had climbed to the seat she occupied. All else wraps and furs, that are more than clothing,—that are masks behind which women conceal the caste and soul. No, stay,— there was her mouth, sharing a little of the mockery of her eyes; and a voice most pleasantly modulated. If he had actually been Tam Dunn he would have put to the test—for in that he had some experience — a slight suspicion of the gay coquette, due to her free-and-easy manner.

Away from the coast the frosty night-haze lessened; in the east a patch of stars extended: Orion seemed to poise upon the hills; the fervour of the Bull glowed in its eye, Aldebaran. Slyly lifting her head, the lady tried to scan the profile dimly now revealed against the celestial squadrons. Her next remark was to startle him.

" I suppose," she said agreeably, " you know Sir Andrew ? "

" Good Lord ! " he thought, " can she have discovered ? " and not for the first time felt that a practical joke was apt to have an embarrassing termination. A second's reflection on her tone convinced him she had asked the question in innocence, and he answered that everyone in Schawfield naturally knew Sir Andrew very well.

" A little—little eccentric, they say ? " she ventured, as if she had substituted on second thoughts the adjective for another not so delicate, and there she opened for Captain Cutlass the very source of fun.

" Daft ! " said he, with his chuckle. " Positively daft ! I see you have heard of him. But I warn you we'll listen to nothing worse than that to his discredit here in Schawfield "—this last to warn her from any confidence she might regret, rather than from any fear of his hearing things unflattering.

" I know nothing to his discredit," she retorted somewhat sharply, as if she resented the suspicion that she might discuss a baronet's failings with a post-boy. " But one hears so many stories of his eccentricities. They say he courted his first wife by telegraph," and her hearer felt the pang of a sensitive heart that finds its sanctuaries invaded by the mob.

"His first wife!" he repeated. "There has not, you know, been a second."

"Oh, I know!" said the lady. "Not yet; but it's as good as settled that there's to be another Lady Schaw; isn't he busy looking for her?" and Sir Andrew realised that he had been singularly ingenuous in his estimate of the public interest in his affairs. "It's what an eccentric man like Sir Andrew Schaw requires before he's very much older, or he'll get into stupid ruts from which he'll never escape, and every year be more unlike his neighbours."

"You're all for uniformity, I can see!" remarked Sir Andrew, with no thought of irony, and she quickly turned her head again to look at him in the inadequate light of the star Aldebaran: the remark was somewhat bookish, coming from a post-boy.

"Always!" she confessed, like one who has thought a good deal of the point before. "It would save a lot of trouble if you knew that men were all the same, like the hats they wear. I don't much care for oddities, and I'm sure they don't get as much enjoyment as if they were like other people. If Sir Andrew wasn't odd he wouldn't have very much trouble to find a wife: Lord knows there's plenty of women to pick and choose from!"

"I daresay he's too particular," said the driver.

"No doubt that's his own idea. That's men all over! They flatter themselves that they're very cautious, and have a choice even in picking wives and——" She broke off the sentence with a titter of amusement. "Excuse me," she added, "but may I ask if you are married?"

"I'm not so fortunate," said Sir Andrew with sincerity.

"Very well, Tom Dunn," she proceeded with mock

solemnity, "I'm glad to hear it, and let me tell you this—I've travelled, and I've learned it: men never reason about anything that's of the least importance to themselves; whatever they do, they do because they must. We're taught in the Shorter Catechism that men are left to the freedom of their own will, but you'll never make me believe it! Not when it comes to choosing wives! Men's reasoning means no more than what we call an instinct in your horses; they have learned to make doors to get out and into a house by, and so have ants, but a world of human beings must be as droll for God to look at as a skep of bees."

"I used to think that too," said Captain Cutlass, wondering who the mischief he had got.

"And don't you think so now?" she asked him sharply.

"No," he answered, with profound conviction. "Meantime, at least, I'm back to the Shorter Catechism *I'm* left to the freedom of my will; if I didn't know it, if I wasn't sure of it, I would kill myself to-morrow."

"For goodness sake!" cried the lady anxiously, "don't begin to preach; I simply can't stand preaching."

"Neither can I," said Captain Cutlass. "I preach so much to myself all week that I grudge the minister's turn on Sunday."

"And am I left to the freedom of my own will?" asked the lady.

"No," said Captain Cutlass; "nobody but me. Do you think you are?"

"Of course I don't," she admitted. "I'm the creature of instinct just as much as your horses."

"It's a pity, madam, you should think so," said Sir Andrew gravely. "We should all of us be sure of our own freedom and responsibility, though convinced that every one else is the slave of circumstance; it's the only conclusion that will make us happy and courageous, and at the same time leave us pity for others and no heart to judge and blame."

His words astonished her; she had been under the impression that she was talking perhaps a little above a post-boy's head, and here he was talking just a little above hers.

"You must be—you must be fond of reading," she ventured shyly. "It's not every — man who thinks of these things," and the baronet with some chagrin remembered the reputation of Tam Dunn was to be considered.

"Oh! I never got that from reading," he assured her. "I never got from books but what I brought to them; but I'm like yourself: I have travelled, too; I have been a sailor."

"I was sure of it!" she cried triumphantly. "I knew at once from something in your manner at the quay that you had seen the world; it's the only kind of education."

"And yet," said Sir Andrew, "almost all that I ever learned worth learning was got in Schawfield. I have no doubt you are fond of reading?"

"I never read—except a lot of silly stories."

"That's bad," said Sir Andrew; "one should never read any but the very best."

"You mean," said she quickly, "that it should always be Shakespeare or nothing. That's ridiculous, Tom Dunn. Everybody has her own best; and mine is fairy tales and romantic novels. It's just an appetite —the taste for reading stories, a natural hunger of the mind. Some of us are satisfied and healthy fed with common steak and potatoes, and others must have fancy dishes and a lot of sauce. They're very silly if they're proud of it. There's Miss Skene—she thinks because the cheapest kind of little story can make me laugh and cry that I'm to be pitied for my taste. The only difference between us that I can see is that it takes a whole box of books from the library to make her laugh or cry, and I can be as merry as I like or sad enough to shed buckets of tears for a penny."

"She ought to envy you your unjaded appetite," agreed Sir Andrew, and chuckled to himself, this time, at the havoc he played with Tam Dunn's reputation.

His eyes were often on the east, not for Aldebaran and the hunter, but for the moon, that should be now uprising over the farther hills, and in a little he saw her gild the ridge a while, and soar at last to light the lands of Schawfield gladly as if she had been sad away from them. How often had he watched her rise, far down the world in foreign harbours, and he home-sick? But not for her own sake did he want the moon to-night; he sought another glimpse of his companion.

"Tell me," she said abruptly, seeing herself observed, "what is he like, Sir Andrew?"

"In looks, or character?" asked the driver, back to a jocular mood again.

"In looks, of course; it's the first consideration for a woman."

"Not so odd as his reputation."

"And I was sure he would be!" she said in a tone of disappointment none the less. "I told Miss Skene he was likely to be a hunchback."

"Not so very!" he assured her. "There's always a touch of vanity about the Schaws that has made them train like horses."

"He's quite accomplished too, I hear."

"That's news to me! He was beat this very afternoon at curling, and——and you should hear him try to sing!"

" Oh, but there are other accomplishments, Tom Dunn. I'm assured he's quite poetical."

" I've seen some of his poetry—trash, ma'm ! just fair trash, as you might expect from a baronet."

" H'm ! " she coughed ; " perhaps you are not a very good judge. It's plain that you don't very much admire him."

" I've no ill-will to the fellow, I assure you, but we're rather critical of poetry in Schawfield, and I prefer Mr Reginald Maurice's."

" Who's he ? "

" A friend of Sir Andrew's cousin, Norah Grant."

The lady lapsed for a while in silence which she was the first herself to break with a remark that was more embarrassing than any that had gone before. " You haven't told me yet," she said, " anything of Sir Andrew's character."

" The best that can be said for him is that he's quite inoffensive," said her driver, and the words were no sooner uttered than the shying of one of his horses threw the carriage across the road, and the lady was flung upon his lap. With a jerk of the reins he barely cleared the lip of the ditch ; she recovered herself, and he had jumped to the bridles of his plunging charges and led them past the shadow that had startled them.

" You weren't afraid ? " he said as he took his seat again, surprised that she had shown no sign of trepidation.

" Afraid ! " she repeated ; " I was never afraid of anything on earth, Tom Dunn—except myself."

They were entering the village. Its glow shone through a bend of the roadside trees. " I presume you stop at the inn ? " he remarked ; it was a point on which Tam Dunn had forgotten to inform him.

" The inn ! " she repeated ; " oh dear, no ; I'm going to Fancy Farm."

He could hardly trust his ears!

"To—to Sir Andrew Schaw's?" he asked, and she laughed maliciously. "You needn't worry," she assured him; "I'll not repeat a word of what you said about his character or his poetry."

In silence he drove her through the village and across the river, along the avenue and up to the door of his dwelling, with some amusing speculation as to what his Aunt Amelia would say if she saw who brought her guest.

A minute later the stranger stood with hastily ejected baggage under the verandah, and watched him with amazement urge his horses with unreasonable haste back to the Schawfield Arms.

CHAPTER IX.

SURRENDERING his whip at the stableyard of the Schawfield Arms to the legitimate practitioner, Tam Dunn,
the baronet hurried back to Fancy Farm in a fleeting
mood of humorous expectancy, picturing the astonishment of his unconscious fare, and the shocked expression
of his Aunt Amelia when she learned of this latest
prank of which he had hoped to keep her ignorant, since
her vexation was so often the only thing to take the
zest from his vagaries. But the night's adventure was
well worth even Aunt Amelia's grieved expostulations:
how rarely did a man experience the uncanny joy of
hearing his reputation from a woman not his wife! He
had no clue to her identity, but Miss Skene, her friend,
had a name he seemed to half remember as pertaining
to the days of Norah's absence at the school in Brussels:
how those callow girls of various nations thrown pro-
miscuously together quarrelled and *schwarmed*, and kept
a polyglot sentimental correspondence going on for years
after they had wholly lost the much-desired French
accent!

That there was something of a plot on the part of his
aunt and Norah seemed apparent, since they had not
given any warning of expected visitors—or had they
done so in one of his absent-minded hours? In any
case, this was the proper jolly method for a guest's
arrival, to delight a man like Captain Cutlass — the

opportunity of the *alias* and the winter night; no chill
formalities nor wary overtures after the parlour fashion,
where people meeting for the first time pull the vizor
down and prick for openings with a cold stiletto. The
faintly perfumed frank Unknown, jostling him unwit-
tingly on the highway curves, so calm and unconventional,
the lonely ride together, mystery and starlight and surprise! He almost wished that he could have a carriage
of his own in future, and scour the coast at nights for
casual unsuspecting guests for the sake of similar experi-
ences. Perhaps with some of them he should not come
through the adventure with such small vexation to his
amour propre!

The dining-room was lit; its wide, low, lattice windows
gushed their radiance on the snowy lawn; he saw the
table set for dinner——late a little, as dinner was apt to
be with him and Aunt Amelia in spite of Norah's better
habits. Round at the southern gable shone the parlour
windows; doubtless the women waited for him. Two
steps at a stride he climbed the stair to his room to
change, and Norah, crossing the hall with a glass of
flowers from the small conservatory, cried after him some
mocking question.

"Oh dear! I'm quite relieved to see him home,"
sighed Aunt Amelia, following her to the parlour. "One
never can be sure what might happen in such company
——a poacher, Norah!"

Miss Amelia——to tell the worst of her and be done
with a task unpleasant——was in no physical aspect like
her nephew; the women of her family, as we used to
say in Schawfield, "a' slept in short beds and grew wide-
ways," and she was curt in stature though as yet without
the width that was properly her due, with an eager,
anxious eye that never rested long enough on anything
to see its inner meaning; simple to irritation, illogical

absurd. She could not be said to talk so much as chirrup; deaf of an ear, she often heard but the half of sentences, and a million ludicrous mistakes had no way lessened her assurance that she decerned the faintest whisper. Romantic, too, if you please!—no Schaw escaped *that* infantile disease, a sympathetic student even yet of the kind of literature that had been precious to Lady Jean. But of the significance, romance, or sentiment, or whatever it may be called with which the meanest happenings of the day could be invested in the vision of Captain Cutlass, she never got a glimpse; there was none less tolerant of his whimsies, which seemed to her an outrage on his ancestry. "With such a figure, Norah," she would say, bewailingly, "he could be Lord Lieutenant—anything! But he only laughs at the Lord Lieutenant's uniform; he laughs at everything that's proper and becoming. I'm sometimes perfectly annoyed at Andrew."

"Shall we tell him to-night?" asked Norah, shivering a little from the cold air of the corridors, and warming her hands at the hissing logs, "or shall we wait and surprise him in the morning?"

Miss Amelia, who bustled about for the joy of shifting things a moment from their places and restoring them again, looked at her, with two deep puzzled lines between her eyebrows, the analytic glance of the dull of hearing, or it might be in bewilderment at a scheme that was drifting beyond her comprehension.

"I knew that something was going to happen that would spoil her visit," she exclaimed despairingly, with that inconsequence which betrays the deaf's endeavour to conceal their disability. "Something always does happen when I try to plan anything that's the least bit out of the ordinary; I someway don't get such amusement out of it as Andrew."

"It's an awful warning, Auntie," Norah said, with a

quizzing glance at the eager, flushed, and troubled face. "It's an awful warning that you shouldn't try to be ridiculous; Andy's the only member of the household who can carry off his little jokes successfully. You *would* have a dramatic entrance, and keep poor Andy in the dark till the gorgeous vision of the girl from No-where broke upon his startled gaze at the dinner-table."

Miss Amelia flushed more red than ever, if that were possible, and laughed self-consciously in a kind of twitter.

"She is very pretty, Norah?" she inquired, like one who wished a reassurance.

"She's lovely! I'd be content to sit for hours and simply look at her."

"I never felt like that about any woman; I think it's quite unusual."

"Oh no, it's not, though men will tell you so; I always take delight in a handsome woman."

"You can well afford, my dear," said Miss Amelia generously, and Norah was at no pains to conceal that she liked the compliment. "Ah, but Grace, Auntie!" She lifted rapturous eyes to the cornice of the sitting-room, suggesting some incredibly celestial altitude of beauty, and with a flicker of the hands expressed her inability to describe the wonder of the thing. "Even at the *pensionnat* she was free to help herself to—and lose—our very best hosiery, and Madame let her break-fast in bed if she took the fancy. How the German girls adored her! And now she's lovelier than ever! When I met her at Christmas I realised that at Brussels her beauty had been just—just hastily sketched in. It's now completed; I said, 'You'll come right away back with me to Schawfield, Grace, that I can get a whole week looking at you!'"

"I hope she isn't spoiled.

" H'm," said Norah dubiously. " You know you can't have everything."

" But she can, I suppose, if she's so very rich," said Miss Amelia, misapprehending. " It's really hardly safe for her to travel alone about the country."

" There's not much fear of any one kidnapping Grace and holding her to ransom."

" I had *so* looked forward to surprising Andrew, and now my little plot is spoiled ! "

" It needn't be, dear Auntie : Grace may be depended on to make a dramatic entrance any time."

" If you understood your cousin as I do—you maybe will when you're my age—you would see that just to—to spring her upon him is the way to secure his interest," said Miss Amelia, with a ludicrous movement to suggest the spring.

Norah laughed. " You wicked, sly old aunt ! " she exclaimed, pointing a denunciatory finger.

" Have you ever thought, dear, that he may marry again ? " asked Miss Amelia in a whisper.

" So that's the purpose of your scheme ! " said Norah.

" You would never notice, you're much too young ; and besides, you're so taken up with Mr Maurice. But I've been observing Andrew now for months, and he's showing a great deal of sensibility. A *great* deal ! I feel sure there's *something* going to happen. I feel it : I can't exactly tell you how. Don't ask me. It's but natural he should think of marrying again ; he was so happy with poor Jean. He goes to church, and he looks about him ; he's never off that horse unless he's curling. He's always here now when he knows we're to have visitors. I thought a while ago he was struck with Mabel Brooks. Have you noticed that at nearly every house he has called at lately there is sure to be a pretty daughter ? "

"What a suspicious aunt!" cried Norah gaily. "And Grace is to be flashed on him without a single word of warning! Well, I may tell you this—she knows a surprising lot about his character, and she's ready to be fascinated."

"Oh, as for that," said Miss Amelia complacently, "it isn't her I'm thinking of. Andrew may be odd, but with women he has always a fascination. I never could understand it. It's—it's in the family,—among the men, I mean. What I'm not so sure of is if your friend is likely to attract *him*. You never can tell with Andy."

"Indeed you never can!" said Norah. "Hu-s-sh! here he comes."

Sir Andrew came slowly down the stair with his mood of gay expectancy completely dissipated. The only sort of fun he had little taste for was the kind that made another look ridiculous; and he realised that the lady must in the circumstances experience some embarrassment. That she should at once identify him he was certain, and she would reasonably feel that he had taken her at a mean advantage. Had he not been confident when he let her make himself the subject of her conversation that he should never meet her again he would not have indulged a spirit of fun that now seemed cruel, and sadly wanting anything like dignity. He was heartily ashamed of himself. He heard the laugh of Norah, and the imminent exposure terrified him. At the foot of the stair he paused a second, half inclined to fly from the ordeal; but he was a little too late. His aunt and cousin hearing him come, emerged from the sitting-room, and a moment after he was conscious of a thankful feeling of relief when he found a dinner set for three. What had come over his mysterious fare?

"Dear me, we're very grand to-night!" said Aunt

Amelia, looking with some surprise at his costume. It
was rarely he conceded so much as a dinner-jacket to
their private meals. Even Norah looked at him with
curiosity. Herself the evening lights invariably made
wonderfully pleasant to the eye. Lovely at any time,
her loveliness, that seemed sometimes wild and hoydenish
out-of-doors—perhaps at times a little too robust,—was
added to enormously by the simplest arts of her looking-
glass; her hair, arranged anew with artful artlessness, of
itself appeared to give her a fresh identity; refinement,
elegance, and poise were in the shoulders and the tilt
of the head. Aunt Amelia plagiarised her taste in fab-
rics, colours, and the cut of things; but the right effect
so seldom waits on the best intentions of our Aunt
Amelias!

"You haven't gone through the ice, have you?" she
inquired.

"No," said Sir Andrew, "that was only the luncheon;"
and glad of his respite he gleefully told of the lost pots.

They gave no hint of the visitor; manifestly his first
suspicions were correct, and they had plotted some surprise. Well, they would not be disappointed in one
respect; the surprise was coming, though with a different
complexion from what they had anticipated. Doubtless
the lady had been tired and had gone to bed; when it
was plain that for a little at least he was to be kept in
the dark about her presence, he played up to the situation and asked no questions. His aunt betrayed an
uneasy feeling of conspiracy; she chirruped with even
more inconsequence than usual, or sat with long intervals of unaccustomed silence. Norah, too, had a sparkle
in the eye that might have roused suspicion under any
circumstances; the plot, he felt sure, was hers.

"A glorious day!" he told them. "Ice perfect;
Paterson was in splendid form."

"And yourself?" asked Norah.

"Oh, middling, middling!" said Sir Andrew, "not so well but that I once came in for his frankest criticism—he said I was an idiot!"

"Tchk! tchk!" said Aunt Amelia, shocked, "if you will mix up with vulgar people!"

He laughed. "Vulgar! Dear aunt, there's nothing vulgar about Paterson—a delightful man, who is good enough to overlook my disadvantages in social intercourse as a landlord, and is even capable of most gentlemanly consideration. He scrupulously leaves the best pools for us, keeps off the river when the fish turn red, and more than once you've had to thank him for a replenished larder."

"With Mr Beswick's pheasants," remarked Norah.

"Mr Beswick understands; I have made that right with him. I learned more woodcraft as a lad from Paterson than from all the gamekeepers. Our poacher's a survival of the antique world, and a sportsman; I never grudge him a dinner from the river or the wood; it's all he mulcts me in. And he's a pretty curler."

"But he needn't be impertinent," said Miss Amelia. "You make far too free with him and his class."

"It wasn't a bit impertinent; the shot he criticised was stupid. I admire his frankness. The truth is always wholesome; I agree to-night with Emerson; —you remember, Norah, the man who omitted all commonplace and compliment in his conversation spoke to the conscience of every person he encountered and that with great insight and beauty? He was mad, it is true, or at any rate they thought him so, but to stand in true relations with men in an age of polite dissimulation is worth a fit of lunacy. You always prefer to know the truth, don't you, Norah?" He looked at her quizzingly.

"Indeed, and I do nothing of the kind!" she answered promptly. "There's a great deal to be said for what we call politeness, even when it's dissimulation. The truths that hurt are the truths we know ourselves already."

"It's a point we must discuss on the return of Reginald," said the baronet agreeably. "A poet could illuminate the subject. I had the most interesting exposition of the thing to-night, when I met a lady who talked to me about myself with the frankness of a child. A most exhilarating experience!"

"It must have been if she told you all," said Norah, wondering. "Could she possibly be more frank than I?"

"She was," replied Sir Andrew cheerfully. "In you, even at your most outspoken moments, there is some reserve——I've lately noticed it,"——here Norah flushed uneasily. "My latest friend was as frank as Paterson, quite artless: downright, literal, explicit. She spoke to me of myself as if I were——as if I were a post-boy."

"You meet such dreadful people!" said Miss Amelia helplessly.

"Was she a lady?" asked his cousin.

He reflected for a moment, staring at the table-cloth. "Upon my word," said he, "I never thought of that. In any case I couldn't have told, for it was in the dark, and I couldn't see her jewellery,"—— and Miss Amelia stared with open mouth at his criterion of judgment.

But Norah, who knew him better, smiled. "Do we know the daring creature?" she inquired.

He fixed his eyes on her, and chuckled slyly, then looked around the room inquiringly. "You ought to," he answered. "It was your visitor; I drove her from Duntryne."

"What is he saying, Norah?" asked Miss Amelia anxiously. "I wish you wouldn't mumble."

"You drove our visitor here?" said Norah with up-lifted eyebrows.

"I had the honour," said Sir Andrew. "Where is she?"

"And she discussed yourself with you! What charm-ing equanimity!"

"It's only fair to add that she was quite unconscious who I was," said the baronet; "I fear I owe her a most abject apology. Where is she? Who is she?"

"I fancy she's having supper with the housekeeper," said Norah quietly. "Aunty, your marvellous nephew's dinner-jacket wasn't meant for us; he expected to be dining with Miss Skene's companion!"

CHAPTER X.

MRS POWRIE, the housekeeper of Fancy Farm, was a lady whose attitude to the frolic and ridiculous universe was one, at the cheerfullest, of petulant acquiescence; had she heard that the end of the world was due on Saturday, she would have said no more than "There's a stupid caper for you!" and gone and drawn her savings from the bank. Her views of men were not unkindly, but contemptuous; her standard of the sex being Peter Powrie, whom, speaking French unconsciously, she sometime called "a gniaf! a perfect gniaf!" and she ought to know, since Peter was her husband. Not a bad man in the main; there were worse in the world, we agreed, even in censorious Schawfield, than Peter Powrie, and his wife herself would probably do any mortal thing to please the creature short of living with him, a trial she had ended half a dozen years ago when he sold her cornelian brooch and bought a pup.

"You're lucky to be single, Miss Colquhoun," she remarked with a sigh that was half of feeling, half repletion, as she rose from the supper-table, wheeled her cosy arm-chair to the hearth, and poked the logs on the roaring fire of her private room, which (with a natural loathing of things canine) she had lost her temper more than once to hear the other servants call, in the common *argot* of the underlings, "pug's parlour."

"I'm sure of it!" said the stranger, to whom, in less

than half an hour's acquaintance, she had, in a mood evoked by the sense of understanding sympathy, laid bare her whole philosophy, and roughly sketched a life of trial and incredible endurance. "There's nothing like independence. I've quite made up my mind I'll never marry."

The middle-aged housekeeper looked at her slyly—at the enviably well-set youthful figure, the merry inviting hazel eyes, the refined and mobile face, the elegant apparel; and coughed a little dubiously.

"Touch wood!" she advised, picking up a crochet-needle and stabbing it in her bosom, till she cleared a skene of cotton. "I used to think I felt like that myself, and still-and-on one winter day I went and married Peter Powrie. Men are all silly, but they have a way with them! I'm telling you about my husband since I know very well you'll have the full particulars before you're another day in Schawfield; we're a dreadful folk for clash! If you ever marry, Miss Colquhoun,—and it's like a sprain, you can't tell sometimes how it happens,—see and marry a nice old man with a little money by him. And above all, take my word for it, beware of a man either young or old that's daft for dogs!"

The lady, whose identity was at the moment being indicated to Sir Andrew Schaw in the dining-room, much to his surprise and entertainment, put a pair of the smallest, slimmest feet on the fender, turned up the front of her outer skirt, as much to reveal the flounces of a green silk petticoat as for economy, and assuming a sober, sympathetic aspect, asked if Mrs Powrie had been long a widow.

"I'm not a widow at all," said Mrs Powrie cheerfully. "That's the one vexation Peter ever spared me. But I might as well be, for all the good I get of him. You've

D

heard of men going to the dogs : mine went to them right
enough——nothing in Peter Powrie's silly head but Dandie
Dinmonts !   He would travel a hundred miles to see a
show of the tousy brutes, even if it cost him his situation.
He's always losing his situation.   As good a coachman
as ever wore a hat with a cockade, but daft for Dandie
Dinmonts !   That's men——aye a want of some kind in
them !   With some it's drink, and with some it's temper,
and with most it's the ran-dan generally, but with Peter
Powrie it was nothing worse than dogs.   I wish it had
been horse !   He couldn't put up with the neighbourhood
because the fashion here was all for Skyes and English
terriers.   People talk about love and jealousy ! " continued Mrs Powrie with a cynical laugh ; " the green-
eyed monster, as they call it in the ' Supplement,' never
bothered me till Peter fell in love with the champion
Dandie Dinmont, and him——that's Peter——at the age of
fifty.   For two years back he's been in a job in Fife
at hardly more than half his proper wages, just to be
near his darling !   I wonder sometimes what was the
Almighty's notion making men.   He must have done it
for diversion."

"'His 'prentice han' he tried on man, and then he
made the lasses O !'" quoted Miss Colquhoun.   "It's
mercy there are different kinds of them."

"Have you ever in all your life met a single one you
could be bothered with about the house, except for the
sake of his wages ? " asked the housekeeper, and Miss
Colquhoun confessed that, except her father, she had
not met any.

"A father's different," said Mrs Powrie.   "He's bound
to learn a little gumption from his children.   Perhaps if
Peter——" She checked herself as a maid came into
the room to clear the table ; and sitting stately in her
arm-chair, crocheting, gave Miss Colquhoun an oppor-

tunity to reflect how much of actual life, as in the novels, is taken up with the whim called love and the penny-dip or lottery called matrimony. She had, she realised, been talking nearly all that day of little else than men since she set out for Schawfield in the morning; there seemed to be something in the air to bring the subject ever uppermost.

"What time do you expect your mistress in the morning?" asked Mrs Powrie when they had the room to themselves again, and the other reddened, with a spitfire sparkle of the eyes.

"Mistress!" she repeated, "I don't have any; I'm Miss Skene's companion."

"I hope she pays you decently for——for your company," retorted Mrs Powrie dryly, clearing her throat. "It used to be always 'my maid' and 'my lady' in my days, and I'm afraid, at my age, I'll never learn the difference."

"There's a great deal of difference, all the same," said Miss Colquhoun, "and I'm a Radical — right down Radical! I learned it from my father, and a poem I got at school, called Goldsmith's 'Deserted Village.' And a bit from Burns——"

"Yon dreadful man! I canna stand him! What a carry-on!" interjected Mrs Powrie.

"A maid sells herself, body and soul, for thirty pounds a-year or less to a mistress who can bully her; I have too much temper and conceit of myself for that; I condescend to be Miss Skene's companion——it's an art; and reserve the right to be——to be cheeky," and she smiled delightfully, the spitfire quenched in a flood of humorous self-satisfaction. "I'm not an angel, but I'm just as good a woman as herself. I don't know French, like her, but *she* doesn't know how to cut a bodice; if I'm not so expensively dressed I'm at least as healthy

and a good deal happier.   Happy !   I'm as happy as the
day's long !   And as outspoken as a sparrow ! "

"Dear ! dear !" exclaimed Mrs Powrie, "it's not in
the housekeeper's room you should be at all, but in the
dining-room."

"No, thank you !" retorted Miss Colquhoun with
emphasis.   " I never like to be in any company where
my presence would make it ill at ease.   I was always
one who liked a congenial air, and I never could sit to
be patronised and hold my tongue."

"You would never make Sir Andrew ill at ease," said
Mrs Powrie, "though you might make Miss Amelia ; he
takes folk as he takes his meat——the first that comes
along, and an appetite for anything that's wholesome."

"Why, that's just me !" cried Miss Colquhoun, and
then she qualified it.   " Unless they happen to be downright fools ! "

"That's where you're more particular than Sir
Andrew !   There's not many fools he can't put up with
for a little—only the very vicious.   He thought the
world of my poor Peter.   'If there were no fools,' he
says, 'how would wise men get a living ? '   There's
something in it, Miss——What did you say, now, your
first name was ? "

" I didn't say," replied the other with a smile.   " But
it's——Penelope," and she blushed.

"Penelope," repeated Mrs Powrie, in a tone surprised
and almost disappoving.   "Tuts ! what a pity ! It's—
it's so foreign !   Give me a plain Scotch name like Kate
or Margaret ; I'm Agnes myself.   But Penelope !——what
in the world did they give you a name like that for ? "

"You may well ask !   My father got it in a book ;
he's a clergyman."

"Oh, ho !   Indeed !" said Mrs Powrie, with a new
respectful tone, " I didn't know.   The very best young

ladies are so independent nowadays. I had a girl below
me a year ago who could play a lot of tunes on the
piano. I'm sure it's greatly to your credit, Miss
Colquhoun. A daughter of the manse!"

"Penelope," corrected Miss Grace Skene's companion.
"Just let it be Penelope, if you don't mind, or simply
Pen. The pen, you know, is sharper than the sword:
that's father's joke. I can't help being a minister's
daughter. I wish to heaven I wasn't! Far too much
is expected for the stipend. I'm sorry I mentioned it.
Say nothing about the manse. After all, it was a tiny
one—United Presbyterian. And I quite agree with you
—Penelope is ridiculous. A girl in my position might
as well be called Cleopatra. Even Miss Skene thought
it was presumptuous when she heard it first: I saw it in
her face."

"I hope you're comfortable with your—with Miss
Skene," said Mrs Powrie. "Some of those madames are
pernicketty."

"Oh, she's as pernicketty as most, and as short in the
temper as myself. That's how we get on so well—for
I'm pernicketty in many ways. We understand each
other: that's one blessing. I couldn't put up with her
for a single day if she did not make allowances, as she
expects me to make for her. I'm older than she is, and
I hope I'm every bit as sensible."

"If ever a girl should have a man of her own, it's
you!" said Mrs Powrie, genuinely admiring.

"There we are! Back to the men again!" exclaimed
Penelope impatiently. "I'm sick of the subject. Let
us talk of frocks or crochet-patterns, hens or ducks, or
dogs."

Mrs Powrie winced. "Not dogs, my dear!" she
entreated. "Don't mention dogs to me: I canna
abide the wretches."

"At least they're better than men, for they never contradict you," said Penelope.

"My man never contradicted me: he just paid no attention. It's worse."

"I can't stand contradiction myself, and yet, do you know, I love it," confessed Penelope, in the very spirit of the thing itself. "The man who drove me here to-night,—I quite forgot to tell you,—he was the most contrairy overbearing man I ever met. It was not exactly in his words, but in his manner. He spoke to me as if I were a silly schoolgirl. You know how you feel when you think there's someone laughing up their sleeve at you, and still with a sober face and quite respectful."

"If Sir Andrew had a wiselike sense of what's becoming to a gentleman of his estate," said Mrs Powrie impatiently, "he would have a carriage of his own and not depend on Mrs Nish's shandry-dan. Who was the man who drove you?"

"Tom Dunn," replied Penelope, and the housekeeper seemed surprised.

"Pooh!" she exclaimed. "Tam Dunn! If he had the impudence to contradict you——"

"But it wasn't impudence," Penelope corrected her, more eagerly, as it seemed, than there was any need for. "He was really very nice about it; and he knows his Shorter Catechism."

"I'm surprised to hear it! I would have thought he was further ben in the book of comic songs than in the Catechism; and I doubt he has been drinking. For ordinar', Tam Dunn's a man in mortal fear of women since the shoemaker's daughter nearly had him. I thought it was a curious thing he should drive away and leave you standing there without so much as offering to carry in your baggage, for he knows he's always sure of some refreshment. What set you on the Shorter Catechism? It's a long time till the Fast."

"A question of predestination," said Penelope,—" free will, rather; it's a thing he seemed to have considered."

"I was sure of it' Drink!" said Mrs Powrie with conviction. "When the men hereabouts have more than's good for them, they start to argy-bargy on the fundamentals. Sir Andrew laughs at them."

"Not—not at the fundamentals?" said the minister's daughter, somewhat shocked.

"No, but at their argument about them. I think he has as much respect for the fundamentals as Dr Cleghorn has, if they could only agree on what they are. It's one of the things I was always willing to leave the men to settle. A silly-like thing for Mrs Nish to send a man deboshed to drive you on a night like this!"

"But there was nothing wrong with the man, my dear Mrs Powrie," Penelope assured her, showing signs that the suggestion was displeasing to her. "He behaved like a perfect gentleman: indeed I am surprised that such a man should be driving horses."

"Tam Dunn!" said Mrs Powrie, shaking her head incredulously. "Don't tell me! It's easily seen it was in the dark you saw him."

"You think there isn't much difference between a gentleman and a post-boy in the dark?" inquired Penelope.

"Nobody would think of such a thing except Sir Andrew," answered Mrs Powrie. "'All men are alike when swimming, and in their mothers' laps,' he says to Miss Amelia. I wish myself they were all like Captain —all like Sir Andrew Schaw! He never bothers his head about original sin, predestination, or effectual calling. Still, Dr Cleghorn says there's not a truer Chris-

tain in the parish. He's droll—I admit he's a little
droll.   There was aye a queer bit in the family.
'There's daft folk, there's wise folk, and there's Schaws,'
is a saying hereabout. It doesn't mean half-and-be-
tween, remember, but that the Schaws always went
their own gait, and had no guile."

The housekeeper was started on a theme she had
crocheted into many a yard of lace. It was a vastly
different conception of the baronet Penelope got from
her from that she had gathered from her driver earlier
in the evening. She listened to the panegyric of attri-
butes and graces that as often met her disapproval as
her approbation, but she offered no word of criticism.
It seemed as if, for Mrs Powrie, all the virtues that
were absent in the silly sex in general were concentrated
in her master.

Tired from her long day's journey, Penelope failed
at last to clench her teeth upon a yawn. The front
door banged; there was a rustle of skirts, and they
heard the voice of Norah humming an air as she followed Miss Amelia to the parlour.

"He's out for his smoke. Miss Grant will read till
bedtime, and Miss Amelia will doze as usual," explained
Mrs Powrie. "You're dreadfully tired, I see: I'll light
you to your room."

They crossed the hall, whose hanging lamp and a
flicker from the fire illumined walls that were sparsely
furnished with a few family pictures, some trophies of
arms and the forest. Penelope glanced around, indifferent, unimpressed. The housekeeper guessed her
thought.

"It's very simple," she remarked in undertones.
"Fancy Farm, you know, is only the dower-house. If
you saw the house itself at Whitfarland! You could
put this whole flat in the hall of it. All oak, dark as

a kirk, and crowded with antiquities. A terrible house
to keep clean, I assure you! I like the grandeur of it,
but it left me very little time for fancy-work. Sir
Andrew has taken only a few of the pictures over.
These "—and she indicated two portraits flanking a
trophy of swords—" are Sir George and Sir Andrew
—the present baronet's grandfather."

Penelope looked at the painted figures bullioned and
girt with swords, turning their backs with unconcern on
stormy seas where frigates grappled under wreaths of
smoke and cloud—Cutlass Primus with a foot upon a
cannon trunnion, Secundus with his spy-glass thrust
below his arm; both of them deliberately portentous,
stout, and pompous. "And this one?" she inquired,
turning to a smaller, more pacific canvas, where the
seaman, little more than a lad, in a lieutenant's uniform,
stood against a lichened cromlech with a trailing branch
of cherry-blossom in his hand.

"That," said Mrs Powrie, "is the master: that is
Sir Andrew."

"I like the look of him!" said Penelope. "So
natural and unaffected! Tom Dunn might very well
have been more generous in his description."

"Tam Dunn's a gowk!" said Mrs Powrie.

"The flowers look a little odd in the hands of a
naval officer," suggested Penelope.

"Do you think so?" asked the housekeeper. "Yes,
I daresay that is so. I used to think them out of place
myself at first, but now I feel, someway, they're very
natural. And these are their swords; Sir Andrew's is
at Schawfield somewhere: he would never have it on
a wall since he hadn't a bloody story to hang up with it,
he says."

Left alone in her room, Penelope undressed, said
her prayers a little sleepily, blew out her candle, and

drew her window-curtains back that she might get the first of the morning sun. The garden, bathed in moonlight, looked reclusive, visionary; Sir Andrew, wrapped in a boat-cloak, paced the snowy walk as on a quarter-deck.

CHAPTER XI.

GOSSIP, banned by the righteous even when they most indulge in it, is, in little country places like our own, the very sauce of life, which without it would be wersh indeed. The word itself is noble in its origin, for all its washerwife associations, meaning (as Divvert was the first to tell me) "Sib with God"; if we do not talk about our neighbours there is no proper warmth of fellowship in us, and 'tis likely we are much engaged in the complacent contemplation of our own perfections. Gossip is gossip, whether it be about the private woes of a family up the street or the fall of a foreign dynasty. I have known a very worthy man who, meaning well, forbade his children at the dinner-table talk of any one within the parish; thus he designed to restrain all tittle-tattle, and induce a lofty spirit of discourse. They conversed only of such things as the Roman occupation and the likelihood of life in other planets, and made a fortune later on by printing newspapers. But "gossip on trivial things!" you may say with reprobation, thinking of tongues that wag in malice, envy, innuendo; the mole-hill of our history was a seeming trifle, but it killed a Prince, and plainly you mean scandal when I mean the gush of clean hill-water from the village pump. No other thing than gossip—apart from the catholic heart, the indiscriminate cordiality of Captain Cutlass—kept us all, in Schawfield, from Fancy

Farm to the fiddler's garret, in a blithe relationship that
helped to make the darkest, dreichest winter more than
tolerable.

We laughed at the Shakespearean frolic of the Captain, but we loved him none the less. It was a more
amusing ploy than the sight of him trotting the country
seeking a half-made wife. Tam Dunn, the first thing
in the. morning, got a fine new hat, and his old one
passed to Watty Fraser, who had crushed his own at
a wedding where a wag had slipped it on the floor
below the foot with which poor Watty always beat the
time to his own performances of frantic reels. Orpheus,
who got the story with the hat, blabbed to the lady of
the inn—" In the name of fortune ! did one ever hear
the like !" quo' she, astounded, and straight to the lasses
in her kitchen to give the latest news with an ac-
companiment of excited clicks from her pebbled ears.
But they had heard it all already from Tam Dunn, who
was ever after to be known as Christopher. The story,
as it spread, swept into its current wonderful new gro-
tesque particulars——the Captain had lost a second lady
on the road; he had forced the survivor, willy-nilly,
to the hospitality of Fancy Farm, and thrust her in
on an unexpectant and astounded Aunt Amelia; it
was as like as not he had even found the ideal
woman at last and meant to marry her ! But of
the truth itself, and the bold adventure of Penelope
on the box, the night maintained a loyal secrecy.

Grace Skene's lady Abigail, quite unconscious of
her part in an adventure that amused the whole com-
munity, rose next morning early, and, with nothing
else to do in the absence of her mistress, explored
the neighbourhood. She sauntered past the lodge, and
with a brisker step passed through the village street,
the icicles of whose eaves were dripping from the

warmth of breakfast fires and a change of weather.
Had she been preceded by the bellman or a file of
halberdiers she could no more immediately have been
decerned as the lady who had figured in Sir Andrew's
escapade. James Birrell's sister saw her from her
window; cried her brother hurriedly ben from his
newspaper; he was pleased to say the stranger had
a stylish manner——Style, for him, depending on the
dress and a certain nonchalance of carriage. For nonchalance it were hard to beat Penelope Colquhoun;
she had the pavement walk of cities, and that air of
imperturbability that depends so often on level and
indifferent eyes.

"A home - trimmed hat!" was the more searching
comment of Miss 'Tilda. "I wouldna wonder if she's
another of Norah's actress-bodies."

Actress or no actress, Mr Birrell insisted on the
Style, and even saw a likeness to Miss Norah; 'Tilda
was unreasonably annoyed at the comparison; Norah
never walked as if the street were of no account
to her, and had always an eye for the windows.
"That one," 'Tilda declared, "is fidging to look at
things, but knows that we may be watching her."

"All the more to her credit," said Mr Birrell; "if
she showed an interest in the shops you would be
the very one to doubt if she was a perfect lady."

"A perfect lady," said his sister, "does exactly
what she likes, even if it's perfectly ridiculous, and
she doesn't bother her head what folk are thinking;
that one's studying herself and making an impression.
You never saw a lady with furs on out on the street
at this hour in the morning"——a conclusion which sent
Mr Birrell away to his office chuckling, but wondering,
too, why 'Tilda, not ungenerous in her nature usually,
should on this occasion be so critical.

And Miss 'Tilda, as it happened, was mistaken, as women often are who are foolishly encouraged to believe their hasty intuitions have divine authority, while in truth they are less to be depended on than the masculine findings of pedestrian reason, for Penelope was actually as abstracted as she looked. If one had asked her suddenly for her thoughts she might with honesty have said Free Will, for on that fascinating futile problem was her mind engaged when it was not puzzling over——the loss of an umbrella! The mind undisciplined to concentration is more of an ass in our apparently profound abstractions than when we are on the surface, and Penelope's was grotesquely philandering with metaphysics, umbrellas, and a mental portrait of Tam Dunn!

The veritable post-boy at that very moment when she had come to the end of the street and turned on her heel to retrace her steps was himself bewildered. He had found the umbrella in his carriage when he set about its cleaning in the morning; the ownership was obvious, and, not unmindful of the pantry ale, he went up with it himself to Fancy Farm.

"There ye are!" was the housekeeper's greeting; "I suppose ye would be nane the waur o' a hoop on your head this mornin'," and he sheepishly grinned when she charged him with a carelessness of which, if she only knew it, he was noway guilty. He could have acquitted himself in a sentence of the major charge of conduct unbecoming to a post-boy in leaving Miss Colquhoun to dispose as she might of her summarily ejected baggage, but he knew very well it would not relieve him of the blame of taking even an involuntary part in Sir Andrew's frolic, and if the housekeeper was ignorant yet of that escapade, this, it was plain, was not the moment nor he the man to enlighten her.

"Tak' my advice, Tam Dunn," said she, "and leave

the drink alane! Or if that's no' possible, never touch it till your day's work's done. Ye must have had a royal time at the curlin' yesterday."

He had earned a hat, but plainly it was at some cost to his reputation! "Ye canna drink very deep and mak' much o' a shape at a curlin' rink," he protested. "I never was soberer in my life than yesterday; Sir Andrew himsel' could tell ye, if ye asked him, and I beat him."

"Don't tell me!" commanded Mrs Powrie; "if ye werena under the influence ye wouldna hae been so free wi' Miss Colquhoun—and her a minister's daughter!"

He stared at her, amazed; what had Captain Cutlass done with his reputation?

"You and your predestination!" continued the contemptuous housekeeper. "What's the reason annexed to the Fifth Commandment?" and Tam Dunn scratched his head for a response that had once been there.

"Ye can ask that!" he replied hopelessly. "I'm hanged if I can mind."

"And you're the clever man that's supposed to be up in the Shorter Catechism!" said Mrs Powrie. "Next time ye drive onybody to Fancy Farm see and confine your attention to your horses—they'll understand ye better;" and with that flea in his lug he returned to his stable-yard, unrelieved, by so little as a horn of ale, of the dejection which had come with the change of weather.

For thaw was on, and this, for certain, was the last of the winter's curling. A bland moist wind came blowing from the west; the snow was sliding thunderously from the village roofs; the gutters ran like burns, all snow-bree-flushed; a tinkler clan, with their brown rags dank as if they had been freed that moment from the burial of a wreath, oozed into the village, spreading themselves in quest of alms. The woods gave up a ghost of frost—a silvery exhalation; the arches dripped, the roads melted into yellow mire.

In a warmly sheltered glade of a planting on the braes above the unplayable loch, Sir Andrew, with his coat off, wielded an axe on fallen timber with his wood-cutters. The deep-gashed trunks and the yellow spales smelled acrid sweet and elemental, drenched with the juice of years. He watched the saw slice to the heart of a mighty spruce, the head of the monarch shake petulant for a moment, then the fall. Far through the wood went the sound of the falling; the world shook at the impact. It was, to Captain Cutlass, like a murder. No more the sweetness of the rising sap, the joy of weather, dark night and dawn on the topmost boughs, the brave companionship of a hundred years! The heart of him rose in his throat, and he felt in his eyes the sting of tears.

He threw down his axe and on with his coat impatiently. "Three hundred cubic feet at the mill," he exclaimed, "and there's money in it, but it seems a shame! I would rather, like my grandfather, be at the plantin'."

The foresters were well enough acquainted with that capricious soul to comprehend its sentiment. "I'm never much vexed for firs," said one of them. "They're no' like oaks or beeches, wi' a hearty grip o' the grund, Sir Andrew—they're kind o' like the pauper bairns in the town doon-bye, nae richt roots in the place they grow in. A flaff o' wind and they may gang; but grand for buildin'! grand for buildin'!"

"That was seemin'ly Virgil's notion, too, but someway I see in them other qualities. If they hae but a short grip o' the ground, as ye say, they've had it longer than any other tree in Scotland or in the world. I never see

yon clump on the knowe behind the house but it mak's
me think o' the time when there wasna a leaf in Europe,
and unco beasts went rootin' among the fir-tree needles.
Cut no farther than the fence there; I'll give those
fellows on the other side another lease——for they're an
ancient people," and off he set for luncheon.

Miss Skene had not arrived when he left the house;
she was, it seemed, unused to emerge from her bedroom
till the day was aired: this knowledge had come to him,
not directly from Penelope, whom as yet he had not seen
since he left her standing among her baggage, but had
filtered through the housekeeper and his Aunt Amelia.
To think that Captain Cutlass might blame himself less
for his deception of a woman not in Amelia's category of
" lady " than if his victim had been Miss Skene herself,
would be grievously to misapprehend his character; what
amusement he had found in the discovery of her identity
had been at himself and his dinner-jacket: he ruefully
looked on his escapade now as less defensible than ever,
and was honestly afraid to meet the girl to whom, sooner
or later, he was due an explanation.

The imminence of this was in his mind when walking
along the slushy river-side in a drizzle of rain he heard
a shriek beyond a distant alder thicket.   Immediately he
guessed at some disaster at the pool between the weirs,
where, in spite of his warnings, Norah sometimes skated.
At least a thousand yards were between him and the
pool; it flashed upon him as he ran how death strides
into the house of life in a single breath, and he realised
the horror of her drowning.   It was as his fears had
told him,——she struggled feebly on the edge of the broken
ice, but her cries had brought assistance; she was rescued
before he reached her side, and stood a drooping, pathetic
figure, whimpering.

" I have told you often——" he began impetuously,

taking her in his arms, where she clung to him speech-less for a moment, while Penelope, her rescuer, no less drenched than herself, sat wincing at her feet.

"It was to be the last time, and only for a little," said his cousin penitently, "and it—and it nearly *was* the last time. If Miss Colquhoun had not run down from the garden when she heard me——" she glanced with fervid gratitude at Penelope, who, as pale as herself but without her tears, now stared with surprise at Captain Cutlass.

He took off his cap to her, wondering why she should sit on the sodden bank. "Thank God, you're a good runner, Miss Colquhoun!" he remarked, bending to loosen his cousin's skates.

"Why! it was—it was you who drove me here last night!" Penelope exclaimed, with the colour flying for a moment to her face.

In spite of his anxieties he smiled—a little foolishly. "The very person!" he confessed. "I thought you should have discovered sooner. I had hoped to have a more favourable opportunity to explain and offer my apologies. Last night's exploit was the outcome of a wager, and I had no idea at the time you were to be our guest."

"It was—it was very silly!" cried Penelope, biting her under lip with the spitfire in her pallid aspect.

"Quite!" he agreed. "There was really no excuse for it, but I warned you of my reputation."

"It was cruel," she insisted, at no pains to conceal her displeasure.

"As it happened, yes," he admitted. "I hope you'll tell me yet that you forgive me," and he made to help her to her feet.

She tried to rise, rejecting his assistance, and sat down suddenly again with a baffled exclamation.

"It's—it's nothing serious," she remarked, with a grimace of pain that belied the statement. "I think I have hurt my foot."

They helped her home between them, her plight diminishing the emotion which the more alarming accident to Norah had aroused. The Doctor, summoned from the village, reported a broken ankle.

In the midst of the commotion caused by these alarms in the ordinarily uneventful life of Fancy Farm, Grace Skene's appearance on the scene was less dramatic than Amelia had expected, or herself perhaps had planned. She drove up, at noon, to a house where Penelope was a heroine, and Norah Grant and her cousin were preposterously preoccupied with a sense of gratitude. Warmth was not wanting in her welcome, it was true, but she had, too obviously, no monopoly of the household interest, and her beauty and her frocks, that seldom failed her elsewhere, seemed painfully less important than a common fractured ankle. It was the hour (had she been of a happier disposition) for displaying a philosophic patience and a sympathetic willingness to surrender her magnificent importance to the claims of plain humanity ; but Grace was created otherwise, and she fumed. Penelope was her brains, and as needful to her (as it seemed) as her very hands ; Penelope was inconsiderate to have met with such an accident, and the prospect of weeks without her services seemed an outrage. The chirruping sympathy of Miss Amelia failed to comfort the lady, and the audacious impenitence of the patient, snugly ensconced in the care of Mrs Powrie, was exasperating.

Worst of all was the attitude of Sir Andrew Schaw. Oblivious of her physical perfections, he was looking for vulgar sentiment, and when he did not find it, plainly showed his disappointment. For all his tolerance of the weaklings of the world, who were so from a helpless ignorance, heredity, or the circumstances of their daily lives, and despite his own philosophy that denied him the right to blame, he would sometimes go to the heart of things with a word of bitter condemnation for that sin he esteemed the worst of all—the lack of human kindliness in those to whom the world was more than kind.

Two or three days of brushing her own hair in this distracting atmosphere was enough for Grace; she took her leave at the end of the week in a temper, abandoning Penelope to the care of a household which appeared to think that care a privilege.

CHAPTER XII.

NORAH lost no time in lamentations for her old companion's going; she had found a new delight in life. She packed the unwilling Mrs Powrie off about her proper business, and herself assumed the *rôle* of nurse to a patient singularly docile, nonchalant to the last degree, void of sophistication, merry as a cricket, proud at times as Lucifer, shrewd and sensible in many ways, in others simple almost to absurdity. Penelope appeared to have read no more than a score or so of books—real books; she knew herself the others were of no account but only for amusement. But she had read those twenty thoroughly; and her knowledge of their spirit, with her native wit, her nonconformity, her fearlessness and confidence, gave to her conversation a curious piquant quality, audacious and original. To come from a manse, it was odd to find her lacking reverence—not for the fundamental things, the ancient altars and the sacrifices, but for the very shibboleths and usages that always meant so little to Sir Andrew Schaw. In her, as in him, was the sense of caste awanting: she would not have a different tone or manner for Tam Dunn and for the baronet; to either she would blurt what came to her head, spontaneously, without conformity or conciliation. It might have been intolerable to Miss Amelia, but to Norah it was charming! Even to Norah, who had learned to like the voice of unreserved simplicity from the practice of her cousin, Penelope's rash deliverances on any subject that came up for conversation might have been ridiculous had they not so often evidence of thoughts peculiar, individual, creditable; guesses at truth that never wanted a kind of dignity since they were inspired by the delicious naïveté of a clever child and lit by unusual insight. Penelope, indeed, at times confounded her, exposing the fallacy of an attitude in a simple question, stripping a cherished theory to the buff and showing it had knock-knees. That a certain principle should be generally accepted in the realms of art or social conduct was enough to make it questionable to Penelope Colquhoun; she did not dogmatise, but she always kept the right to doubt.

The girl was beautiful. Norah, looking at the liquid flashing eyes that seemed never surfeited nor weary, rarely dulled by inward speculation, quick, searching, and responsive; at the sensitive sweet mouth that never gave idle compliments nor temporised; at the tiny ears detecting every artificial note; at the faint pink shoulders shrugging themselves from the edgings of her bed-gown in an argument, — found the cultivated loveliness of Grace Skene incredibly diminished by comparison. Her old beliefs in race and breeding were most awkwardly upset; she failed to see in what respect a mansion-house could have produced a finer body; half the mansions in the neighbourhood would benefit by such common-sense.

"Why did you leave home?" she asked her one day, sitting on her bed.

"I'm the youngest of six daughters, all unmarried," replied Penelope. "Six unmarried daughters in a small manse with a kind of dear old Christian Socialist for a father, a love for pretty things, and a decent elementary education, make a very explosive mixture. It exploded, and I found a situation."

"I wish," said Norah, "the explosion had carried you a little farther, and landed you somewhere else than with my friend Grace Skene. Why! you must have been continually quarrelling. *I* know her!"

"We were," confessed Penelope. "It was that which made me stay for the last two years with her. You see, when she was in her tantrums, she was nearly always in the wrong; a woman spoiled as she has been could hardly help it. When we quarrelled it was like a tonic to my self-respect; I felt superior, and forgot all about her wages. It was like being back in the manse again with my sister Peggy. The more she stormed the more composed was I, and it made her mad."

"You must have an enviable temper!" said Norah admiringly.

"I haven't. It's a beast! But it's just the ordinary average temper for a woman. Her furies are all fire; mine are—are splintered ice; that's the only difference," and she laughed with all her heart. "I know I should be sorry; it's a sin," she proceeded, "but I'm not, and I can't pretend to be. I feel it's good for me to quarrel with ill-temper and selfishness. Father used to say that anger acts like poison in the blood; I don't believe one word of it! a good rage makes me feel grand when it's over. If Miss Skene was always dignified, and cool, and what she ought to be, I would have left her long ago. Lord! I couldn't stand that! It would make me feel so small and servile. Wouldn't you feel like that?"— and she leaned across to her nurse with the engaging frankness of a child.

"I daresay I would," said Norah, kissing her, for already they were friends. "But I'm sure I shouldn't put up with more than a week of Grace. I'm afraid she hasn't much of a heart."

"Oh, there's worse! there's worse!" pleaded Penelope,

with a tone that brought out another of her qualities—
forgiveness. "She has as good a heart as can be made
out of brains. And when she's nice she's almost jolly.
I'm certain she's annoyed with herself already."

She could forgive Miss Skene her tantrums, and even,
apparently, her desertion, but not so readily could she
forgive the imposition of Sir Andrew, who had made her
look ridiculous to herself. Even yet her face would
burn when she thought of her indiscretion. It was no
excuse for her, she knew, that she should have chattered
to him only in her ignorance of his identity, but the
offence began with him. "It was too bad!" she declared, "and you can tell him so from me. I abominate
the kind of joke that starts with falsehood."

"But it wasn't exactly falsehood with my cousin,"
protested Norah. "He was Tom Dunn for the occasion,
and if you knew him as well as I do, you would understand that he kept up the character for the sake of
Mrs Nish, whose post-hiring business would suffer badly
if it were generally known that she let jocular amateurs
drive her landau. Why are you so unforgiving?"

"I suppose it's just my vanity," confessed Penelope.
"When I think of it I feel so—so small. I was taken
at a disadvantage; it was cowardly. And I hope I'll
never meet him, for I'll tell him so."

For three or four weeks she was certainly not to
meet him, but still he got to know her day by day
more intimately; day by day with more surprise and
curiosity. Norah would come from the patient's bedroom betraying her amusement at some new phase of
that rebel nature; Captain Cutlass had a full report of
everything.

"Why!" he would cry, "she's splendid! I'm sorry
she won't forgive me, but she's right. When will she
be able to be out? I'm all impatience."

"Tchk! tchk! Andrew," said Amelia in despair. "A saucy—" but she suddenly checked herself, at the disapproval of his countenance.

"What are her imperfections?" he demanded from his cousin. "You've been telling me of nothing but her merits."

"I didn't say she had any imperfections," answered Norah, smiling.

"Good Lord!" said Captain Cutlass hurriedly, "I hope she's not inhuman. But no: I remember! At least she has a fiery temper; I heard it in her very first words to me on Duntryne quay, and I saw it in her eyes when I made to help her to her feet on the river-side. But after all, temper's hardly an imperfection. There's a frightful kind of tame submission in some of your sex compared with which the violence of a virago is a virtue. There must be something else— ah! I remember: a strained, high, unrefined inflection in her voice, not quite pleasant, when she was con· tradictory. Women should have quiet, sweet, level voices, even when they're furious."

"I see nothing wrong with her voice," protested Norah. "It seems to me rather pretty and musical."

"Probably; but you never had the chance, perhaps, to hear it with the piccolo-stop out. I thought it pretty most of the time too,—at least it had possibilities in it, with a little training. Why women shou_d learn to sing before they have learned to speak is a thing I could never understand. They're speaking all the time, and they're only sometimes singing. They might as well learn to dance before they have learned to walk."

"Oh! if it's a highly cultivated young person you expect to find in Pen," said Norah, "you'll be disappointed. She's quite untutored and undisciplined, as naïve as a child."

"Ah!" exclaimed Sir Andrew on a high note, hopefully, "that's good! That's promising! I like that! Your amiable friend Miss Skene has made me more dubious than ever of what passes for cultivation and the discipline of conventional good breeding."

"Nonsense!" answered Norah bluntly. "You cry for a disciplined speaking voice in one breath, and condemn discipline and good breeding in the next. You might at least be consistent."

"Please God, not!" he exclaimed. "I'd sooner be impulsive."

"She's impulsive enough, if that should please you. She says what comes into her head first."

"Better *and* better!" exclaimed Captain Cutlass, rubbing his hands together between his knees. "I never know myself what I'm going to say till I have said it;" and Miss Amelia turned up her eyes in despair at such a scatter-brained confession.

"But Penelope's impulsiveness," said Norah quietly, "is apt to be followed by the same regrets that it brings to common mortals. Her annoyance with you is wounded pride; she feels that you had her at a disadvantage when she was indiscreet."

"Yes," said Sir Andrew, "that was another thing. Even if I had been Dunn, she was indiscreet. She hurt me a little twice—by a reference to my marriage, and—another matter. Never mind! I could never have been so indiscreet as that myself, nor you. But of course we've had advantages."

"Oh, she's imprudent——"

"I'm glad to hear it," said Sir Andrew. "Prudence is nearly always fear. 'I was never afraid of anything —except myself,' she said when my horses jibbed, and I could believe her. She's a perfect Stoic. You've been trying to show me her imperfections, and——"

" I haven't," protested Norah.

"——I find they're all virtues. She's independent, contradictory, self-willed, confident in her own convictions, spontaneous, with no duplicity, clever. I believe a year of your society and the run of your book-shelves would make her perfect."

" But that would be to spoil her, wouldn't it, Andy ? " said Norah mockingly. " You wouldn't have Penelope inhuman ? "

" You don't exactly catch what I mean," said Captain Cutlass, looking with abstraction at his cousin's profile and a little curl of hair upon her temple.

For a month the room where Penelope lay was the heart of the house, for every house has a special chamber whence the pulse of it is derived, even if it only be the kitchen. She had kicked Mrs Powrie's pillows to the foot of her bed, impatient at the very sight of embroidered monograms representing weary hours of foolish fancy-work that spoiled the pillow for its proper purpose, and sat for hours reading Miss Amelia's novels. Mrs Powrie would go in to her, and be, for twenty minutes at a time, a kind of mother ; Norah's frequent, longer visits, were the visits of a sister, and made the days too short : a broken limb seemed to be the best of fortune.

By-and-by she could rise ; a little later, venture out of doors to see the gold of the lilies and hear the lark and the mavis singing, and no longer could her meeting with her enemy be averted. He came upon her one day sitting under the verandah. There is a happy eye continually making pictures out of things familiar, even commonplace, and Captain Cutlass, coming on her suddenly, thought the unpretentious front of his house enlivened by her presence. It seemed as if she had been there for years—since the old unrepenetrable times when he was a sailor coming home with eyes sea-wearied, to look again with delight on the green of the rhododendrons. Jean had sat there sometimes; Norah often —how like, in some respects, the stranger was to his cousin!

"I'm delighted to see you out," he told her, taking her hand and sitting down beside her.

"Thank you," said Penelope, and then, more warmly, "everybody has been so good!"

"Though we began badly," he suggested, and saw at once he had blundered, for she reddened.

"It's not improving the situation to bring that up again," she said coldly. "I have been trying to forget it."

"Pardon me," said Sir Andrew softly; "that was not what I was thinking of; I was alluding to your accident. I've said all I mean to say about—about the other thing. That's past; that's finished. *Fugit!* I've forgotten all about it. And now I hope we're going to be friends. Why not?" He beamed on her so jovially, so far from any spirit of contrition, that she had to smile.

"Why not?" she replied. "Except that you—you told me a lie to begin with. I didn't like it. I don't like it. I suppose it's because I never could lie myself. I've tried it; sometimes it would be useful, but somehow it makes you feel as if you were dirty. I'm always for the downright truth!"

She spoke with a flurried ardency, breathing short between her sentences, looking him straight in the eyes without a quiver of her lashes, and he was seized with a tremendous admiration.

"That is right!" he said, "absolutely right! And I hope that you will learn by-and-by that dissimulation is as distasteful to myself as it is to you. Why! Fancy Farm is quite an inappropriate name for this place; it is the palace of truth. Norah's exactly like you in that particular; she hates any form of falsehood, either sentimentalism or affectation, and I'm——" He stopped, reflected for a moment, and chuckled. "I reserve the right to be harmlessly mendacious when the wind's north-west. . . . I like you!"

He delivered this finding with a hot impetuosity, and she could not doubt the candour of his eyes; but neither could she forego the obvious retort.

"That's nice!" she said. "But I suppose the wind's north-west at present."

He was charmed; he had never before met any one quite like her, except in some respects his cousin. She made him think of the free wild moor and morning walks there, for folk to Captain Cutlass often had some spirit of a certain place and weather. For half-an-hour they sat together in the forenoon sun; Miss Amelia, disapproving at a window, wondered at what they laughed so much. Penelope put all his whimsical ideas to the test of prose, like another Jamie Birrell; he delighted in her spirit of dissent, in one who spoke without reserve, with the bold unconsciousness of childhood.

"I envy Miss Skene the stimulation of your contradiction," he declared, and a shadow came to her face.

"Miss Skene," she replied, "will have to dispense with that sort of stimulus in future; I'm not going back to her. I told her so before she left, and she probably doesn't believe it, but I always ride when I saddle, as my father says."

"Norah!" he cried, running into the house, and his cousin came hurriedly to see what caused this peremptory manner.

"Do you know," he asked eagerly, "that Penelope is not going back to your friend Miss Skene?"

"I don't," said Norah, smiling. "She seems to have taken you into her confidence again pretty readily, considering the way you have already abused it."

"You must keep her here!" he went on impetuously.

"In what capacity?" asked his cousin quietly.

"You are as much in need of a companion as Miss Skene."

"Not quite," she replied. "I've always you and Aunt Amelia, and — there's often Reginald. I like Penelope immensely, she's so like myself in some respects, and seems sometimes to remind me of a sister I never had. But I couldn't engage the girl who saved my life to put up my hair, even if I didn't find it better for my health to do so for myself."

"If you don't make some arrangement whereby she'll stay, I'll marry her, offhand, myself!" said Captain Cutlass.

CHAPTER XIII.

THE Hunt, it would seem, was ended!

"Sir Andrew is the sort of man who wants what he wants when he wants it," was a saying of Mrs Powrie's, and she was right: a dogged resolution will be found in men who seem to drift good-humouredly through life, accepting without demur what the gods may send them. The gods, so far as I can see, are pretty busy at the heels of seeming pliant and irresolute men who relinquish trivial positions with an air of generosity, but are dour to surrender an idea. Even Norah Grant, with a will of her own and an assertive personality, had often to submit to that capricious, amiable domination. It sometimes looked as if she had trained herself, without suspecting it, upon his theories, at least upon the sanest of them. Lady Jean, poor soul! (and sometimes Miss Amelia), had been the sad example of the kind of woman Heaven plainly meant to dwell alone, and Norah made herself as different as she could. She opened the windows of her being and let the air blow through; she kept a heart of wonder, curiosity, adventure in her bosom; never relaxed in peevish moods or apathy; she sang, danced, rode, or gardened, filling each hour of the day with duties to herself and others; knew no idleness of brain or body; left no chinks between the flowery hours for the weed *ennui*.

But resolute and self-contained, and free, as she might

appear, from her cousin's crazes, often she submitted to them, and she did so now.

Penelope was induced to stay. She liked the unpretentious, odd, old rambling house, where Sir Andrew's humour had insisted on an almost Japanese simplicity —no idle ornament, no effects of ostentation,—and was attracted, too, by its contiguity to a village full of character. She found in the spirit of its occupants, apart from Miss Amelia, much that was in harmony with ideas she had had to fight for with Miss Skene. To her whilom nurse, the lady she had saved from drowning, she took the fancy of a secondary Providence, and her consent to stay was all the readier since she felt that the office of companion to Miss Norah, though it entailed a salary, had no menial understanding. One of her first instructions was to call her simply Norah—were they not actually companions, friends ? Even Miss Amelia, blissfully unsuspecting what this movement might portend, soon lapsed, herself, into a chirruping recognition of a kind of equality in the protégée. Penelope, she agreed, at least had manners. So thought Captain Cutlass too, but he thought them capable of improvement.

With all his democratic tendencies, he liked fine manners as he liked good clothes. For him an ill-made coat on a man who could afford a better was a kind of self-depreciation ; as for manners, he could find them without surprise in places where for other folk they might not be expected—in self-reliant shepherds who knew their business thoroughly, and were, in the dipping-fold or the shearing-shed, equal with the best and at their ease : even the blacksmith, fitting a tyre upon a wheel, was, in the act, a gentleman to Captain Cutlass. Norah had the natural good manners that invariably attend on kindliness and trust, but she had the cul-

tivated kind as well, though they sat on her so naturally
they seemed so far from artificial that her cousin failed
to see the difference. It was his wish to have Penelope
another Norah: he thought that manners were infec-
tious, like the measles, which, at their best, in truth
they are, except for the unhappy, born immune.

Yes, yes, the Hunt was ended.

We guessed it in the village long before Amelia did,
indeed before the baronet himself. He rode about his
land, that spring, as gallantly as ever, boyish-hearted;
smiled on every woman on the road with yon fine air
of true beneficence, not a scrap of condescension in it,
almost a congratulation on the common joys of mere
existence; he battled with the sea in his yawl in moods
exultant, haunted the dark ways, mused about the cromlechs, accompanied his women-folk on social rounds that
bored him, and seemed as whole of heart as ever; but
the roving eye of the kirk was now subdued, and wherever he went with his cousin Norah, there went Miss
Penelope!

We have but a single touchstone to affairs like these
in Schawfield—was the woman anyway like the thing
in looks, and was she willing? The most unfriendly
critic, even Mrs Nish, could not but confess that Miss
Colquhoun was, in appearance, all that could be wanted,
and in deportment wonderfully taking. With these
two gifts alone, we knew in Schawfield that the Captain,
just like any other man, must, if the lady willed it, feel
attracted: love with the rich and with the poor is first
and last a matter of propinquity.

'Tilda Birrell alone was dubious. "Stop you!" she
said with a kind of crafty gusto when gossip threw
Penelope into the very arms of Captain Cutlass,—"stop
you! and Sir Andrew will surprise you!" an attitude
looked upon as unaccountable in a woman of experience.

E

Penelope was unconscious for a while that she was a pupil to be trained on Sir Andrew's patent System; had she thought it, she would have proved indignantly rebellious, for still, to her, he was a little daft; the nonconformist in her never went the length of approving his particular kind of eccentricities. In truth, a thought of his possible interest in her personality never entered her mind; she was Miss Norah's friend, and made the most of that companionship.

There is, in the love of girl for girl, a spirit sweeter than the grosser loves of men and women,—something of the passion of the early morning world and of the Garden; they were, those two, like sisters reunited. Penelope dressed herself like Norah, happier in her imitation than poor Aunt Amelia; she learned her songs, became familiar with her thoughts and sometimes echoed them. Even in gait and general movement she showed unconsciously the other's influence. Sir Andrew often stood apart and watched them walking waist-encircled over the neighbouring fields or standing on the bridge, conventual white in airy garments, their hair let down, as was his cousin's favourite schoolgirl whim, and streaming on the warm west wind. He could look on them thus, he felt, for ever: so lean angelic creatures on the parapets of paradise, nor is there age nor separation there; or so, on Grecian terraces, scanning the foam for the loom of coming ships, stood women uncorrupt with Time — clean, cool, and exquisite! Sometimes in woods he saw them through the trees, incredibly remote from a life of chatter, shelter, food, and all the brutal mean demands of life on a wearied planet, seeming solemn in the glades as in a temple, dryads overlooked or nymphs forgotten in the exodus of the first immortal tenants.

And then he would laugh at himself—at such absurdly pagan bookish fancies gathered about two girls intensely practical and human; girls who ate their food with huntress relish, joyed in the conflict with ungrecian Schawfield weather, trudged the wet hills in thick-soled boots; bold disputants, hearty laughers.

This laughter troubled him—not his cousin's, which was like the plash of fountains, musical and decorous, restrained to a certain register, but Penelope's pealing unconstrained, all in the air, often with no depth to it.

"Look here!" he said to Norah, "our Pen spurts and screeches far too often like one of Mr Birrell's quills; stop it! If it goes on much longer she'll infect even you with that kind of preposterous laughter."

Norah reddened. "Would you mind very much?" she asked with an elusive note of hope in the question.

"I shouldn't like it," he admitted, "but I'm more concerned for Pen herself; that kind of rustic merriment, though I rather like it in a harvest-field, doesn't go well with cultivated gardens and the song of birds."

"Nature, Andy—Nature! Don't be traitor to your life-long convictions!" Norah smilingly warned him.

"Oh, to the deuce with Nature!" he exclaimed, hurriedly jumping his own convictions as he sometimes jumped his fences, tempted by their very opposition. "If we were all to laugh in key with Nature we should squeal."

They were coming from the stables, where they had been looking at a pony Norah had bought for her companion—at a quite ingenuous hint from Captain Cutlass of the good Penelope should derive from a share in her equestrian exercise. They walked across the lawn with the baronet lower on its slope than Norah; he stared before him like one hurrying to overtake a phantom scheme, his aspect ardent; she could look sideways down on him, and she looked with curiosity, bewildered, and perhaps a bit annoyed. For the moment it seemed as if for him she had no existence; that was so unlike him!

"You have got in Pen," he said in a little, "the very finest stuff for a great creation—a perfect woman."

"There's always a certain drawback in the fact," said Norah, "that I never could make anything without a model. Out of poetry, now, have *you* ever seen a perfect woman?"

"Yes!" he replied emphatically. "Once I dreamt her in my sleep. She came and sat a moment on my bed; her face I don't remember, nor do I think we said a word, but in the very core of me I felt that her face and soul completed something that was me. Eh? You know the unfinished feeling one carries about as if one needed another eye or some stupendous inkling into outer things, eh? Sometimes you almost get a hint of it in poetry, or an extra eye appears to open in the brain when the weather changes on the country,—but that's an ecstasy, blackguards perhaps may feel it; this that I felt when I saw the nameless lass at the foot of my bed did not give me ecstasy, but a far more delicious sense of self-fulfilment. We shall not die—no! no! we shall not die; at least, not the light black out and the worm triumphant: for having felt that satisfaction, I can swear it will be well with us yet. God gives those glimpses just to hearten us."

He turned to her with a quickened face, whose skin seemed quivering with emotion. Norah drew her eyes away and sighed.

"I don't share your dreams, Andy," she remarked in practical accents. "What I meant was a human model."

"Look in your glass! look in your glass!" he blurted, hastening his step, flicking his leg with his riding-crop. "You've got in Pen the ideal basis for the kind of thing. First, she has health—that is the best of wealth, and more than half perfection. Nearly all the women I see are out of the rhythm of nature, just because of ill-treated stomachs, customs that enervate, bad feet that prevent their walking, flaccid limbs, waists over which they have lost all power. Show me a man who does not feel omnipotent in his lower ribs and I'll show you a physical wreck. Everything's in the torso—in the poise and rhythm. We should flow, eh?" he raised his arms and gave a sinuous movement to his body. "You understand? Everything in unison with the pulse— the rhythm. 'Hearts, like muffled drums, are beating funeral marches to the grave'—rubbish! It's the beat of universal and eternal life; the very stars keep true to it in their twinkling, and it agrees with the beat of ocean tides."

"If Pen is to flow like ocean tides to please you, we'll need to put up some breakwaters," said Norah, and he chuckled.

"What I mean is this—she has a good beginning: she has rhythm, and the use of her ribs yet; she has not been spoiled by social pleasures, nor made herself a martyr to fancy work and domestic drudgery. She's as near being a child of nature as the parish school will let you have in our time, and she hasn't any accomplishments to unlearn. You recall my fiddle?—I taught myself to play it horribly in the East, and once, when I was home, I went to a real musician thinking of lessons. He looked at my fingering, bowing. 'How long have you been learning to do zis?' he asked, and I said a twelvemonth. '*Blitzen!*' he said, 'it will take a lifetime to get over it; I recommend ze flute.' Now

Pen has little to unlearn except her laughing. In anger and in laughter we lay bare the heart, and there's something wolfish in squeals of joy."

"She got that, I fancy, from Grace Skene, as she may have got the high inflection when she warms in contradiction."

"That's gone, I notice. You didn't——" he stopped, as if alarmed at the possibility of deliberate lessons.

"Oh, I didn't do anything foolish, you may be sure," said his cousin; "but Pen is not a fool, and she has an ear, and——and she likes me. Like all of proud, independent, and impulsive nature, she's as soft as butter if she's sure of your affection. I could get her to be anything I was myself. First, she contradicts——that's to give herself the dignity of self-assertion, and partly a relic of Grace's tantrums; next day you find she has added the very idea she contradicted to the big bundle of convictions for which she is prepared to lay down her life."

"By George! that's like yourself," cried Captain Cutlass.

"I daresay it is," she agreed; "it's a common characteristic when we're among our friends. All nice people have but one idea about everything of importance; the only difference is in its expression. I wish your politicians knew that fact."

"Inflection, laughter, poise——that's another thing," the baronet went on; "she wants poise. Nine hours out of ten she has it when she's quite unconscious, doing any useful thing in which she's interested, but she hasn't had experience of the ladylike art of graceful lolling; she can't sit down like you as if she was to have her portrait painted."

"Do you suggest that I pose?" asked Norah.

"No, no!" he hurried.

"Why not? I do as a matter of fact, and so do you;

it's part of the proper action of the lower ribs you speak about. I began deliberately, but it has long since become instinctive. The thing is not to pose in the mind—no, no, I'm wrong! For instance, I adopted a pose of imperturbability just for effect when I was at school, and it became second nature, greatly to my comfort."

"I am not speaking of pose, meantime, but of poise. Look out your foils, my dear, and set our protégée to fencing. She must fence, swim, ride, and dance; these are the prime accomplishments. She wants command; courage she has to spare already. A woman who can stand upon her feet and lunge will never worry about her stomach nor feel that the world's all yellow; and if she learns to take a fence flying, and swim, she has added two elements to her empire—air and water. Self-reliance is the beginning of all good manners. Eh? Does she dance?"

"Not a step! They didn't approve of dancing, it appears, at the U.P. Manse."

"Tut! I thought so! Something in her droop when one opened a door for her suggested that in that department she had been neglected. Lord, what fun she's lost! When I was a youth I got more unhappiness out of my inability to go through a quadrille than I got from any of my sins. How the devil can one have rhythm if one can't dance?"

"Oh, dear me!" exclaimed his cousin with a comical note of resignation, "I'm afraid we are all imperfect creatures."

"Good heavens! I should think so!" he retorted. "Everything that's of interest in life has something of imperfection, or it would terrify us, or shame us into hatred. God is a good Artist; He leaves a bit in every work of His for the imagination."

"But, after all, Andy, what you aim at is a work

of art," said Norah,—"the perfect woman, the living Venus."

"Well! well! well!" he replied impetuously, "in every work of human art, as in divine, our most passionate admiration demands a little of obscurity—something of the magic casements opening on the foam, eh? and if the lady in the Louvre had her arms she wouldn't be half so charming."

"Your argument proves nothing but that you are better at it than I am," said Norah.

They had come to the stile which gave an access to the back parts of the garden; she was upon its upper step when something made her pause, a figure of unconscious grace, a lesson in poise herself, arrested by the sight of the girl they spoke of, busy, without a protective veil, about a skep of bees.

"There's Pen," said Norah, "quite unconscious that she's to be reconstructed. If she guessed, wouldn't she be mad! By the way, is it only in the poise and rhythm, the laughing and the lower ribs, you're interested? You haven't said a word about her character and her mind."

Sir Andrew, leaning upon the fence silent a moment during which his cousin felt herself neglected, watched the movements of his protégée.

"Her character is all right," he replied at last; "for, like yourself, she has a passion for the truth, and that, with courage, is the best part of all good character. As for the mind, I'm for the physical graces to begin with; afterwards we may begin to think of stuffing her head with words and lists of names, which is what passes for education with the most of us. The proof of a sensible education is obvious—the power to construct or recreate, even if it's only a wheel-barrow or a pair of boots. A scandalous lot of money was spent on me at the school and university, and as yet I haven't learned to make anything. I missed my mark because I was brought up on the system which is based on the theory that everybody should learn the same things—a silly notion for a complicated world. Pen's mind is all right."

"Then we needn't bother about the book-shelf?" said his cousin.

"The devil created three-fourths of the books to waste our time," replied the inconsistent Cutlass. "There is so much in life that is far more interesting! I'm much mistaken if Pen hasn't found it so already. I admit that I like to have books about me, but the older I grow the less I learn from them. I can be happy thinking. Imagine that bookish idiot Pliny poring over a book while Pompeii was being destroyed before his very nose! And yet I like to see some poetry in women. There isn't very much of it in Pen; you might do worse than give her an introduction to the poets."

"I know what I'll do," said Norah, jumping from her pedestal,—"I'll send for Reggie Maurice."

"H'm!" said the baronet dubiously. "There's almost nothing poetical about Reggie but his poetry— and his devotion to you."

"All the same," said Norah, smiling back, "I must have Reggie."

CHAPTER XIV.

SEARCHING my mind for the right impression of our Schawfield Sabbaths, I find myself thinking of them always as a silvery grey in colour—the ominous, hard glitter of the mornings slowly fading away in a blur of misty clouds by the time the bells were ringing, and the afternoons made pensive by a thin persistent smirr or drizzle. Pensive—sweetly pensive, not burdening the spirit much, but charging it with quiet sentiment as do the memories of old things unrecoverable, nigh forgotten—days of youth, the yearning of the family psalm at evening worship, good men and women dead, and many things accomplished. It was a holy day in Schawfield, even if we had played at dambrod or the cards, which I give you my word we never did. But still a day with the finest opportunities for gossip.

"So solemn, so religious a day—I feel it a kind of wickedness to spoil it all by sitting in an atmosphere of peppermints and mildewed Sunday clothes," said Sir Andrew once to his Aunt Amelia: the sentiment gave her the first alarming impression that, in spite of his morning prayers (which he often bellowed fervently in a high Gregorian chant as he plashed about the bath-room), and in spite of Dr Cleghorn's guarantee of the genuine Christian spirit, her nephew might be little better than an infidel. Herself, she never missed a diet of the village temple; she felt her attendance was a

sacred obligation, and, besides, she shared the feeling of
Cattanach, the factor, that it helped to "break the back
o' the day so nicely."

"I go to the church regularly because I know I ought
to go," she assured Sir Andrew, with the air of a martyr.

"That is often my own excuse," said he. "One might
have better; but, when everything is said and done, 'I
ought' is the root of all religions. I'll go, myself, to-
day, *pour encourager*, like a decent landlord, but first I'll
have a bathe."

"Oh, Andy dear! You shouldn't swim on Sunday!"
she protested.

"Why not?" said he, who always felt that the mire
of the world washed off when he went swimming.
"There's nothing the devil hates like clean cold water,
and a bathe is a moral baptism."

Sabbath, as he had seen it elsewhere, in other lands,
a pompous interregnum in the hurry of the world, had
seemed no more than the formal mood of an hour or two,
confined within the walls of churches: here all outdoor
nature herself appeared to revere the day, from the rising
of the sun to the going down thereof. A hush came
even to the woods, or at least their tenants seemed in
their songs and cries in harmony with the sober thoughts
of men; the very rooks, cawing above the trees of Fancy
Farm, evoked no secular associations.

The morning would flood the empty street with wasted
sunshine long before the fires went on, and glint upon
brassy knockers, and beat upon curtained windows, and
wash to a clean, new ochre all the eastward gables of the
sleeping village. Vacant fields, deserted highways, gardens lonely within their high old walls; a dog or two
extended idle in the gutter beiking with breast against
the heated sand. And then the faint blue reek of
chimneys, and the blacksmith coming out to stump the

street with his jacket off, vainglorious of his Sunday linen.

"There is no lonelier thing in all the world than a Scottish village street on a Sunday morning, with a single citizen pacing it slowly on a wooden leg," was Sir Andrew's verdict, having seen that moving spectacle.

Splashing of soap and water at the backyard wells, a bit of balm or appleringie from the garden as a marker for the Bible, a chink of coppers changing, and then the clinkum-clank of the rival bells, our two in Schawfield being as much in dissonance as the churches they adorned have always been in other things.

"That's the one thing that worries me about it all!" would the Captain say to Norah as they followed the crowd of decorous whispering worshippers to church. "Those Sunday clothes! Those hats! This dreadful sense of a custom petrified! This fierce suppression of the natural self! Surely to God we shouldn't go to church like this, but rather with our holiday garments, and with cheerful drums and flying banners!"

"You sometimes talk a lot of nonsense!" would Norah reply composedly.

"Quite probably," he would agree with the utmost cheerfulness. "I find a little nonsense in other people singularly refreshing. But still, my dear, I'm right about the petrifaction. There goes Clashgour; *his* idea of piety is that you mustn't have the odour of beer about you on a Sunday, so he makes it brandy."

Then, almost certainly, would the drizzle come on at mid-day, as if by some beneficent joke of Providence to give the folk of Schawfield an excuse for their universal nap——the sweetest of the week——which broke the back of the day a second time. Again the street abandoned; only far off a sound of human life——the

calls of children plucking the honeysuckle wetly scented
from the hedges, wisely left to the care of God by their
parents fast asleep in warm and window-blinded chambers;
and an odour of scorching wood from the baker's oven.

But a drizzle never kept us from our walk when the
nap was over, the graveyard our objective, — though
why, with all the beautiful living world behind our
gardens, we should choose to meditate among the tombs
it were ill to fathom. Perhaps the custom grew from
a compromise with that narrow spirit that one time
would not let us walk at all on Sabbath, the graveyard
being looked upon as an eloquent epilogue to the sermon.
It lay about half a mile from the village; sooner or
later we landed there, even lover and lass would tryst
to walk between the low green mounds and read again
the long-familiar names upon the foggy sepulchres.
From that sedate engagement comes perhaps a part of
my conviction that the Schawfield Sabbaths have been
always sweetly sad and moistly grey.

The greyness was certainly real enough one Sunday
afternoon when Mr Birrell, refreshed by his nap, a figure
of plump integrity and decorum in a frock-coat, walked
with his sister 'Tilda to the popular rendezvous, gallantly
holding his umbrella over the fine new bonnet which—
to tell the truth of 'Tilda—was the chief excuse for
a daunder in such weather. There was another excuse,
as may fully emerge hereafter, but neither of them, to
Mr Birrell, would have justified the half-mile tramp
ostensibly to look at epitaphs he knew by heart already.

Such weather might delight a Captain Cutlass, with
his curious relish for the abstract thing we know as
weather, quite regardless as he might be of its character;
but except for angling in the Kettle Pool it seemed a
kind, to the lawyer, quite objectionable. *He* could not
see with the Captain's eyes the charm of that silvery

vapour through which the village faintly loomed—a vision unsubstantial, and the trees appeared like phantoms, and the churchyard, like the vague chaotic churchyard of a dream; *he* could not think the beads on the gossamer actual jewels, nor discover in himself, as the Captain swore he did, a physical pleasure in the smack of the rain-drop on his face.

There were fewer of the quick than usual in the churchyard this particular Sunday, since it was not everybody who could boast of a fine new bonnet like Miss 'Tilda; but among them was Mrs Powrie, who was as regular in her visitations there as if she were a trysted maid or a veritable widow. The eyes of 'Tilda brightened when she saw, as she had expected, the housekeeper of Fancy Farm drooping like a willow over the railing of the family's last mortal tenement.

"H'm! I see!" said Mr Birrell dryly. "I'm hauled away from my book on a muggy afternoon like this, on the pretence that my health demands it, just that you may have your crack wi' Mrs Powrie!"

"Right you are, James! I wouldn't miss it for the world," confessed his sister frankly. "She'll can maybe tell me the reason for a thing that's bothered me a' the day—no' a body but Miss Amelia in the Schawfield pew this morning!"

"They didn't miss much," said the lawyer cynically. "Dr Cleghorn—decent man!—was more than usually anecdotic. I always notice that when he's in despair of making us any better than we are by nature by keeping to the Gospel truths, he falls back on his wee bit stories, and there's nothing in them. The pulpit, for stories, canna compete with Mrs Nish's parlour—but, of course, one canna expect the clergy to have the advantage of comparison. For the love of goodness, don't get on to Peter and his dogs with Mrs Powrie, 'Tilda!"

The housekeeper could have been no more abstracted in a picture-gallery than she was in her contemplation of the monuments of the Schaws of three hundred years, her sense of art agreeably engaged by the sculptured figures carved with minuteness to the very waistcoat-buttons; noses on a level with the cheeks; plump cherubs hovering, bodyless, above the epitaphs, with the soul of human prank in their roguish faces rather than angelic raptures; and the country mason's tribute to *macabre* sentiment in skulls and bones.

"A sleepy sort of day," said Mrs Powrie, as if that was not to be said with truth of all our Sundays. "I just forced myself to come out."

"Ay, it's like settling down to rain," said Miss 'Tilda; and her brother, taking off his hat politely to the house-keeper, marvelled at the conversational tactics of their sex. For a while they maintained the appropriate grave-yard manner, as they walked, with him behind them, along the narrow weed-grown path between the lairs, stopping here and there to recall the personal traits of old acquaintances now no more than a turfy mound and a name cut deep in granite; or to moralise (with a due regard to their skirts being clear of the clay) on a text adorning the plinth of some new headstone.

"'A few short years of evil past,'" Mr Birrell quoted, unctuously, from a slab. "It's scarcely the happiest sentiment to put on the tomb of Robert Grieve the maltman; after all, he wasna so very bad a fellow!"

They came down the road together from this Sabbath relaxation wonderfully cheery.

"I noticed," said Miss 'Tilda, "there were none of your folk in kirk to-day except Miss Amelia; they'll be from home?"—a point on which she had satisfied herself to the contrary hours ago, but then a reconnais-sance must have a feint at opening.

"No; they're all at home," Mrs Powrie assured her earnestly, quite well aware it was a feint, respecting her none the less for it. "Miss Norah had a headache."

"Indeed, and I thought of having one myself!" said Miss 'Tilda nonchalantly. "When the Doctor's away from home all week, and only gets back on Saturday, there's nothing to be looked for from his sermon but cauld kail het again, or a parcel of stories about great men that led good lives and left a great deal of money and a valuable object lesson. He was gey thin this morning, as I expected. I havena seen Miss Norah down the town for a fortnight; she'll be busy?"

"She's never otherwise," said Mrs Powrie. "Everything wi' her's a hobby. Her and Miss Colquhoun are galloping on horseback, like to break their necks, or dancin' even-on for hours in the drawing-room, or fencin' wi' Sir Andrew, or plowterin' at the garden till their faces are like sodger's coats. It can't be very good for them, I think! At their time o' life I was glad to sit down wi' a seam and rest mysel'."

Mr Birrell realised that 'Tilda was now in the thick of it; she had forgotten her bonnet, even his existence —the mightiest of us are out in the cold when the hens of gossip start to clock.

"Dear me! she must be talented, Miss Colquhoun!" she remarked with the right inflexion of astonishment.

"Oh, she's talented enough, I'll warrant," Mrs Powrie agreed,—"a minister's daughter, mind! She's grand company for Miss Norah, more like the thing for her, I think, than Mr Maurice. He's here now, and helping at the dancing. 'Deed! we're all at the dancing," she added with some amusement; "Sir Andrew made me join them the other night to make up a set o' Lancers. And me!—I havena danced for years, since Peter——"

"Oh, heavens!" thought Mr Birrell, scrupulously walking a little apart from this undignified clocking, "we're in already among the Dandie Dinmonts!" but a sigh stopped the lady's current of reminiscence, and Miss 'Tilda lost no time in restoring the conversation to more novel topics. "He was aye a very good dancer," she remarked; "I mind o' him at his Home-coming—took the floor like a dancin'-master. Perhaps it's as well he should keep in practice for the next occasion."

"The randy!" said her brother to himself.

Mrs Powrie sighed again. "I doubt," said she, "he'll never marry," and "Well done, the loyal Powrie!" thought James Birrell, trudging on the edge of the grass beside them. "One marriage in a lifetime is enough for any reasonable man or woman," continued the lady, who had found that one was more than enough in her own experience.

"Nothing of the kind!" retorted 'Tilda. "Give the like of me a chance. The first is always an experiment, —a second wife's more likely to be the pick of grim experience."

"No, no; there's a lot of clash, I know, about Sir Andrew looking for a wife again," persisted the faithful housekeeper, "but there's nothing in it. Dear me! think for yourself; there's a houseful of women there in Fancy Farm with nothing for us to do but to look after him,—not that he's hard to please, I admit! It's all a matter of clothes laid out and ordinary comfort; I don't believe that half the men would marry at all if it wasn't either that or lodgings."

"I daresay you're right," admitted Miss Birrell, and her brother waited for the unmasking of the second battery. "All the same," she continued, "I hope your dancing-practice at the Farm will not be thrown away; of course, there's always the prospect of a match between

Miss Norah and the poet," and she smiled with roguish suggestiveness at the housekeeper.

"Perhaps!" said Mrs Powrie, "Perhaps! They're very chief wi' one another, and he's most attentive, as he well might be, for she has the siller; but for myself I could never be taken wi' him; he's a peerie-heided soul—I suppose that that's the poetry. They may have an understanding between them, and then, again, they may have nothing of the kind; you can never tell wi' a hearty girl like Norah. I sometimes think he's just another of her hobbies. It would be more like the thing that he should take up wi' Miss Colquhoun; *she* would take the poetical nonsense out of him. What do you think, Mr Birrell?"—and the housekeeper turned with deference to the gentleman who would have it understood that he preferred to remain outside these cackling hen conventions.

"I don't know anything about it, Mrs Powrie," he replied, pursing his mouth to prevent an escape of his further sentiments.

"Neither do I!" she said, alarmed at this obvious disapproval on the part of Sir Andrew's agent. "I was only venturing an opinion."

"Pooh!" said Miss Birrell impatiently. "Never mind my brother! If you werena listening, James, you wouldna be affronted. Let me tell you this, Mrs Powrie —I can't put up wi' your Miss Penelope. I doubt she's a deep one."

"I'll speak of the girl as I find her," retorted the housekeeper with spirit. "So far as I can see, she's as open as the day. She fears the face of neither man nor woman."

"That's the depth of her!" said the Writer's sister with asperity. "If she wasn't deep she would pretend she did, like the rest of us," and a parting with the housekeeper being imminent, now that they were close to the gate of the lodge, she put the question that gave Mr Birrell the second reason for her insistence on the afternoon's excursion.

"She has never missed a Sunday in the Kirk since she settled here; what was the matter wi' her to-day?"

Mrs Powrie flushed and hesitated, with a glance at Mr Birrell, who seemed himself a little interested. "There was—there was a little accident yesterday," she confided in an undertone. "Nobody knows of it but myself, and she bade me not to mention it. Sir Andrew was fencing wi' her and he hurt her arm."

"And he doesna ken of it?" exclaimed Miss 'Tilda with astonishment.

"She never said a word, though it must have hurt her sorely, and he hasn't the least suspicion. She wouldn't even tell Miss Norah. I'm glad to say it's nothing very serious."

"That girl," said Miss 'Tilda in an accent of despair, "is the deepest or the unluckiest that ever God put breath in!"

She went down the street in silence with her brother: even he, it seemed, got something to reflect on in the news of Mrs Powrie. The village clock was chiming five, and the smoke of mended fires for tea hung low upon the slates and sank like a haar within the lanes, making the day still greyer than it was by nature. The tenements stood like cliffs with fortress apertures. 'Tilda took the key from her pocket and opened one of them, her brother with his umbrella still solicitous of the bonnet she had quite forgotten.

"As sure as fate, James Birrell," she said as they entered the lobby, "if she goes on the way she's doing she'll have him!"

CHAPTER XV.

THE training of Penelope proceeded briskly; never before was there such jolly times in Fancy Farm. Jolly times there had been, it is true, when some of Norah's actress friends would launch themselves upon her in the summer, which is the winter of their art, and romp among the harvesters, where their romping had a spirit of sophistication that was not of Arcady, and lacked the true pastoral unconsciousness of the natives. "They bring," said Captain Cutlass of those city Chloes and Phyllises, "the scent of the footlights over the hay-fields." But it was jollier with a genuine country spirit like Penelope's. She had, in the fields, the courage to seem what she was, a daughter of the people, and had no desire to shine. The same was true of her horse-manship; she quickly learned the art, at the cost, at first, of many tumbles in the paddock. "Oh lassie! lassie!" cried the panic-stricken Mrs Powrie, "ye'll kill yoursel' for certain; that'll be the end o't! I would sooner see ye married." "No fears!" said the ardent pupil, breathless, tousy, and dishevelled, but unconquered; "and it's worth a killing, anyway, to do something that I'm almost terrified to do!" This desperate courage charmed her tutor, who was no less delighted at her growing skill of fence. He never learned of her injury in the first stage of her lessons, though every one in the village knew of it, somehow, and he kept her at the foils

for weeks before he handed her over to the further care
of Norah.

"That girl's got legs!" he proclaimed to his cousin
gleefully.

"I've always suspected it!" said Norah.

"She stands upon her feet; she has craft, finesse, and
sleight of touch; there's nothing in her attitude of the
dancing-master." Norah, all the same, was the better
fencer, having learned the art from him when his interest
was less divided.

And they danced—oh! they danced, I assure you, till
it seemed as if the evenings passed to the step of a
saraband. Watty Fraser's fiddle was engaged for
Saturday afternoons to play to the harvesters and
the woodmen in the barn, and then would you see
Sir Andrew giving to Petronella all the elaboration of
a minuet. He danced with everybody, most notably
the eldest and the plainest of his folk; daffed with the
young ones till they all adored him.

Penelope danced by nature; the manse had no more
suppressed the rhythm and ear of her than it had
destroyed her appetite for bread and butter. But still
we agreed that she did not dance so well as Norah, who
brought to the thing a stately swooning kind of grace
that made even Cattanach, the factor, swither to venture
an arm upon her waist. Maurice gyrated round her,
posturing grotesquely, laughing at his own unhappy
incapacity, which was one of the defects that made Sir
Andrew doubt his qualities as a poet, since poetry is no
more than a joyous reeling prose.

Indeed, where anything was to do, their protégée was
docile and adroit; it was only in their abstract arts,
where some conventional theory was to be conceded—
those hypotheses that make existence possible for cultivated people, keeping them from going utterly astray,

—or where views were to be expressed in the accepted jargon, that she sat in silence, often out of it completely, sometimes a little obviously uneasy.

That was the trait in her that Aunt Amelia liked, since it made her own aloofness, due to that unhappy ear, the less conspicuous. "They chatter such a lot!" she declared. "And mumble. Reggy Maurice mumbles worse than ever; I can hardly make out a word he's saying."

"You wouldn't be greatly edified if you did, perhaps," said Penelope. "I never knew a man talk such nonsense, with such a wonderful flow of quotations. He's like a birthday book."

"You better not say that to Norah," Miss Amelia cautioned her.

"Why?" Penelope asked.

"Oh! just because she wouldn't like it. You can see they're—they're very friendly, she and Mr Maurice," and she nudged her with a meaning there was no mistaking.

Penelope looked surprised, and then she smiled to herself inscrutably.

Especially was she silent (except on one occasion) when it came to poetry, of which the gentleman in question was a fountain, gushing it from other wells, and even trickling now and then from a little cistern of his own, without, as it appeared, permitting much of it to soak into his system. He was a dapper little fellow, with a ruddy boyish face that had not got a single line as yet from anguish or from midnight contemplation, ready with merry jibings, the derisive chaff of four-and-twenty, and had come at first to Fancy Farm in its days Bohemian in the wake of a lady artist who had meant to paint the portrait of Lady Jean, and had taken half a summer to discover that her subject was incapable of sitting in one position longer than a minute. The artist disappeared and drifted thenceforth out of the poet's life, but he had found in Sir Andrew and his cousin friends to solace him for the extinction of a passion which, like a good deal of his poetry, was an end in itself and not a furious impulse. Norah, who at first had been inclined to laugh at him, took to him at last with an impetuous ardour that astonished the baronet and his wife. They could hardly credit it! The fervours of the poet were so manifestly artificial, his fun was of a cynic quality. "A perfect treasure on rainy days; if the cabinet-makers made such things, we should all have minor poets, like weather-glasses, in our country houses," said the Captain, paraphrasing Diderot. But scarcely the man for Norah! Yet, at last, she had him constant at her heels, and seemed unhappy in his absences. "I really believe you're in love with him!" exclaimed the baronet's good lady, and her latter days were cheered to some extent by the fact that Norah would not deny it.

Maurice came with less than his customary promptness to the whistle of Norah when the training of Penelope began.

"I thought you would have been here on Saturday," she said with mock imperiousness.

"I would have been if—if—" he stammered, unprepared with a plausible excuse.

"If you had started," suggested Norah. "Don't trouble to think of some poetical impediment; we're all for prose and plain speech now in Fancy Farm," and she told him about Penelope.

"I want you to be nice to her. Andy's taken a tremendous fancy to her, and thinks she'd benefit by

a little of your highly intellectual and poetic nonsense."
But she took the sting from the remark by a kindled
manner that appeared to take him to her very arms.

"Good!" he replied, with his hand on his heart. "I'll
roar you as gently as any sucking dove; I'll roar you and
'twere any nightingale to please the lady. I'd rather than
forty shillings I had my book of songs and sonnets here."

"My dear Reggy," said Norah, "we've got half a
dozen copies in the house, so that needn't worry you.
And Pen has had a copy in her bedroom for the past
three days."

"Of course! Of course! It's the usual prelude to
a meeting with an author; fully primed, I've no doubt
she'll be rapturous."

Norah mischievously smiled. "If she is I'll be very
much astonished. Pen, let me tell you, didn't betray
the slightest alarm at the prospect of meeting a poet,
and wouldn't prime herself to meet the Psalmist David.
She doesn't even know that Reggy Maurice and 'Wilfred
Ford,' the author, are the same individual."

"Excellent!" he exclaimed. "Don't enlighten her,
and I'll be sure of a frank criticism."

"You'll be sure of that in any case," said Norah—
"that's to say, if you ask one. If you're any way tender
of your *amour propre* I should advise you to be cautious.
But I really must explain to her."

"Don't! Please don't! What the good-year! a poet
and afeard! Not I, Miss Norah, faith not I!" said
Maurice. "Do you like her?"

"I simply love her!" said Norah heartily. "She
brings out the best that's in me, like a walk on a
stormy day."

"Happy girl! Is this, may I venture to inquire, the
final result of Sir Andrew's quest for the true Dulcinea,
or is she one of your Aunt Amelia's discoveries?"

She looked at him with disapproval. "There are considerations, Mr Maurice, which it is indelicate for a poet to touch on, though they may quite naturally engage the gossip of a village. My cousin is not the gentleman to compromise a woman in Penelope's position by discussing such a thing with me."

As if to make amends for this *faux pas*, the poet entered cheerfully into the dancing-lessons, where his aid, indeed, was scantily helpful, and played accompaniments for duets, and helped with picnic fires, and spouted poetry not his own, and "clowned" (as Pen described it) in the hay-fields round the Farm with loyal self-suppression. A week or two of his practised entertainment as a ladies' man, and Captain Cutlass stood in the background with his office gone. He felt, in the presence of Maurice with his effervescing spirits, just a little elderly, and sought within himself in vain for an earlier self in whom such facile arts were possible. He had never in his life been quite like Maurice.

Out with the mare, then! The old roads, and woods that never alter, and understand! Out with the mare! The tang of old withered leafage, and the sweetly acrid odour of the woodman's chips! Of all the birds that had rendered the spring-time gay and hopeful, only the robin and the linnet seemed to be left, companions of the melancholy afternoon. The linnet thinly cheeped unseen on an upper bough of hazel; the robin, like a tiny spirit mutely begging human fellowship, followed him along the dykes. Oh, the sea! the sea! How greedily he looked for it as he rose to the pass above Whitfarland Bay; it seemed as if the iron gates that prisoned him in space and time flew wide apart when he saw again the dim horizon. The crash and rustle of ocean, and the long withdrawing lisp of tired waters backing from the sand, and the farther islands stretched across the west like a picture washed in milk. Appearances! Appearances! Expressions of a thought unfathomable formed in that *pia mater* of the which the sky is fibrous membrane, our life-long dreams the momentary movement of an infinite cell.

While Captain Cutlass followed his crazy fancies, Norah and Penelope would be raking in the meadow, and the poet mooned about the garden, gleaning straws from the stubble of the fields of poesy long since swept of their crop by other reapers. At midday they would lunch together on the river bank.

"How's the Muse this forenoon, Reggy?" Norah asked him flippantly.

"Coy. Distinctly coy. It's something in the weather. Here will we sit upon the rocks and see the shepherds feed their flocks——incidentally, I'll have another scone. How is it, by the way, that the shepherds about Schawfield look so deucedly unpastoral and unpoetic?"

"Do they?" asked Norah, sipping milk with deliberate relish, as if it had the flavour and bouquet of a wine. "I've never noticed it, except at the end of a fair day, when they're sometimes a little unsteady on their dear old legs. And even then Andy insists that they're quite in the poetic spirit."

"Oh, everything's in the poetic spirit to Sir Andrew," agreed Reginald. "If he'd got to give it form in decent verse, he'd see that nowadays Phyllis is a slattern and Damon is a lout. Don't you think so, Pen?" He lay back on the grass with his hat off, leaning on his arm, balancing a glass of milk on his knee.

"I don't know," said Penelope simply. "I never tried to make poetry myself, and I know I couldn't, for more than half the poetry I see I don't understand it."

"That is the test of the very best kind of poetry. I often write poetry so confoundedly subtle that I don't understand it myself. Still, everybody else who reads it does, and it's thought to be very fine. But perhaps you don't care for poetry?"

"I don't," admitted Penelope. "I always skip it in a magazine or a story. 'Oh, bother!' I say when I come to it." At which confession the bard upset his glass, and Norah gave way to laughter at his astonishment.

"Why?" he demanded.

"I can't say why," she replied, with a moment of reflection. "Don't you skip, too, Norah?"

"I'm afraid I do," admitted Norah. "But I always feel it's a sin, like skipping the church on Sunday for a headache. Now, there's Aunt Amelia—she delights to come on a good thick slab of original verse in the newspapers. She usually cuts it out and carries it about in her purse for a month or two. When she finds some day that she hasn't a sordid prosaic pound she's been calculating on, those bundles of inoffensive verse are treated very badly."

"You really don't mean to tell me you dislike poetry?" pressed Maurice.

"No," said Penelope; "I don't dislike it. I like Pope, and 'The Deserted Village,' and——"

"Oh!" groaned the poet, "that is little better than the heartiest detestation of poetry. Have you read, by any chance, 'Harebell and Honey'?"

"By Wilfred Ford?" said Penelope, and Norah nervously cast her a warning glance that passed unheeded.

"Yes," said Maurice.

"It's in my bedroom; Norah put it there, I suppose. I've looked at it, but I didn't care for it."

"No?"

"It—it made me sleepy. It's so full of gorgeous words and names like Eurydice and Perse—how do you pronounce it?—phone. It might have been written hundreds of years ago, it's so musty."

"How darkly, deeply, beautifully—true!" said Maurice. "I sometimes feel like that myself about 'Harebell and Honey,'" and Norah gave him a look of gratitude.

"I suppose it's clever," proceeded the unconscious critic. "It looks as if it might be clever; but then I don't much care for cleverness in poetry—I mean the gorgeous kind of thing. It looks like mere display. I think Wilfred Ford said to himself, 'It's a lovely day, and I have a lot of nice words,—what will I make a poem about?' Don't you?" She swung her sun-bonnet round her head and smiled deliciously at him.

"Bravo, Penelope!" cried Norah, clapping her hands, and Maurice still retained her gratitude by his good-humour.

"You would have the poet sing because he must, and pipe but as the linnet sings?" he suggested airily.

"Something like that," replied Penelope. "I'm sure Mr Wilfred Ford didn't sing because he must, but only for display."

"Hadn't we better go and finish that rick?" said Norah uneasily.

"Oh, never mind the hay just now!" said Maurice. "Pen's just got her views on poetry sketched in; let's see them finished. What do you want in a poem, Pen?"

She looked across the field to its further side, where the harvesters sat resting in the shade of trees.

"I want simplicity, love, and truth, not too elegant and sweet, a little wild—like a bramble-bush. But I don't know: sometimes I think there's only one poem after all, and that it's not in written poetry, but inside everybody waiting to be stirred. It's the hearer makes the poem."

"I quite agree with you," said Maurice; "at least he makes the best part of it. But here and there in 'Harebell and Honey' you surely found simplicity and truth?"

"Certainly not in the poem called 'Ardfillan Priory,' for that is near my native place."

"Pen," said Norah abruptly, "before you say another word let me tell you that Mr Maurice is 'Wilfred Ford'."

Penelope turned crimson. "How stupid of me!" she exclaimed. "I beg your pardon. I didn't mean———"

"Oh, you mustn't back out," he protested, laughing. "That's the sort of thing that makes a poet's friends quite useless to him unless he hears their real opinions at second hand. I assure you I've got an extremely durable hide."

"I had no idea of backing out," said Penelope firmly.

"And what is wrong with my poor 'Ardfillan'?"

"It's all pretence. It's one of the things that make me sure a great deal of poetry's just an infant's game. 'Ardfillan's' only words and make-believe. You pretend to be very melancholy about its crumbling walls and empty windows———"

"A melancholy of mine own, compounded of many simples," quoted Maurice.

"And say you wept as you walked in its ruined cloister."

"So I did," he protested. "Those ruins affected me very poignantly."

"When?"

"Last summer," he replied, betraying some uneasiness.

Penelope looked at him with widely open eyes. " Ardfillan Priory ! " she exclaimed indignantly. " You've only
read about it in a book or seen it in a picture. There
isn't a stone of it standing on another, and there hasn't
been for eighty years : they were taken away and built
into dykes and byres."

CHAPTER XVI.

CAPTAIN CUTLASS laughed immoderately when Norah met him that afternoon returning from a cavalry charge against the dolours, and told him how Penelope had made the artist in affected ecstasies look like a boy found surreptitiously playing with a doll. "You ought to have seen poor Reggie!" she exclaimed; "I never saw a pinker poet. First, he tried to make out that his melancholy had been got in another ruined priory, and that he had only borrowed the name of Pen's Ardfillan for the sake of its associations. Pen declared that such poetic licence was a crime; it was no better than to write an elegy and then go out to murder a man to fit it. Then he said the origin of a poet's emotion did not matter, so long as it was fervent and articulate. 'You're pretending to be very anxious to justify your poem, but really that's not what is troubling you,' said Pen. 'You're vexed that I found you fibbing.'"

"H'm," said Sir Andrew, clouding slightly, "I don't like that. *You* wouldn't have said that. It suggests that cursed sentiment, self-righteousness."

"No, no, it wasn't said like that," protested Norah. "She was genuinely shocked. You should have heard her say 'fibbing,' it sounded like a word that meant a compound fracture of the ten commandments."

"I should have expected a little more sympathy with the bard from you," said Sir Andrew, sorry for the bard's discomfiture.

She blushed, and bit her nether lip. "Am I unkind?" she asked anxiously. "I shouldn't laugh at it if I didn't think it was for his good. Reggie's poetry is full of stylish affectations, and the very faults that Pen discovered in a twinkling. I often wanted to tell him so, but never had the courage. That's one result of being brought up in an atmosphere of conventional good manners, we are nearly always fibbers to our friends. There was positively nothing rude in what Pen said to him: she did not seem to be blaming him so much as protecting herself from contact with ideals not quite decent. And as for Reggie,—oh, Reggie doesn't care! He has the practice and belief of so many poets to back him up in a theory that Art is only an ingenious make-believe."

Norah was right; so far from evading another rencounter with his critic, Mr Maurice merrily opened up the subject again that evening at the dinner-table.

For two of the human arts alone had Captain Cutlass something like contempt—that of the cook and of the lapidary. Unhappy men, he argued playfully with Maurice, developed a new palate by resorting to pungent spices, piquant flavours, high-savoured, hot, bitter, and even putrid things, when they had exhausted the old one which delighted only in the simplest foods. In the plain and natural life of the forester or the seaman, all that the body craved was in half a dozen edibles, to be found with ease wherever fortune took him. Set the clubman and the gourmet before a dinner of herbs, salt junk, or oatmeal cakes, and he should be wretched, since he had bought his discrimination in kickshaws, curries, and wines at the cost of a simple palate ruined. Both seaman and gourmet sought but to gratify a natural hunger; that it should be gratified was the main thing, and considering the cheapness and accessibility of the seaman's fare as compared with the gourmet's, who, he asked, should deny that the sailor had the best of it?

"We will now have your favourite strawberry trifle, Andy," innocently intimated Aunt Amelia, who had imperfectly got the drift of his remarks; and everybody laughed, including himself, at the unconscious retort, for in truth his sailor palate always watered like a boy's to sweets and trifles.

"There have always been strawberry trifles, praise the Lord!" he said. "I was thinking of peacocks' tongues and ortolans, olives, truffles, caviare, and rotten cheese. The hunger of the workaday world has always been satisfied by commoner stuff, at which the gourmet is apt to sneer, and which, like bread and milk, has never gone out of fashion; while peacocks' tongues, and the monstrous salads of Lucullus, have long had their day, and now create a nausea to recall. Eh? I'm all for the old earth flavours: to the devil with your sauces and cruet bottles!"

"Andy!" exclaimed his aunt, whose ear was always marvellously quick for an impropriety.

"Well, well," he amended genially, "I withdraw the sauces; let him have the cruet bottles."

"I believe in a Good Table," said his aunt, as solemnly as if it were the opening of the Creed.

"So do I!" he answered gaily.

"I sometimes think you don't believe in anything that's natural and nice," said his aunt. "You have talked of the sin of jewels till you have made even Norah stop wearing any!"

He looked at his cousin with surprise; he had never noticed that she had lately fallen in, apparently, with his views in respect to jewels; she flushed, and he recognised immediately that the change betokened no capitulation, but a sacrifice in the interest of Penelope.

"Norah," he said, taking up a glass of water, " I drink to you ! I've never seen you look more charming. You confirm my belief that gold is only good for making into sovereigns, and that diamonds are rather vulgar bits of glass. No jewels you ever wore became you so well as this, their absence. It is not for any actual beauty in them women cherish jewels, since the meanest flower of the ditch is much more beautiful than anything that ever came from the hands of the goldsmith or the lapidary, but for vanity, avarice, and display ; too often, I'm afraid, to rouse the covetousness of other women. No woman was ever better or more beautiful for a necklet or tiara—useless and barbaric things. . . . Don't you think so, Pen ? "

He shot the question at her over the dinner-table, and her hand instinctively went up to the string of little amber beads upon her neck as if he were to snatch them from her.

" I don't know," she said with hesitation. " I like to see jewels—on other people. I suppose they're not more useless and barbaric than a lot of other things that women delight in—men too. Whether they're good or bad, barbaric or beautiful, depends, I fancy, on the way we think of them ! "

" Exactly," said Sir Andrew, peeling an orange. " There's nothing really in them but a jaundiced ore and carbon turned to crystal. I should sooner have the gold of a dandelion, or this orange, and a drop of dew for in them there is the destiny of ourselves—brief life a little of the sun, and then—Phew ! " He popped a part of the orange in his mouth and gulped like an all-devouring Providence. " I can't get into the soul of minerals and metals," he proceeded, " except good honest coal—the fire in it, you understand, eh ?—and the old dead summers, and the primeval forest, and the tiger burning bright, and the flame waiting, waiting, waiting, buried in the bowels of the earth. Now, I can be a flower——"

"Oh, you are perfectly ridiculous, Andy!" said his aunt. "I wish, instead of being a flower, you would be sensible."

"No, dear aunt," he said with a laugh, "it's a jolly sight better fun to be a flower. Eh? I can be a flower, if I look long enough at one, and I've looked at a rose and guessed all its feelings till my heart was almost breaking, to think that together, the rose and I, we should have that strange heat in us, and be so wonderful and weak, and bud, and grow, and bloom, and perish, except in the mind of that inscrutable skyey Gardener. Eh? But I never could be a diamond brooch; there's nothing of me in it,—no human touch or tingle, no juice, no sense of tears, as in the commonest vegetable."

"As the onion," broke in Maurice with his usual flippancy. "Diamonds are what you make of them in your mind, as Pen says. They are, like everything else, a symbol——"

"True! true!" said the baronet reflectively. "I catch your point, Pen. Quite! Perhaps it isn't always vulgar possession that makes folk eager for diamonds and emeralds. Eh? Everything material is the expression of a thought, particularly all precious things, like the flag, for instance, and diamonds may be a kind of poetry. Those sparkling stones typify a superlative and unearthly purity; all the dross of the earth is out of them; they are nearly as imperishable as stars—why! they are just tiny stars when you come to think of it!"

"Exactly! Polished up by your detested friend the lapidary," suggested Maurice pleasantly. "There's not a hint of poetry or the stars about your diamond till the lapidary brings it out with a wheel. That's like poetry,

Pen; I took that priory of yours from a chapter in the 'Old Statistical Account of Scotland,' where it was described by a man who was interested only in the lineal measurements of it and had no idea of its pathos; and I brooded on it as Sir Andrew did on the rose till it almost broke my heart. That's how poetry's made.

> 'Point me out the way
> To any one particular beauteous star,
> And I will flit into it with my lyre,
> And make its silvery splendour pant with bliss.'

Yes, that's how poetry's made."

"Perhaps it is," she agreed. "But I think the poetry would be better if the priory had really been there, and you had actually seen it."

"I can always feel most poetic about a place I haven't seen, or a voice I haven't heard, as Milton could, or Keats—the other poets, you know," said Maurice.

> "'Mombaza, and Quiloa, and Melind,
> And Sofala (thought Ophir), to the realm
> Of Congo,

and

> 'Heard melodies are sweet,
> But those unheard
> Are sweeter——'"

It was then that Penelope proved that apparently all in vain had been Norah's introduction to the poets of her book-shelf and the influence of "Wilfred Ford." She vehemently contended anew that the sense of poetry in things was just a satisfaction of a natural human thirst, and that she got that satisfaction for herself in a chapter of Isaiah or a popular old country song. It was all nonsense, she protested, with a heightened colour, and at times a stagger on the edge of the high inflection now

almost cured in her—it was all nonsense to imagine that
a poet could dispense with truth, and make up for it with
ornament, which was often an obscurity. It might give
a versifier great delight to make ingenious poetry out of
moonshine, but poetry so made would never quench the
thirst so well as the verse of a simple psalm. There
were single lines of the psalms, she said, that almost
made her cry—they touched the heart so!

"The heart is not a very safe guide when it comes
to poetry," Reginald informed her. "What have we
got heads for?"

"My father would call that blasphemy!" she cried.
"You might as well say the same of love. You'll
never get genuine poetry out of your head if it isn't
bubbling first of all from your heart, and no one on
earth ever really loved a woman or a poem except
in his heart. however much he might admire them in
his head."

"*Touché!*" exclaimed Sir Andrew to the poet,
delighted with the spirit of his protégée. "My boy,
you're face to face with the oldest fact in the world,
that the heart is an infinitely better guide for man
or poet than the head. When I attempt a poem on
my head it's apt to turn out a triolet or a villanelle,
both charming forms of exercise, but scarcely to be
called arterial."

The interruption gave Penelope time to recover a
calmer mood, and she pursued her thesis now in a
spirit of gaiety. It must be sad, she said quizzingly
to Maurice, to be a poet by profession; to be going
round all day and every day looking at things not
full face with open eyes, but sideways, or upside
down and through the eyelashes, aiming at a state of
mind, continually torturing, not spontaneous thoughts
but painfully constructed ones, into pretty lines. One

might as well be trying to fall in love or doing Mrs Powrie's fancy-work.

"Tut! tut!" said the troubadour, with genuine vexation, "you're giving expression to the most commonplace opinions."

"That's the kind I like; don't you, Sir Andrew?" she inquired, with merry eagerness.

"By George!" he said, "I do! Emphatically! Haven't I told you often, Norah? Every-day opinions are more likely to be in harmony with the mind of God than the opinions of the superior people who scorn them. I couldn't convince you, but here Pen jumps to the truth instinctively."

"Oh, it isn't a new discovery: *vox populi*, you know," said Maurice.

Norah said nothing; she was listening to the daring Pen with some amusement. Aunt Amelia found the discussion unedifying, and withdrew to the parlour with a novel where the issues were more obvious. A crimson-shaded lamp upon the table tinctured the room with a winy light through which the face of Penelope Colquhoun, surmounted by the umber masses of her hair, seemed like the face of some sunburnt calm Olympian creature. The cosy nest-like warmth of the room was rendered the more perceptible by the dash of rain at times upon the windows; withdrawing himself for a moment from the subject of their argument, Sir Andrew thought with satisfaction of his hay-crop safe in rick.

"You've helped to save my hay, you folk," he remarked, "and that's to more human purpose than making poetry, which, when I'm engaged on it myself with a pen, occasionally strikes me ludicrously as a childish game, so that I sometimes have to stop and laugh at myself. My own verse, Reggy, always reminds me, as Pen has said, of Mrs Powrie's fancy-work; she cuts up a useful thing to make it into something ornamental; I cut a happy thought, which is quite sufficient in itself, into four-line lengths, and make it a very indifferent stanza. The thought is none the nobler for the process, and I'd be better making hay."

"All flesh is grass — or hay, and the flesh of your beeves is the food on which you nourish yourself," said Maurice. "It makes you live. And when are you most alive? When you're elate with high poetic fancies. The poet gives you these directly; he provides a short-cut to the very top of life."

"With some assistance from the butcher," said Sir Andrew. "But yes, I see your point. We must give the poets a chance, Penelope—capital fellows! I love them all—well, nearly all, if it's only for their good intentions. If they happen to be obscure, and I miss an appeal to the heart in them, I find my reward in admiring my own intelligence in grasping what they mean. And a cultivated taste——"

"What *is* a cultivated taste?" asked the girl whose word or deed was never to be predicted.

"It's—it's a cultivated taste," he answered laughingly. "It's one that's in agreement with our own. But seriously, one doesn't appreciate the finest kind of poetry except by a cultivation of the taste."

"Like the sauces and fancy foods?" suggested Penelope mischievously, and Sir Andrew slapped his knee in a transport of delight at a shot from his own locker.

"I remember! I remember!" he exclaimed with animation. "It is your old defence of novel-reading. There's something in it; haven't I said so to you sometimes, Norah? But one can over-eat one's self; one can't have too much poetry."

"I don't agree with you at all," replied Penelope.

" My father always told us too much art, romance, or poetry, or music was a poison, a narcotic, and I'm sure it isn't good for Mr Maurice. If it was he wouldn't laugh at my getting a satisfaction which he can't from Pope and ' The Deserted Village.' It may be bread - and - butter poetry, but it feeds me very well ; it's beautiful."

" What is Beauty ? " asked the poet senatorially.

She hesitated for a moment, seemed to search her mind, and then flung out the answer, " It's anything that satisfies our own imagination and finds us at our best. Whatever it is, it's something in ourselves, and the things outside ourselves only help us to find it out. God gives, but He does not carry home for you. Nothing in the world is in itself more beautiful than another : the shabbiest things are beautiful to somebody because——because they quench the thirst inside."

" But some things quench more finely than others," said Maurice.

" Nothing beats plain water : there is only one wholesome kind of thirst and one condition of quenching."

" But hang it all, Pen ! " protested the troubadour, " you must confess that Shakespeare's poems are beautiful."

" Do they know they are beautiful ? " she asked quickly.

" Well, no, of course not," he admitted.

" Then the beauty is in the reader's mind," maintained the eager advocate of the exclusively subjective. " And it makes me happy to know it is so, that everything is mine to make what I like of it, that I can waken my sense of poetry and beauty by looking properly at the commonest things on earth."

" My dear Penelope," cried Sir Andrew, " who the devil told you that ? "

"I think it's very obvious; it's the truth," she answered. "Everyone in his heart believes it."

"It's true! Of course it's true; but for heaven's sake let us not admit it, otherwise the Search were done and we were clods," said Captain Cutlass.

CHAPTER XVII.

In wet or shine, and more like maidens of the sea than equestriennes, with little cowls upon their heads, and jerseys which divulged bewitching lines of waist and gracious bosoms for the nourishing of heroic generations, the girls would ride each afternoon to the gates of the Schawfield policies, or amble in the turfy canters cut nearer to their home, between the forest trees. Beautiful beings! Radiant things! Cattanach told James Birrell once how he one time watched them there in the quiet green colonnades, their ponies stepping high and soft on the foggy sward; behind them, stretching distantly, the vista of the sundered trees. Poor Cattanach! how he rebelled at the scurvy trick of fate that had made him fat and middle-aged, and had reared those social barriers that compel a man to smother his inclinations. They seemed to him, he indicated in his luscious Gaelic accent, strange alien creatures of a different country and complexion from his own, controlled —if controlled at all—by a different kind of destiny; feeling different wants, provoked to every act by inclinations quite unknown to such as he.

"And yet," said Mr Birrell, "just women after all! Just flesh and blood like the rest of us; moved, like ourselves, by common wants and appetites, pushed on by a multitude of children crying to be born. When I was tempted as a youth to believe a woman was an angel, I had only to look at the lugs of her to remind me that for a' that and a' that she was just a human animal. We're the awful fools, Cattanach, to be afraid of any of their sex—ay, even the loftiest of them,—as if they had some tremendous secret that we canna share. They don't know anything that we do not know oursel's; they don't have any finer mainspring. Marry the most majestic of them, and you find it out. It's only a lad's illusion, not for the like of you and me."

"If I thought it was that way of it, I would gather them in my arms and fly with them to the Outer Isles," said Cattanach, the undying savage Celt.

"And which o' them would ye have?" asked Mr Birrell.

"I would have them both," replied the natural man. "But I canna help it; I'm afraid o' them."

"And that's the way ye never married, I suppose! There's many another man in the same position; but it's all a fallacy of vision. I've had it; sometimes (between oursel's) I have it even yet. But I doubt, when all is said and done, if the game is worth the candle."

Those canters had been cut by Sir Andrew's grandfather, who liked to feel the turf below his horse's feet. Such turf!—so green, so soaked with flowery perfumes after rain! And never was there a more inviolate sylvan privacy: here alone, of all Sir Andrew Schaw's estate, the folk of the village rarely ventured, from some tradition of Cutlass Primus's sentiment for the place as a kind of sanctuary where he galloped down his liver and his private fiends. Even the red deer from the hills along the coast—the noble, the august!—when they came, as they sometimes would, to the woods and pastures in the neighbourhood of Fancy Farm, ventured timidly across those mossy avenues, lifting their heads with startled glances, throwing out their breasts, twitching their ears, and sniffing the air with some mysterious surmise.

But it was not to the canters that Penelope went alone on Saturdays, while Norah went with Aunt Amelia through the village tenements, dutifully acting in the *rôle* of Lady Bountiful that custom has imposed upon a landlord's women-folk.

" I could never do it," cried Penelope, reddening furiously when Amelia asked her company. " Oh ! I could never do it; I—I think too much of the people; it would hurt their feelings. You'll excuse me; I feel I haven't a right to walk into their houses when they haven't a right to walk uninvited into ours."

" Tchk ! tchk ! you are as bad, I declare, as Sir Andrew !" exclaimed his aunt. " He'll not set foot in a workman's house to which he's not invited, or if he does, he'll have the man to tea in the Farm immediately after. Tea with an egg to it !—not a Christian dinner, mind, but tea with an egg to it, to give the visitor a homely feeling. You'll not come with us, then ?"

" No, thank you," said Penelope, without a moment's hesitation. " I'm sorry to refuse, and I know it is very kind of you; but for me it would be cruel, for after all I'm only one of themselves."

" My dear, they expect it of us," said Miss Amelia, who always went about the tenements in her grandest clothes on principle, believing that it pleased the folk, oblivious of the hopeless envies roused, the discontents created, the bad examples set in silly and expensive fashions. " They like to see us taking an interest, don't they, Norah ?"

" Let us hope they do," said Norah quietly, dressed simply in her blue serge gown. " But Pen is right. . . . You Radical ! You Radical !"

And left to her own devices, terrified lest the troubadour should catch her, Pen would trot away on the horse she saddled for herself, into the farthest confines of the parish. She loved the wilds as she loved the night or the moonlight on the sea; the horse was most a joy to her when it bore her into the uncultivated country where the whaups went screaming over lands unfenced, expressing desolation. In the neighbourhood of Fancy Farm she felt at times an irksome sense of artifice, paths too trim and hedges dandified; of nature subjugated to the whim of a single family for generations. There was, for her, no path for miles around that did not, far too obviously, lead to the gate of Schawfield House.

Far better for her the lonely moor, with its lochans dozing in the sunshine, wild-fowl splashing through the reeds, the windy voices in the heather, glance of the asphodel, and nodding heads of the cotton-sedge, the cannach. The myrtle breathed upon her there its perfume like a benediction, better than all your garden flowers; God's blessing, oh! God's blessing on the myrtle of our hills, hardy as men should be, and unassuming! Her father's people had been Highland shepherds, and some secret chain of sentiment brought her back, upon the moor, to the state of life they knew—their homely joys, their great endurances. Pictures and books, and poems battered from the brain in rooms luxurious; the sloth of elegance and the vanity of intellect—how remote were they from the lives of these her people, and the blood of them went coursing through her body. She felt herself upon a pinnacle that broadened as it sank below her feet, deep down in centuries through the multiplying generations — hunter and shepherd, shepherd and hunter, humble and frugal women, simple-minded, self-sufficient men: had she the very morning's wings, she would not at that moment ask to fly from off that pyramid of heredity.

She would sit upon the knolls, with her pony standing by, and think, not in the terms and sentiments of other people's poetry, but in great cloud-masses of elation, awe, and wonder, that went surging through her soul, of sadnesses and gladnesses, of matters inconceivably remote from the daily life of Fancy Farm.

"As droll as the laird himsel'," said the village, which was not long of learning of the superficial aspects of those weekly flights.

"A lad, I'll warrant!" Tilda Birrell conjectured. "What in the name of mercy would a body scurry from the best of company for, if it was not gallivanting?"

"I hope to the Lord it is!" said Mr Birrell fervently. "With an account for the saving of Norah's life, and a broken ankle, no' to mention the accident at the fencing, we're in a bonny mess in Fancy Farm; and no one settles an account so heartily as Captain Cutlass. To hear that the lass had a lad already, would take a load off my mind."

Only once Sir Andrew met her on those Saturday excursions, for he never sought her company abroad unless she was attended by his cousin; and yet when he saw her riding towards him from the moor one afternoon, he felt most singularly quickened by her coming. She had pinned a little tuft of mingled heath and myrtle on her cowl, and had cocked that Cap of Liberty, as he sometimes called it, slightly to the side with an arch effect of challenge. She rose and fell in her cantering like a wave, and her pony bore her lightly, as the wave bears on the sapple of the sea. Not for the first time he was struck by her peculiar harmony with certain backgrounds: the flat plain broken up in fields, and the rises fringed with pine, and the great white leaning clouds beyond, appeared to have designed themselves in such a manner as to make of her their focus.

Putting off the purpose of his own excursion, he turned him round about like the knight on the Irish shore, and rode with her back to Fancy Farm. For a while they went side by side without much conversation. He felt like one who had achieved a work of art, for already she revealed the influence of her training. There was none of the high inflection; if she laughed, it was with a pleasant gravity. There was even a touch of poetry in her, due (though he could not guess its cause) to her solitary thoughts among the myrtle. She was quiet, she was restful, and for the first time he discovered in her possibilities of shyness.

On the road they met a hawker with a little cart of cans and baskets, which, with quite unnecessary solicitude for gentlefolk, he backed into the ditch to give them all the highway's width. Its wheels sank over the hubs in mire, and the horse and its owner were unfit to extricate it till Sir Andrew had jumped down to their assistance.

The man stood with his hat off, full of abased humility, too fulsome in his gratitude.

"Put on your hat," said Captain Cutlass, who would leave a road and take to the fields sooner than encounter mean subserviency. "Put on your hat, my friend; it doesna make my head any the warmer for you to stand wi' yours uncovered. I'm a wonderful man, but I'm no' exactly God. The road's no' mine."

"That is the only sort of thing that makes me furious with wealthy people," said Penelope as they rode away. "They have taught poor folk to cringe."

"And he hasn't the excuse of Fleming: once I met Clashgour at the end of a sheep delivery, where the spirits had been circulated freely; he took off his hat and was beat to find his head to put it on again. . . . And am I included in your detestation?"

"No, no!" she said, "you're different; you may be wealthy, but——"

"Wealthy!" he broke in with a laugh. "That poor fellow with the cart is doubtless wealthier than I am, if it comes to that. I probably eat and drink as little as he, and spend no more on personal pleasures. My vices cost me nothing, and my only luxury is a decent coat. What do I get from this estate? The rents, you say!—I never see them: that is a luxury reserved for Mr Cattanach. The land is the great joker; it seems to be giving out a constant crop of guineas every term, but it always wants them back immediately as a kind of top-dressing. That's what the fields are smiling at so slyly—our illusion that anything is to be got from them but the simplest living, and a shelter, and a grave."

"But you have money," she said; "you have investments——"

He chuckled again, and turned over a coin or two in the waistcoat pocket we used to be familiar with when we were boys and he was a lieutenant. "I have," said he, "exactly eighteenpence, and a little credit. I used to think like that of my father's wealth when I was a lad at sea—that it was an actual thing imparting an exclusive kind of happiness, a thing to give a hundred and twenty minutes to every hour of joy and make the sunshine warmer than it was for common people. But I found when I came home it was only stewardship. I got no more out of it than I could eat and drink; a slightly bigger house than Watty Fraser—less for my own convenience than to give work to servant-maids. Money is like that river,"—and he pointed to the stream by whose side they were advancing. "I can turn the wheel of a mill with it, but I can't stop it, and I can't drink more than a glass or two at the most. It's long since I ceased to understand it, having only a sailor's head for figures. You speak of my investments—you should hear Norah on that point! They don't even turn a meal-mill for me, though I'm glad to think they may be turning some one else's."

"Yes, yes," she persisted, "but you have what that poor man in the cart had not, nor any of my people; you have security."

"From what?" he asked her quietly. "From care? From pain? From the ultimate common lot—a hole in the churchyard yonder? There is no security but for the soul. If the hawker knew the facts, I doubt if he would change with me. I have only this advantage over him, perhaps, that I know where I am, and have seen the folly of grumbling and rebelling. . . . Heavens! Pen, I'm becoming homiletical; let us trot!"

The trot became a canter, the canter changed to a gallop; together they felt that sense of power that comes to confidence on a saddle. The road went through arcades of foliage or crossed between successive fields where harvesters were working. To the harvesters they seemed, those two, to be impelled by the same force, to be blown as withered leaves are blown before the wind.

"By George, you ride!" said Captain Cutlass, slowing down upon the summit of a rise, and he looked with admiration at her animated face.

"I love it!" she exclaimed, exalted. "But I know now what my father meant when he said that every man on horseback was a tyrant, and every creature meeting him on foot a knave."

"Why should you think that?" asked Sir Andrew,

who was ever unconscious of his class except when
the foolish cringed.

"I can't tell. I know what I think, but I can't say
why I think it. I'm afraid if I were rich I should
be hard and cruel."

"God forbid!" he said fervently. "Why?"

"Again I don't know why. One has so many thoughts
which one hasn't sensible words for: I feel them often
when I'm on the moor. That is why I can't say much
about poetry or religion: there are no ready-made sentences that seem to fit, and so I like the company of
folk who talk about little else than the weather and the
news."

"So do I," he confessed, "unless I happen to be in
the mood for my own homiletics. But try to tell me
why you think that to be rich would make you hard and
cruel."

She thought a moment, with knitted brows, hands
low, head and heart high, as he had tutored her in
riding. "Because," she said at last, choosing her words
with great deliberation, "I have seen nothing worth
while in the lives of what I call wealthy people that I
am not fit to enjoy, myself, tremendously. I could
indulge myself far more than you or Norah can, so
much indeed that I fear I should grow heedless of
less fortunate people. I can see that all my beliefs in
which I get a lot of comfort, and which I got from my
father, would weaken and entirely disappear. I couldn't
help myself. The thought of it shakes me. Do you
know I have even wished I could be wealthy?"

"The wish might be very creditable to you," said Sir
Andrew. "There are many fine things to be got with
wealth, though I never had enough, myself, to prove it,
nor perhaps the inclination. Sometimes the wish for it
is the worst of vulgarities. It depends on your ideals."

"They go no farther, at this moment, than a horse of my very own, and—and—and a string of pearls," she confessed with an honesty that pleased him. "That shows you I was never meant for riches, which should only be for those who understand them."

"I wonder," thought the baronet, without reply, as they entered the village street.

CHAPTER XVIII.

THE village had been built by Cutlass Primus on the
plan of a town he had seen upon the Baltic: its central
tenements ranked like companies of infantry along the
street, and massive as bastilles, of a slate-like stone or
lapis-ollaris (as the Dominie called it), which, when
wetted by the rain, gave them an aspect singularly
sombre, and the more remarkable since each peering
little window had its lintels, jambs, and sills white-
washed. The upper flats were reached by ponderous,
thickly-parapeted outside stairs, beneath which draughty
passages went between the street and the shabby lanes
we call the wynds, behind; and midway in its brief
career the street divided, taking the narrow kirk, as
it were, with its dumpy steeple, in its arms. "A h——
of a place to put a kirk, the middle o' a street!"
Clashgour had said when he blacked his eye against
it on the first dark winter night on which, a stranger
to the district, he had walked bedazzled out of the lights
of the Schawfield Arms. From end to end the little
town was paved with cobbles; let a horse or carriage
trot or trundle in at the southern end where Alick
Brodie had his smithy, and the bruit of it was heard
instanter at the other end where Cattanach had his
office. You knew, in Schawfield, at the breakfast hour,
when herrings had been got along the coast, even if you
never saw the herring-cadger's cart. You knew, if you

stood in the midst of it at night, whose bairns were teething. But yet the place had a secret inner life enclosed within the fortress walls of its tenements, and up their windy closes and their blue-flagged stairs—a life that, on the summer days, when the hens were in the fields, and Watty Fraser's gander stood, a still sentinel, in the wynd, and the street was silent, you could hear in muffled tones like drumming of the rabbits when the ferret penetrates the warren and you lie with an ear upon the hole. So sounds the beeskep when the days are wet, and its little people pack the cells more tightly with the sweat of heaven or the moisture of the stars, as the elder Pliny thought it.

There was something in this stifled indication of the people's inner lives that used to make Sir Andrew yearn to know them closer. He knew them at their work— none better; every man by name: he knew them in their outdoor recreations, but he felt that there was more to know, more vital things and paramount, within the poorer dwellings of his village, which he could not enter. How he wished it was a ship again, and he at liberty to take a lanthorn and go through the crowded depths, asking if all was well with comrades!

But that, on land, was a joy reserved for a Captain's women: Aunt Amelia stood his watch, more of the martinet than he had ever been on the *Bellerophon*, chiding the sloven, menacing the ne'er-do-well with threats of trouble at the factor's office. She undertook the duty in a missionary spirit; felt herself a daring soul, landing (backed by Norah Grant) on jeopardous sands in Raratonga. I would not say exactly that the people loved her,—how can you love a lady who asks what the dinner-pot contains, and has views of a maiden kind about the ease with which the size of a family may be restricted?

They would fly from the open stairheads when they saw her coming, to put fresh pawns on the bed or hurriedly pile the unwashed breakfast dishes in the bunker. And Watty Fraser, being a lonely man without a woman-body, only with a fiddle, which is sometimes better company, had been compelled to train a gander. "Jock" they called it—a bachelor bird of great antiquity, hating the very sight of frocks. He lived upon the gutter, and he held the entrance to the wynd where Orpheus and the fiddle shared a garret. 'Twas a stirring thing to see the bird with his neck extended, and a baleful eye, padding with nightmare feet in chase of bairns whose naked legs were pimpled with their terror. His hiss expressed a very orgasm of fury that became more sinister at the sight of women, who never ventured down the wynd but fearfully, prepared to pull their skirts about their ankles.

"Well done, Jock!" would Orpheus cry, looking out at his garret window.

The blackness of the heathen isles lay, therefore, on the wynd where Watty dwelt, for Aunt Amelia daren't venture near it. She appealed to Captain Cutlass for an edict from the factor's office to proscribe all geese of either sex, and he only laughed at her. "What, Jock!" he cried, "my old friend, Jock! I couldn't look a goose in the face again if I deported Jock. The gander is a sacred bird; the Romans used to carry a golden one in their processions."

"The Romans would do anything!" said Aunt Amelia.

"Look out! There's Jock!" cried Norah, warningly, that Saturday afternoon: he stood at the head of his master's wynd, lifting his beak already at the sight of Aunt Amelia's splendid raiment, and they had to take the other side of the street as usual, leaving the fiddler's wynd in its hopeless heathendom.

The game of Lady Bountiful is one that must be played according to the rules, and Captain Cutlass made it difficult for his aunt. Her most devoted efforts for the welfare of the people were handicapped by influences of his. What is charity? what is mercy? what affection if it is not dealt with justice? Her nephew gave them oftener to the undeserving and impenitent than to the nice, clean, humble poor, whom he thought, with strange perversity, did very well out of his aunt, and had quite enough good fortune in their virtues. Oddly they liked him none the worse for it. "I would rather have a joke wi' the Captain than a pound o' tea and a good advice frae Miss Amelia," the wife of Paterson the poacher put it. Charity!—he loathed the word; the very sight of it in a dictionary made him furious. "It looked," he said, "so devilish like a sneer." But coals and bread were often to be had by the very useless poor of Watty's Wynd at prices out of all relation to the market, and the coalman and the baker sent a monthly bill to Cattanach. Once a-month, on the pay-days, every boy engaged in the harvest-fields got a brand new or polished shilling in addition to his wages; the baronet had polished the coins himself in the workshop, where at intervals of a year or two he spent some weeks inventing a reefing gear. "There you are, my bully boys!" he cried, when the shillings lay in shining rows on the work-bench.

Polished shillings for truant boys who didn't deserve them, and a night at times with the rabbit-nets with Paterson the poacher; jobs restored to futile characters properly dismissed by Cattanach; fantastic occupations set agoing to keep some interesting vagabond about the place; hail fellow with the broken men, the failures,— those things rather spoiled the village for a zealous missionary. Had Schawfield House, the stately mansion of the Schaws, been nearer to the village instead of half-a-dozen miles away, the village doubtless had been different in its character, for mansions have a domineering influence on a country-side; but Fancy Farm was such a couthy, unpretentious place, and the ways of its folks so manifestly human, that the very gardeners sang and whistled on the lawn. In truth, the village took its tone from Captain Cutlass — easy-osy, and we're a' John Tamson's bairns!

Even Aunt Amelia, though the slattern fled before her, failed to create the proper feudal atmosphere. "Sit down and draw your breath; and how are they all up-by wi' ye?" was a characteristic salutation in the very topmost "lands," where a husband was known as "my yin." The feudal days were gone, and 'Tilda Birrell, with Miss Amelia in her room, swithered to lay down her knitting till she reached the middle of the needle. Perhaps the affable Norah's presence helped a lot in the nonchalance of this reception: Norah was a universal favourite, and she liked Miss Birrell's tea, which always tasted like a masking from the Cranford urn, though made in a wondrous pot that her father had carried in his knapsack from the looting of Pekin.

"You're not married yet, Miss Norah!" said the lawyer's housekeeper, as usual, twinkling with her brother's fun. "You must haste-ye and look about ye, and no' be left in the lurch like me!"

"Oh, there's many a splendid chance at fifty," was Miss Norah's joke—an old one among maids of hopeful spirit.

But never a word, you may be sure, about the poet: in Schawfield one might joke on anything except a rumour of engagements, far too serious a thing.

That day Amelia was unusually deaf, sure sign of a

change of weather, and her eyes kept darting restlessly in search of hints. It was impossible for any human being to be so alert in following a conversation as she thought herself at that particular moment.

"And how is Sir Andrew keeping?" 'Tilda asked, plying the Pekin teapot.

"I asked that this morning," answered Norah, "and he said, 'I'm feeling so well that if I felt any better I should be heartily ashamed of myself.' He couldn't very well be more emphatic, could he?"

"He's well looked after," pointed out his aunt—the common boast of wives in the "lands" she had just been visiting. "He was saddling the mare to go to Mr Beswick's when we left."

"But Andy does not always ride when he saddles," said her niece. "And whether he gets to Schawfield House or not depends how long his conscience operates. You drove him to it, aunt; he admitted he had been remiss with Mr Beswick, but you never can tell with Andy: who knows but he may meet a charming caravan of gipsies?"

"And Miss Colquhoun? I saw *her* gallop out this afternoon," said 'Tilda genially, at which her elder guest gave a little start and cocked an ear.

"To the moor as usual," said Norah. "Pen loves to haunt the moor: she's a great dreamer."

"Eh? What!" cried her aunt, astonished. "Schemer, did you say?"

"Dreamer, aunt, not schemer. I'm saying to Miss Birrell that Pen is a terrible dreamer."

"You always mumble, in the town," said Miss Amelia querulously. "I wondered what you meant," and she helped herself to another cookie. She looked relieved, but from that single word misapprehended rose a thought before unknown to her in spite of her great experience in vicarious romance. 'Tilda Birrell's cookies weren't quite so good to-day as they used to be. In another moment they would seem a good deal worse.

"How's her arm, Miss Grant?" asked 'Tilda, unreflecting that a matter gossiped of in Schawfield village might be a holy secret in Fancy Farm.

"Oh, better long ago," said Norah, not surprised that what had been a secret from her aunt should be known to calmer people in the village.

"What is that about Pen, Norah? I didn't catch——" said Miss Amelia quickly.

"It's Pen's secret, aunt; only a scratch; Andy expected her to parry."

"A match! Marry! What *are* you talking of, my dear?" cried her aunt.

Miss Birrell had no sooner got her guests to the foot of the stair with decent circumstance than she was up again and stamping on the parlour floor, the signal for her brother in his den below. "I'm a sinful woman, James," said she; "but I thank the Lord for Miss Amelia's sad infirmity."

The clatter of horse on the noisy causeway filled each window in the street: she ran to hers, and saw the Captain and Penelope ride past.

"They'll overtake the ladies," she exclaimed to James, looking out behind her shoulder. "Isn't this the busy day wi' Providence?"

CHAPTER XIX.

THREE days after, a joyous sun-scorched band of the village children, all the care of the world unknown to them,—dear hearts!—pattered with bare feet behind a barouche which had never once previously emerged from the coach-house of the Schawfield mansion since the days of the late Sir George. It might have been the golden chariot of Mumford's Circus by the interest it awakened as it made its way without an occupant except its driver towards Fancy Farm, whose yard had never seen a carriage with the family crest before. The children cheered, and Captain Cutlass, suddenly appearing, helped them at the cheering, "with one more for bare young legs and good old walking!" The lad who drove looked uneasily self-conscious, as a lad might very well do who had not previously been charioteer for anything more glorious than a timber-jonker, and flicked in his rear when he felt the slightest jerk upon the springs, and heard the shouts of "Whip behind!" from envious youngsters who were pushed away by older ones from the joy of hanging on.

"Losh! is the Captain takin' to a carriage?" cried the village in a tone of apprehension; he had so long appeared among them otherwise that the notion of his separation from a saddle-horse was painful to contemplate, like a centaur cut in two.

A week or two more and Peter Powrie was restored

to the grateful arms of his lady; he came from Fife
with the champion Dandie Dinmont, whereof, it appeared,
Miss Norah Grant was now the owner, and he was to
spend the rest of his days in driving Miss Amelia, who
thus got the darling wish of her life. Her happiness
was only slightly clouded by the fact that Captain
Cutlass all his days refused to share it.

Watty Fraser and the heathen people of the Wynd
were the only ones who suffered from the innovation;
the sentinel Jock could make no pretence at holding the
fort against a carriage, and when Penelope learned that
this last redoubt of the very poor was forced by a
contingency she had not anticipated, she almost rued
her share in the expansion of life in Fancy Farm. She
availed herself, however, of Miss Amelia's longer absences
by going to the kitchen to be rebuffed at first by a cook
whose art had long been lapsing from desuetude because
of the baronet's indifference to a Good Table, but soon,
by cunning wiles, to rouse again the spirit of art, which,
in cookery as in painting or in poetry, must be kept
from sleeping by applause. Cook and Pen, between
them, fashioned dinners which defied the culinary
theories of Captain Cutlass. He blinked at mysterious
and chromatic dishes. "Astounding!" he exclaimed;
"I wish I weren't really hungry, and I'd try them;
please pass me the bread again, Reggy." But no more
lectures on the simple life of the seaman and the forester,
since fancy food it seemed was a taste of Pen's.

There was even a grand party!—a diversion which
had not disturbed the calm routine of Fancy Farm since
the death of Lady Jean. Norah shone, magnificent and
commanding, all her jewels on. She took her company
in her hands, and played their happiest notes as if they
were an instrument of strings—a singularly cheerful
evening! The women seemed so tender and so sane,

the men so witty and so humanly fraternal. Sir Andrew thought the time on a ceremonious dinner well expended if it took the stilts from people, and showed his cousin to such great advantage. Never had he seen her look the same before, serene and regal, all the more conspicuous against the foil provided by Penelope, unreasonably quiet and self-effaced. He rallied all his social charms that night, to the support of Norah; he was the best of hosts, and his courtly graces to the golden ones, the Brooks and Beswicks, made his happy aunt relinquish the last of those vague unrests aroused by the incidents of that Saturday when her nephew and Penelope came riding up the street together. Who could think that there could ever be anything between Sir Andrew Schaw and the parson's daughter?

"Now, Andy, you see how nice a dinner-party may be, if one goes about it sensibly," she said to him with a smack of satisfaction when the company had dispersed. "Everything went off so beautifully, and I never saw you more like *my* idea of Sir Andrew Schaw."

"Oh, parties clearly have their place in the puzzling scheme of things," he admitted. "I got as close to the heart of Mr Beswick to-night as if he had been a ploughman, and we were sitting on a dyke together sharing the same tobacco. There's a lot to be said for a glass of wine. I'm glad you're pleased, aunt, but indeed you owe me no gratitude: if the God of things-as-they-should-be is appeased, we have to thank Penelope."

Luckily for her peace of mind the last phrase failed to penetrate Aunt Amelia; she went off to bed elated. The night wind breathed outside among the trees; it bore in its louder flaws, *diminuendo*, sounds of rolling carriages, passing into distance over devious ways; Sir Andrew, Norah, Pen, and Maurice gathered round the hearth and softly laughed at some common secret understanding.

"Well, madam," said Sir Andrew to Penelope, with a deferential bow, "we are getting on famously. I admit I found your guests exceedingly agreeable and entertaining. When one has no ulterior motives, even Mable Brooks has a certain depth of soul in her."

"Even the very rich are human, Andy," said his cousin. "There are times when they should be pitied, they are so forlorn. You are far too prone to be on agreeable terms with every class except your own; that's very narrow-minded."

"I trust I comported myself to them all to-night like one with as much good-will as I sincerely felt for them? But what is the next of your august behests as a lady of rank and wealth, Penelope?"

Pen had thrown off her self-effacement; she answered gaily, a humorous acceptance of the dignity in her tone. "I want more punctuality at meals," she said. "You almost spoiled the soup, Sir Andrew. It upsets everything. A person can be unpunctual and irregular only at the expense of other people; my father used to tell us it was a kind of theft."

He comically knit his brows. "H'm! There's something in it! If I have hitherto failed in this respect, it was, honestly, not for want of trying to do better. I'm afraid those minor virtues are a gift, like a head for mathematics; you have it or you have it not. I must certainly buy a watch; my instinct for the exact breakfast hour is not what it used to be. And I hate a watch, for many reasons; I spoiled the only one I ever had as a boy by using it, in fishing, as a sinker. But I foresee, in the possession of a watch, a lot of trouble; it's got to be wound, for one thing. More than that, it stamps the owner as a man of system, parcelling off the day and its duties in a way that's foreign to me. Confound it, Pen! I always just do what I like and when I like!" He put on a ludicrous air of protest.

"That's all very well for gipsies, but I could never think it very wise or right in a gentleman," said Penelope, the loyal slave of the everyday duties. "All the good work of the world is done by men and women who know the value of time."

"You're as much as ever for uniformity, I can see," he answered, shrugging his shoulders; "but as Mistress of the Keys you shall certainly be obeyed."

That was the joke—Penelope, the parson's daughter, for the nonce was regent queen of Schawfield, demure and self-effaced so far as any open indication of her office went, but actually in power to indulge her theories, and command resources, with Miss Norah and Sir Andrew for her agents! Had Aunt Amelia known by whose influence she had got her carriage, how dreadful would have been her indignation!

This grand caprice had occurred to Captain Cutlass on the day they rode from the moor together, inspired by Penelope's views on wealth and her confession that she sometimes longed to test its power. "Look here!" he exclaimed impulsively, after pondering on it for a little; "I've a great idea—you shall manage Schawfield for a month, absolutely! You'll be Mistress of the Keys in everything except the vested offices of Aunt Amelia; you can do what you like, and, as far as my bank account goes, indulge yourself in pearls if you find your nature cry for them."

She drew herself more upright on the saddle, reddening furiously, and stared at him with sudden and disquieting doubts; his honest face was lit with boyish fun. "My dear!" he cried ecstatically, "it would be splendid! splendid! Ha! ha! You'd see then I was right about the stewardship, and I'm ready to swear you wouldn't want the pearls. I ought to have done something of the kind that night with good Tom Dunn, you know; as it was, we only got half the possible sport of that escapade."

Despite her sense of humour, which in many things could be as active as his own, she flatly refused at first to have anything to do with such a wild vagary. " It's the maddest of ideas ! " she exclaimed.

" Well ! well ! " he retorted heartily ; " isn't that the beauty of it ? And it's only east by nor'-east of dull sanity ; if I did half the mad things I am sometimes tempted to do, I'd put the ship about and sail for Atlantis, where the folk who sit for ever singing on the sands never do anything like anybody else."

" Norah——" she began.

" Norah understands," he broke in hastily ; " I never devised a good joke yet but Norah wanted a hand in it. She'll be just as delighted as myself to delegate her powers for a week or two."

He was right, too ; Norah entered into the scheme with the liveliest alacrity ; swept away the last objections of Penelope, and stood by to watch the fun to which she was contributor in a way the author never once suspected.

" I want the barouche at Schawfield House brought out," was the first demand of the regent lady. " It's only proper that Sir Andrew Schaw should have a carriage, even if it is only to prevent his guests from awkward adventures in Mrs Nish's landau."

" Who that has ever known the glory of a saddle would want to sit and joggle in a wheeled arm-chair ? " he asked, disappointed at her selection.

" Your aunt has wanted the carriage out for years," replied Penelope.

"She has never once said so," he exclaimed with genuine surprise.

"No, because she knows your views about a carriage; she was afraid to press the matter. I'm afraid of nothing," but she glanced at Norah with some sign of perturbation, as if she looked for her support. "And then I want—I want a dog for Norah, if I can get the one she fancies—the champion Dandie Dinmont."

"Good Lord!" he cried, "I never suspected you of a taste for Dandie Dinmonts, Norah."

"It has been the guilty passion of my life," said Norah. "You are so wrapped up in your own fancies that you seldom think other people may have fancies too. I'll pay myself for the dog if we can get it, Pen; it needn't come from your bank account."

"If we can get the dog, we can get Peter Powrie, too, as coachman," proceeded Pen with more nonchalance. "Of course one wants a good driver for one's Aunt Amelia. I was almost thrown out of a landau once by an inexperienced amateur."

He smiled at the reminiscence. "Mrs Powrie will not thank you for bringing back her Peter," he suggested.

"I think I know Mrs Powrie a good deal better than that," replied Penelope. "It is only the absent Peter she is angry with: that's a woman's way, and I feel certain she'll be glad to share his fidelity with a well-bred dog."

"Very well, madam," he agreed "And après? What next?"

"I insist on good cooking," continued Pen, who had now entered a little breathlessly into the spirit of domestic autocrat, supported by the obvious approval of Norah and the imperturbable good-humour of Captain Cutlass. "I think it is a shame to spoil good cook by not giving her an opportunity to

keep up her practice; she may not always be at Fancy
Farm, you know, and all other houses are not so easily
satisfied as this. . . . And I want a dinner-party to
show off Norah—and her pearls."

"No pearls for yourself?" asked Captain Cutlass
smiling slyly.

"No. Now that I can have them,—I suppose,—I
don't seem to want them. Besides, I can see them
better on Norah."

And thus by a playful acceptance of the situation
into which his whim had forced her she had given joy
to Miss Amelia and Mrs Powrie, gave Norah an opportunity she had not had previously to show herself at her
best, and made a great success of the dinner-party whose
component parts were now scattered to the night.

"You seem to have thought of everybody except
yourself, so far," said the baronet.

"Oh, no!" she answered cheerfully, "I have thought
of myself too, and sent for a dozen of the very latest
novels."

"And not a single poet!" exclaimed the mocking
Maurice.

"Not one! I'm determined I shan't encourage
them. I'll not be renegade to my Goldsmith."

"I'm beat to understand how you, Pen, with a head
like yours——"

"Thank you so very much, Mr Maurice!" she broke
in with a flicker of the spitfire. "You don't expect
much of a head of any kind on a woman, do you?"

"I'm beat to understand how you can bear to waste
your time on such trashy stories," he persisted.

"I can easily tell you why," she said. "It's because
they are quite untrue to life. The good men in them
are always handsome, brave, chivalrous, and true, and
the heroines are always beautiful and fortunate. Th

bad people are so transparently wicked that they could not deceive a kitten, and everything ends in joy. Real life is not like that, but it ought to be. That's why common people — like myself — read common novels. They get quite enough of real life by living it."

Sir Andrew listened with amusement, but brought back the conversation to the subject of its opening. "Most of the satisfaction of wealth, I'm told, is in the power it gives over other people," he remarked. "As your guests here, we can be so only on your own terms. Remember you are absolute monarch."

"Then," said Penelope quickly, "I am not going to encourage those gipsies who come about the place. Every tribe that comes into the parish looks upon this as an almshouse."

"There's nothing in it!" he protested. "To give them a bone occasionally is surely not wrong; why, it's actually biblical!"

Penelope was firm. "I have convictions," she insisted. "And I'm taking you at your word. And there should be no excuses for men like Paterson. If he had not been encouraged by you he might have been an honest workman, whose wife could go to bed at night with an easy mind. I don't believe in countenancing vagabonds."

"I always loved a vagabond," said Captain Cutlass; "I don't know why."

"So do I, sometimes, but they are a luxury Paterson's wife can't very well afford, and she has told me all about him. Is the estate *all* mine?"

"Certainly."

"Then I insist on Mr Cattanach taking a firmer hand with those farmers at Barbreck; they are shamefully neglecting their dykes and hedges. When it was not my estate"—she smiled—"I thought it very picturesque, but now I have to think of my successors, and hand Schawfield down to them in as good condition as when I got it. I think I'll plant the whole brae-face behind the mill with timber."

"Haven't the money, Pen; haven't the *gelt!*" said Captain Cutlass, shaking his head.

"Yes, you have—in that diamond mine that paid a dividend the other day for the first time," broke in Norah eagerly. "Now's the time to sell out of it, plant trees, as Pen proposes, and watch them grow. Diamonds! remember, Andy; you can't have shares in a diamond mine and hold the views you do on diamonds with any consistency."

He threw up his hands in a gesture of surrender.

"There is another thing," said Penelope, bracing herself to a greater effort. "I think every one should earn his or her living somehow, and———"

"Why, Pen! I do, surely. It takes a good deal of my time to qualify the excessive zeal of Mr Cattanach, and keep an eye on my cattle."

"You do, Sir Andrew, and I'll — I'll allow you a modest salary. So does Norah; so do I, but — but Mr Maurice———" She broke down here, apparently appalled at her own temerity.

Maurice reddened; her thought had come to him even before she gave it halting expression. "There's the new book, you know," he suggested, with a smile, and his good-humour restored her courage.

"I am speaking of real work," said Pen. "Work people want. Does one make a living from poetry?"

"'Harebell and Honey' cost me exactly £70 to publish," he informed her. "If I made anything off poetry I should be sure there was something very far wrong with it."

"Then," she pursued, with relentless logic, "you don't even pretend to try to earn your living?"

"I don't," he admitted quite amiably. "I take a remote half-yearly interest in a business established more than half a century ago by my people, and it seems to prosper very agreeably in my absence. You have heard of the shipbuilders Maurice?"

A delighted smile irradiated Pen's face. "Oh!" she exclaimed, "I didn't know you were a shipbuilder. That makes a difference. But if I were a shipbuilder, I would think it so splendidly poetical that I would never dream of bothering with make-believe poetry at all. I thought you did nothing else!"

Maurice flushed a little under the mildly satiric eye of Norah; in truth, for several years he had done practically nothing else.

CHAPTER XX.

PEN would have ceased to be queen regent for the *farceur* in a week were it not for Norah's ingenuity and delight in thinking out a hundred ways in which the pleasantry might confer some benefit either on Sir Andrew or on Schawfield. The two of them conspired with Justice (truer friend to the world than Tolerance, Sir Andrew's favourite); in a fortnight they had, between them, established a *régime* in Fancy Farm where all things went like clockwork, and where fads were stringently discouraged. Aunt Amelia couldn't understand it: "I'm sure that Andy's going to be ill," she wailed, "he grows so sensible." Indeed he played his part in the joke with honesty; smothering many an inspiration which would make the prank more laughably ingenious, relinquishing that moral domination which is sometimes found in the tenderest men; for the nonce a pattern of conformity and regular ways.

Norah, abandoned by her aunt to the vulgar claims upon manorial ladies, induced Penelope to go with her one day among the tenements, while Miss Amelia swept magnificently away on more stately social rounds, of which she compassed many in the first few weeks of her barouche. They even defied the gander: "Get away, you stupid goose!" cried the fearless Pen, contemptuously; the savage wynds revealed themselves as after all hum-drumly like to other places where the mission flag of Miss Amelia waved: the native tribes proved friendly. Watty Fraser, coaxed from his shyness, played them "Clean Pease Straw" and "The Smith's a Gallant Fireman," to show from what celestial heights Italian music had degenerated. "They havena the snap, them foreign fellows, and the snap's the main thing. I canna stand them gliding capers." "And quite right too!" said Pen; "the snap goes best with the Scottish climate." "Stop, you!" said Watty, screwing up a peg, "and I will give you a splendid one of my own contrivance! I was thinking for to call it 'Lady Norah'"—whereon that lady blushed tremendously, and Pen was very sly.

Norah sat amazed at the art with which her friend set people at their ease. 'Twas not an art, in truth, but an effluence from an artless nature that disarmed suspicion and dispelled alarms by sheer simplicity. Pen, above all, could restrain the roving, curious eye that breeds dislike in humble dwellings, and be oblivious to dirty jaw-boxes and—in Paterson's—to pots of salmon-roe, at which Sir Andrew always laughed as a harmless superstition of illicit anglers. She would lean, to the manner born, on counters, marvellously learned in un-bleached cottons and the cost of remnant woollens; sheep-dips, saddlery, potatoes, smoothing-irons, cheap baker's "dumpies"; loin, hough, and entrails; or balance on a kitchen-dresser, telling all about herself and her sisters in the manse, showing herself most humorously experienced in economic household make-shifts, hard times, the making-down of garments, old-fashioned cures, half superstitious, for children's ailments. In half an hour she could be further into the confidence of the folk than Aunt Amelia could have been in a hundred years, and all without a single conscious effort.

"*How* do you do it?" Norah asked her enviously.

"I have never seen that woman so genial and unreserved before."

"Have you not?" said Pen, surprised. "She seemed to me very natural."

"I don't know how it is, but they trust you," said Norah. "With us—with Aunt Amelia and me—there's always some aloofness, some acting of a part. They speak to you in a different accent almost."

"Perhaps you unconsciously act a part to them," suggested Pen. "There's nothing they discover sooner. I have no necessity to seem but what I am with them; I know them, and I like them; they remind me of my mother. She had been a servant-maid when my father met her first,—one of the class to whom rich people leave the beautiful art of domesticity, the first, the highest. It was sometimes pretty tight with us in the manse; you have no idea of the grandeur and hospitality expected off a stipend less than a blacksmith's earnings! But my mother pulled us through. Father philosophised, but she did better; she turned garments outside in. She didn't know much about poetry, except the Psalms and a song or two. She taught us to love the humble, though I'm not a bit humble myself, and prefer the shy and quiet, though I happen to be neither. I learned from Miss Skene how stupidly the rich may think about the poor, who have sentiment and pride, and many compensations, just like other people. The one thing you must never do is to pity them."

"Surely for what they miss of beauty in the world?" said Norah.

"Lord bless me, no!" cried Pen. "Not that! Do you imagine God's unfair? Do you think all the sweetness of the world, the hopes, dreams, gaiety, are only for the well-to-do? There's not a tinker on the road but has his moment. 'People like you,' I told Miss Skene once, 'never really see the poor, but only yourselves in the places of the poor. You credit them with privations and discontents you would feel yourself in their position. They're really just about as happy as yourself. And at times as sad. Their real sufferings you are not likely to hear anything at all about.'"

"Then we should leave them as they are?" said Norah, cunningly political.

"No," said Pen. "You can't. They can no more remain what they are than you can; they must move. They don't want pity, which is often quite misplaced, but you, to be really happy, must be generous to them. No, not generous, I mean just. Whether they're at their ease with you or not depends upon yourself. I know, because my people have been always sharing trouble, and fun, and soup with people I can never look upon but with affection. Most folk change their friends when they change their clothes. If they rise in the world they can find a thousand very plausible reasons for throwing off their old acquaintances. I hope I should never do that. I like to make new friends, but I'd rather not make them at all if it meant I was to turn my back on old ones. I hope that if I came into a great fortune to-morrow I should feel none the less at home in a but-and-ben."

"I'm sure there's not the slightest fear of it," said Norah warmly. "You have as great a genius for fidelity as Andy. It extends even to some trivial songs which I'm sure you can only tolerate because you knew them when a child."

Pen laughed. "That's so!" she admitted. "Ought I to turn my back on them now that you have taught me to love Schubert 'and them gliding capers'? The trivial songs are not trivial to me at all; they bring back the past like a perfume, and they let me play again with a little girl who was Penelope Colquhoun."

"Another phase of the pathetic fallacy!" said Norah mischievously.

"What's that?" asked Pen, who was never ashamed to show her ignorance.

"You should never bring your own joys or your own griefs to the appreciation of nature or art; they should be loved for themselves alone."

"Good gracious, that seems awful nonsense! One can't love anything for itself alone. Even a baby likes the daylight just because its brains recall the dark. I defy you to look at anything or listen to any song in that inhuman abstract way. Everything is shaped by our experience. A song has two tunes—one that was made by the composer, another you make for yourself, that has no notes to it, but is full of sad or happy things remembered, which nobody could understand except yourself."

Penelope did not require to have authority as Mistress of the Keys to find her way to the homes in Schawfield village; long before that prank had come to the freakish brain of Captain Cutlass she had made acquaintance with the people—in the shops and in the fields and at the wells, where they emptied stoups and waited to fill them up again for the chance of a palaver. And wherever there was a child she knew the passport to its mother's hearth if she had wanted there. But there were no bairns — more's the pity! in the house of Mr Birrell, and as yet she had not drunk from the Pekin teapot. Norah baulked at an introduction there, doubtless for private reasons.

Pen suddenly suspected something of the kind, and as usual did not beat about the bush. "I'd like to meet Miss Birrell," she said; "she seems to be the one out-

standing female personality in Schawfield. It's always
her the other women quote. Can't we call on her this
afternoon ? "

" Of course," said Norah. " You'd have met her long
ago if you hadn't your Radical scruples about going
round in state with Aunt Amelia. I'm certain that
she's dying to make your acquaintance, for she doesn't
say so. And you must be sure to like her teapot."

" If I do, I'll say so," answered Pen. " If I don't, I
can praise her tea at least, for there I'm not particular
if it happens to be reasonably warm."

The day was sultry, and the world lay panting all the
fervent afternoon. A landrail in the field behind the
village kept continuously craik-craiking, like a salmon
reel—voice, it might seem, of the parched earth; no
other note was audible. Jock Fraser waddled from his
post and sought the Midtown Burn, now withered in its
courses, stood in the surviving tiny pools and cooled his
scaly legs. Across the street skipped Wyse the saddler,
from the licensed grocer's, dangling a bottle, frank and
honest, from a string about its neck, suggesting oil, but
really the receptacle for beer, good cooling beer. A
street of windows with the blinds all down : happy the
people in the massive, vault-like lower dwellings of the
tenements and wynds !

Miss Birrell welcomed her visitors with effusion, in a
room that won its way at once to the heart of Pen,
with its dark mahogany, its shining cupboards, and its
flowery chintz. " And this is Miss Colquhoun ! " she
said, looking up with kindly penetrating eyes at the face
of Pen, whose own had always a communicable and
appealing candour. " I have looked at you often in the
kirk, Miss Colquhoun, and thought to mysel', What a
bonny lassie ! What did you think of yon young minister
from Perth on Sabbath ? Birds ! Birds. and the wisdom

o' them, and the fruitful summer breezes ! Lord bless my heart ! Fancy a young man coming here from Perth to tell us about birds and summer breezes ! As I said to my brother James, ' What have birds and summer breezes got to do wi' the blessed gospel ? ' Faith, we've had more than our share o' the summer breeze this fortnight ; now that my blanket-washing's by, I'm sure the country would be nane the waur o' rain."

" You're always the busy woman, Miss Birrell ! " said Norah, fanning herself with a ' Missionary Record ' which the lawyer's sister always cherished for the sake of Jimmy Chalmers of New Guinea. " Do you never take a rest at all ? "

" There's no rest for the wicked, Miss Norah," answered 'Tilda cheerfully, searching for the best spoons in the cupboard, bringing forth the Pekin teapot. " There's no rest for the wicked ; we have Scripture warrant for it, and there's seldom any rest for the like o' me, that's only middlin' good. I'm aye thinking that when I die, it'll just be my ordinar' luck if the resurrection doesna happen on the morn's mornin'."

Pen laughed, and felt a curious gush of liking for the little woman who reminded her immediately of her mother. " I wouldn't think of that at all, if I were you, Miss Birrell ; it would give any one the blues."

" It does, but there's a cure for the blues," said 'Tilda blythly, measuring the tea from a lacquer caddy.

" In Buchan ? " suggested Pen, who had found that amazing medical vade-mecum in every other house in Schawfield village.

" No, nor Buchan ! In the Bible—thirtieth Psalm," replied Miss Birrell. " And how's your aunt, Miss Norah ? "

" She's fine ! " said Norah.

" We haven't seen much of her of late since she

took to carriage exercise. A carriage must be a great convenience."

"So Pen decided," answered Norah. "Sir Andrew would let the old barouche lie rotting for another generation if it hadn't been for Pen."

A host of eager questions cried in the mind of 'Tilda, but she held her tongue, and while the Pekin teapot plied, Penelope realised that the air of the afternoon had suddenly become a little chilly in the room, however it might be outside. Miss Birrell seemed watchful, and the mood of fun was clean departed for the moment. When she thought herself unobserved she scanned the stranger closely over her teacup edge, or under cover of a flourish of the cookies. She was looking for those faint airs that in woman the jealous discern so rapidly— an accent of self-complacency, a trivial boast, a disparaging droop of the eyelids, vanity about a neat shoe or a well-fitting pair of gloves; a saint could not have come more creditably through the scrutiny than the unconscious Pen, who admired the Pekin teapot and showed it in her manner without a word, the subtlest kind of flattery for a lady like 'Tilda Birrell.

"I see," said their hostess in a little, having brooded darkly, "that you have gotten Peter Powrie back. His wife's quite new-fangled wi' him. They go for a walk in the forest on the week-days. Did you ever——!"

Pen looked puzzled.

"Men never walk with their wives on week-days," Norah explained to her, twinkling. "It's a solemn rite reserved for Sundays. But I'm afraid it's not so much for the company of his wife as for the welfare of my Dandie Dinmont that Peter walks at any time. He's married far too long for maudlin sentiment."

"Coming on twenty years," said 'Tilda. "It was the

time when women wore the dolmans. A fine, big, breezy
fellow he was thought—I suppose because he was always
blowing. If you took his word for't, there was only one
man knew the breed of a dog in Scotland, and his name
was Peter Powrie. And I'll allow he *did* know dogs.
Women, too; he couldn't have got a better wife than
Aggy Cameron—poor long-suffering lass! He was so
daft about her, she could lead him round the country
with a cobweb,—that's the way with men before you
marry them." She saw a smile on Norah's face, and
laughed herself. "I'm not pretending, mind, that that's
the way I'm single; no indeed! I would be glad to do
the leading wi' a rope, and risk the hanging o' mysel' at
the end o't. Peter Powrie was a disappointing husband
for a while, but we all have our own bit failings, and
I'm glad to see him back. It's real considerate o' Sir
Andrew."

Norah, with a gesture of her teacup, indicated Pen.
"There again, Miss Birrell, the fairy godmother! Mrs
Powrie might never have had her man restored to her,
nor I be owner of the darlingest of dogs, if it weren't
for the magic powers of Miss Colquhoun."

"In—deed!" exclaimed Miss Birrell, bewildered and
astringent: Pen wondered why. It seemed to her, on
reflection, that the lawyer's sister did not like her.

"And have you heard," asked Norah, patting the
teapot-lid, as she used to do when she visited the parlour
of Miss Birrell as a child, "that Paterson isn't to be a
poacher any longer?"

"In the name of fortune! what's the matter wi'
him?" asked Miss Birrell, recovering.

"He's going to Mr Beswick's as a gamekeeper."

"Well done, Mr Beswick!" cried Miss Birrell, delighted. "I could have told him long ago there was
never a cheaper way to cure a poacher, and he couldn't

get a better man for the job than Paterson. He swears
and he drinks, he poaches and he loafs, and they even
say he beat his wife once, but there's not a word against
his moral character."

"Beat his wife!" said Norah. "Shocking! I never
heard of that."

"Perhaps she needed it," suggested Pen calmly. "I
have often thought there are wives to whom a beating—
not too hard but noisy—would do a great deal of good."

Miss Birrell looked at her with something like admiration. "Fancy you saying that!" she exclaimed. "I
could never have the daring to admit it, but I've often
thought it."

"Every woman thinks it sometimes. Of course I
would never say so to a man, for it isn't every man
who's qualified to use the power, and perhaps on the
whole it's better to let men stick by their idea that it's
chivalry to let a wife go utterly astray for the want of
a little mild correction. All the same, it's as logical to
whip a foolish wife as to whip a naughty child. And I
know the wife of Paterson."

"There are faults on both sides," admitted 'Tilda, her
favourite summing-up of such situations. "One night
he came home none the better for his company, and she
was ready for him in the morning, but he hurried for
the first word. 'When you and me were married, Kate,'
he said, 'didn't the minister make us one?' 'I suppose
he did,' said Mrs Paterson. 'Then let me tell you this,'
said Paterson, 'we had an awfu' skinfu' yesterday!'
Another time the banker saw him throwing in his hat
at the open door o' his house, and waiting on the landing. 'What do you do that for, Paterson?' asked the
banker. 'If the hat comes bungin' oot again,' said
Paterson, quite joco, 'I ken the weather's coorse inside,
and bide awa' till it calms. If she keeps it in, I ken

she'll be glad to see me.'　There's a lot o' fun in Hughy Paterson! I'm glad he's going to settle down; I suppose it's for his good, poor man! but many a one'll miss his pranks, forbye his partridges. It's very good of Mr Beswick giving him the chance."

"Once more," said Norah triumphantly, "the potent hand of the fairy godmother! Sir Andrew got Paterson the situation just to please Penelope."

This time there was no mistake about the jealousy in Miss Birrell's eyes; even Norah saw it with amusement. The jollity of their hostess fled with no returning; her manner grew punctilious; they were shown to the foot of the stair when they departed with far too ceremonious professions of the pleasure that their visit had conferred, and not too fervent invitations to repeat it when they happened to have time. 'Tilda, returning, washed her tea-things furiously, and snapped the cupboard door on the Pekin teapot like a woman who never meant to bring it out again.

"And what do you think of our friend Miss Birrell?" asked Norah, as they took the shady side of the street for home, threading their way among the hens.

"I like her," answered Pen. "She isn't dozing, and she is herself. I'm not surprised one hears so much about her."

"I like her too," said Norah. "Always did, though she treats me like a child new out of school. I don't suppose she has noticed that my hair's been up for half a dozen years. Her idol's Andy; I thought it odd that she never asked for him to-day."

"And she's a very good friend of yours, I notice," said Penelope.

"I haven't a doubt of it. What makes you think so?"

"Because she was doing her best to like me too, for your sake, and all the time would rather not."

"I think you're wrong," said Norah feebly. It was the very thought that a moment ago had given her amusement when she watched the bewildered, disapproving face of 'Tilda Birrell.

CHAPTER XXI.

CAPTAIN CUTLASS, with his coat off, and his rolled-up shirt sleeves revealing a tatooed figure of a dolphin on his arm, came sauntering through the shrubbery from the kitchen-garden, found the girls on the verandah fondling the Dandie Dinmont, gave a sailor's whoop for salutation, and threw himself, exhausted, in a chair. He looked at them with envy: they were cool as mermaids, being such as carry about with them their own breeze, and he was melting.

"I feel," said he to Pen, "that to-day, at least, I've earned my living. Humphrey and I have spent the most arduous afternoon at what I begin to think the degrading task of sheuching leeks. Why should Christian men, who were meant to stand upright, squat on their hunkers on a day like this, so plainly meant for swimming, and prod holes in the inoffensive earth for the sake of a wretched weed that happens to be esculent?"

"Because they like hotch-potch and cockie-leekie, I suppose," said Norah. "The curse of Eden rather spoiled us for a diet of thistles. But you haven't been sheuching leeks?"

"So to speak, my dear: you mustn't be so literal. Simply to watch old Humphrey doing so was quite enough to make me sweat. But I stuck manfully to the noble, dignified, and essential business of superintendence, which is always highest paid, for some mysterious reason that I hope to learn in heaven. Meanwhile, mum's the word! let us still dissemble and pretend that superintendence calls for some peculiar kind of genius. Humphrey, poor devil! never suspects the truth or he'd have thrown a dibble at me. The fun of it is he didn't take off his coat or tuck up his sleeves, and yet he didn't see the irony of my doing it. So I brought him out a jug of beer; if the working classes don't have a sense of logic they have an excellent capacity for beer. I felt, out there, thus sharing in the travail with nature, something of the old husbandman wrestling with the stubborn glebe for my existence; that I was a good man. It is a reflection singularly soothing. I might have been busily engaged in squeezing the means for a sybarite existence from unhappy tenantry; penalising poachers by making them do for wages what they loved to do for fun; turning gipsies away to sorn on other people less well able than myself to feed them; poking my way into village houses where I wasn't wanted. . . . Oh, Pen! Pen! are you not ashamed of your position?"

"Yes, I am!" she answered, "and a little bored by it."

He assumed a look of apprehension. "You mustn't be bored yet," he said, "I'm just beginning to enjoy myself. Mr Birrell and Cattanach plainly begin to think there's hope for me yet; they never suspect that my concurrence with all they think good business and common-sense is due to the fact that temporarily I'm another person. For the first time, honestly, in ten years, I wish I hadn't broken up that fiddle; there's a sense of liberty that's only to be expressed by making noises. The jolly thing is to learn that, after all this time, I find it quite as easy to be a person of no importance as it is to be a landed gentleman; it's most consoling!"

"But then you never had many of the habits of a landed gentleman," Norah reminded him.

"That's so," he agreed, with pleasure. "Amn't I lucky? I don't have any habits at all, and you may take it from me that that's the secret of an equable and contented life. Never contract a habit, even a good one, or you become its slave."

Penelope put up her chin, opened her mouth and shut it again; he saw in her look the hint of a thought suppressed.

"Out with it, ma'm!" he ordered. "You don't agree with me?"

"Not having any habits is a habit in itself," she remarked with a smile; "and it's the worst of all, for nobody knows when they have you, or what you may do next. For that reason I'm going to bring our little diversion to an end. Why not make Norah play the part? She could do it ever so much better; indeed all the ideas are hers to start with. Oh, you needn't frown, Norah; you know they are! I find I don't like playing a part, in a joke, even; it seems to need a lot of cunning." She stopped, breathless.

"And so you propose to hand the *rôle* on to me," said Norah, smiling. "It isn't quite a compliment, Pen."

Pen showed no distress. "You know very well what I mean," she said. "I'd never have been so bold, demanding all those changes, if it hadn't been for you; and I don't see why you couldn't have made them for yourself; with you it need not call for any pretence. I just feel horrid!" She grimaced in a way which showed the sentiment was not assumed. "For the first time in my life to-day I found a woman who was anxious to dislike me!"

"Nonsense, my dear!" cried Norah. "Miss Birrell is the dear good friend of all of us."

"I'm not mistaken," firmly insisted Pen. "She was quite nice till you gave her the impression that I was seriously of some importance, which is nonsense. At every other revelation of my influence (which was really yours) she grew colder to me. I should say it takes something very serious to annoy so naturally jolly a little woman as Miss Birrell. She thinks I'm a meddlesome upstart, and I know her feeling. She is so loyal to you all that she resents my interference. It's very natural. She's quite right."

She could have told them more—of a recent *hauteur*, sometimes, on the part of Miss Amelia; but on that she was discreetly dumb.

"My dear Pen," said the baronet, hastily jumping to his feet and turning down his sleeves, "I have been an ass as usual. I ought to have known that the Elizabethan joke is no longer practicable without involving somebody in trouble, and I'm sorry. I looked for its development on other lines; I wanted to see if you were really going to be hard and cruel, as you feared you would be, in such a position as you have figured in for the past few weeks; and of course you weren't, as I might easily have anticipated."

"I really feared it!" she exclaimed.

"Yes, yes!" he said, "I know! Upon a horse. The thing's proverbial. Set a beg—— How does it go, now? I forget; but the philosophy of it is, that we all of us have only to go thirteen hands higher than our fellow-men along the highway to feel ourselves their masters. Heaven help us all! I know you better than that." He put his hand upon her shoulder—the first time he had ever touched her, save upon the fingers, since the evening he had raised her from the grass beside the treacherous ice. "Thirteen hands, Penelope, just thirteen hands, and think upon the height of the nearest stars! Eh? There's not much danger that the like of you and me will ever gallop down the multitude on foot from any poor delusion of our own importance."

"My people," said Penelope, "have always gone on foot."

So the mummery of the Mistress of the Keys abruptly ended, but not before Penelope, at Captain Cutlass's desire, had chosen one last self-indulgence, this time really for herself, with none of Norah's prompting. The two companions went to Mr Divvert's school; broke in, impetuous and resplendent, on the serried ranks of youth—who love resplendence—humming sleepily like bees among the lindens.

"We think of giving a children's garden-party," intimated Norah. "The berries are over, so there isn't any danger."

It was a *fête* to charm the heart of Captain Cutlass, who devised details whose fantasy discounted, for his neighbours, all the recent symptoms of his change to sanity. "We want the thing at night," he said; "that is the time for children's *fêtes champêtres*, for the whole of the day is gained additionally in the joy of anticipation. Beds, dear aunt! Pooh! I've been a boy myself, and I haven't even yet got out of the way of it; bedtime's an adult tyranny, and who ever heard of fairies getting up for a daylight garden-party?"

"Fairies?" said Miss Amelia helplessly. "I hope you don't expect me to be a fairy?"

He laughed good-humouredly. "You'll be expected to be nothing, aunt, but what's hygienic and respectable; the night air's chilly, and I only thought of fairies of the mind. There are! you know; there are! and

'. . . the trumpeter, Gadfly, shall summon the crew,
The revels are now only waiting for you.'"

He put his arm about her waist and made to waltz her round the room.

"You're cracked!" she exclaimed indignantly, releasing herself, and looking with irritation at the girls who shared his merriment.

"I know," said Captain Cutlass. "It isn't a crack, exactly,—merely a little chink, and it's rather useful, for it lets the light in."

The night was star-bestrewn and warm, but the very heavens paled their splendour in the rivalry of lanterns that were blooming on the trees and by the borders of the paths round Fancy Farm. The house itself seemed filled with radiance that escaped from every window; young fragile moons of gorgeous colour hung suspended over tables on the lawn. The children stood at first in groups within the gates, and stared incredulously: it seemed unreal and magical, a scene deserted. Only the rivals of the stars were there, and the plash of the little burn that ran behind the dairy, sole familiar thing; they heard it every morning that they came for milk. They stood abashed and dubious till a rocket leaped from behind the shrubbery, seeking to reach that pale fraternity of stars, but failing in the effort, and expiring in a rain of emerald and gold, and the bairns all laughed a moment after, with hearts relieved, and the night made friendly by the chuckle of Captain Cutlass, standing with Penelope and Norah, fiery spirits, in the blaze of Roman candles.

CHAPTER XXII.

WEARYING for sisterly dissensions, sweet in retrospect and absence, and the tonic influence of her stringent father; for the compact little manse, square - built like an oven, adorable (as she thought now) in its contempt for any grace that might detract by a single corner from its stark utility, and for the crowded garden-patch that never had known the trim propriety of bedded-out or coddled flowers unfit without the early aid of glass to bloom in the rigorous airs of the bleak north - country parish whence she got the half of her own unconquerable spirit, Pen went home for a fortnight's holiday. For the first time in her life she was secretive; a cloud of doubt in her father's face at one first tentative hint of Sir Andrew Schaw's eccentric character roused in her all the cautious Schawfield loyalty; it would be impossible to make her father understand.

"The thing is, Has he the grace of God?" asked the clergyman dryly. "I'm not set up with his merriment and pliant manner; the times are sick with men who cannot make up their minds on anything. Easy-osy to themselves as well as others, overlooking others' follies just because they want to palliate the same ones in themselves, what are they but drifters? I can stand a strong man hard as whinstone if he has a principle, but I never could thole your drifters, and your jocular jack-easies least of all!"

"At any rate he is a good man, and a gentleman," said Pen, surprised, as she said it, at the fervent feeling of defence that brought her back, for the first time in many months, to her high inflection.

"A gentleman—pooh!" said her father, in an acid humour. "Pilate himself was a gentleman, and what a job did he make of it!"

"I mean what I say—a gentle man—and it's not the least of his credentials," said the daughter firmly.

"I have seen gentle men, as ye call them, jump through girrs at a country fair, and making a bigger company laugh at their posturing than Sir Andrew Schaw could entertain with a month of his fantastics. Let us hope that it's nothing worse than a bee in the creature's bonnet, Pen. I'm more taken up with your friend, Miss Grant."

Pen gladly turned to this safer and more favourite topic; there was nothing in Norah's character but would meet with his approval.

She came back to Schawfield from the treeless moor that hardly showed the seasons' difference, and was astonished to find the autumn almost gone; perished leaves in the ditches, the hill-sides rusty with the withering bracken. Miss Amelia met her at Duntryne with the barouche, and—"I hope you have brought some books with you," said that insatiable student of romance, who always found Penelope's resource in this respect a comfort. "I haven't had a thing to read for weeks except the newspapers, and everybody else in the country except ourselves has gone to London. At this time of the year one might as well be in a prison as in Schawfield."

Pen was sorry; she had brought no novels back with her; that was a commodity hardly to be expected in the manse. "I've scarcely looked at a book since I went home," she said, "but father, every afternoon, read a chapter or two of Motley's 'Dutch Republic' to me; he has been doing it since ever I remember, and I almost like it—for the fights."

Miss Amelia grimaced. " I can't stand history ! " she exclaimed, " and I'm starving for a nice new novel."

" I'm tired of novels," said Pen. " It came to me lately that most of them are ridiculous. At any rate I've lost my taste for them in the meantime."

" Dear me ! " said Miss Amelia. " Why ? "

" I don't know. I fancy it's because of late it has taken me all my time to keep track of Mr Maurice. The amusing thing is that in a month or two I'm likely to know as many quotations as himself, for I've discovered in a bookcase at home the chief source of his—Leigh Hunt's 'Imagination and Fancy.' " She laughed gleefully. " If I can get most of that book by heart I'll very much astonish Mr Maurice."

" Oh, he's gone," Miss Amelia informed her. " He went off two days after you left for home, of all places in the world to go to the shipbuilding yard where he hasn't spent a week since he published his book of poems. And Norah's quite disconsolate."

A feeling of disappointment—not acute, but something like the numbness of the spirit that we feel when first we wake from a sleep that has followed on deprivation, and while yet we can't recall—fell upon Pen. He was a bundle of affectations, but he had some amiable parts. As, at Portnahaven, the country people pluck the larger feathers from the tails of fowls to keep the winds of that stormy coast from blowing them out to sea, she had, from time to time, in sheer candour and common-sense, divested him of many a plume from the gorgeous peacock-tail of his artistic conceits, so giving him a more stable foothold on the common earth whereto even that glorious poet the lark is ever dragged back by love and hunger. He

did not drift to sea so much of late—she had found his
cynicism less manifest; Fancy Farm, she honestly told
herself, would not be quite the same for a day or two
without him.

But Norah's welcome quite dispelled her brief regrets,
and Sir Andrew met her almost boisterously. She had
come in the nick of time, he said, to join them in the
last cruise of the season, for he laid up the yawl on
Monday. "How the days pass!" he exclaimed ruefully.
"It looks as if it were only a week or two since I put
out the moorings, and now it is time to snug *Kittywake*
down for winter. . . . Gnats! Gnats! We should need
a hundred lives to do justice to the variousness and charm
of things. And after? Dr Cleghorn said on Sunday,
with that literal mind of his that fancies all the truth
may be packed into a single Scripture sentence, that
hereafter there shall be no more sea. A blue look-out
for the sailorman who makes a pier-head jump at peni-
tence, and finds on the other side that he's booked for an
eternal job of holystoning mansion fronts! Eh? Hard
lines on the Galilean fishermen—think of them, walking,
even-on, the golden streets, remembering the slat of sails
and the wash along the bows!"

"Oh, there will probably be a sea," his cousin assured
him blythly; "but the winds will always be sou'-west-
by-west."

"If winds were always sou'-west-by-west, women might
be skippers," said Sir Andrew. "And there's you, Pen,—
you haven't learned to hold a tiller or belay a sheet yet;
it's high time you had your lesson. What were you born
for, on an island, if you want the skill to go round the
edges?"

They rode next day to Whitfarland, and stabled at a
farm. An east wind, tempered by a blazing sun, was
blowing over the archipelago; every islet clapped its

hands; the straits were deeply, darkly blue, and high white continents of cloud filled up the west, hanging above the hilly isles beyond the Sound, sun-silvered, splendid. The bays were full of happy noises—plashing breakers on the pebbles, sandpipers in the dunes. The dim lights, shaded waters, fading reeds, and melancholy moaning marshes of her native parish seemed incredibly far-off and undesirable to Pen: she sat in the well, silent, as they ran, close-hauled, from *Kittywake's* moorings and opened up the portals of the sea whose farther ends thrash coldly upon Labrador, or feel the chafing of the ice about the Pole. The sense of space—the magnitude of nature and the smallness of herself—possessed her. They sailed for a while along the mainland, where Sir Andrew pointed out his marches. The drystone dyke that marked them rose from the sea-edge, dripping; ran through alder thicket, gorse, and withering heather to the summit of the hills, and there was lost to sight as it plunged down the inner glens.

"'The Lang Dyke,' they call it," he informed her. "Made by my great-grandfather, who seems to have thought he would live for ever and maintain possession of a substantial swatch of God's world in spite of time and revolution. And the fun of it is he's dead. Ha! ha! There's his dyke, indifferent to time, and useless to repel a mortgage, and Lang-dyke Geordie's only a little dust in a leaden shell on a shelf in the mausoleum in the grounds there, just behind the ice-house. These are the considerations that make me wonder, sometimes, if it's worth while marking anything on earth as our possession; aye, if it's worth while even to possess, more than ourselves, and a nook to sleep in, and a pot to boil our kail."

"You might add a little yawl and a friend or two," suggested Norah, practically. "Isn't it time to put about ? Stand by!" She kept the yawl a point or two off for a moment and then put the tiller slowly down with a "Helm's alee!" The boat shot up into the wind ; Pen got a hurried first lesson on the cleat from Captain Cutlass.

They were steering now for the largest of the inner isles ; the lands of Schawfield lay upon their weather ; Schawfield House itself abruptly came in view through an opening in the timber, its inconsistent towers and rambling wings a testimony to the freakishness of its various builders, but yet preserved from incongruity by the ivy crowded on all its walls. High on its terrace on the steep peninsula it looked august and arrogant ; Captain Cutlass, who loved it, strangely felt that it called for some apology. "As great a lesson in human vanity as the Lang Dyke," said he, with a look across his shoulder at it. "People imagine I own that house, when in truth the house owns me, as Mr Birrell or Cattanach could tell you. If you could turn that monstrous shell upside down you would find a snail below it—Andrew Schaw, with a budget of liabilities left for his amusement by the previous members of his family. I'll wager Mr Beswick lies on my bed at night and laughs when he thinks how easily himself and his ironmoulders have turned out the Schaws, who got in with swords. . . . Pardon our ostentation, Pen——; good heavens ! how many chimneys ! What are you thinking of ?"

"I was thinking of a saying of my father's," said Penelope, scarce looking at his house, but on the scene around. "It is a day of glory ; the Lord is abroad."

"And I was thinking only of myself and things material ! I fear I'm like Clashgour, who told me once he never thought so seriously of the Lord as when he had just got a clout on the lug from Him." He cast a sailor's eye aloft at the fluttering vane, and swept his glance along the far-off alps of cloud that now seemed less benign and stable. "We're just in time, I think, to close the season handsomely : when the wind comes round with the sun this afternoon we may have a different story ; it looks as if there were a lot of dirt behind there, somewhere."

Presently they opened out more spacious mainland stretches,——remoter inland peaks and jutting promontories, flaming with woods now voiceless, autumn-burned. On one of them there stood the ruins of a keep, with tiny ash-trees, wind-blown, seeming feeble seedlings, growing on its crumbling walls, its window-openings blue, like innocent young eyes, only the sky beyond them ; its rude foundations like a portion of the rock. Daws chattered as they hopped about the broken crenels of the turrets, but the place appeared the very soul of loneliness and silence, unspeakably indifferent to sunshine and to time. Gardenless, unfenced, neglected, and their doorways choked with rubble and with weed, such castles numerously stand on western beaches, keeping the secret of their origin and darkly brooding, blind to sunsets, deaf to storms. Pen's eyes fastened on this one with inquiry and delight ; every chord of the romantic fancy answered its mute appeal.

"Built by some of our folk, too, but by which of them exactly I possess no knowledge," said Sir Andrew. "The sennachies, those wondrous cock-sure gentlemen, attribute it to one David Schaw of the fifteenth century, but who was the dainty Davie ?——there's nothing left of him but his name in several generations."

"I had no idea your family was so old," said Pen, who had never thought of lineage but as something which, as in her own case, could be traced for only a hundred years or so.

He laughed. "It's as old as your own, and not a

single generation older," he informed her. "Three sons of Noah came out of the ark; I'm descended from one of them, but have always been unable to discover which."

Norah, keeping the little vessel full and bye, her face sparkling with the pleasure of her occupation, looked at him where he lay stretched upon the deck and cryptically smiled. "I hope you're not deceived by those fine democratic sentiments, Pen," she said. "Behold in the humble gentleman one who is absurdly proud of his long descent."

"Not proud of it," he corrected cheerfully; "neither glad nor sorry, like a dog at its father's funeral, but just contented with a genealogy which depends, for its identity, on some delightfully musty parchments. Were it not for the parchments, Norah, and that old castle, and the grip our people fastened very early on this coast (let us not inquire too closely how they got it), I probably wouldn't have known the name of my great-grandfather. All the same he would have been there, and was bound to have a name too. It's not the Schaws who have been continuous, but Schawfield, and I am honestly glad to think of that—of the old castle faithful to all the girls they brought in as brides, giving them a strong warm home, a rugged welcome; but their names are forgotten —of no account; Schawfield turned them all to Schaws. I'm telling you! I'm telling you—Schawfield is the master! and makes of us what it will!"

"I think I understand," said Pen. "But I never thought of it just like that before."

They sailed between the islets, theirs the only sail in vision: with a piece of marling he taught her Carrick bends and Blackwall hitches, he told her the names of sheets and halyards, the principles of tacking, and the helm's command.

"Oh, it's just like a horse!" she cried, enchanted with

the power to make the white wings poise or flutter at her slightest pressure. " I love it ! I love it ! "

She caught the trick of it as she caught the trick of all they taught her, instantly : for hours, with only a hint at times from him or Norah, she steered between the little isles, and even bore out to the Sound. The beauty of the scene now lost on her, she set her whole attention on the flapping vane and on the sails. Sir Andrew watched her, wondering at a skill so speedily acquired. He had never to tell her the same thing twice : " there's a Viking somewhere in your genealogy," said he.

" Am I doing right ? " she asked him anxiously.

" You never do anything wrong," he answered, " that's the alarming thing about you,—Luff ! Luff ! For the Lord's sake, luff ! "

So intent had been his observation of her pleasure in the new - learned art that he had not seen the squall come racing blackly over the sea, and Norah had been looking, equally abstractedly, in the wake that creamed behind. The boat careened ; Pen strove with all her might against the windward helm—here was a lesson that had not as yet been taught her ! and the yawl lay over suddenly as if the power of flight had been arrested in its wings. The sea, fierce green, swept over the rail and frothed along the coamings ; the windward hull rose high as if to topple over them and to whelm ; Pen for a moment looked into watery depths astonishingly near and sinister ; a great wave burst upon the quarter, sweeping the yacht from end to end. A woman screamed.

" Damnation ! " cried the baronet, once again a seaman, feeling the chill of the drenching in his back, and jumping to the well with a hand to loose a sheet, and another to grab the tiller which Pen, apparently oblivious to their hazard, was reluctant to relinquish. The yacht

ecovered, shaking herself with petulance in a wind that
eemed pervaded with the sting of sleet.

"I was sure the dirt was there!" said Captain Cutlass.
Who cried?" he looked at them both with disapproval.
That's a thing that's quite intolerable. Quite! It's
gly; it's unpardonably vulgar in the circumstances!"

Norah, who had been sitting on the lee side of the
vell and leaning on her elbow, had got the wash of the
eeling vessel up to her very shoulder. She had looked
or a giddy moment into a sea that seemed to reach
he level of her lips, and her hair was blowing wetly
rom its fastenings.

"I must go below to patch my reputation up with
airpins," she said a little breathlessly, restraining hands
pon her rebel tresses; thrust back the companion hatch,
nd disappeared.

"Did I do wrong?" asked Pen, with some anxiety,
harging herself with the incident.

"Wrong!" he repeated gruffly. "Nothing's wrong,
ut some things are abominably silly, and a shriek in the
rcumstances makes me rather sick. We are not chil-
ren, are we? I thought you were quite devoid of nerves,
en; why did you do it?"

"I don't know," said Penelope reddening.

CHAPTER XXIII.

It is the sense of smell that often conjures back ou
happiest hours, and Pen, for ever after, never had a whi
of clean ship-canvas but her heart expanded with th
recollection of that day among the islets, the sweeter fc
its shocks and perils, though of the latter she was not t
guess until Sir Andrew had her safe on shore. Sh
learned of it more from his evasion than from word
"Why did you swear?" she asked him. "A sailor
always apt to swear when things look blackest," he in
formed her; "it's only Jack's equivalent for an *ave;* h
would quench the fires of Hades with a curse. Thei
was a moment, yonder, when——" But he went n
further. The silver of the cloudy alps had turned t
ebony before they landed; the beach was clamorous wit
surf, and through the bent where the meadow pip
cheeped some hours ago the sandy wind went whistling
Norah had come from her toilet in the cabin as trim a
if it hung with mirrors; her cousin looked at her a
provingly: that was the way that Captain Cutlass like
to see his women—under the strictest self-control an
neatly flemished down. Poor Pen, with the intuitic
that she was disgraced to him by her admission of tha
craven scream, was heedless of her wanton locks, ar
came ashore in a curious mood, half vexed, half happy

The breathless roads at morning had been laced wit
gossamer; now the wind was blowing over leagues

sea, and every withered bell of heather rustled; when
they rode into the forest, night ascended like an exhalation from the roots of ancient trees, and full of undistinguishable blended voices, as of beasts that harboured
for the night, or anguished boughs that whipped each
other; of muttering of rocks, and creak of boles, and
whimpering wakerife hidden burns. Those beings of the
night and forest Cattanach has told me of from his
mythology—the phantom things that took their shape
and character from mankind's earlier terrors,—breathed
in the thickets, peered from stony clefts, amorphous
creatures neither man nor beast; the grumblers and the
snarlers and the blood-red-eyed; all the chuckling little
bodies of the caves.

The road was quite invisible; they trotted, with the
baronet in front, by the guidance of the vague grey ribbon
of the sky that showed above them through the rift of
trees.

> " Oh, soon we'll hear the Old Man say
> (Leave her, Johnny, leave her !)
> 'You can go ashore and take your pay,'
> (And it's time for us to leave her !) "

That chantey of discharge, the parting hymn of landfalls
homeward bound, broke on the night incongruously—a
seaman's vesper shouted by Captain Cutlass. A piece of
doggerel, but to Pen his singing of it there and then conveyed a sense of something tameless, swift, and proud;
it was hopeless to understand him.

They clattered down upon Fancy Farm in time for
supper. Mr Birrell, with documents immediately calling
for his client's signature, had been waiting there for
hours, bawling to Miss Amelia in the parlour. " Have
you seen about the Athabascas ? " he inquired. " That
should be welcome news for you ! "

" The bottom out of them, and another call upon

shareholders, I suppose," exclaimed the baronet without surprise.

"It's time for us to leave her!"

"It's not the time for leaving her at all!" retorted Mr Birrell; "they're doing fine! they're doing marvellous. So far as they're concerned, you're a richer man by twelve per cent than you were at this time yesterday. I'm not going to say another word disparaging about your craze for—what do you call it?—portages and voyajoors, Red Indian trappers, prairies, and the rest of it; my doubts of your holding on to Athabascas, or going into them at all indeed, have vanished, over the hills to Badenoch."

"Who told you?" asked Captain Cutlass, neither up nor down.

"I read it in the morning paper which came here this afternoon," said Mr Birrell.

"What a curious taste you have in reading!" said his client. "The very look of a Stock report in a paper makes me wild; the page would be so much more handsome if they left out all the beastly figures."

Aunt Amelia, who had a tiny interest in Consolidated Stock that kept her figuring nervously every afternoon when the papers came, "tchk-tchked!" at such preposterous views, and shook her head to Norah. "Did you ever hear," said she, "such nonsense? Who could understand without the figures? I only wish they would print them larger."

Norah's interest and pleasure in the lawyer's news made up to him for his client's seeming unconcern. "Bravo the fairy and romantic, after all!" she cried. "I wish we could expect as well of your diamond mine."

"We're out of that, you know," said Mr Birrell gleefully, rubbing his hands and twitching his eyebrows rapidly. "We sold our shares in those abominable liamonds more than a week ago with a view of planting arch behind the mill."

Sir Andrew nodded confirmation, ravished at Pen's astonishment. "Wasn't going to say a word about it till the woodmen started trenching," he proceeded with a chuckle. "A little surprise, you know, for the recent much-lamented Mistress of the Keys."

"It was only a joke!" said Pen impetuously, alarmed to think what great commercial mechanism she had tampered with at Norah's prompting. She had not, for a moment, dreamt that he would act on the suggestion.

"A joke, at times, is about the only thing that a man should act in seriously," said Captain Cutlass, "and I was bound to carry out my part of the agreement. It wasn't so much of a joke after all, when I come to think of it, for some poor devil lost on the transaction, as Witwatersrands went down as soon as I cleared out of them. So far as the planting is concerned, your views coincide with mine exactly; it's some time now since Norah gave me an idea of it. We should all plant trees, and never lose an opportunity. 'There's nothing more delightful you can do with a hole in the ground when you come on it than to pop an acorn in,' was a saying of my grandfather's. The forest is the proper garden for men like me; it needs no weeding."

"But we needn't be in a desperate hurry now about the planting," said the lawyer. "The money's making more in Athabascas than it's ever like to make in larch."

"What! did you put the diamond money into Athabascas?" Norah asked delightedly.

James Birrell nodded, pursing his lips triumphantly. "Every penny, ma'am! My suggestion! Better than to have it dozing in a bank till Whitsunday."

"By George!" said Captain Cutlass, "I had forgotten

that! There's quite a pleasing income to be made from Athabascas now, and I owe it all to your agreeable participation in the crude Elizabethan joke, Penelope. . . . I wish," he added quite irrelevantly, as it seemed to all the others—" I wish you didn't scream."

Pen winced at this reminder; Norah blazed, thinking he was back again to his views on women's laughter.

The portraits of his folk, that had been borrowed from the walls of Schawfield House to furnish forth the hall for Miss Amelia's approval, and to gratify that family pride she cherished upon grounds that made him laugh, were almost the only pictures to be seen in Fancy Farm. The rooms were beautified by other things—proportions, mouldings, panels, native woods unpainted, polished; soft harmonious colour; most of all by windows which, no matter what the season,—winter's snow or summer's splendour,—framed such pictures as no art could ever rival. 'Twas this severe restraint of the unessential and the merely pretty, obvious in everything selected by Sir Andrew Schaw,—his interest in the ribs and lines and poise of things, his apathy to the showy ornamental,— that had first appealed to Pen in Fancy Farm. In that respect she had recalled to her the manse where straitened means compelled a like simplicity, without, however, as she confessed, achieving such a suave and restful atmosphere. Her father had another home to beautify— the palace of his soul. Furthermore, it was a joy to Pen to find that Fancy Farm was, in its absence of deliberate ornament, not wholly so to please Sir Andrew; Norah shared the taste that (not without some pensive sentiment) had swept the house of some wondrous ugly Oriental treasures—dragons of delf, crude-painted josses, preposterous fans, and a myriad cumbering nick-nacks that the Lady Jean had never once suspected were her husband's detestation. His wife now dwelt so tenderly in his remembrance that he could not bear to think of her with such associations.

But Aunt Amelia, though she did not care for dragons and for josses, longed to see their walls adorned like those of other people. The tiny book-room, facing the pergola, where he smoked a pungent sea-tobacco which he found his casual wayside friends preferred to any aromatic mixture, had, above the mantelpiece, a single picture which was her abomination. In truth its art was primitive; the painter was the seaman whom Sir Andrew's swimming had preserved from the maw of the Roaring Forties. "He was not exactly Tintoretto," said its owner, "but I never knew a man who could better lay a gun than old Tom Drake. I prize his picture more than any medal, and, after all, barring the oakum pouring from the funnels, you have only to stand a little way back and it's almost the *Bellerophon*. At any rate, it's near enough for me."

Amelia sometimes was inclined to wish Tom Drake had drowned, and so averted such an outrage on her sense of the artistic, but she daren't say so. She desired another kind of picture than the able gunner's—many of them, richly framed, like Mrs Brooks's; and the temporary affluence of her nephew, due to the soaring Athabascas, seemed a providential opportunity. She went into the book-room on the following afternoon, where Pen was learning chess from him as the five-hundred-and-fiftieth solace for old age, and Norah scribbled nonsense rhymes for Mr Maurice.

" Phew ! what an odour of tobacco !" she exclaimed.

" I am at present enjoying the best smoke of the day, which is always the one that one is at," he told her. " The second best is the one that is coming, leaving the one you had formerly a poor third. Perhaps the best smoke is the one you were about to have had when you find that you have left your matches in your other waistcoat. This is the Preterite Subjunctive Smoke and only to be enjoyed in a negatively Preteritish Subjunctivistic way."

"Your grammar is most remarkable," said Norah, as he put his pipe away and threw the window open.

"It ought to be," he retorted. "I make it myself as I go along. The common grammar always stumped me; I never could remember more than a single rule—that the noun must agree with its nominative in number, gender, and case, as 'John,' 'London,' 'dog.' Let me see, now—was it really 'dog'? Talking of dogs, my dear, what has become of Brownie? I haven't had a sight of him since Tuesday."

"You must ask Peter Powrie," answered Norah. "My only claim on Brownie seems to be confined to the privilege of paying for his licence. Mrs Powrie came to me imploring me to let him have a kennel in the yard. Her husband was growing restless again, with a tendency to Airedales. 'Brownie and me between us surely can keep the man at home,' she said with great emotion."

Miss Amelia put the window further up, and disdaining artifice, boldly preferred her claim, as housekeeper-in-chief, to some mural decoration in the dining-room and parlour. "You must get pictures, Andy," she informed him plaintively, "even if it's only three or four to break the walls up."

"Nothing beats a hammer," he suggested. "But why break up an inoffensive wall, my aunt?"

"One might as well be in a barn," she proceeded, heedless of his humour. "You can quite well afford to have some decent pictures now; they'll give us great enjoyment in the winter."

"And whence, dear aunt, am I to get these alleviations of our wintry terrors?"

"From the people who sell them," she replied with readiness. "You have only got to send for them."

"Good heavens!" said he. "By post! 'A dozen assorted landscapes of a cheerful tone, with a human note in them. About five-by-three. No battleships. Thanking you in anticipation.' Dear aunt, let us be really serious when it comes to art. It's the only Faith that's left for half our fellow-creatures. There are people who think their rapture in a picture is a thing to exculpate them from the wrath of God."

She flung herself out of the room impatiently: this was a mood of her nephew's she could never bear.

"That's the only argument of an aunt's that there's no retort to," he remarked with some contrition, falling back upon his pipe. "I suppose she'll have to have her pictures too—if I can find what she will like and I can tolerate, next time I'm within range of studios. That's the worst of a carriage, Pen; it extends the interest in art as presented in other people's parlours. By the way, now, how does it stand with you in regard to the painter's stuff? It's a facet of your engaging mind that I have not yet seen. What do you think of my authentic Drake?" and he glanced complacently at the gunner's masterpiece.

"Now's your opportunity! Smite, my dear child, and fear not!" counselled Norah.

"I think it's ugly," answered Pen, without a moment's hesitation. "But of course my thinking that does not make it so: it must be beautiful to you, or you shouldn't value it."

"Not, strictly speaking, beautiful," he amended. "It doesn't quite respect the canons, which, I'm assured, are devilish stiff, and I'm often tempted to regret that Tom attempted to depict the smoke, a thing elusive and perplexing to the sailor-artist. His stays are a little too a-taut-o, and his waves are somewhat tesselated; had they been like that about the Horn, he might have walked aboard again, dispensing with my gallant services. But still—but still——" He looked with a softened aspect at the picture. "I don't know that I'd change it for a veritable old Italian masterpiece. . . . I love it, for the sake of the ship, and the honest man who did his best with it. It moves me sometimes like a voice from youth; I never weary of it."

"In that case, then," said Pen, "of course it's beautiful."

CHAPTER XXIV.

"A MUCH-APPLAUDED trait of human nature I could never value quite so highly as my friends, is gratitude," proceeded Captain Cutlass. "Yes, yes! I know the proper sentiments about it — the ingrate child and all the rest of it, but I hold that the merely thankful feeling towards a benefactor has been foolishly exalted to a virtue. Love—affection, ought to know no gratitude, which the rascal, Rochefoucauld, very wisely said is too often merely a lively sense of favours to come. When we are warmly conscious of the benefits received from others, we are on an infinitely lower plane than when we simply like those others out of sheer humanity, having nothing got from them and nothing to expect. Our brother the dog and all those humble fellow-creatures of the fields are devoid of that meretricious sense which is an outcome of possession, of the greed for property. Unconscious of possessing anything, luckily unaware of the moral difference in *meum* and in *tuum*, they accept benefits as they grant them—as a matter of course, and without desire to retain the benefit in their recollection. And so with children; till they have been spoiled by the knowledge that the foolish world recognises individual property, that the toy may be *theirs* and not another's, they are exempt from gratitude. Thankfulness they have, of course, but only as a vague emotion, flowing out to no one in particular, like the contented purring of a cat in a patch of warm sunshine in a chilly room. This absence of a grateful feeling in the child persists through life in the relations between offspring and their parents; search yourself minutely, and you'll find that your love of your father has no scrap in it of what we know as gratitude. Knowing that all you have is his, you feel no emotion to reflect that all he has ever had has been always yours. The vice of individual property creeps into the household last of all; there nearly everything is held in common. To be grateful is to be infinitely less than fond, but to look for gratitude for our benefactions is to render them of no account and claim what is due to God alone. If I give, expecting gratitude, it were better that I kept my money in my pocket. A kindness should have no reaction; we are meant to pass it on to those who need it more than ourselves or our benefactors."

"What *is* the text for the day?" Norah interrupted flippantly, looking up from her nonsense rhymes.

"I'm not quite sure that I've discovered yet," said Pen, "but it seems a bit remote from the picture with which we started."

"Have patience, child! have patience!" said Sir Andrew soothingly, tapping his pipe on the hearthstone. "I am leading up to it. Tom Drake confirmed my worst impressions of that weakness gratitude; his picture is by far the least embarrassing of the votive offerings he laid on my unworthy altar. Perhaps his manner was more disconcerting than his gifts; he had a way of shifting his plug and following me about with his eyes that made me miserable, since I was bound to realise how far I fell short of being worthy of such devotion. And the truth was that if gratitude were justified in any case, it was rather due to him than me. I dived to pick up a sailor who was ass enough not to have learned to swim, and along with him I picked up Andrew Schaw. I learned that I was capable of terror. He caught me by my arms and almost drowned me."

" Did you scream ? " asked Pen quickly, in an undertone.

" No, thank heaven ! A scream implies surrender and despair ; that's why in any peril seamen hate it. We should die with dignity and not with the squeal of a netted hare. So long as the squeal is left in us, our discipline, our training, our cultivation, and our religion are in vain ; there's a white spot somewhere in the liver. But I tell you I was, for a moment, terrified. Not at the thought of annihilation ; but at the vision which came to me, in a flash, of what a botch I had made of myself and my opportunities. And there was never to be another chance to clear away the raffle of the deck and start anew ! It was patent to me, there and then, that all my life I had been after the wrong things, confusing values, using my youth in such a way as would have made my old age miserable. Bankrupt in faith, a pauper in conviction, nothing accomplished— I could think of no virtue that was in me except that I loved my fellow-men. I have never been quite the same man since, though I fear my constant efforts at amendment are like a child's attempt to remove a dent from an india-rubber ball ; the dent is only shifted to another place. Can we ever change ourselves materially ? Eh ? But at least I have the grace of trying, and I'm not in the appalling state of self-content. . . . It's not a picture to please an artist, Pen, but I never weary of it, 'or the sake of the old ship and the honest fellow who under God,' as Cleghorn puts it, was the means of shaking my conceit of myself."

" Pictures are not for artists," said Penelope. " We needn't bother our heads what they may think."

He laughed. " You're as dead against the canons there as Drake, Pen. My painter friends assure me that their work at its best is only to be understood by specially qualified fellow-practitioners. Art is a mystery which in every age can only be enjoyed by a very few by right of birth."

" You don't believe it, surely ! " she exclaimed with genuine surprise.

" I don't suppose I do," he confessed ; " and neither do the artists, or they shouldn't send their works to picture-galleries : they would paint them strictly for the entertainment of their gifted friends, the gentlemen who mix their colours with brains and theories and a little delicious moonshine. Tom Drake didn't mix his with brains or theories either, but with absurd affection for my unworthy self : that's why I value every line of it done with a straight-edge. I rather hoped you'd like it, Pen ; it's one of my tests of genuine friendship. There's Norah, who came from Brussels stuffed till she could hardly walk with the History of Art by those amazing folk her teachers, and she prefers my Drake to anything by Raphael."

Norah looked up, reddening. " I do ! " she said warmly.

" Oh, my opinion of pictures isn't of the slightest value ! " said Pen quickly. " I'm no art connoisseur."

" I know," he said. " I'm rather glad of it. It would be most distressing to find that you knew more about it than myself. There is no one so narrow-minded about the Arts as your enthusiastic amateur. While broadness of view, tolerance, and universal sympathy may be regarded by him as virtues in religion, politics, and the particular arts he has not studied, he has no sooner acquired a taste for Browning, Wagner, and the Primitives than he becomes contemptuous of all who do not share his preference. That the world had every possible joy in poem and music and some scratches on an elk-horn ages before Browning, Wagner, or the Primitives were born, and will have it from art of a totally different character after they are quite forgotten, does not seem to occur to him, or he wouldn't always take himself so seriously."

"I used to tell Miss Skene art was all a question of fashion, like ladies' bonnets," said Pen. "She jeered at anything that was popular. If Schubert's music ever got the length of the barrel-organs she would hate it. I think the best music and the best pictures are those that most people understand and like."

Captain Cutlass doubtfully shook his head. "That's a theory that will lead you into a lot of difficulties, Pen."

"I don't care."

"There must be progress, movement, in the arts, as in everything else, and the novelty at first is only to be appreciated by a small and shrewd minority."

"*Is* there progress?" Pen asked eagerly. "I don't think it. There's only change. We get tired of the too familiar song and picture, and welcome something fresh, for the very same reason that we change our millinery every season. I could destroy your apprecia-tion of the finest piece of music in the world by having the finest musician in the world play it and nothing else to you for a week on end."

Norah threw down her pen with a noisy indication of impatience and joined in the debate. "I don't know when I had to listen to such nonsense!" she exclaimed. "Both of you! Fancy comparing art to millinery!"

"I'm comparing it with what I best understand," said Pen. "I don't believe any woman would give her new spring hat for the best old picture in the world!"

"By no means nonsense, Norah," said Sir Andrew. "Pen is on the verge of mysteries that have puzzled myself for years, but which I have long ago despaired of penetrating to my own satisfaction. Our reasons for preferring certain things in art are not very easily discovered——"

"I know them!" said Penelope, with assurance.

"Tell us, then," said the baronet, smiling.

"No. Not now; you would only laugh at me. I'll tell you sometime."

"Well, I, at all events, find the problem quite insoluble. The arts are our intellectual toys, and I daresay you're right in saying we break them up from time to time and look about for new ones simply from a wanton love of change. No quality is more common than vanity and self-delusion. I sometimes think that the vulgar hunger for exclusive possession is as manifest in our attitude to art as to other things. Though we have contempt for those who don't agree with us, we would not share our emotional pleasure in painting and music and poetry with the common herd. If they have the presumption to gratify themselves with the same things that have gratified us, we will change our tastes. . . . I'm very sorry you can't approve of my *Bellerophon*, Pen, any more than Aunt Amelia. I hope I've made it plain that I regard it not so much as a work of art as a relic. I'm so fond of pictures, generally, that I can't bear to see them continually about me; they're wise people the Japanese who roll them up and take them out only now and then to look at. Aunt Amelia has the common delusion that walls were made to hang pictures on."

"I don't like pictures on walls at all," said Pen. "I always think the strings look silly."

"You have noticed that!" said the baronet with

pleasure. " I'm glad. There you agree with Norah and me. The room is not properly designed whose walls need to be ' broken up,' as Aunt Amelia puts it ; the better they are, the more of an intrusion seems a hanging picture. All our pictures nowadays are economical makeshifts, more or less cheap compromises. We can't afford a fresco, the only tolerable kind of painting for a room, and so we have to content ourselves with scraps of canvas stuck in gorgeous golden frames, and hung on cords with an inclination outwards that is apt at times to set my nerves on edge. There's something wrong with it, and if artists were consistently artistic they would not lend themselves and their charming gifts to such gimcrackery."

" I love whitewash," said Pen. " For pleasant walls there's nothing beats a decent kitchen. I can't stand patterns and ornaments ; I like things simple, strong, and useful."

" Add the touch of grace that should come from the thing being made with pleasure, and your preference is as sound as if you had gone to Brussels and studied the entire history of art from a nice little book in French," said the baronet.

Norah smiled satirically. " This passion for bare walls, Pen, doesn't extend to Schawfield House, as you have seen. I hope you liked the ancestors ? "

" Relics, Norah, relics ! " said Sir Andrew. " And admirably designed to keep us humble. Did you ever see such a grim assortment of old gentlemen combining every facial quality of the cut-throat and the Covenanter, Pen ? They made my early childhood horrible at night —the Schaws who never slept, but were always staring with wide-open eyes that saw all things, even in the dark. Portraits are by far the best of any family inheritance ; you see in them from what you came.

Those cruel, proud, licentious, amiable, gallant, handsome, and ugly effigies prepare you to understand how many of their qualities are lurking in yourself. They always watched to hear if I should scream. If I had screamed the Siccar Schaws would have come leaping from their frames and killed me."

"I suppose they would never forgive my scream on the yawl?" said Norah nervously.

"You scream!" he exclaimed incredulously. "It was Pen."

"It wasn't; it was I."

He turned to Pen. "And why in Heaven's name did you give me a different impression?" he inquired, but she fled from the room without an answer.

CHAPTER XXV.

IT was like the man, that, finding his protégée pursuing, as it seemed, for private reasons of her own, some inexplicable line of equivocation, he should be inclined to set the incident aside and ask for no explanation. He was ever one who shrank from the revelation of any weakness in the things of his affection. A worse poltroonery than any screaming ! — her flight was so ungracious and so rude. First she had flushed and then she had blenched at the disclosure; gave a frightened glance of mute appeal to Norah, looked angrily at himself, and then dashed wildly from the room, a shocking figure of inelegant and coward haste.

He whistled his surprise and had recourse to another pipe, which he began to fill in silence. Norah watched him curiously, waiting in vain for questions.

"Did she really charge herself with that ridiculous scream ? " she asked at last, incapable of bearing any longer a silence worse than wild denunciation.

"H'm ! " he muttered. "Not exactly ; but she tacitly confessed when I accused her. I'm puzzled to understand."

"How good of her ! How generous ! " cried Norah warmly, preparing to run after her.

"Yes, yes ! " he exclaimed, with a start, as if that point had not before occurred to him. "I suppose she *did* take the blame of it to shield your reputation.

That doesn't, someway, make the situation any better; I'm sorry you should have given her the occasion for that particular kind of generosity."

"What! would you rather she had screamed than I?" asked his cousin, with eyes averted.

"It's a double shock to find that you're a little weaker than I thought you, and that Pen is capable of dissimulation," he replied. "I'm half inclined to wish I had never been undeceived."

"Why?" she asked, and he looked uneasy.

"That's a secret of my own. But why did you scream? It's so unlike you!"

"That's *my* secret," said Norah, abruptly.

"And why should Pen, who seems to be your superior in physical courage, be so timid morally as to fly from the revelation of her magnanimous deceit?"

"That's *her* secret," said his cousin. "I fancy I can guess, but I'm not going to tell you," and she left the room to seek for Pen, whom she found in the refuge of Mrs Powrie's room, darning furiously, as if a stocking were a reputation.

Sir Andrew, full of troubled thoughts that might have seemed ridiculous as emerging from an incident so trivial as a girl's dissimulation in the interest of her friend, rode that afternoon over half the parish; galloping down misgivings, conjectures, and chagrins that astonished and alarmed himself. To any casual observer it might seem as if the Hunt were up again. The outer man of him busied itself, here in counsel with the woodmen trenching already behind the mill, or with drainers knee-deep in morass, burying Athabascas in the shape of tiles; there with his herdsmen tending the shaggy cattle whose sullen fires appeared to him to indicate the prisoned souls of clansmen in a brutal incarnation; but deep within him, all the time, was an unrest that abides even in the uproar and horror of battlefields. The day abetted his discomforter; the afternoon was cold, a touch of frost already was on the kail of wayside gardens; leaves were dropping without a breath of wind; a grey sky lowered upon the glens; melancholy disengaged itself from coppice, field, and ditch. For months he had been happy—how serene and glad from day to day he only now discovered; here were the old brown devils back again! Past the cromlechs in whose shadows, circling from age to age upon the plain, he had stood so many wondering hours in youth, he sped by things unholy and abhorrent, blameful and portending; communion with them now would only add to his despondency; he desired to speak with men!—with men!—with men! It was with a feeling of satisfaction he found, as he neared the village on his homeward way, that the mare had cast a shoe and given him an excuse for stopping at the smithy.

Already it was gloaming round the fire of Alick Brodie; that hour when all the morning's birds of gaiety fly home with battered wings to roost in hearts disconsolate. The low black felted smithy roof dropped a sleepy eyelid of wide eave above the doorway; its front was stained with pitch that always gave to it externally an aspect of the dusk and slumber. Within, its shape and bounds were lost in sombre shadows; only when Captain Cutlass bent low on the saddle to peer across the shut half-door, he saw in its depths dim faces against the jetty beams in the glow from the hearth when Alick blew his bellows; heard the low roar among the cinders, and sepulchral voices. 'Twas like a glimpse of the workshops where the gods are ever fashioning the shackles and the gyves of men, themselves condemned and helpless, toiling bitterly, or a cavern of the early world, pungent with ancient rites, with sizzling iron and seared horn. To those within, himself stood out against the pensive landscape like a refugee from Flodden, like a beaten rider fled from the sack of towns. He dropped from the saddle wearily, and led in the mare. The blacksmith stopped his blowing; the flame retreated from the hearth, and in the trivial glow from the sooty sky-light window the baronet looked about him, seeking to identify a company such as loves to gather on chilly autumn evenings round the warmth of smithy fires.

"It's no' a smithy, Alick!" he exclaimed whimsically. "It's no' a smithy, but a parable."

"Oh ay! it's a smiddy right enough, Sir Andrew," said the blacksmith, pinching a cooling shoe; "but it would be a better smiddy if it had some sclates on't. The sarkin's done, and what the randy wants is a new roof a'thegither, if I could get it oot o' Mr Cattanach."

"Ye'll get that!" agreed Sir Andrew readily. "Never heed Mr Cattanach. A bonny-like thing if the rain drowned out the fires o' Cyclops or o' Vulcan for the want o' a sclated roof, and business so brisk ower yonder in Athabasca! I was thinkin' there, when I saw the shop for a minute lit wi' the lowe o' your fire, that life itsel's a country smiddy: maist o' the time we're in the shadow, hardly seein' each other's faces clearly, but now and then a wind blaws through the coal slack o' the spirit and we stand revealed."

"Whatna wind, Sir Andrew?" asked the blacksmith, clapping the mare upon the neck.

"God knows! I'm only haiverin'. Everything's a guess except to the conceited idiot. But still-and-on there's a bellows somewhere, and some one yerkin' now and then upon the handle to heat the job that's to be hammered on the anvil. D'ye catch me, Alick?"

"I'll be dashed if I dae!" said Alick honestly. "But I was only meant for bashin' airn and ca'in' nails." He picked up a leg of the mare and looked at the hoof where the shoe was missing. "That was nae job o' mine, Sir Andrew!" he exclaimed contemptuously; "I fit the shoe to the hoof and no' the hoof to the shoe, and somebody's been slashing awa' here wi' a knife. That's the way guid horse is spoiled."

"Ye're right!" agreed the baronet. "I had her shod in a hurry at the farrier's in Duntryne, and he talked about brittle feet, and hacked awa' like hey-my-nannie wi' his gully."

"There's naething bates the rasp!" said the black-smith, blowing up his fire again. "There wasna a knife in my faither's shop, and the farrier that uses yin should be kept to the job o' singein' sheep's-heids. But the chap in Duntryne was right in ae thing—the meare *has* shelly feet that's ill to shoe—a delicate constitution."

"And what's the cause o' that, my ain Great Alexander?" inquired the baronet.

"Fine bred!" said the blacksmith drily. "Ye'll never can get the breed without a flaw in't somewhere, and it's often in the horn."

"Better in the horn than in the heid or in the heart," said the baronet. "The flaws o' breed are no' confined to cattle, Alick; whiles I see them comin' out in folk. It's a world where naething's perfect."

"Exceptin' mongrel blacksmiths. And even they hae sometimes wooden legs," said Alick cheerfully.

In the volcanic flare from the fanned dross of the hearth Sir Andrew nodded to the men who sat on the stilts of ploughs or on discarded stithies. He passed round his tobacco while the blacksmith wrought; no unnatural restraint was in their manner, for the presence of Captain Cutlass never embarrassed any one in Schaw-field, even when he idled away the time for which the Captain paid him wages; but he noticed in them signs that his advent had the nature of an interruption. They had been debating volubly when he rode up to the door, now their disputation was suspended.

"It's a wee cauld the nicht, Sir Andrew," said the miller's man, who had a horse in, too, for shoeing, and a feudal right to the smith's immediate attention, second only to that of the laird himself.

"As cauld's a heidstane," said the baronet, and the blacksmith chuckled.

"That's what they ca' a coinsydence," he remarked, taking the foot of the mare between his knees. "It was just on heidstanes we were talkin' when ye cam' in. There's mair nor horse-shoes to be made at a country smiddy, and we were thrang composing at an epitaph. What dae ye think, Sir Andrew, would be suitable for the grave-stane o' a man? Naething flash, ye ken, and nae parade o' superhuman excellence in the corp—just a middlin' decent, middlin' sinfu' creature like the lave."

Strange are the subjects of the talk in smithies! Sir Andrew, thinking the epitaph desired was one for mankind in the abstract, answered playfully.

"'Here Lies a Man,'" he suggested. "That's a sufficient epitaph for the best and worst o' us. The hale o' the story's there—the fun and the tribulation, health and sickness, the wind and the weet, the sun and the sleet, the lass and the glass maybe, and the job at the hinder-end of course half-done. 'Here Lies a Man!'—it sums up a'. And it's mair than an epitaph,—it's an apologia, —it asks for some allowance on the part o' the Lord Almighty Who might hae made an angel."

"'Wi' the sure and certain hope o' a glorious resurrection,'" suggested the miller's man, who was an elder; and the blacksmith, wiping his brow with a grimy hand, stood up and looked at him apprehensively.

"No' o' the body, Rubbert!" he exclaimed. "If ye

say it's o' the body—a pheesical resurrection, I'm in a
bonny habble, for I'll be like a man twice mairried, and
I'll hae to choose between the leg I lost in 'Seventy-twa
and Jessie. I would be sweirt to mak' ony preference.
And, forbye, I've lang ootgrown the ither."

"There's nae risin' for timber" said the miller's man
authoritatively.

"What! What! Then where'll Watty be withoot
his fiddle? Is there no' a soul in fiddles, laird?"

"I'll warrant ye that!" said Captain Cutlass. "There's
a soul in a' things tangible, even the mute things o' the
earth, and what for no' the fiddle that has laughed and
cried? I'm only fear't my ain'll rise in judgment up
against me. But I didna guess your epitaph was for a
fiddler, Alick. To the epitaphs o' artists we should
bring some art, and the 'Hic Jacet' o' a fiddler should
clink. What do ye say to—

> Here lies a man was fond o' fiddlin',
> As man and fiddler only middlin';
> Lord grant that by divine election
> They may be baith raised in perfection!"

"Well done!" cried Alick Brodie, plying his hammer.
"I'd like to gang and show't this very nicht to Watty.
It would cheer the body up to see we're gaun to dae the
right thing by his memory. But I doubt the wife'll no
let me—there's the weans."

"I hope it will be long before we need to compose an
epitaph for Watty," said the baronet, suspecting some
bucolic joke, and Alick Brodie grew very grave.

"A done man, Sir Andrew! Have ye no' heard the
news? Fever! Got it frae a tinker clan he gaed to
fiddle to in the quarry."

Vulcan spoke with an abated breath becoming to a
sad calamity; in Schawfield visitations of the kind were

rare, and always terrible, turning the bravest into cowards.

"Good Lord! who's looking after the poor fellow?" asked the baronet impulsively, and his company betrayed confusion.

"The puir soul's done!" said the smith defensively. "And he has the doctor."

"And never a woman near him!" cried Sir Andrew furiously. "Don't tell me those old craven terrors still persist in Schawfield, or, by heavens! I'll tear the roofs down on your heads and plant the site o' a town wi' turnips!" His chin thrust out like a ram of a ship, and his nostrils spread; they had touched Jack Easy on the proud-flesh when they showed him of what dastard cruelty his folk were capable, and he quivered at the smart. At no time was he more admired than when he was the righteous and commanding autocrat, when he stung them like a conscience; one roar of the quarter-deck in crisis, and the spirit of democracy himself had fostered shrivelled at its roots and they were the slaves of Captain Cutlass.

The blacksmith rose to the encounter manfully. "It's no' sae bad as that, Sir Andrew," he explained. "It's only the married women that are frichtened—no' for themselves, but for their bairns."

"Such women should have no bairns, then," said the baronet, still with his anger unabated.

"It may be so," retorted Alick Brodie wisely; "but they hae, and we canna help it. There's no' a mother in the village that'll venture into Watty's Wynd."

"What about the unmarried women, then?" asked Captain Cutlass. "Surely there are plenty."

"Far ower mony for Watty Fraser! What did he keep a gander for, if it wasna to scare them aff? He never would let a spinster ower his door in case she'd grab him when his back was turned and marry him."

"This notion that women marry men in spite of themselves seems curiously prevalent in Schawfield," said Sir Andrew, cooling.

"It's no' peculiar to Schawfield, sir; it's universal," said the blacksmith grimly. "And whether it's right or wrang, there's no' a wanter that'll dare gang nearhand Watty."

"He swears like a dragoon," said the miller's man, and the baronet breathed more freely.

"That's hopeful!" he exclaimed. "It's the sign o' no surrender."

He hurried round to the attic in Watty's Wynd and found the fiddler sitting up in bed with his instrument upon his knees, plucking the strings at times with nervous fingers, the fire of his trouble lighting up his face with an unnatural ardency, his tongue hysterical and uncontrolled. "Ken ye fine, Captain! Kent yer faither!" he exclaimed. "They wouldna let me play at his weddin', but, the Lord be praised, I was guid enough for the servants' ha'. I'm no' carin'—they understood me and they liked me fine in the servants' ha'. I doot I'm a done man, Captain, when the doctor's at me, damn his eyes! Talks about bringin' in a woman! Have I no' my ain wee fiddle?"

The visitor felt the coolness and the sanity of his flesh, the power of his body, a taunt to the broken minstrel. "Nae man's done, Watty, till the wright has got him. How did this come on ye?"

"The doctor says it was playing to the tinklers in the quarry. He's maybe richt, confoond him! I never played before to tinklers—just a wheen o' cattle! But ye ken yersel' the feelin', Captain—a fiddler maun be fiddlin', and it's meat and drink to see the creatures dancin' . . . I'm trying to mind a tune——" He hissed a bar or two of an air between his parched lips. "Damn me! that's 'Monymusk,' it's no' the tune at a' . . . and the warst o't is I canna tune the fiddle." He pushed the instrument away from him with irritation.

"I'll tune her for you, Watty," said Sir Andrew, lifting it from the bed and screwing up the pegs. He tucked it below his chin and drew from its strings the needed harmonies. "If that was a' there was in fiddlin'," said he, "I would tak' the road for't, even to the quarry." He restored the violin to its owner, who idly plucked again upon the strings.

"You must have some one to look after you—some woman body, Watty," said Sir Andrew gently.

"I'm no' sae bad's a' that," said the patient anxiously. "Good Lord! they're easier to get in than oot. If it wasna for Jock I would be pestered wi' them and their tantrums. Guid enough for dancin'! There was never a woman in this house for a dozen years, except Miss Grant a month or twa ago and Miss Colquhoun. They hae a bonny taste for fiddlin', and they're welcome to come back, but never another petticoat 'll flaff across the door o' Watty Fraser!"

Sir Andrew's news at Fancy Farm that night affected the ladies variously. Miss Amelia's feeling was one of wroth that he should have come to them—even with all precautions—from the side of a fever-bed, and Norah had a share in her apprehensions, though for a different reason. But Pen amazed them all by eagerly volunteering to go down herself and nurse the fiddler in the absence of any more experienced aid to a distracted doctor.

CHAPTER XXVI.

Pen came like a blast of wholesome wind to Watty's
Wynd; burst open windows in the flats that had never
been really aired since the builder left them; loosed
cataracts of soap-and-water on the stairs, swept sanitary
tides up to the highest attics. Marvellous was her
power to influence and command! That she should be
brave enough to hazard risks they feared themselves,
and look upon a fever and Jock Fraser with the same
contempt, secured their admiration and docility. Miss
Amelia Schaw was used to preach what the tenements
called "highjinkics"—a gospel of hot baths for Saturdays, carbolic powder, flannel next the skin, but not
directly in the unregenerate wynds, since she never had
got there; they laughed at her highjinkics as they
laughed at her calves-foot jelly which she thought was
indicated, as the doctors say, for every village ailment,
from whooping-cough to broken legs. Highjinkics
seemed entitled to more respect as Penelope Colquhoun
commended them—a girl who could say, "For Heaven's
sake, give me a pail of water and I'll wash your stair
myself!" She found an empty garret on Watty's flat;
rendered it habitable in an afternoon, made it the base
for a great campaign against the forces of unimaginable
squalor. For a fortnight she kept away from Fancy
Farm, and Sir Andrew, who had one day taken off his
hat to Jock with a droll apology for breaking through

the lines, had climbed the attic stairs to find himself
rebuffed. Pen was too busy to see him, he was told,
and he could on no account have parley with the fiddler.
A fever was a fever, and the terrors of Miss Amelia for
infection must be decently respected.

The need for epitaphs seemed speedily averted.
Watty Fraser got the turn, and swore no longer; he
was the most tractable of patients, though he grudged
her every hour she stole from nursing him to carry on
the campaign of hygienics in the neighbourhood. "If I
had known that women were so handy, I would never
have got a gander," he informed the doctor. "Give me
a nurse like her for the rest of my days, and I'll never
ask to get up again; you might burn my clothes.
She's splendid, man! she's splendid!"

"A man like you should have married long ago,"
Penelope told him. "Your way of life is pitiful and
unnatural. It is not good for man to live alone."

"So they're always telling me!" he answered. "But
hadn't I my fiddle? When ye're tired o' a fiddle ye
can hang it up. And there's plenty o' time, forbye, for
me to think o' marryin'; a man can mairry ony time.
It's different wi' the women,—that's the way they're sae
deevilish desperate when they're young; naething in
their heids but husbands."

"Nonsense!" she cried merrily. "I'm not so very old
myself, and yet I've never fashed my head with thinking
of a husband."

His lantern jaw slipped down grotesquely; a spasm
suspiciously like a wink came to his parchment countenance; he coughed ambiguously, then slyly laughed with
crackling incredulity.

"Ye needna tell us that in Schawfield!" he exclaimed.

"At least," said the stickler for strict veracity, "I

never allowed myself to think of such a thing a moment longer than I could help. Of course there are thousands of silly thoughts that come into one's head uninvited, and that take a moment or two to expel. . . . It's time for your medicine, Watty!"

"Might as weel sup saep-sapples!" he protested, grimacing; but where the doctor had failed to coerce, Penelope could coax successfully. "We'll dae Mrs Nish between us!" was his boast. "If I was allooin' mysel' to be hurled to the kirk-yaird in yon crystal hearse o' hers, I would never be able to show my face in another warld."

But this harmless chaff on matrimony went one day a little further in a stimulated hour of Watty's, and Pen was shocked to find from the manner of her patient in a pawky humour that her position in Fancy Farm was liable to misconstruction. The fiddler's innuendoes revealed that the village gossip linked her name with that of Captain Cutlass, anticipating a romantic and immediate close to the Hunt, on which she had not once reflected after the recovery from the chagrin she had felt at alluding to it on the evening of her drive with the fictitious Tom Dunn. She flamed at the suggestion. Blissfully unconscious that he stung her to the quick, poor Watty followed up the theme with rustic humour. "So you'll hae to have me on my legs in time to fiddle at the weddin'," he went on, "though I didna get playin' at his faither's and only got the Haymakers at Lady Jean's."

"It's not very respectful to Sir Andrew, and not very kind to me, to talk such nonsense!" she remonstrated breathlessly. "Who could be so cruel as to set about such silly gossip?"

"Naebody set it about at a'," said Watty shrewdly. "That's the usual way wi' gossip—it never tak's a wing

to itsel' unless it's just what everybody's thinkin', and
this has been in the air since ever ye cam to Schawfield;
it couldna weel be otherwise. We used to jalouse it was
boun' tc be Miss Norah, but she's taen up wi' the poet,
and the Captain onyway wouldna mairry money. What's
a' the trainin' for—the dancin', and the ridin', and the
fencin', and the rest o't, if he didn't mean to mak ye
Lady Schaw? . . . What! me'm, are ye angry?"

He could not mistake the shame and indignation of
her countenance; she looked for a moment like shaking
him, and, speechless, left the room. It was not the
association of her name with that of Sir Andrew Schaw
that rankled, so much as the revelation of deliberate training. A hundred things were now made plain to her—
subtle emendations and suggestions towards improvement,
artful leads to more accepted standards from Norah;
the baronet's enthusiastic interest in deportment and in
tone. The pride of the Colquhouns was touched; each
family, even the humblest, has its own variety, and hers
revolted at the thought of being moulded to a pattern,
even though it might be elegant and pleasing to her
friends. She felt ill for hours that afternoon — sick
with vexation, exceedingly lonely and insignificant, a
pawn in a game of chess she did not understand. All
the plain old ways of home came back transfigured to
her recollection, the humdrum hours, the noisy sisters,
the lamp at night, the strict routine of useful duties.
What had she learned in the past nine months from her
assiduous and cunning teachers? To fence — whose
father hated warfare of the body! To ride—who must
trudge through life on foot as her people had done before
her! To dance—who seemed at the moment quite unlikely ever to have the mood of a quadrille again! To
swim—who henceforth should never see the waves without recalling that she had been found deceitful! To

prattle of books, pictures, music, in the passing and
conventional jargon of the times, making art a fetish!
Was she the happier for her new accomplishments? No;
life, that now seemed more complex, had not a gladder
hour to give her than she knew before; cells of the heart
and brain that had tingled hitherto at simple combinations
—warm wind and running waters, evening psalm and
moving shadows, the scent of a flower and the memories
it awakened,—often now were unresponsive but to moods
sophisticated; she found herself suspicious of intuitions
just because they were her own, and not in seeming
harmony with canons of the educated world as repre-
sented by the baronet and Norah. She had learned at
last that there were divers ways through life and time,
and lost confidence in her own. How her father would
storm if he knew she had given up the citadel of her
individuality!

She had for a day a wild idea of deserting all and
running home; and she wrote to him telling him of her
present occupation, hinting at a weariness of the spirit,
doubts of her usefulness. He wrote her back immediately, scolding and imperative. "The only wise-like
task you seem to have had since you left us!" was his
verdict. "Stick by it till it's done—till your fiddler's
dead or back again at his jigs, poor body! You're not
content with yourself, you say. Capital! That's the
very best news you could tell me; you had aye a
good conceit of yourself, and self-improvement always
starts in discontent. Stick by the fiddler! Till you
drop! The dreicher the job the greater the bliss in its
accomplishment. Keep a cool head and an open body,
and don't forget your prayers."

Even this paternal injunction probably would have
failed to keep her longer in an atmosphere that meanwhile seemed to choke, and Duty itself appeared to

relinquish any claim it had on her, for Watty was so much himself again that he began to chafe at a woman's presence. Just when some decision seemed imperative, either to return to Norah or go home, she became more indispensable to the wynds than ever. Hygiene's *régime* was a little late of starting in the Schawfield tenements, and by the end of the week Penelope was nurse to several households. She flung herself with joy into a task that helped her in the fight against her own alarming new disease of introspection. She toiled unwearyingly; the doctor sang her praises; a scheme of Captain Cutlass's for professional nurses met with the disapproval of the village, which was now more willing to assist, shamed to humanity by Pen's devotion.

Norah came down now from the Farm to see her every day, and would implore her to come home and rest; commands were out of the question with an imperious paid companion who maintained that Sir Andrew Schaw as landlord of the village was in a great degree to blame for its condition. And he himself experienced some qualms of conscience on the point; in truth, his hatred of intrusion had too long concealed from him the internal state of things among his humbler tenantry.

"She's right as usual," he said to Norah, "and I feel that she's pluckily shouldering far too much of my responsibility. I found to-day, to my perfect horror, that some of the lower houses in the wynd have iron-stanchioned windows at the back. A relic of barbarism! It might be medieval Italy! Cattanach never once gave me the slightest inkling. Those people might have been burned to death like rats trapped in a granary. Good heavens! fancy children growing up behind iron bars! Babies having their first glimpse of the world between them! Marriages and funerals in a jail!"

"How dreadful!" said his cousin, shuddering. "I

never knew of it; Aunt Amelia and I were never allowed to see the back apartments."

"Of course not; the poor souls were ashamed that you should see their degradation. Little wonder that the iron enters in the soul of people cradled behind stanchions. Pen showed me those places to-day—a score of them, all on Cattanach's rent-roll. She seemed to do it with gusto. 'That's the price of refinement,' she said, as if she hated me. 'We vex ourselves about the wrong wall-paper, and we must have pretty, modulated voices, but we shut our eyes to the shame of people who depend on us.' I seemed to distinguish a certain tone of irritation. Surely she hasn't guessed, Norah; surely she hasn't guessed!"

Norah reddened. "I fear she has. In fact, I find that she's quite aware she had been in school of late without her knowing it. How she learned I don't know, but you may be sure she doesn't like it. I'm afraid we haven't overestimated the penetration of the people round about us here: Pen's education, since she came among us, has been far too obviously on lines to agree with the theories of Sir Andrew Schaw."

"You mean that it has been the subject of speculation?"

"Certainly, Andy. There is no new move of yours that is not the subject of speculation."

"Good heavens!" he cried, profoundly touched. "How sickening for Pen!"

"Yes, it puts her in an awkward position I never foresaw, or I shouldn't have so amiably fallen in with your fantastic scheme of cultivation. My only consolation is that she is no discredit to her tutors; she was incapable of being spoiled."

"But it means that—in a sense—she's compromised!" he cried excitedly.

His cousin hesitated, paled, looked at him anxiously. "That is the conventional way of putting it—in our society," she confessed reluctantly.

"The convention," he said, "has its start in a sentiment of honour which is as applicable to Penelope as to a princess of the blood-royal."

She would have given the world, had it been hers, to read his mind.

He could relieve himself immediately of the pangs of conscience in the matter of the stanchions. Alick Brodie went to break them down, when—so curious a thing is habitude!—the householders, born and bred behind the bars, were half inclined to resent the removal of a feature which, they held, contributed to their security. But not so easily was his wounded moral sense placated in regard to Pen. She grew heroic and pathetic to his fancy, battling down there in the village tenements with the consequences of his negligence, while he was able to do nothing. They were wretched days for Norah. Willingly would she have shared the attic and the cares of Pen, but she was too painfully aware that, whatever her accomplishments, none was such as qualified to help in an epidemic.

Her infelicity sought relief in a letter to Reggy Maurice.

CHAPTER XXVII.

THOSE who know Maurice now, the great shipbuilder, with his name in enduring brass on ships that are found in every port of either hemisphere, would wonder did they know of his youthful predilections for the muse of verse. No saccharine sham emotions now for Reggy Maurice! 'Harebell and Honey' must be mentioned by his friends only with caution, the very name of it a rebuke for early follies. Veritable ruined priories now affec his friends less remarkably than the wrecks of ships that in their brief career on ocean have, by the travail and endurance of their men, been glorified and rendered holier than any of those dateless old monastic piles consecrate to sleep and prayer. 'Tis not unlikely that to-day a living shipyard seems to Maurice infinitely finer than a dead cathedral; he will stand (they say) below the struts and baulks, and glory in the swelling lines of the leviathans that fill his stocks——so much of himself, his labouring hours, his cogitations, his anxieties, elations, inspirations in the work, and find more joy in the sheer of a prow than he ever found in a well-turned couplet of his own. The youth of him was spoiled by luxury and indulgence, and the flattery of his friends, who took his pretty echoes of the genuine poets for genius; let the fathers of green-sick sons be hopeful; four-and-twenty is the age when some convulsion of the mind may turn the puling dreamer into a man of action!

Keats and Byron in the breast-coat pocket of twenty-one
—I say nothing about the inner heart—is only a kind
of measles all the healthier constitutions will survive.

"Good stuff!"—that is the motto of the yards of
Maurice; it rings like the bells of churches from the
hammers of his engine-shops. "Men depend on us in
storms!" he tells them. "Don't betray them! a dubious
bolt's a crime," and the exaltation he discovered once in
a sentiment conjured up from some trivial conjunction of
a night of stars and a hackneyed verse remembered, he
finds to-day in the eye of the microscope with which he
looks at the metal surfaces, pondering on molecules, and
stresses, and the shock of seas.

A little of this change was already apparent in
Maurice as soon as Penelope had plucked a few of the
feathers from his tail; her flash of inspiration that the
making of ships was a kind of poetry to which perhaps
he had a truer call than the making of sonnets, fou..d an
open suture in the skull of four-and-twenty that is apt
to close ere thirty, leaving us impervious to influences
that might be blessed. He had burned his note-books
and gone back to the shipyard, nursing strange emotions,
and found the place, as it were, an epic—new meanings
in the giant cranes, the oozy piles, rhythms unsuspected
in the beat of mallets, inspiring cadences in the throb of
riveting-machines. Their influence, though for some
weeks only in operation, was manifest vaguely in his
manner on his return to Fancy Farm immediately on
getting Norah's letter.

She drove to meet him at Duntryne on such an
evening as ever found responsive moods of wildness in her
bosom—

> "The country ways were full of mire,
>   The boughs tossed in the fading light ;
> The winds blew out the sunset's fire,
>   And slowly dropped the night."

Aunt Amelia was struck with the eyes of her before she started——emeralds glinting; the eager mouth, the thought-chased brow, the hurried movements, something turbulent and tameless in her manner——and marvelled somewhat that a spirit usually so cool in the presence of Reggy Maurice should become so agitated at the prospect of his coming.

"Never admire too much!" she counselled. "At least you shouldn't show it, Norah. Reggy Maurice is quite conceited enough without your giving him the impression that he is indispensable."

"There are times, dear aunt, when he is!" retorted Norah, "and this is one of them."

Maurice found her waiting on the quay, tramping it impatiently, the salt wind buffeting her garments; they had to shout their greetings over the crash of waves. Her hand was wet with rain, but her clasp was fervent warm. She seemed to take possession of him; her atmosphere was more ascendant than that of the autumn night itself. He discerned internal tumult from the manner with which she hurried into questions about himself like one who shrank from touching on her own affairs. And yet his answers to her inquiries hardly seemed to reach her; plainly she was little interested in his new engagements.

"You have been having some extraordinary excursions and alarms since I left," he said at last, as the carriage rocked on its way up the windy stretch of unsheltered road that led from the shore, and immediately she seemed to overflow with feelings pent. Hurriedly she reviewed the situation of which her letters had already made him partly cognisant. Pen was well; her patients were progressing favourably; nobody was going to die. As for herself, oh! she was miserable! She made the avowal violently. Sitting beside her in the darkness of the carriage he had a sense of crisis.

"I can understand how anxious you must be for Pen," he said.

"I'm not!" she answered curtly. "I'm anxious for myself. Pen comes through everything scatheless; she meets every test like an elemental force of nature. One might as reasonably be anxious about the wellbeing of an earthquake. You're surprised, no doubt, that I've permitted her to go down alone and establish herself Sister of Mercy to the victims of Andy's ineptitude as a landlord?"

"A little," he confessed. "Not surprised that Pen should want to go—that's only what one might expect from Pen—but there might have been other arrangements. In our place"—here spoke the shipbuilder—"we never put a ten pound man on a two pound job, as a matter of economics, and Pen's too valuable to be spent on a fight with squalor and disease."

"I might have gone myself?" she suggested cynically.

"I don't mean that, but now that you mention it, I admit that I thought at first you would be with her; you have quite as strong a feeling of humanity as she."

"Have I?" asked Norah reflectively. "I wonder! There are stronger feelings. Perhaps you're like Andy, and are half inclined to think that I'm a coward. So I am. I shrieked like a fool on the yacht, not because I thought of any danger for myself, but because I thought of him, and Pen had the magnanimity to shield me, with the consequence that my position's worse than ever. I'm at home comfortably while she's nursing, and it does not escape even Aunt Amelia that Andy looks on it as a kind of shirking. It's not. Not altogether, at all events. Pen won't have me, for one thing; she has discovered one situation at least in which I'm absolutely

useless. She has, herself, the placid nerveless system of
an ox, and just at present the tanglement of things makes
me incapable of settling down profitably to anything.
I'm tired, Reggy—tired ! "

Had the night been calmer, he might have heard
her sob. But that humiliating evidence of her state
was concealed from him by louder noises of the night—
the booming of a wind that seemed to bear the carriage
in a vortex ; the splash of hoofs in the flooded road, the
drumming on the carriage roof, the rattling of the
window she had partly lowered in a feeling of suffo-
cation, though the rain was thereby driven in her face.

It was a certain quality of sympathy, none the warmer
though concealed at times behind his superficial affectations, that had first attracted her in Maurice ; to-night
he somewhat failed her, like a person wrapt too much in
his own reflections.

" The main thing is," said he with a wish to relieve
the tension of her mood, " that Pen is well. There was
something about your letter that made me think you
were apprehensive."

" She was never better," said Norah, gulping. " An
engagement of this kind brings out all her strength.
She's the heroine of the village ; the only person who
refuses to be impressed is Mr Birrell's sister. I'm a
little afraid of 'Tilda Birrell, Reggy ; she's far too quick
to discover things."

" Yes ? "

" She has discerned already that a part of Pen's
enthusiasm for nursing is due to the fact that it gives
her an excuse for evading Andy."

" I can't imagine Pen in a spirit of evasion ; what's
the matter ? "

Norah hesitated : they were on grounds on which they
had studiously refrained from stepping hitherto. " Since

Pen came here," she said, " she has been the unconscious subject of an experiment. You know my cousin's fad for that perfection which is always the object of his worship so long as it's ideal, though actually his heart is with the imperfect, the incomplete, the failure? Between us we have been training Pen—oh, you know! you must have seen it! Fancy Farm for months back might have been a seminary. Why! even you were supposed to help; it was expected that the author of 'Harebell and Honey' would impart a proper interest in poetry."

Maurice laughed, incredulously. " Don't tell me I was Sir Andrew's selection on that score," said he. " He always had a saner estimate of the value of my poetry than I had myself."

" No; the idea was mine," admitted Norah quickly. " And it hadn't really anything to do with poetry; perhaps I'll tell you some day what I mean. Anyhow, Pen has discovered, somehow, that we have been moulding her after a system of Sir Andrew Schaw's, and her pride resents it. Do you wonder?"

" I don't! It never occurred to me that there was the slightest necessity for tampering with Penelope; I thought her a quite satisfactory personality," said Maurice, with emphasis. " So far, at least, from my teaching Pen, I found I had something to learn from her. Nobody had the courage to show me before that I was a useless idler, and that there's a great deal of genuine poetry about the business I was drawing money from without contributing a single constructive idea. . . . Ships, Norah! I've got a new outlook; I find there's as much artistic joy in putting the last possible touch of finish on a hull as there is in perfecting a sonnet —if I were capable of that. And it was only a hint from Pen."

He spoke with heat, almost crying against the rude

contention of the night which seemed to infect them both
with its tempestuous humour; the girl inhaled deep,
gusty draughts that seemed to fan her inward turbulence,
and the heart of her kept time to the beat of the horses'
feet.

"Yes, yes!" she said impulsively. "She's fine! she's
fine! I should not deny it if I could. I'm the better for
her influence. And so is Andy! Nothing will ever
change his temperament, which, to most people, makes
him a kind of nursery puzzle incapable of solution, though
amusing to play with for a time. She couldn't change
the pieces, but she has been shifting them about of late,
till one almost sees a pattern and harmonious colours.
He has done more commonplace, sensible things in the
past three months to please her than at any time since
I have known him; now he's getting as great pleasure
out of improving the wynds as you can possibly get from
building ships. . . . I'm the only miserable! Nobody
looks for the slightest benefit from me! . . . Nobody,"
she added bitterly, "cares the slightest rap for me." She
spoke as if with—

> "The desire of the moth for the star,
> Of the night for the morrow,
> The devotion to something afar
> From the sphere of our sorrow."

"My dear Norah!" exclaimed her companion, lapsing
into his old humour, "if the fealty——"

"Nonsense!" she interrupted impatiently. "Don't
begin to be poetical again; I much prefer the shipbuilder. The finest poetry in the world never relieved
an aching head, far less a really aching heart. I'm
wretched, and the worst of it is, there's nobody I can
blame. . . . I'm in love with Andy! There! I'm in love
with his very follies and his whims! . . . Open that
other window! Open it! Never mind the rain!"

She spoke as if she wished to fly away upon the pinions of the storm, from ruins of her pride. She had given up the last vestige of reserve, and was the elemental woman with an elemental passion. The rain, for the time, was gone, but the gale drove through the carriage, whooping, as it drives through halls deserted.

"I know," he said quietly. "I have known it all along."

"Isn't it shameful?" she inquired, panting. "It began too soon. I can conceal nothing. Can we help our feelings? I was loyal to Jean, his wife; he never got a word or a glance from me that would do her wrong, but she seemed to suspect my infatuation, and I took steps to convince her that her suspicions were unfounded. You—you——"

"I was never under the slightest misapprehension on that score," he broke in.

"I have done my best to make amends by the strictest faithfulness to his purposes and projects. I have sunk my own interests so far as even to help him to look for a wife! Was there ever such a farce! It will be the climax of my punishment if he now concludes he has found her in Penelope Colquhoun."

"Who evades him! You are being carried away by your imagination, Norah," Maurice cried, but with a note of hesitation she discerned.

"That matters nothing! I evaded, too, and yet I was in love with him. Who can tell? The maddening thing is that nearly all he most admires in Pen is to be found in myself, if he had only eyes to see it. I did not teach her courage and frankness, for these she had already, but the superficial things he seems to think indispensable were got from me: there's a way of dressing her hair she has that seems to fascinate him, and it's simply

an imitation of my own. . . . Are you laughing, Reggy?
Amn't I disgraceful?"

"No," said Maurice. "I'm not laughing; I'm sorry.
There are occasions on which the temperament of either
the poet or the shipbuilder is unable to see any humour."

"I'm afraid! That's the long and the short of it,
Reggy; I'm afraid! There's always a fate pursuing
Andy that drives him to the most serious acts on the
hasty impulse of an admiring or generous sentiment. If
I had not been his ward, and burdened with an inheritance I don't want, he might have — he might have
thought of me; but everything of late appears to be
pushing him into the arms of Pen. It is she who is
always having the opportunities,— she saved my life
and tried to save my reputation; now she's nursing
his blunders. What's the monster, Reggy?—the thing
that was made by Frankenstein? I've made an adorable monster, and, quite unconsciously, I'm sure, she's
doing her best to make me wretched."

"I am sure you exaggerate the gravity of the situation," said Maurice, yet sharing her agitation.

"I'm not! He has only to brood for a day or two on
the idea that she is compromised in the eyes of some
gossiping villagers, and Quixote would marry out of hand
without any better reason! . . . And whether he does
or not, if ever you say a word to me on the subject again
I'll hate you, Reggy Maurice! I hadn't another soul to
speak to on the matter, and now it's done. . . . Tell me
all about your shipbuilding."

CHAPTER XXVIII.

LIFE in Schawfield is at its best when the first of the winter fires are lit, and we sit in the privacy of the lengthening nights, hearing the rain upon the roof, the gurgle of the rhones; or when the snow is deep upon the gardens, drifted on the highway, muffling sounds of traffic. 'Tis then we know each other best — cut off from the stranger, members of a single family; to no travel or adventure tempted, content to look at the fire, read the old books, hear the old stories, muse as in the cave where our fore-folk hugged the embers till their legs were freckled. I speak of common people; not those restless soaring spirits who make history—heaven help them! Late autumn always stirred the maggot in the brain of Captain Cutlass, his whims strengthened as the night lengthened; he grudged the hours that darkness stole from day, chafed at the lamplight, lapsed into moods of utter nonsense, became, to his Aunt Amelia, incomprehensible. Often he seemed like a man in drink —he who but rarely drank anything save water, and could find in it, at an effort of the mind, the flavour of the hills, the stimulus of wine. In those days was he more peculiar than ever—finicky in neckties, savagely unsystematic in respect to food, standing up to snatch a scrap of what was nearest to his hand when hunger took him, staving it off like a shameful passion.

" I wish I could feed on grass," he said to her once;

" there is some unholy brute within that thrives on flesh and cannot rest; I would have the imperturbability of oxen. Don't you wish, aunt, sometimes, that you were a cow ? "

" Eh ? " she exclaimed, quite startled, unbelieving her own ears.

" A cow," he repeated loudly, looking from the window at the little herd of Ayrshires munching placidly upon the river-bank. " Life's no puzzle to a cow, nor has it any sense of duty. It is self-contained and self-sufficient, incapable of sin, without the need for self-examination, repressing no desire, just flowing—flowing——"

" You are positively indecent Andy !" she exclaimed nervously.

" Am I ? " he said anxiously, regarding her reddened visage. " I didn't know. Beg pardon ! That's the worst of being so long at sea : it makes a man indelicate. I'm afraid I shall never understand women."

" Why don't you get married ? " she asked him bluntly. It was the first occasion on which she had broached a theme so personal, though it was often in her mind.

" Why don't I get married ? " he repeated in a non-committal spirit rare with him. " Why does the miller wear a white hat ? Why—oh ! it is a long story, aunt. You see there is the north-east wind, likewise the sou'-east ; then there are the Trades, the flying-jibboom, and the little pink parakeets that flit among the bushes. Also there is Great Circle sailing, and the how, and the why, and the when. Eh ? Especially when the button is on the top, and there is no soap, and the powder runs out at the heels of the boots."

" Heels of the boots ! I don't understand one single word you're saying !" said his aunt despairingly.

" Well, that is exactly the reason why," said Captain Cutlass.

It was the day on which Norah had gone off to meet her poet, and a mood of devilment had possessed him more or less since he learned that Maurice was returning. He played an unseemly prank on Peter Powrie, who had, for the first time, got a livery, high tops, cockaded hat and all, to the manifest pride of his wife and Miss Amelia's satisfaction. It was she who had, without consulting him, imposed this dashing innovation on the unpretentious baronet's establishment. He surveyed the gorgeous coachman with amusement; Peter himself was obviously unhappy, having imbibed the Schawfield sentiments about the folly of ostentation, and he turned the cockaded hat about in his hands like a boy at Hallowe'en caught stealing apples.

"Oh, Peter! Peter!" cried his master, "what hae they gone and done wi' ye? Stamped, by God, for a flunkey! Buckskin breeks and a'! Put on the hat, man! Put it on! Now, just awa' oot wi' ye, the way ye are, and sweep the yard!"

And the glorious coachman, clad immaculately, had to sweep the yard in a raining torrent. Sir Andrew watched him, grimly, watched the livery soak, and the hat give up its shining splendour. It was in garments more befitting the weather that the driver drove that evening from Duntryne.

An odd restraint, something indeed of coldness, was in Sir Andrew's welcome of the visitor, but it lasted only for a little. To find a man wildly in love with shipbuilding and garrulous on the subject when he had expected a cynic and a poet, bereft him of the only fault he had ever found in the lad. He had always liked Reginald, even when he chaffed him on his more affected humours; now he could not but recognise a beneficent change of character. They sat up late that night and talked of ships; it seemed to the younger man as if his host, at times, was talking simply to cry down internal voices. They disputed on a point of bulkheads, neither budged an inch from his first conviction, as is the way in disputation which is only dear to men with their minds unalterably made up. "Let us reason!" said the shipbuilder.

Captain Cutlass laughed. "We may reason, Reggy," he replied, "until we're black in the face, but our reason —as we call the feeble enemy of our intuition—never guides us; that is in other hands, the hands that rule our appetites, passions, and emotions. I have taken the word of Pen for it; we are no more rational than a skep of bees when it comes to the vital acts on which our lives depend. Had our elaborate reasoning any influence on destiny, we should long ago have been the equal of the gods."

"We think——" said Maurice.

"Yes, yes, we think—in words! And what are words but the gibbering of apes elaborated? It is not logic that controls the actions of the best and wisest men; I'm sometimes half inclined to think, like my grandfather, that it is the liver. I can see the logician in me stand aside and politely shut his eyes when the reins are handed over to inclination—that's the true postboy of destiny!"

All of which seemed irrelevant, and far from the theme of bulkheads to Reginald, but who shall guess the chain of thought in a man like Captain Cutlass? If his mind was ever upon Pen in the wynds, he never mentioned her in that connection, and Maurice seemed as ready as himself to leave the topic till the morrow; Norah's fears and Norah's outburst endowed it with the character of a powder-magazine.

Next to his own shipyard, it seemed the wynds to Reginald were most interesting; he had to go down to see them at the earliest opportunity. And it was, of course, impossible to see the wynds with the conscience-

stricken landlord's workmen freeing windows from their
iron bars, and opening drains, and storming, generally,
the redoubts of insanitation, without meeting Penelope
Colquhoun. A little wan with recent cares and close
confinement, the snap gone from her eyes, her manner
less assertive, it was well her patients had begun to
make less claim upon her service or she would have
fallen ill herself. She used to come out in the afternoons and shop for half-a-dozen families; " the regular
cut of a housewife!" said observers when they saw her
trudge from shop to shop with a basket; " she's the boy
to drive a bargain!" said the flesher.

Maurice met her suddenly, with her basket, in a
throughgoing close; it was he who blushed for the
basket, as if he had found her in deshabille, but a silly
shame like that could never lodge in the mind of Pen;
the basket might have been a Grecian lyre. She greeted
him almost joyously; he was not in the plot to hurt her
pride, and he was all that was left unchanged from those
happy unsuspicious months in Fancy Farm.

" I'll carry it," he said, reproached by her unconsciousness.

" Carry what?" she asked, and smiled when she saw
his embarrassed glance at her burden. " My basket!
Oh, not at all! It's not the thing for men to carry
shopping baskets in the tenements; it looks effeminate.
And a poet would carry it consciously; a basket must be
carried naïvely."

He persisted.

" No," she said determinedly; " it isn't heavy. It's
only your politeness. Men will insist on carrying a
woman's trivial little bundles just because it is the
fashion, but they're quite prepared to thrust on her
heavy burdens no one sees. Let us not be merely
polite for once, but only sensible. I didn't expect to

see you quite so soon again in Schawfield, but I'm quite delighted."

" Are you ? " he asked.

" I wouldn't say so if I weren't. I was sorry, when I came back, to find you gone ; you have no idea what you lost in the way of poetry ! "

" And you have no idea what I gained in the way of shipbuilding ! " he retorted, attending her down the wynd.

" I heard of it from Norah. She says I have spoiled you as a poet."

" I'm afraid you have ; at least, you helped. Are you sorry ? "

She looked at him ; there was something fresh and resolute in his manner—the cheerfulness that attends on men with new discovered aims who find themselves progressing. " No, I'm not sorry," she said bluntly. " One knows where one is with a shipbuilder. I could never quite trust a poet. But all the same, when I think of it, I'm ashamed that I put the thing so rudely. What right had I to interfere in any way with your pursuits ? I like to be left alone myself, to follow my inclinations. I must have made you very angry."

" On the contrary," said he, with a sincerity almost vehement, " you made me very glad. You were the first person I ever met who seemed to have sufficient interest —sufficient faith in my commonsense, to let me know the truth, and I hope I'm grateful."

She frowned, remembering Sir Andrew's sermon. " Grateful," she repeated dryly ; " I have lately learned that gratitude is not what I used to think it was, but a poor substitute for something better." She checked herself, with a blush he failed to notice, and bit her nether lip. " In any case," she hurried on, " you're crediting me with an influence that was not really mine at all, but

Norah's. I'm discovering more and more that I have been nothing but her mouthpiece. She gave me the ideas, and all I had was the effrontery to express them; she was too polite to tell you that you might be doing better work than making poetry."

"It's the effrontery, as you call it, that gave the idea any value; a too polite monitor is as useless as a mute inglorious Milton," answered Maurice, thrusting gently with his stick at Watty Fraser's gander, faithful still to his post though the citadel was long ago surrendered. "I'm certainly not prepared to credit Norah Grant with my discovery of the fascination that's in building ships. That, I'm certain, was an inspiration of your own; she has known me for two or three years and she never once suggested it."

"Perhaps that part of it was mine," Penelope agreed reflectively; "but in almost everything else I had Norah prompting me." She reddened again, but this time angrily. "I was a fool!" she burst out. "Did you know I was a mimic, Mr Maurice? A silly parrot?"

He laughed so boisterously that she glanced with apprehension up at the overlooking windows with whose espionage she was familiar. "A curious parrot!" he exclaimed. "Who always contradicted!"

"All the same, I've been a mimic," she insisted. "Aping Norah without my knowing it, just because I loved her and admired her. I'm only counterfeit. Oh, I hate to think of it! Do I carry myself gracefully? That's Norah, you know! Have you noticed my intonation and the pretty new way I laugh? Picked up from Norah! My clothes are an imitation; my manner of doing up my hair, till a week or two ago, was a shameful copy. Norah! Just Norah!"

He was shocked and grieved at the bitterness in her

voice ; she seemed to scourge herself with salted thongs of accusation.

"At least you had a good model," he protested weakly.

"I conceal nothing from you; I'm determined to be my real self in one thing at anyrate, and that's in making no pretences. The only pleasure I have known for weeks is in telling you now that what you saw on the surface of me was simply a veneer stuck on to me when I wasn't looking, and that below I'm the old Penelope Colquhoun as God and her father made her. Give me a few months more away from Fancy Farm, and I'll laugh as—as vulgarly as ever, if I can ! "

They had come to the stair at which she must leave him to rejoin her charges ; she put out her hand and forced a smile, unwilling to end the meeting in a key of agitation ; he was determined not to go.

"My dear Pen," he said, "some stupid vanity is making you talk very foolishly, a thing I have never known you do before. You seem to be annoyed that in a few superficial respects you have changed yourself, as I humbly think for the better, by the only process which effects a change on character—an imitation of the character you most admire. We all acquire our arts and graces from our Norahs, and Norah herself in her turn must have had exemplars——"

"Have *you* ever been to school since you grew up, Mr Maurice ? " she asked him sharply.

"Mr Maurice ! " he repeated with a grimace. "And it might so much more easily be Reggy ! Haven't I been to school, Pen,—with yourself ? I'm at school now—in the shipyard, too, getting up the rudiments of an education under the tutelage of men who haven't read even your precious Pope and Goldsmith, and laugh at me, I'm sure, behind my back, for what they must consider a kind of half-indecent boyish frolic with the Muse. They're quite entitled to; let them! So long as I can learn from them, I'm not so proud as to grudge them their amusement. By-and-by, perhaps, they'll learn from me."

"But without your own consent, I mean," she explained. "If you were at school without your knowing it, and being drilled like——like a Dandie Dinmont, to sit up on your hind legs and beg prettily, and give a paw——"

She broke off, indignant at the amusement with which he fairly shook.

"I beg your pardon, Pen!" he said, putting out a hand to prevent her going. "I'm ashamed to seem so unsympathetic, but it is really too funny to think of you thinking you could possibly be drilled like that. One doesn't drill the nor'-west wind."

"You mean that I'm incapable of training?" she inquired with inconsistent irritation.

"Look here, Pen," he said warmly. "You're tired with all your labours and your anxieties, and you're worrying about trifles. What you want's a rest. Now that your patients are recovering, don't you think you might come home?"

"That is exactly what I contemplate," she answered.

"Norah will be so glad! It really isn't a bit like Fancy Farm without you; it wants the nor'-west wind."

"I meant really home——where I'm best understood," she explained.

"You're not going back to Norah?" he asked incredulous.

She shook her head.

"It looks a little like ingrat—— It's not quite kind. I thought you were very happy with her."

"I was——very! But, I'm more at my ease now in the wynd, where the people appear quite satisfied with me. You see they know no better, poor souls! They are not critical. They have no particular preference for an ideal lady."

"Yes they have!" he retorted. "But I think they have monopolised her long enough."

She hardly listened to him, filled with her own distress. "What is your notion of an ideal lady, Mr Maurice?"

"In a single word or in detail?" he asked.

"You can't tell me in a single word, of course; it's bound to be a very complicated character."

"The view of a poet or of a shipbuilder?"

"Is there a difference?"

"Vast!" he answered airily. "A very minor poet's ideal lady is apt to be as visionary as—as a Priory; he'd perhaps be rather sick if he saw her in the flesh. A shipbuilder's is not so unsubstantial; I could make the drawings for her like the sheer-draught of a ship, and the first considerations I insist upon are buoyancy and a quick recovery of her equilibrium when the winds of vexation make her heel. Stability—resistance—trim—speed—strength; these are all-important in a lady as in an ocean liner. But I can't pursue the figure, Pen; I want my lady beautiful and calm, self-disciplined and good, above pretence, evasion, and deceit. A womanly woman—that's the thing!—the kind that has always overcome my sex by the power of continual quietness and self-possession."

"Have you thought so long?" asked Pen, with a troubled aspect.

"Since ever I saw her, and I've come back to Fancy Farm to tell her so," he answered.

"Oh, I'm so sorry!" said Pen with genuine grief, if a troubled countenance was evidence. "Didn't you know? You ought to know! Her—her affections are set on another person," and without another word she left him and ran up the stair.

CHAPTER XXIX.

HE stood for a little where she left him, confounded by her parting words. At first they repeated themselves again and again to his ear but not his comprehension, as syllables alone, with a rhythm but not a meaning. Suddenly, at last, they transformed themselves to an idea which eclipsed immediately the sunshine of the afternoon, dispelled a buoyant spirit of adventure that had come to him some days ago amid the clatter of the shipyard. He was dismayed. Till now Penelope had appeared an object of affection only; interesting, attractive, worthy of further investigation, but not absolutely essential to a shipbuilder's existence. Now that he had, at her own suggestion, summed up all the qualities he admired in her in his sketch of the Ideal Lady, he, for the first time, clearly realised how vividly they had been in his mind, and all they meant to him. And now she was remote and unattainable! Commingled with his disappointment was a feeling of the ludicrous that almost made him laugh. He was so absurdly situated there at the mouth of Watty Fraser's close, with the eyes of the opposite tenement upon him, and a gander pecking at his calves.

"Well done, Jock!" cried the fiddler with his head out at an upper window. Maurice summoned all his dignity, and, followed by the bird, went up the wynd, unreasonably hating the sight of every stair and close

in it, and yet so conscious of the folly of the feeling
that his sense of the ridiculous prevailed above his
disappointment.

In spite of the storytellers, the discovery that the
woman of your fancy may be meant for some one else
is no irrevocable blow to four-and-twenty; the stunning
blow is reserved for the hour when the lady, having led
you on, at last discards, and Maurice must confess to
himself that Pen had never once encouraged him to
think of her in any tender sense. He blamed himself
for his precipitation. It would look to her as if he had
sought to take advantage of her wounded loneliness. He
could, with patience, have discovered how things lay
without exposing himself and causing her embarrassment. How shrewdly she had guessed the purpose of
his speech; how delicately sustained with him the
fiction of the third person pronoun; how kindly she
had cut the revelation short!

"By heavens, she's a trump!" he said at last, irra-
tionally more in love with her than ever.

It was only when he got back to Fancy Farm and
saw Norah, even more wan than Pen, walk languidly
between the dead and dying blossom of her garden, that
he remembered her foreboding.

"Well?" she said, without periphrasis; "you have
seen her?"

"How do you know?" he asked, surprised.

"There's nothing remarkable in that," she answered.
"I'm not stupid enough to think you deserted me this
afternoon to look at the windows of the village shops.
You're full of tidings, Reggy; I can see it in that
evasive eye. Aunt Amelia is over at the Ludovics;
Andy's heaven knows where; I'm left even without
the company of a dog, since Peter Powrie has him
away on some excuse of medicinal balls, and I'm

sick of myself. . . . And how do you think she looks ? "

" Like a Virgilian goddess ; a priestess carrying sacred vessels," answered Maurice readily, with enthusiasm, thinking of the basket ; and Norah quietly laughed.

" Oh, Reggy ! " she exclaimed, " how you forget ! That one has done duty with myself before now. Your new ideas of economy as a shipbuilder mustn't lead you to make the same highly poetic compliments do for everybody. *I'm*——if you please——the only real and original Virgilian goddess, and —— oh, I wish I hadn't such a headache ! "

He followed her into the house. Her deer-like tread was wanting. A torpor seemed to hold her limbs, but her intuitions swooped with kestrel-wings on the cause of something reticent in his manner. It was too significant that he should have hardly anything at all to say of his interview with Pen.

" Ah ! " said Norah, with the light of penetration in her eyes, " it dawns upon me now that it wasn't to comfort me you came to Fancy Farm on this occasion. Relieve my fears at once, and assure me that you haven't been proposing marriage to Penelope Colquhoun."

" You——you wouldn't mind if I did, would you ? " he stammered.

" Mind ! " she exclaimed with vehemence. " Oh, you silly fellow ! What do you think I brought you here for almost as soon as Pen had joined us ? "

" Good heavens ! " he cried, " what a designing woman ! "

" It's the nature of the sex, Reggy. We women can only get married by helping one another, and in any case I had quite made up my mind that Pen, without a scrap of guilty makebelieve, or pose, or prevarication in her composition, was the very woman to make the best of you. I knew I was a charming person myself, of course, but rather spoiled for taking a chronic poet in hand, and how was I to guess you would recover? I thought it would be good for Pen, and good for you, and—I'll not deceive you—maybe good for me. . . . Andy, you know." She flushed, regarding him with eyes that expected disapproval. "Does it shock you? We're not supposed to practise stratagems like that—it's never mentioned in Aunt Amelia's novels, I understand—but it isn't for your sex alone that everything is fair in love and war. . . . Now, tell me, did you propose?"

He shook his head. "I started out to do it, but I didn't."

"Coward! You're just as tall as she!"

"I was a day behind the fair, Norah. Pen's engaged."

The little colour that was in her face, brought there by hope, fled instantly; he was shocked to see her agitation.

"Are you sure?" she asked, in what was hardly more than a whisper.

"She said so. At all events she let me know that her affections were engaged by another man."

"Another man! I told you, Reggy! Oh, I told you! . . . Andy!"

He felt happy that it was in his power to contradict that natural conclusion. "No, no," he said; "whoever it is, it certainly isn't Andy," and the relief he witnessed in her face was so good to see that the rest of his speech was pitched deliberately upon a key of greater certainty than was warranted by his actual knowledge. "With what you said last night," he went on, "I might myself have fancied it was your cousin if it hadn't been that Pen made it very plain that she's as near hating him as a Christian from a U.P. manse may go. I never before realised how much ferocity can go with the wounded pride of a woman. She's bitter, Norah, bitter!"

"About the training?"

"Yes."

"I know; I told you. She made that plain to myself. You're sure it isn't Andy?"

"Just as sure as I am that it isn't Reggy Maurice. It's so far from being Andy that she's never coming back again to Fancy Farm."

"Nonsense!" cried Norah. "Not come back! She must. I could never bear to let her go away with any rankling feeling that we have no regrets for the vexation we have caused her. You don't know how much you have relieved my mind, Reggie. I was afraid, you understand—it is so natural to fall in love with Andy! She must come back, immediately. And it isn't any high commanding goodness of heart that makes me say so, though I love her and really want her. If Andy thought she suffered from his scheme so much as that he would chase her to the other side of the world, if necessary, to make amends. . . . Tell me again, you're sure it isn't Andy. . . . And to think she never told me! Who would have thought that Pen could have been so sly?"

Maurice listened patiently, but she saw he had no share in her elation, and at once she realised.

"Oh, Reggy, I'm a brute!" she cried, running forward and taking him by the hands. "I'm so selfishly engrossed in my own shameless schemes that I'm not giving a single thought to your disappointment. Are you *sure* it's hopeless?"

"She ran away. She didn't give me a chance to pursue the subject," said Maurice blankly. "I felt like a fool, you know, with nothing of any importance said, and that abominable goose pecking at my legs, and rows

of windows staring at me. If she had only given me
an opportunity to explain that I wasn't talking merely
poetically——"

"You'll have the opportunity!" said Norah hastily.
"Pen may think at this moment that she'll never set
foot in Fancy Farm again, but I'll have her here to-
morrow."

Maurice looked dubious. "She seemed on that point
quite emphatic. How are you to induce her to return?"

"I'm unwell, Reggy; don't I look it? I'm really
unwell. I haven't slept for a fortnight. Never mind
the reason! I'm unwell, and I'm off to bed, and somebody's got to send down to the village to Pen at once to
tell her she must come at once if she wants to keep her
friend from dying."

The confidence of Norah that Penelope's affection was
a more commanding force than wounded pride was justified by the quick appearance of the nurse from Watty's
Wynd. The news that her friend was ill put every
other thought immediately in the background; she took
leave of her convalescents with a parting word of counsel
on the prophylactic virtues of fresh air, soft-soap, and
water. "Are ye sure that they're salubrious?" asked
the fiddler doubtfully. "Yes, yes," she cried behind her,
hurrying down his stair; "make no mistake, they're
quite salubrious." And twenty minutes later she was
mirthfully recounting it to Norah, who was languorous
and pale enough, in truth, to rouse a nurse's zealous
sympathy.

Pen might have had some magic spell, so swiftly did
the burnished hue of health come back to Norah's cheek,
her eye regain its sparkle. It was the miracle of a
single night through which they shared the same bed-
chamber. Once Aunt Amelia wakened, and heard what

seemed alarming sounds come from their room; she rose and hurried across the lobby, breaking in upon them without so much as a warning knock. They were laughing in the darkness.

"What on earth's the matter?" she inquired. "It does not look as if you were very ill, Norah," and Pen, with a pillow, smothered the uncontrollable amusement of her patient.

Maurice, upon reflection in the morning, which so often gives the high emprises of the previous day a new look altogether, was for going home. The right deportment for a broken-hearted gentleman at a breakfast-table with a lady who had had the painful task of telling him so recently she loved another was, he felt certain, quite beyond him. Norah, apprised at an early hour by Mrs Powrie of his sudden resolve to leave before his hosts were stirring, immediately threw off the invalid and descended on him with the old coquette imperiousness. Astonishing! Here was he aching from a sleepless mattress, mortified more than ever by the night's reflections, and she was radiant.

He mustn't go. There was no earthly reason why he should go. On the contrary, there were considerations of the most ponderable character which made it imperative that he should stay where he was in the interest of everybody concerned. And the lady who last night was languishing on the verge of despair sketched out for him with great vivacity a programme for a week's-end entertainment hardly consonant with the mood of a disappointed lover.

"We're quite forgiven," she said gleefully. "At least, I'm quite forgiven. I must leave Andy to make his own peace, if he can get the opportunity. Whatever you said to Pen yesterday on the subject of self-improvement, it has modified her resentment. She sees

things in a new light, and she can't deny that she has
benefited by our wicked scheme of cultivation."

"That's all right so far as it goes," said Maurice,
"but——" He looked at her ruefully, wondering that
an intellect usually so alert should fail to see the difficulties that more immediately concerned himself and
Pen.

She took him by the sleeve and shook him.

"Imbecile! A poet has five hundred and fifty
different ways of telling a woman that he likes her;
but if he put the whole of them into the form of a
sonnet it wouldn't please her half so much as if he
simply said, 'I love you,' like a ploughman. Why were
you so oblique with Pen? You ought by this time to
have understood her better. She's under the delusion
that you're a pathetic victim of unrequited love for——
Who do you think? . . . For me!"

"How could she possibly think so?" he inquired
incredulously, and Norah grimaced comically.

"How could she possibly think? How could she
possibly think?" she repeated mockingly. "Oh, Mr
Maurice, am I so utterly impossible? Pen does not
think me so, at anyrate; she's obviously of the impression that if there's any one on earth who could
meet with a shipbuilder's requirements in the way of a
Perfect Lady it's myself!"

"She plainly told me her affections were set elsewhere!" protested Maurice, somewhat shaken.

"She did nothing of the kind! It's an almost incredible example of feminine modesty, I admit, but all
along she thought you referred to me. She had been
quick enough to guess how I felt about Andy from the
very first hour she saw us together, but was quite
deceived by your philandering. I thought I should
have suffocated, laughing, when the situation dawned on

me. It required a solemn oath that I hadn't been consciously trifling with your young affections."

Maurice paced the floor, immensely agitated. The boy in him was always what had pleased her most,—something immature, dependent, wistful, calling for a woman's tactful guidance, had invested him with charm as an idler, and still remained to some extent with the shipbuilder; she felt peculiarly maternal.

"Then there's no one—there's nothing—— Did you explain?" he asked nervously.

"I was just on the point of doing so," she answered, "when I thought better of it and left her unenlightened. It wasn't for me to put your sentiments into prose—that would have been indelicate and injudicious, and I leave it to yourself."

"Good heavens!" he cried, alarmed. "Have I to go all over it again?"

"It looks like that," she answered. "Next time be explicit. And from all I know of Pen, I think you'll find her more interested in your pathetic state of a hopeless lover than in your eloquence."

He turned from the window with a sudden resolution. The housekeeper crossed the hall. "Oh, Mrs Powrie," he said, "on thinking it over I find I—I needn't go till Monday."

CHAPTER XXX.

It was the year of the Storm, for so we have always definitely called it, as if storms were rare phenomena. In truth the hills that lift to the north of Schawfield plain are the very breeding-ground of tempest; we have cradled on the blast and suckled on the cloud, as Dr Cleghorn puts it, but this was the year of storm transcendent—Boreas's masterpiece. The woods came down in swathes as to the shearer's hook. They say that Captain Cutlass almost grat when he rode to the coast on that November morning, and saw, from Bishops' Offrance, a landscape smashed, the noblest trees destroyed, great plantings of his father's time made flat as sodden oats. He wept, they say, or was as near on weeping as a man may be, and went about the ruins mourning as a man will mourn for old companions fallen in disaster. Possession has its penalties: he loved too fondly every feature of his countryside, and here was it trampled on and scarred. Years have gone by since-syne, and still John Baillie's woodmen labour to remove the timber levelled by that hurricane. Bairns have been born in the village, and have grown to men and women, never thinking he was not a native like themselves, but a stranger brought to the place on an orra job whereof even yet he sees no culmination.

Nor was the damage to the Schawfield woods the only thing that made that season memorable, though in the

local calendar whereby we count the ages of our children
it stands out epochal and paramount like the dates of
battles or Disruptions. The Storm has not entirely
puffed out the memory of the fire at Fancy Farm.
When Sir Andrew rode that day to Bishops' Offrance,
and put his arms about the stricken bodies of his
favourite trees and called them brothers, he had ridden
from a house astringent with the smell of char. Only
the tragedy of his woods could for a little lift his mind
from those contending moods that answered now to
reason, now to inclination, and were more contentious
than ever through this accident of Pen's.

The girl, since her return from Watty's Wynd, maintained with him a careful distance; she was never to
be got alone, and, so odd a thing is human nature, he
was glad for this even when he planned it otherwise.
What he should say to her to mollify, while yet unable
to explain the origin of that presumptuous scheme, was
more than he could easily decide upon; the thing must
be left to the moment's inspiration. Norah refused to
discuss it; Norah, indeed, was sure discretion, delicacy,
kindness, counselled an evasion of the subject altogether.
And Pen's demeanour, in the general company, seemed
to favour that contention; she showed no signs of nursed
resentment; a little less inclined to smile at his random
theories, perhaps more ready to contradict him—that
was all. But her *tête-à-têtes* were all reserved exclusively
for Maurice or for Norah, Aunt Amelia, or the amiable
Mrs Powrie.

Three days had passed, and Maurice found it possible
still to stay away from his drawing-office, much to the
baronet's surprise, considering the fascination that was
now supposed to be in shipbuilding. Aunt Amelia was
the first to see a difference in his manner to her niece;
the young gallant was not so manifest; deep-learned in

"symptoms" through the study of romance, she missed the persiflage with which they used to treat each other, and, singularly, Norah did not seem to care. Aunt Amelia wondered. When Aunt Amelia wondered thus, the world seemed in a mumbling conspiracy. But if she failed vexatiously to catch the quieter passages of those bouts of pleasantry that now seemed always going on between Penelope and Maurice at the dinner-table, her eyes could discern a nervous warmth in the young man's manner, a deferential droop of the shoulders, a meekness that was new. She even thought she saw a softer light in the eyes of the parson's daughter. She took immediate alarm, in Norah's interest.

"Norah," she said to her niece with tremulous mysteriousness at the earliest opportunity, "don't you think Penelope's bolder since she has been mixing with those people in the village?"

"Only the very nicest kind of boldness would have sent her there, aunt," said Norah. "What makes you say so?"

Her aunt was wrapt at once in Delphian vapours, her air was charged with portent like a thunder-cloud, in hints and innuendoes the oracle breathed a doubt of Reggy's faithfulness. He was not so much to blame, of course, as the bold, designing girl who led him on.

Norah maintained her gravity with an effort. "Are you not mistaken, aunt?" she asked with a subtlety of which she was herself ashamed. "Has—has Andy noticed?"

Her aunt cast up her eyes in a manner to indicate the utter hopelessness of getting Andrew Schaw to notice anything really worth his observation. A man who even now appeared to have no interest in the febrile rise of Athabascas would notice nothing—even what was passing beneath his very nose. And she was right; Sir Andrew had not noticed.

He frowned when Aunt Amelia, as Norah had expected, came to him with inklings; for the first time in his life he was almost rude to her. "What! what!" he said, "do I notice anything! In a tone like that! Damn it, I would sooner put my eye to a keyhole. No, ma'm, no, ma'm—blind! stone blind!" He grew very red; he spluttered, and Norah, when she heard it all from her astonished aunt, ran up to her room and foolishly kissed a worn-out slipper.

But all the same it spoiled his meals to know that his aunt was spying, and in spite of himself he realised a quite unusual spirit of conciliation in his guest's address to Pen, in Pen a singular vivacity. Norah, moreover, was at times quite flagrantly deserted, he would meet them in the avenue: together, he learned, they had visited Watty Fraser; it was Pen who naïvely told him, it was Reginald who blushed.

"Can a man be in love wi' twa women at the same time?" the fiddler, later in the day, asked Peter Wyse. "There's naething easier," said the saddler, "if they bide in different places."

Miss Birrell, on the Sabbath, in the church, nudged James at the opening psalm; when the occupants of the Schawfield pew were standing, she could see that they were only Pen and Maurice. Her brother wondered at the triumph of her eye.

> "A bird was in the breast of me,
>   Until the day we met;
> And now its wing is broken,
>   Since you so soon forget—"

Sir Andrew came upon his cousin one day singing this to herself at the piano, with a feeling that seemed poignant; he was beset with pity and annoyance.

But though Norah might sing of broken wings with all the expression she had learned from her music-master, loading the words with a fictitious despair, the bird was now as strong in the breast of her as ever.   Maurice and Pen might have their own enjoyments; hers were secret joys unshared with any one—sweet intuitions, lively hopes, though sometimes they were oddly blended, as it might appear, with very common pleasures.   For instance, Athabascas.   If Mr Birrell could never rouse his client to his own great state of excitation at the way that marvellous stock kept climbing over the eighties, over the nineties, over the hundreds, he could always count on Norah's glee.   That, if you please, was the lass with a pencil!—she summed the ascending profits of her cousin with the relish of a Jew.   Himself, he only vaguely understood the Writer's figures; he would run his fingers through his hair and say, " Quite good!   Quite good!   I see they have opened a new post farther north at a place deliciously called Wealth-of-Waters; a name like that enriches the map of Canada."

" But the thing is, stupid, that you're getting rich! " said Norah, losing patience, and Jamie Birrell crackled with exultant laughter at the baronet's bewilderment. " We're fairly rollin' in't," he said, with a heave of his shoulders, as if with his client he swam through seas of wealth.   " It was well for you that your father took the fancy for the voyajoors, Sir Andrew, and got in so soon, and that you were wise enough to back his fancy."

" I had aye a fancy for Athabascas," said Sir Andrew. " I liked the name.   It's spoiled for me in the meantime, but I liked the name.   It had the ring of romance in it. There are names we should support though they never brought a penny to us. . . . Athabascas——" He rolled out the word lusciously.   " Snow-shoes and tepees, Red Indians and furs! "

"It's no the furs that we have to thank, Sir Andrew, no the furs," said Mr Birrell. "It's the land. They're breaking it up in farms; there's a better skin on a farmer than on any beaver."

"H'm!" said Captain Cutlass, visibly depressed, "I don't like that! It takes the gilt from my Athabascas, do you know? My poor voyageurs! I notice of late the name has lost its charm for me. It's not a name to be bandied about in the commercial columns. It used to brace me like a fine spring day; the sound of it was a poem with lakes and forests in it; now it leaves me cold. Eh? How's that?"

"Association," answered Norah readily. "You're confirming Pen's æsthetic theory that beauty's only in one's mind, depending upon memories evoked."

"Ay, ay!" said he, amused. "So that's Penelope's philosophy! . . . Alison, and Jeffreys! How did she discover *them*?"

"I'm sure she has never heard of them, any more than I have done," said Norah. "It's the rule of her life, in nature and in art, to seek in herself and her past experience for every thrill she feels."

That afternoon he saddled the mare, on a sudden impulse, and, indifferent to the frost, bathed in Whitfarlane Bay, a sacrament wherein he often worshipped God and purged his sins. He had ridden west on roads as sonorous as seasoned wood, with fairy-bells of tinkling ice-drops on the wayside trees, but the sting of the brine was yet upon his skin, and the sea's rejuvenation in his breast, when the change of weather that his sailor eye had earlier foreseen came with amazing quickness. The night had a worn-out moon that staggered across the scud of clouds a while and then was whelmed. He sheltered from torrential rain, and supped in Clashgour Farm; the rain abated, but the night, when he emerged again and trotted out of the light of Fleming's lantern, appeared the very throat of tempest.

Powrie was waiting up for him. "A wild night, sir!" he cried, throwing open the stable-door.

"Wild's no' the word for't, Peter," shouted back his master in the tumult of the yard. "It's wicked! Wicked!"

"We didn't expect you the night, sir; we were sure you would put up at Beswick's, and they're all in bed except the mistress," Powrie told him in the stable, which was like a haven consecrate to calm.

He crossed to the house, despondent, feeling a widower's loneliness; Jean had sat up for him always, no matter how late the hour. The spirit that had tingled in him as he braced to the storm's antagonism, and made him almost shout in fellowship with the roaring forest, immediately died down; he looked at the dark front of his home, in whose eaves the blast went moaning—cliff-like inhospitality!

The feeling vanished on the threshold and gave place to consolation, for there was Norah waiting him in the hall! She seemed the very soul of loving-kindness, like a beacon set on a harbour-bar.

"I knew," she said, "you would come home." She radiated warm waves of welcome.

He had hardly lapsed into actual sleep when a hammering on his door set him wide awake again, and above the gale, that appeared to shake the house to its foundations, he heard her agitated voice. "Come out immediately," she said, "the west wing is on fire."

The household, when he had got outside upon the lawn, was gathered before the dairy, Aunt Amelia bleating like a sheep, unconscious of the oddity of her vesture; a flaming window lit the garden, the servants ran with buckets. In the storm's supremacy the fire seemed insignificant, but it belched from Pen's bed-chamber, and Sir Andrew sickened with apprehension.

"Good God! has Pen got out?" he shouted.

A shivering figure at his elbow reassured him. "Reggy got her out in time, no more," said Norah. "She had been reading a book in bed and fallen asleep, and the candles caught her curtains. You know Pen's foible for open windows."

"I do not see her," he cried, with a hasty scrutiny of his company.

"That's the silly thing," said his aunt. "She has gone back to her room again with Mr Maurice for the book that she was reading."

"The ineffable Pen! If she hadn't fallen asleep I'd have sworn it was her Bible. . . . Wasn't it, Pen?" he added as the girl herself, with Maurice behind her, breathlessly joined the group.

"It wasn't," she answered haltingly, with the rescued volume in her hand. "It was 'Harebell and Honey.'"

CHAPTER XXXI.

THEY breakfasted that morning in a littered dwelling, for the village folk, who had helped to quell the fire, in an excess of zeal had emptied threatened rooms of furniture, and, in the way of hurried flittings, heaped where the notion took them. Pen's room alone had suffered serious damage; she wept at the havoc when she saw it in the grey light of the day, a kind of symbol bearing meanings for herself alone, and Captain Cutlass found her among the ashes guiltily regarding them, with Miss Amelia expressing the severest censure by her silence. He came in upon them whistling, exuberant.

"There's something tonic in a fire," said he; "it's as near on war as we may attain in those pampered times. We ought to have an annual one to keep us from losing the early virtues. Eh?"

The reddened eyes of Penelope stopped him; he realised an attitude of accusation in his aunt.

"I never was more ashamed of myself in all my life!" said Pen, and Aunt Amelia breathed heavily, visibly a martyr to restraint.

"Wouldn't have missed it for a hundred pounds," he told them buoyantly. "There's a certain calling forth— a stimulus—an excitation in a fire which gives me my one regret that we can't all live in cities and see other people's fires each evening. Some pleasing terror is in conflagration, eh? You saw the fine delight of the village boys ? They liked it even better than the garden-party. What the world wants when it's young is bonfires—to see the ravening beast uncaged : Chinese lanterns are all very well for timid age."

" I can't conceive how I should have been so stupid ! " lamented Pen, but little comforted by his humour.

" If people *will* read in bed——" said Miss Amelia sardonically.

" I always do ! " said Captain Cutlass. " The thing is, Pen, to avoid somnolent books for such occasions. A rapid action ! It's the hour for breathless incident, if we're to avoid the risks of burning curtains. Never mind ! It is probably the first time Reggy's poems have roused intense excitement."

" Reggy's nonsense ! " said his aunt impatiently, and Pen's lips hardened.

" I think," said she, " they're very clever. They're beautiful ! "

" Of course they are ! " said Captain Cutlass.

He had not learned as yet of the wounded forest. The morn was beat upon by tatters of the storm. Gusts eddied round the house, strewing the lawn with twigs and whistling in the chimneys; wild ragged clouds went scurrying across the sky. Rooks gathered in the fields with scoffing sea-gulls from the nearest port; they rose at times in the air in clanging masses. The garden had lost its tameness ; every bush appeared to struggle to escape and join those elemental revels. To the relish of their meal that morning every sense contributed; they saw the boughs thrash, and the tree-tops rise and fall like billows round the village; the swollen river at its weirs resounded like a cataract; a scent of freshened earth and herbage seemed to find its way indoors, contesting with the scorched wood odours.

All things considered, they were a cheerful party

lifted a little above themselves by the night's adventure, inspirited by the morning's weather; only Pen was contrite, Miss Amelia sour. Maurice should have basked in their approval of his vigilance and gallantry, but for one who had averted tragedy unspeakable he seemed ill at ease whenever the night's events were recapitulated. Norah alone observed it.

"If you say a word," she whispered hurriedly, "I'll not forgive you!"

"Can't keep it up much longer," he muttered. "It makes me feel an arrant humbug," and regardless of her clutch upon his arm disclosed the cause of his embarrassment. He had been credited with the first alarm; Pen's feeling of obligation, obvious in her manner to him, gave him pain. "I did the shouting," he explained, "but Norah was the first to see the fire. She roused me, you understand. I'm sorry for your knuckles, Norah."

"And I'm sorry for your stupidity," she said in an undertone of disappointment. "You have thrown away the best part of a beautiful reputation and robbed Pen of half her admiration, and you're going to make me look absurdly silly in another moment."

"And all the time we have been thinking Mr Maurice was so clever!" cried Aunt Amelia. "How did you waken, Norah?"

"I was not in bed," said Norah, looking with blameful eyes on Maurice.

"But we all retired together, to bed, hours before," said her aunt, astonished. "We had quite decided Andy would not come till morning."

"I thought, again, he would," said Norah, very red, "and decided to wait up for him. So I returned downstairs and stayed till he appeared, a benevolence for which he has to thank me, since Fancy Farm might have been burned about his ears if I had not seen the flame

from the west wing on my window-blind as I was pre
paring to go to bed again."

"So it's Norah you have got to thank," said Mis
Amelia to Pen, whose manner to the hero had impressec
itself on her as rather warm.

"At all events it was Mr Maurice who rescued me,"
said Pen impulsively, her aspect a defiance of Sir Andrev
Schaw's theories of gratitude. He, on his part, seemec
at once immersed in contemplation, with his eyes upor
his cousin.

She turned uneasily to Maurice. "I hope you are
glad now that I gave you the opportunity," she
whispered.

"You think of everything," he said to her humbly.

"My wits have been on edge for weeks; I *have* to
think of everything; amn't I a woman? But it was
not altogether to give you the joy of rescuing Pen I sent
you to her door; I was afraid myself; I was afraid!"

Cattanach appeared before their breakfast ended; he
brought from every part of the estate along the coast the
tidings of devastation. At once Sir Andrew mounted
and was off, the fire forgotten, but a vision in his mind
of Norah standing in the hall to welcome him from the
storm, of all the household she alone solicitous.

He had mourned the fallen comrades and returned to
Clashgour Farm where his mare was stalled, when the
ravage of the storm appeared of little consequence compared with that which was created in his breast by a
foolish sentence from the lips of Fleming.

Together they were leaning on a dry-stone dyke before
the steading, looking upon a flooded meadow whose condition made the farmer even less urbane in manner than
was his wont. To him the spoiling of the woods was of
less account than the loss of a stack of hay that was now
on its way to sea, swept off by the river spate. He

snuffed with his ivory ladle without the usual courtesy of the proffered box, and talked of the ruined plantings as if they were a blessing in disguise.

" No' much to complain o', laird ! A windfa', a perfect windfa' ! It's time thae trees were doon in ony case ; now ye can turn them into money. It's no' as if the hale ing-bang were sailin' doon the river like my stack."

" I would rather have my trees," said Captain Cutlass sadly, as he turned about to get his horse. " And misfortunes never come single ; you'll have heard about the fire ? "

" Yes," said Clashgour indifferently. " It's a mercy t's nae waur, and that naething happened to Miss Colquhoun to put aff the waddin'."

" The wedding ! " said Sir Andrew, stopping. " What wedding ? "

His tenant fortified himself with another snuff : a man made coarse by his convivial habits, the delicacies of perception blunted, he had long since lost the instinct to refrain from a dangerous familiarity.

" Naebody should ken that better than yoursel', Sir Andrew," he replied, with a cunning leer. " The clash o' the country's sayin' she played her cairds gey weel to nab a landlord."

Next moment Captain Cutlass had him by the collar and shook him like a rat. " You blackguard," he exclaimed. " To say such a thing about a lady ! "

" Lord keep us, laird ! " gasped Fleming, " I'm no' misca'in' her. If it comes to that, I was nabbed mysel', and I'm no' regrettin' 't."

Incapable of answer, Captain Cutlass left him. The tempest of the mind awakened thus prevailed until he reached the village. From the lips of Norah the hint that Pen's tuition had occasioned chatter, though enough to make him bitterly regret his scheme, was not so overwhelming as this brutal revelation. Pen was more the victim of his whim than he had first imagined. . . . And Norah had waited up for him—the home personified, the soul of the hearth; that dream he had one time told her of, revived by her living presence when he came from the storm into the warm-lit hall. . . . Brave Pen! Honest Pen!—in all respects so close upon his own conception of the perfect woman, how must he atone for the consequences of his folly? His errant sense of honour promptly gave an answer.

If Mr Birrell was capable of surprise at any act of Captain Cutlass, he had occasion when his client, having trotted up to the office door a little later, fastened his mare to a ring worn thin by his litigious grandfather before James Birrell was born, and burst into the writing-chamber with the question, "Mr Birrell, am I well enough off to marry?"

The Writer, who had seen him earlier in the day in the huddle of Fancy Farm with his mind preoccupied with other things than matrimony, thrust his glasses back upon his forehead, peered at him under shaggy eyebrows, rubbed his hands, and gave a pawky smile, in which were blended pity, fellow-feeling, and amusement.

"It's a point that didna bother you much last year Sir Andrew, when the topic was discussed between us in this very room," he answered. "I'm glad that such a humdrum commonplace consideration has occurred to you at last. Famous, man, famous! You see romance itsel must come back at last to a question o' bawbees. If you had half as much interest in your own pecuniary affairs as Miss Grant has gotten, you would know that Schawfield was never in a better state to warrant such a step as you suggest. I thank the Lord for Athabascas! And now I hear the very winds are blawin' in your favour

What's the good o' me keepin' books if you'll no' take the trouble to understand them?"

He moved to a deed-box stamped in gilded letters with the name of the estate.

"For Heaven's sake don't go into that again!" said his client hastily, pushing the deed-box back on its rack with a thrust of his riding-crop. "This thing ought to be in the family mausoleum. Full of ghosts, man, full of ghosts! All I want to-day is an assurance from my man of business that I'm not insolvent. I have the utmost confidence in your judgment."

The Writer sighed and sat down again. "And yet folk wonder at defaulting lawyers!" he remarked. "My trade exists on the presumption that the world's dishonest, and that every man's a rogue unless his name is on a parchment, stamped, and yet you'll put such confidence in a lawyer that you'll never fash yourself to check his documents. It's a marvellous compliment to my profession, but whiles I can't deny to myself that it's idiotic."

"I'll risk it," said Captain Cutlass.

"Yes, yes! you'll risk it! You'll risk anything, Sir Andrew—that's the worst o' you! But it's no' a way that's justified by reason" Mr Birrell insisted.

"We are driven to all our vital acts," replied the baronet, "by forces quite outside our reason."

"Indeed!" said his agent dryly. "Even marriage, the most vital act of all?"

"Even marriage," agreed his client. "You'll admit I never attached a vast importance to ratiocination. Nature knows best what we're fitted for, and I'm almost come at last to your philosophy that it's women who make the matches."

James Birrell chuckled. "And what for no'?" he asked in the homely idiom. "It's no disgrace to the man that he should come like the mavis from the tree to his natural charmer. And am I to congratulate you, Sir Andrew ? "

"That remains to be seen," said the baronet. "I have yet to consult the lady."

His old friend smiled again and looked at him with a father's eye. "It's almost necessary," he remarked with irony. "Just *pro forma*, you understand. *Pro forma !*"

"I'm not so sure," said his client. "It's a point that's extremely doubtful, to judge from the lady's manner," and again James Birrell chuckled.

"I'm up in years," he said, "and I've just been an observer, taking no share in the game mysel', but I always understood that coyness was a part of it. Hoots, man ! get awa' wi' ye ! "

Sir Andrew walked about the room restlessly, surprised in some degree at his agent's sympathetic humour. "A year ago you would have called the project sheer romantics," he remarked.

"A year ago your mood was not so sensible : you were then for training fish to swim tail foremost."

"Not a word about that presumptuous folly !" said Sir Andrew. "It's a painful subject. I find it has not escaped the observation and the comment of the village gossips. An inquisitive and babbling place, Mr Birrell ! "

"In that respect it's just like other places," said the lawyer, up in arms for his native village. "Remember your position, sir—you're no' an ordinar man ! you're like a steeple standing up in the midst of us, and a steeple canna grumble if it's stared at."

"To see how goes the weather-cock," said Captain Cutlass with a smile, as he made to leave the writing-chamber. "Well, I hope the move I contemplate will meet with their kind approval."

"I can guarantee you that," said Mr Birrell heartily, with his hand upon the door to show him out.

"I am glad you have come to my view of it, that what we comically call race and fortune on the lady's part are not essential," said Sir Andrew. "But not a word to any one in the meantime. You understand the situation: after all, it may come to nothing," and he left the lawyer, quite astounded, on the threshold.

James Birrell stood for a moment like a man of stone, all the pleasure roused by his misconception of Sir Andrew's project dissipated. His wish had been the parent of his thought, which had been nursed assiduously by 'Tilda. Was it possible that that amazing woman's faculty for probing to the heart of local things with little more than glimpses from her window had at last betrayed her! For weeks she had been more and more convinced each day that the Hunt was ending as she wished it; innumerable portents which had missed the observation of her neighbours had conferred on her a pleasure that could not have been exceeded, as she told her brother, by the capture of a husband for herself.

He respected his client's wish for secrecy on the subject, but he was unable to forego the melancholy pleasure of a douche to his sister's confidence.

"I suppose you are still of the idea that his lordship's bound to make a match of it with Norah?" he said to her at their midday dinner.

"I seldom had more than the smallest doubt of it," she answered calmly, "and never a doubt of any kind since Mr Maurice came up the wynd wi' Watty Fraser's gander, lookin' like a goose himsel'. He'll have a jauntier step, I'll warrant, now that Miss Colquhoun is in his reverence for savin' her this mornin'."

"There's aye the chance that Sir Andrew may forestall him," said her brother cautiously. "He's just the man who would think himself bound to marry her because such a thing was rumoured."

Miss 'Tilda laughed derisively. "He may think what he likes," she said, "but I ken better. You men! You men! Indeed I wouldna wonder if he hasna found out yet that he's daft for Norah. All the same, James Birrell, you may take my word for it that he's goin' to marry her."

CHAPTER XXXII.

THE hunter ran his quarry down that afternoon in the heart of a wood which has known that kind of chase since ever its trees were old enough to keep a secret, and will doubtless lend its privacy to the ancient sport so long as there are lads and lasses left in Schawfield; while back gates of the village lead to it, and the glades entice, and the howlets keep their counsel as to what the answer is when they cry "Who? Who?" No storm would ever spoil Strongarra wood for lovers : let the silly young pines come down in squadrons elsewhere, the oaks stand fast in old Strongarra—ah, the old rogue oaks! the sly old wrinkled fathers shaking with pagan fun!—and the foggy paths which intersect it, a monument to the spendthrift days of William Schaw, will never have any obstacle to the feet of young romance.

It was not romance, either young or old, that took Sir Andrew there, but a resolution forced on him by events as ludicrously unromantic as if they had been planned by some malign and mocking providence. When he let himself reflect upon them, even he was bound to realise that the thing he contemplated was in keeping with the spirit of the joke wherewith the drama opened on the curling-pond a year ago. A proper culmination to a prank that now seemed childish! He could only face it smiling, like a man, as he had done before when his impetuousness had brought Jean Jardine home from

India to stagger him with dismay. But then, the issues were not so complicated; duty presented no alternatives.

A while before he had got back from Mr Birrell's office, Norah, having paid a hurried visit to the tenements to assure herself that no one was the worse for Pen's withdrawal, was returning through the avenue, when she saw her friend at a distance crossing the fields in the direction of the lower of the hunting-roads that wound themselves about Strongarra. Pen's obvious haste amused her: had she not been aware that the wood was the winter substitute for the moor where Pen so often betook herself in summer on her solitary rides, she would have thought the signs propitious to Reggy Maurice, who had, earlier in the day, displayed a flagrant craft in vain attempts to see the lady by herself. But Maurice was not in the wood, a trysted knight expectant; across the lawn she could hear him playing the piano in the house —perhaps another artifice to gain his purpose, for Pen was always ready to be lured by music.

Aunt Amelia stood in the verandah, looking worried. The irritation that had mastered her all the morning since the shouts of Reggy Maurice woke her from her dreams appeared to have reached a fever height, for her cheeks were patched with crimson and her manner was a little incoherent.

"Have you seen that girl?" she asked irascibly, looking round the garden. Norah discerned the symptoms of an outbreak she had feared for several days.

"Pen, you mean? She's gone across the fields to the hunting-roads. And she seems in a dreadful hurry."

"Flurry," said Miss Amelia. "I have no patience with such a spitfire! For all that I said to her!"

"What did you say to her?" asked Norah anxiously. Affairs were at that juncture where an injudicious word from her aunt might have the most unhappy consequences.

Her fears were justified : Miss Amelia rambled into a petulant explanation that she had in the friendliest spirit taken it on herself to warn Penelope that a certain circumspection was expected from a person in her position in the household.

Norah pressed for more details, with a sinking at the heart.

"Her manner to Mr Maurice !" said her aunt significantly. "I think you must be blind ! Or you haven't any natural feelings. Don't you see the way she looks at him ! She went back to her room this morning for his book for nothing else than for effect, and I told her so. A bold, designing girl ! Still, I had no desire to hurt her feelings ; I like her well enough ; and all I meant was for her good. But she flared up at once, and told me she would leave the house immediately. ' I'll leave to-morrow,' she said, as if she were a kitchen-maid, and dashed away before I could say another word to her. . . . And now I wish I hadn't spoken," she concluded, nervously repentant.

"Indeed I wish you hadn't !" said her niece, appalled at this latest wound to her friend's susceptibilities.

She hurried in to Maurice, who stopped his playing at the sound of her entry, turning round with eager expectation. "No, Reggy, it's only me," she said to him. "You're sitting fiddling while Rome is burning. Take my advice and find yourself at the earliest possible moment walking along the lower hunting-road."

A moment later he was off in Pen's pursuit.

She went to the garden foot to watch him cross the fields. There had come to the world an hour pacific : after the night-long roaring of the tempest, nature's silence seemed oppressive, for the sense of hearing still was strained in expectation. Blue scraps of sky were showing through the rifts of clouds that hardly moved, but yet at every upward glance displayed Protean changes. The wearied landscape slept. Her heart was sore for Pen's distress, but she could not help a smile at the way in which her umquhile poet the shipbuilder hurried across the grass as if it were without his own volition, neither poet nor builder now, but a man submissive to the destiny of men. She thought of his new importance to the world; of the distant shipyards clamorous with labour and engaged with mighty interests, and she smiled to see the man who should be there plunge like a faun through rushes, chasing the dryad of the wood, responsive to the law of nature that has no regard for human dignity nor a sense of humour. He broke impetuously through the hedges, leaped the ditches, plunged into the forest.

A curious feeling came to her. It seemed to her then as if her friend and her pursuer had become immortal, having passed from a world of doubt and conflict into some enchanted realm of certainty and single purpose, to emerge no more, but wander for ever on mossy paths below the oaks entranced. Some withered leaves, blown from the hedge beside her by a flaw of wind, came rustling to her feet with a motion as of life, like little frightened things; the universe, outside the wood, appeared exceeding huge and purposeless and cold: she felt forlorn.

Suddenly there was a sound behind her, footsteps on the gravel; she turned to see Sir Andrew come from the front of the house with a haste precipitate as Maurice's: he, too, had come home to learn from Aunt Amelia of her officious intervention, and was furious.

"Have you heard of this latest outrage?" he inquired,

and needed no other answer than the perturbation of her face.

"Where has she gone, do you know?" he asked, with his vision ranging over all the fields.

"I saw her go into the wood a while ago," said Norah.

"By which of the roads?" he asked abruptly, not looking at her.

She hesitated for a moment. "By the upper road," she answered weakly.

Without another word he left her, and quite as resolute as Maurice, though with more deliberation, cut across the fields. She watched him, too, but not amused; aghast, indeed, at the facility with which, on an impulse not of her better self, she had deceived him. Remorse inflamed her; she was ashamed to her finger-tips. When he reached the wood and disappeared, he seemed to violate a sanctuary; externally it looked the same as ever, but it had become the haunt of warring passions.

With a half-formed notion that the forest's sanctity must be preserved, and partly a wish to correct the error of her guidance, as if a falsehood could be turned to truth by immediate retractation, she tore into the house and hurriedly assumed her cloak and hat to follow him. Her dog came barking at her heels as if conscious of the chase. She ran across the fields more urgently than Maurice; when she reached the entrance to the hunting-road she cried her cousin's name. Her voice resounded through the verges of the forest, appealing, clarion-clear; but the only answer was from echoes. The road rose steeply through the wood: she had climbed it a thousand times as lightly as the roe, but that was without this pack of cares. Expecting to come in sight of him at every turning, at every turning she was disappointed; it seemed as if by some enchantment of the place he had evanished. She cried no longer— climbed more slowly, gave herself to a mood of wonder and expectancy. No birds were to be heard, no brute was stirring in the undergrowth; it seemed as the stillness of the wood had never been disturbed or never would be broken any more. She felt aloof from all the noisy interests of mankind and heard her own heart beat.

Where the road bent back upon itself the easier to reach Strongarra's top, she saw him first standing above her on the upper level. He had not seen her. He stood as in a listening attitude, staring through the trees. Not a stone-throw of distance separated them; had he lowered his glance a little he would have seen her there, immediately, but his search swept over her, in among the thick growth lower on the hill.

"Andy!" she cried, and hurried round the bend to where he waited for her. It might have been herself he had been hunting, by his aspect of relief.

"You haven't seen her?" she asked him, breathing fast.

"No," he answered, looking at her strangely.

"I'm sorry that I misled you about the road she took," she exclaimed. "Pen took the lower road, as she always does. I deceived you wilfully."

"Wilfully," he repeated, with surprise. "I don't understand."

She turned her profile to him and stood in an attitude of guilt. "I didn't want you to make Pen's position more awkward than it is," she said. "There are small untruths that are surely justified if life is to be tolerable at all."

"You Jesuit!" he exclaimed, but with a smile. "I

should like to hear you make such a plea with Pen."

"I know," she answered. "But I'm only an imperfect woman. I would be a better one if I could. I'll be a better one—to-morrow."

She was flushed with the haste of her pursuit of him; there was a flutter in her breast; her eyes were large and anxious. Into her voice had come a quality he had never perceived in it before—a softening, a sweetening, an intoxicating tone of confidence and dependence. She put up a nervous hand to replace a strand of her hair whose mutiny he now discerned as something that had interested him since ever she was a girl, without his realising it, and she looked at him with unfamiliar shyness, then hastily turned away.

She walked as if regardless whether he followed or not, along the path that narrowed as it bent about a granite scaur to be seen from Fancy Farm in the sunny blinks of rainy days like a wall of marble, and he came behind her, compassing her figure with his glance, perplexed by something in her manner. Her dog ran on ahead, questing among tufts of the bleached long grass with which the Schawfield folk made up their beds in spring.

Suddenly she stopped for a second, withdrew as it were in alarm from the ledge to which the path diminished, wheeled round, and retraced her steps.

"Let us go back," she said. "After all, you can see Pen any time."

"I never wanted to see her less than at this moment," he exclaimed, and walked obediently beside her.

But when they had got down the path a little way he observed that the dog had not turned back with her. He stopped and whistled.

"Never mind! He will follow us by-and-by," said Norah quickly.

"I'll find him," he said, relieved by the opportunity of doing anything to break a spell that seemed to have fallen on them, and hastily returned to the spot where the dog had left her.

"Come back!" she cried, peremptory, and a moment later he stopped abruptly as if in response to her command. But it was for a very different reason.

From the point where he stood—where she had so suddenly paused and turned—he could see a stretch of the lower road. The dog was dashing down the slope pursuing rabbits, but his interest in the dog was lost immediately by reason of a spectacle revealed between the opening in the trees.

He stared incredulously: Pen was standing in the arms of Maurice!

CHAPTER XXXIII.

ONLY for a second he gazed with a startled eye, doubtful of the scene that he beheld or of the pair's identity; but of that there was no mistake. They stood on the road, surrounded by the trees, confident of its privacy, and oblivious that any part of the higher path could overlook them. Chance had made him witness of the very climax of the joke he had himself originated, and at the same time made the purpose of his chase ridiculous. He felt immense relief, to be followed instantly by bewildering thoughts of what this meant for Norah. The abruptness of her turning back was now accounted for; she had seen what he had seen, and yet she had said nothing—shown neither grief nor indignation.

Or, on second thoughts, had she really seen? With the dog at his heels he rejoined her quickly, holding himself composed, intending to keep silence, Sooner or later she must know of Maurice's disloyalty, but it would not be from him.

No, she had not seen,—the glance with which she met him when he joined her seemed conclusive: she was undisturbed; she had regained her old serenity.

She chided the dog that gambolled round her quite unconscious that it had a vital part in the comedy of mankind: they went down the road together.

The wind, that had scarcely rustled the sheltering hedges of Fancy Farm, had risen a little, or was more

apparent on those higher levels. It filled the woo
with rumours; all the trees communed in their loft
tops. There were murmurs in the undergrowth an
whispers in the dry bog grass. The trunks of th
oaks, the gnarled old rogues, maintained their attitud
of motionless indifference, having seen so much of th
ways of hart and hind and men and women; the innu
endo was all on the part of their giddy branches.

"We were talking about perfection," he remarked
"Do you know, I have discovered that while I'm alway
fascinated by perfection as a goal, as an ideal, I prefe
the imperfect for everyday use."

Norah smiled. She could long ago have told hir
that. There was never a man on earth who bette
loved the broken melody, the column incomplete, th
first rough sketches. His family motto, *Non inferior
secutus*, was a motto that for him referred to incorporea
things.

"There is no perfection," he proceeded, "and a goo
thing too! The dream of it compels us always to b
striving forward like the donkey with a carrot hun;
before his nose."

"It is the imperfections of our friends that mak
them tolerable—unless we are monsters of righteousnes
ourselves," said Norah. "I think you told me tha
yourself, a year ago, with a good deal of inconsistency
considering what you wanted was a perfect Pen."

"Quite so!" he agreed. "I overlooked the fact tha
I wasn't worthy of a perfect Pen or perfect anybody
else. But even Pen is incapable of perfection: I can'
say yet whether I'm glad or sorry to find that out."

"I have yet to discover any weakness in her," answered
Norah, generously warm.

He glanced from the corners of his eyes at her with
pity, thinking of what he had seen. "I have though

f late," he said, " that she was hardly loyal to your-
elf."

She stopped immediately and faced him with a pene-
rating scrutiny. " Oh!" she exclaimed, " you saw them
up there, then, when you turned ? "

" Good heavens ! " he cried, " did you ? "

She nodded, smiling and confused.

" I'm sorry," he said with genuine feeling.

" Why ? " she asked him.

" Maurice——" he stammered, and she laughed.

" Exactly ! It was I who sent him along the low
road after her. The penetration of the surviving Schaws
appears to be confined to Aunt Amelia. What do you
ancy Maurice came back to Schawfield for, leaving his
darling shipyard ? "

He took off his hat and ran his fingers through his
hair, bewildered; his eyebrows almost met. " Am I to
understand," he asked, " that everything is over between
you and Maurice."

" Maurice and I are friends, as we have always been,
and nothing more," she answered hurriedly. " How
often have I tried to make you understand ? "

" My dear, you let me assume——"

" My dear, I let you assume ! It was you—or Jean,
who first suggested, in so many words, that I was in love
with Reggy, and all I did was not to contradict you.
In any case it takes two to come to an understanding,
and you might have seen that Reggy never had more
than a philanderer's interest in me. Had there been
the slightest danger of his feelings being more ardent
he should not have been so often here."

" But why——? " said Captain Cutlass.

She would not stop to listen, but hurried down the path.

" Why did you let me think——? " he persisted,
keeping step with her.

Still she was silent. Strongarra was full of merri
ment, derisive glee. Waggish life was in the underwood
the hazel bushes shook as in hilarity. Something of th
antic mood of the wood was in her mind; she was afrai
of his questioning, she was tingling with expectation, bu
also she was amused as she had been amused to witnes
Maurice running across the fields; men were all in som
respects like one another. It seemed to her that th
underwoods knew what he was blind to,—that the ver
oaks, the ancient ones, with difficulty kept themselve
from mocking; she grew shy of those old rogues.

If she had come up the hill with a pack of cares sh
went down it as if her footstep could not bruise th
moss. He looked at her sideways with delight, as if h
had never seen her hitherto, released himself of thos
constraints imposed on him so long by his delusion, an
saw her frankly with a lover's eye.

"Stop!" he said, with a hand upon her shoulde
She faced him shyly, all her amusement gone.

"I come back again to my whim," said he. "Tha
vision of perfection. You remember the qualities
wanted—an exceedingly fastidious and exigent gentle
man! There was that in Pen that seemed to make
good beginning, she was in so many respects like you
I thought I wanted a new creation, and all the time
find I was thinking of a duplicate. The more she be
came like you the more I liked her. Could she hav
been exactly you, I would have loved her."

"Oh, Andy, Andy!" she exclaimed. "You are a
circumlocutory as Reggy Maurice. I had to tell hir
that the ploughman has a better way of putting thing
at times than the poet has."

He looked vexed. "Then Maurice——?"

She broke in hurriedly: "No, no, not to me. Let u
have no more misunderstandings. He was trying t

make Pen see that he wanted her, and he did the thing
so stupidly that she thought he referred to me."

He still had a hand on her shoulder, gripping now so
tightly that it pained, but she bore it without complaint.
He caught her other shoulder and looked into unflinch-
ing eyes, profound as wells, but only for a moment: her
lashes fell to keep the deeps of passion from his
scrutiny.

"Oh, Norah!" he said—"Lord! the very name is
like a song! and I've been making a fool of myself as
usual. If I knew you loved me, I swear you have seen
the last of my caprices."

"I hope not," she replied. "Without an odd vagary
at times you would not be Andy Schaw. What else
should I love you for?"

He drew her to his arms and kissed her. For a
moment she stood in his embrace, and then released herself, shy of the espionage of those sly old trees that were
looking over his shoulder.

"You kissed me last on my eighteenth birthday," she
faltered, as it seemed irrelevantly. "When my nine-
teenth came and you stopped the practice, I was sorry
that I was growing old."

"I remember," he exclaimed.

"Yes, you remember, when I tell you," she replied;
"but I was different, I never forgot!"

"I feel," said he, "like a man that has been dragged
from the brink of a precipice. Do you know what I
contemplated?"

She nodded. "It was because I knew that I sent
you the wrong road. You see I have lost all shame,
now that I am confident."

"But yet I want to know," said he, "why you let me
think so long that you were in love with Maurice."

She bit her nether lip. "If you can't guess that,"

she said, " I'll never tell you." And whether he guessed or not, he asked no more.

The wind grew fresher in the forest's privacy. The tree-tops hummed more loudly; surviving little trees in a patch of coppice that had seen the coquetry of young folk peeling bark in summer, nudged when they remembered. And when the two were gone, and the kissing wicket clashed behind them, Strongarra gave itself to merriment from end to end.

THE END.

Printed in Great Britain by
WILLIAM BLACKWOOD & SONS LTD.